# Finding the Beautiful

## TRUDY SAMSILL

*In Christ Alone,*
*Trudy Samsill*
*Phil. 4:8*

*Text Copyright © 2017 Trudy J. Samsill*

*All Rights Reserved*

## acknowledgments....

~ I never know where to begin, but at the beginning. This book would never have found its way to these pages without God first bringing the story to my attention or Him giving me the passion and gift to write. May my passion bring Him fame.

~ Without my husband and children supporting me, I doubt I could ever do this writing-thing. Their love, encouragement, and sacrifices allow you to hold this book in your hands. Steve Samsill is my greatest fan, my wonderful husband, and dearest friend, the one who has helped shape me over the last 31 years of our marriage. Thank you, Steve! You are my rock. My children, nearly all grown now, are so patient and supportive of their "Mum," "Mom," and "Mommy" that I find it difficult to write adequate words enough to express my heart-felt love and gratitude for them.

~ I have the best support group in my editors/friends/sisters who, without their eyes, questions, comments, and suggestions, this book would hold many missing pieces and errors. (Please forgive any you do find!) You know your names, your part, your commitment to help me see this through to the end: Jane, Amy, Jana, and Sharon....I love each of you and appreciate you so very much!

~ I am so thankful for my cheerleaders and prayer-warriors. There are too many to name. If you prayed this through or cheered me on....THANK YOU FROM THE BOTTOM OF MY HEART!

~ Lastly, to my readers, YOU....without my readers, this writing venture would be pointless. Thank you for pressing me for the "next book" and for sharing my books with others you know. The emails of encouragement I have received after each book keep me going! And to the dear ones who pour your heart out to this unknown author, someone you have never met before, I pray for you often. I pray the God of hope will continue to fill you with all joy and peace as you believe in Him.

*Romans 15:1*

Sometimes you meet a hero unexpectedly, not face to face, but through the words of another. That's how I met the main character of this book, Samantha.

*"A hero is someone who, in spite of weakness, doubt, or not always knowing the answers, goes ahead and overcomes anyway."*
--Christopher Reeve

THOUGH THIS IS BASED ON A TRUE STORY, ALL NAMES, PLACES, AND SOME EVENTS WERE CHANGED WHEN THIS STORY WAS WRITTEN. MANY FACTS ARE TRUE, MANY IMAGINED, BUT THE HEROINE'S HEART OF COURAGE WAS LEFT UNTOUCHED.

# PROLOGUE

Twenty-five years is a long time to wait. Little did I know, today on this hot, humid, afternoon our Postman Reggie would bring an end to my waiting.

I watched as my dear husband and soul-mate meandered down the cracked sidewalk with each of our two tow-headed children by the hand. Stan has always been a good man, an excellent father, and even better husband.

So when he asked me to join him and the young'uns for a walk to the ice cream parlor, I feigned a headache, saying the Mississippi heat had taken its toll on me that day and all I wanted was a tall glass of sweet tea and a spot in the shade. Stan knew the humidity and heat left me with a usual end-of-the-day headache so he gladly took the kids, fixed me a glass of sweet tea with two lemon slices and extra ice just the way I like it. After giving me a lingering kiss on my sweaty brow, my three loves headed for ice cream. Amidst shouts of "Bye, Mama" and "Love you, Mommy," they took the four block walk to *Mary Jane's Ice Cream Parlor and Soda Shop* for root beer floats.

Retrieving my glass of tea from the porch railing, I walked slowly to my favorite bright yellow metal glider that sat under the massive branches of my beloved tree I lovingly nicknamed "Maggie." I loved beautiful things and made it a point to find at least one thing beautiful to my eyes each and every day. This magnolia was one of my beauties. The tree and I have shared many secrets under her flower-studded branches. So beneath Maggie's sheltering arms, I sought solace from the foreboding feeling I had endured the past five hours.

Unbeknownst to Postman Reggie, his usual noon delivery to my mailbox had started a swirling in my stomach that had ebbed and flowed all day. Quickly I had retrieved the small white envelope and crammed it in my skirt pocket. The butterflies flitted around my gut straight through lunch preparations of bologna sandwiches and apple slices, through hanging the wet heavy sheets on the taut clothesline, and all the way to turning down an ice cream cone at *Mary Jane's*.

Setting my tea down on the matching metal table, the glider squeaked under my 120 pound frame. Gently pushing the warm chair into motion, I heard the crinkle of paper in my pocket.

*It just has to be him*, I mused. *I would know his writing anywhere.*

Retrieving the white rectangle from my pocket, I cast a wary glance at the envelope once again. I had stared at the cramped manly cursive often as a young girl. My mind flashed back to a handful of old square photographs that pictured three people walking on the Mississippi coastline. A young mother, an equally young father, and me, as a two year old girl. Sadly none of the three were smiling in any of the photographs. The little girl had her thumb stuck in her mouth in every one; the mother, my Mama, shaded her eyes and probably her soul in most of them; and the young man, my father, wore a hard scowl. Though you couldn't tell in the picture, mother and daughter had a matching set of large violet-blue eyes and the straightest, strawberry blonde hair. On the back of each was scrawled in a manly script *"Mississippi Coast: Waylon, Sam, Lily, July 1946."*

Time tugged me back to the present and the reality I probably only had an hour to myself while Stan and my two angels were gone. I *knew* without a doubt who had written the letter I held in my trembling hand. I *knew* whose writing I would find on the pages the envelope contained.

*But why? Why now?*

There was only one way to find out. I ran a coral painted fingernail under the envelope's seal and withdrew the single piece of paper it contained. I quickly could tell this was not written on custom stationery paper but on a piece of cheap, common, lined, school paper. Nothing fancy, just purely functional.

Before I allowed my eyes to read the first line, I flipped the sheet over to the back page and read the signature:

*Regretfully,*
*Your father, Waylon Graves*

My heart thudded out the truth that I had guessed right on the letter's author. It was from Waylon. I couldn't bring myself to think of him as my father or Daddy or Dad. The words were not there in my heart nor my memory.

Lifting the envelope from my lap, I saw the corner of a photograph peeking out. Grabbing it I stared at a picture I had never seen before.

One of Waylon and me.

I was standing on a large rock, thumb in my mouth, same little plaid jumper on I had worn in the pictures in my memory that my Mama had shown me years ago. Waylon had an arm wrapped around my waist so I wouldn't fall off the large rock; he was wearing the same scowl and white t-shirt he had worn in the other photographs.

Flipping the small yellowed square over, I saw his handwriting. It simply read, *Mississippi Coast: Waylon and Lily, July 1946."* No wonder it matched the others from my memory. It belonged to that same set of pictures that had Mama, me at age two, and Waylon at the coast.

Sucking in a deep breath of the heavy air, I retrieved an embroidered handkerchief from my waistband and wiped my dripping brow. I held my ringing wet strawberry blonde hair up off of my neck hoping to cool down a bit. My tea glass was sweating as much as I was.

The ever-present paper fan on a wooden stick lay close by on the table. I worked at creating a semblance of a breeze with the cardboard picture of Jesus and a dozen children around his feet, while one perched on each of His knees.

A thought flitted through my mind. *What happy children they must have been.*

The words on the back of my makeshift fan flashed before my eyes with each motion of my hand. *Childress Baptist Church, Childress Mississippi.* The address and phone number blurred in my vision as I wondered what to cook for this Sunday's potluck. Childress Baptist is where Stan and I had taken Jack and Bethie each week, Stan driven to be a good father, me driven for my kids to be raised in stability and love and out of harm's reach their entire young lives.

I paused to listen to the cicadas start their evening chorus, their haunting sound only adding to my emotions. My eyes wandered back to the letter in my hands as I smoothed the corner back out that I had unknowingly wadded up.

And so I began.

*August 20, 1971*
*Dear Lily Ruth,*

*I know this letter will come as a surprise to you, it being twenty years or more since I last saw you or your mother Sam.*

Well, he was pretty close. It had actually been twenty-five years ago. I was merely two years old the last time I laid eyes on Waylon, though snatches of my memory contained very unpleasant memories involving the man.

My mother, Samantha Jean, was a mere nineteen years old.

Part One: **Looking for Beauty**

*"The voice of beauty speaks softly; it creeps only into the most fully awakened souls."*
--Friedrich Nietzsche

# chapter 1

*April 1941*

Sylvia Owens knew that if she closed her eyelids she could continue the fifteen minute walk to her husband's workplace blind. Most days she enjoyed the walk and the break from the duties of home.

There was always an endless list of chores to do: washing, ironing, cooking, canning, floors to clean, and dishes to do. For a house so small she was surprised at how much work there always seemed to be. But with six of them crammed into two bedrooms and the back porch converted into an extra bedroom, they all created dirty floors, heaps of laundry, and piles of dishes.

Sylvia knew better than to complain though. She knew of families of ten to twelve crammed into homes smaller than the one she lived in. Luckily she and Henry were one of the first dozen or so families to occupy one of the coal mining town's cookie cutter houses.

Henry's "smithin' skills" earned him a job as blacksmith for *Watson and Whitaker Mining Company* which in turn earned Sylvia peace of mind that he would do the dirty work *above* ground instead of deep within the black abyss of what she referred to as "the inner bowels of hell itself." Too many of her closest friends had lost either husband, son, or brother to the coal mine. If not loss of their lives, others lost fingers or developed the never-ending "miner's cough" from the evil black dust. Eternally grateful, Sylvia was proud her man had secured the coveted job of smithy; all the miners' wives coveted this job for their husbands' safety so their men didn't have to descend into the unknown depths of the coal mining world. Henry's position wouldn't leave Sylvia wondering if he would return home each night alive or uninjured.

Though today's calendar had marked the day as the 4th of April, 1941, it felt more like the month of June to Sylvia. Not a breath of breeze stirred the thick, heavy, Mississippi air. Sylvia shifted the basket of food from one hand to the other and dried her sweaty palm on the front of her blue checkered apron.

The scent of freshly baked cornbread, lima beans, and two fried slabs of salt pork floated up from the basket. Henry would be pleased with the strips of fried meat to go with his noon meal. Each day Sylvia or one of their two older girls, Bernice or Claudia, would make the short trek from the edge of their mining town of Wataker to bring lunch to Henry. At least, a month ago, Bernice would have, but she married her sweetheart just a few short weeks ago so now Sylvia and Claudia shared the job. On days Claudia and her little Geoffrey were able to take the short walk, Sylvia would find another chore to occupy her time. Many days she let Claudia escape and take Henry his lunch while she stayed back with her grandson Geoffrey; such a walk was difficult for the almost three year old joy of her life.

Passing the brightly painted sign that read *"Nearing Watson & Whitaker Mining Company, Wataker, Miss.,"* Sylvia, along with most of the small mining town's residents, scoffed at the name of their town. Whoever heard of such a name anyway?

The two coal mine owners, Watson and Whitaker, had gotten into an argument after taking a full week to decide whose name would be first in their 50/50 partnership. Finally they drew straws, Watson ending up with the long straw so he got his name listed first in the company's name. Then the same thing happened when it was time to decide the name of the mining town. Some suggested the men combine their last names for the mining town's moniker; again Watson drew the long straw. Thus the name Wataker, a combination of Watson and Whitaker. *Hideous* was the word Sylvia used to describe their town's name.

The loud, harsh staccato of hammer beating on iron brought her back to her surroundings. Sylvia looked up at the crooked hanging sign that read *Watson & Whitaker Mining Co., Blacksmith* as she neared the outer reaches of the coal mine.

Waiting outside her husband's shop, Sylvia sat down under the shade of a sprawling post oak tree, appreciative of its thick limbs and intertwined branches that created a cooling canopy overhead. She knew Henry preferred for her to wait for him until he could finish his work, then he would join her at the makeshift table under "their oak." Tucking a graying strand of fading, wavy, golden-brown, hair back into her bun, she did just that. She waited and enjoyed every second of the sit-down time.

Just a couple of minutes passed and she saw Henry emerge from the smithy shop, red handkerchief swiping across his face. A large grin broke out on Henry's face when he saw Sylvia sitting at the table, basket awaiting him. Flopping down across from his wife, Henry sighed deeply.

"I'm getting too old for this, Sylvie."

She loved the way he shortened her name and left off the "uh" at the end. He simply called her "Sylvie" instead of the usual "Sylvia." She smiled at the way Henry had of nicknaming everyone close to him. Never did he call those he loved by their given names.

Reaching into the basket, she withdrew a large, sealed mason jar of sweet tea with no lemon, Henry's favorite. She found the cloth napkin and swiped at a long, black, smudge on his cheek and forehead.

"Missed a spot."

"I always do, Sylvie. Can't seem to get rid of the black no matter how hard I try." He grabbed her hand then kissed the back of her soft skin and teased her some more. "Let's get to the real reason you came here. I know it wasn't to give me a bath, though I will let you do that later."

A slight blush crept over Sylvia's cheeks. She smacked Henry on the arm playfully and reached for the tin plate of food and uncovered it.

"Sylvie, you just made me one happy man! How'd you know I was craving meat today?"

"Lucky guess. I would bring you meat everyday if we could afford it, Henry. You deserve it. Now finish your lunch and I might give you a piece of apple pie I saved." She raised her trim eyebrows teasingly and got a laugh in response.

"Apple pie, huh? I thought you said last night it was all gone."

"It was. No one had to know the last piece went in the cupboard for your lunch the next day."

"You sure do take good care of me, woman." Henry's eyes softened as he enjoyed his meal and relished sitting across from his beautiful bride while he emitted satisfied grunts with each taste of her fine cooking.

Resting a moment in silence while Henry ate, Sylvia began staring off into the surrounding trees. Her face clouded with trouble like a storm cloud gathering over the sun.

Henry laid down his fork. "Uh-oh. What is it Sylvie-girl? You've got that *look.*"

"I do not! I don't have a *look!* Now hush up and eat."

Eying her suspiciously, Henry pulled out an old pocket watch from the front of his bib overalls and clicked it open. "You got twenty minutes to hand over my pie and tell me why you have that look on your pretty face. You know the one.....you get all starry-eyed and stare off into space, then you bite your bottom lip—"

The second smack he received was less playful than the first one he earned.

"Enough!" Withdrawing the pie from the basket, she handed it over hoping to give Henry something else to occupy his mouth with instead of teasing her about worrying.

Huffing loudly, she began. "Okay. You caught me. I do have something on my mind......It's Samantha Jean. She's—she's......I don't know, different lately. And I'm worried."

"How do you mean *different*? I haven't noticed any change in Sammie." Stuffing another bite of cinnamon and sugar topped pie into his mouth, Henry waited for her to gather her thoughts and answer. Sometimes getting his woman to talk was like pulling hens' teeth.

"Of course you wouldn't notice. You're a *man*," Sylvia said as if that explained his lack of awareness that his daughter might be having a problem.

"Why, thank you, Sugar. I'm glad you noticed I'm a man." Henry never let her get one over on him.

Sylvia rolled her blue eyes and continued. "I can't put my finger on it, Henry. She's been late getting home from school, she's absent-minded, she's quieter......" Struggling for the right words, Sylvia stopped short.

"Sounds like a normal fourteen year old girl to me."

"Which reminds me of another thing. What are we going to do for her fifteenth birthday? It's only a month away. Bernice's wedding a few months ago used any extra money we had. And when Mel enlisted in the Navy and we helped move Claudia and Geoffrey back in with us, well, that took the rest of our money. You know we did what we had to and we couldn't leave our Claudia home alone with a two year old to raise."

Hating to see her fret and worry, Henry covered Sylvia's small hand with his larger, calloused one. "Don't you worry your pretty head over money, Syl. That's my job. All our girls are fine. Bernie's married to a good man, a rich man by our standards for that matter, and he will take care of her just fine. I know you didn't want her to marry just yet, but she's in a nice apartment and has a good job." Pausing for a sip of sweet tea, he then continued. "Our Claudia has a good man too. I know she and Mel will get back on their feet soon enough when his stint with the Navy's over. Claudia's just not able to raise a baby alone. It was just too much for her and she needed her mama and papa's help again. Plus I like having the little guy around. We have to catch lightning bugs tonight so I hope you saved me that pickle jar."

Sylvia deeply appreciated Henry trying to cheer her up. It did little to erase the worry over Samantha though. She was Samantha's mama and she just *knew* something wasn't right with her girl.

Gathering Henry's lunch things, Sylvia kissed his cheek and told him 'bye. Both went back to the remainder of their day, one sweating and smithing, the other stewing and worrying.

# chapter 2

Straightening her skirt and reaching to unbutton the top button of her blouse, Samantha Jean Owens knew her mama would highly disapprove of a fourteen year old girl wearing her blouse open so low in the front. Especially a girl as developed as she was. Flipping her strawberry blonde hair over her shoulder, she flicked away the pesky thought as well. Mama was home washing breakfast dishes and about to begin the eternal laundry so Samantha had no reason to worry about her mama's opinion right then anyway.

*I'm nearly fifteen so that makes me a woman,* she reminded herself as she took the long way to school alone again that week. Samantha missed walking to school with her girlfriends. It had always been one of the highlights of her day, but now she had a good reason to walk alone.

She and her friends had agreed that if one of them wasn't at the designated meeting spot on time waiting by the huge sweet gum tree at the bend in the road, the late person would have to walk alone instead of making all of them tardy. Lately, Samantha's friends had been quizzing her for the reason for so many missed morning walks. She had used Geoffrey as her excuse, which was partly true since she had been helping her sister Claudia get him fed and dressed for the day.

Claudia's husband Melvin had joined the Navy last month to avoid the draft and to provide a source of income for his little family, so since then, Claudia couldn't do anything for herself as it was and seemed to always need someone's assistance. This gave Samantha a believable excuse that her friends bought hook, line, and sinker, as her Daddy would say.

Thinking of the real reason she now walked alone to school the long way, Samantha blushed furiously at the scenes that played across her mind, all things she would never tell even her two closest friends.

She and Waylon Graves.

He was the real reason Samantha walked alone.

~~~~~~~~~~

"Hey, Graves! Slow down, man!"

Footsteps pounded behind him as he continued hurrying forward. Waylon Graves was on a mission and wouldn't be deterred.

"Where you headed so fast? I was going to see if you wanted to join me and the guys for poker tonight." Waylon's buddy shoved him roughly to get his attention as they walked.

"Cut it out, Lenny! And no, I don't want to play poker tonight." Waylon increased his pace.

"Slow down, Way! Why the rush? You never wanted to get to work this fast before. What does the *Roadside Gulf Station* have that I don't? Why the race?"

A starved, greedy smile spread across Waylon's handsome face, the look of a hungry wolf about to devour a helpless ground squirrel.

"Oh, if you only knew," Waylon replied.

"So tell me, pal. What's got you all excited," Lenny pressed.

"You mean 'who' not 'what.'" Waylon clapped Lenny on the shoulder and took off in a sprint. He called back over his shoulder, "See ya later!"

Before Lenny could utter a response, Waylon darted down a side alley and into the field behind a row of buildings. Taking a quick left path, he forced himself to slow to a halt. Removing a black plastic comb from his hip pocket, Waylon did his best to slick his hair back into place and re-tuck his shirt tail.

Last night's lengthy stay at a friend's party did nothing to help him get out of bed on time this morning. He had to rush if he was going to reach their meeting place on time.

Already Waylon could taste Samantha's sweet young lips. She was a flirt and a tease, but so far Waylon could do no more than sneak a kiss or two at each secret meeting before she had to leave for school. The thrill of the chase was about to get the best of Waylon and he knew it. If Sam wouldn't give him more today than a few kisses, he would just have to be a bit more aggressive. She was young and needed to know what a man needed from a girl. He wasn't some schoolboy to be led around by the pigtails of a sweet young thing.

He was a man and it was time Waylon showed Sam who was boss and in charge of this relationship. But he knew he had to do it without scaring her off like he had the last two girls. These young little beauties with the bodies of older women were tricky.

And Sam was proving to be the trickiest. One minute she teased him mercilessly and the next she pushed him away. Rounding the curve to their secret meeting spot, Waylon saw her and most of his devious schemes melted away at the sight of Sam.

Not seeing him first, Waylon stopped on the path and stood watching her straighten her hair, check the buttons on her blouse, and apply another layer of red lipstick that set off her strawberry blonde tresses even more. She drove him crazy and didn't even have a clue.

Samantha turned around in his direction and instantly caught sight of Waylon, her face lighting up with a coy smile. "There you are! I wondered if you had forgotten all about me." Putting on her prettiest pout, Samantha batted her long eyelashes at Waylon.

Not able to stand himself another second, Waylon grabbed her arm and drug Samantha behind a tree that was off the path. "Baby, come here...."

Samantha allowed him to lead her away. She noticed he had caught sight of her lower than usual neckline and it excited her to see his reaction.

Hungrily, Waylon pulled Samantha into his arms and brought his lips to hers. Kissing her roughly she pulled away after a moment and placed her delicate hands on his heaving chest.

"Slow down, Way...."

Ignoring her protests, Waylon began kissing her neck.

"Waylon! Stop! What's the hurry?" Samantha hated the nervousness she could hear in her words. Clearing her throat, she tried to draw his attention away from kissing for a minute. "Hey, guess what is coming up soon?"

"Hush, Sam, and kiss me. I've missed you. A man misses a woman when they are apart."

No one had ever called her a *woman* before. Distracted by his flattery, Samantha allowed him to resume his search for her red lips. When things began to get out of hand again, Samantha shoved at his chest again.

"You're going to get me all rumpled before class, Waylon. I have to go in a minute anyway. And you aren't listening to me....I asked you a question. Do you know what's happening soon?"

Releasing her, Waylon drew in a frustrated sigh. Speaking sharper than he had intended, he asked her, "No, I don't know! What's happening soon, Sam?"

Sometimes she loved to hear him say her name, but not in this tone. The past month had been mostly heaven to Samantha, but more than she cared to admit, Waylon was becoming increasingly frustrated with her, often spoke harshly to her, and occasionally pushed her to do things she was uncomfortable with. Yet she knew she was a flirt and a tease.

Grabbing both of his hands in hers, she looked into Waylon's eyes, drawing him into the depths of her violet blue orbs. Shaking his head slowly, Waylon let his frustrations dissolve away. Gently, he asked again, "What is so important that is coming up, Sam?"

A huge smile lit her face. "My birthday! In a week!"

"That's wonderful! Sweet Sixteen Samantha! All grown up and beautiful as ever."

Her face dropped instantly. "Sixteen? Way, I will be *fifteen* in a week.....I thought—"

Shocked, his face matched hers. "What? You told me you were fifteen when we met. Three months ago you said you were fifteen." Anger clouded his eyes. "Did you lie to me, Sam? I hate lying."

"No!! I—I only said that I was fifteen because I nearly was—does it matter, Waylon? We are together, right? What's age anyway? It's just a number." Fear closed in around Samantha, making her afraid she would lose the one thing that meant so much to her, the one thing that brought her joy and excitement and made her feel like a woman. "Don't you still want to be with me, Way?" On command, tears pooled in her purplish-blue eyes.

He did the one thing she hated. He turned his back on her. It had worked countless times in the past when he was mad at her and wanted his own way. Samantha reached for him and cuddled up to him as close as she possibly could then began kissing Waylon on the neck. She felt him soften in her arms.

Waylon emitted a low moan. "Sam, when you do that I forget how old you are. You're right; should age really matter? Fourteen, fifteen, sixteen--I want *you*, Sam." He began letting his hands have their way until she stopped him yet again.

"Waylon, stop, please. You know my rule. Not til we are married.....please."

Caught up in the moment, he replied, "Then let's run off and get married! For your birthday! I know somebody who will marry us. Then we can be together like we both want and start a life with each other." Persuasively he kissed her again, only softly and gently this time.

"Married? Waylon, you don't mean it, do you? Now?? Us get married?" Samantha was incredulous at the thought of his suggestion.

"Why not, Baby? Unless—you don't *want* to marry me.....I know plenty of other girls....." Waylon let that sink into her head a minute.

"Yes! Yes, I do! But now? How?"

"Trust me, Sam. Just trust me. Can you do that?"

"Yes. But what about Mama—"

Smothering her protests with another kiss, Waylon scooped her up off the ground and twirled Samantha, his prize, in the air. "No need to fret. Your parents will be happy if you are happy. Now! I say we marry today!"

Laughing, Samantha was so caught up in love and Waylon and the moment, her school books and sack lunch lay forgotten under their secret meeting tree as she allowed him to carry her off to get married.

# chapter 3

The hot, steamy, two hour drive to wherever they were headed gave Samantha Jean Owens plenty of time to rethink her decision about this impromptu marriage to Waylon Graves. Her mind raced with questions as she watched the fields of wilting wildflowers speed pass them.

*Find the beautiful,* Samantha reminded herself.

She glanced over at Waylon and couldn't find it.

The beautiful. The good. The lovely…..something she had vowed to search for each day she woke up since she could remember. That's what made life in a dirty coal mining town bearable. To look for the beautiful.

Today, of all the days in her fourteen years of life, she *should* be able to find the beautiful. But where was it?

The roaring of the old car's engine returned Samantha to the present. Her *wedding* day.

But why didn't it feel like she had imagined all those many nights as she stared out of her open window into the star-lit sky above? What was missing?

Already her young mind knew the answer to these questions. What was missing was her parents, her sisters, her friends, a softly lit chapel, a preacher, flowers, a specially decorated cake…..

Today, she had none of that to show for on her wedding day.

*Find the beautiful!* Again, she reminded herself to look for it.

It took some effort on her part, but finally she saw it. Something beautiful.

As the rattling car slowed to a halt, Samantha saw it.

A red balloon. Tied to a little girl's left hand as the girl's right hand held tightly to her father's. The father was smiling at the little girl as he watched her upturned face smiling at the bouncing red balloon.

Samantha had found the beautiful in this day and then suddenly it vanished with the sound of a voice breaking into her staring at the floating red orb.

"Sam! I said we're here so let's go unless you changed your mind!" She looked to her left and saw the scowling face of her future husband awaiting her answer.

"Oh…..yes, we're here. No, of course I haven't changed my mind." Samantha plastered a smile on her face and quickly forced herself to kiss Waylon on the cheek. "What are *you* waiting for, silly man? Let's go; it's our wedding day!"

27

"That's my girl," Waylon replied.

Reaching for the car's door handle, Samantha inhaled a deep breath as she fought to still the pounding of her heart. Could she really do this? Marry a man without her parents' knowledge? Without even yet turning fifteen? Without her family and friends there to witness her special day?

Waylon reached her side and placed a kiss on her forehead, momentarily erasing her fears and tumultuous thoughts. He had that effect on Samantha and she knew it.

Giddiness, queasiness, and uncertainties all vied for attention in her young gut and this time giddiness won out. It was her wedding day! And she was marrying Waylon Graves, for Pete's sake!

Maybe she *could* find the beautiful.

Looking around the stuffy room filled with stale cigar smoke, Samantha shivered involuntarily as she glanced repeatedly at Waylon. She shifted in the hard wooden chair where she was sitting by the man she loved, his arm draped around her chair back.

An image from one of Geoffrey's picture books came to mind.

A sharp-fanged wolf, walking on its hind legs with a thin string of drool slipping from his lips. The wolf was quietly sneaking up on a small pink piglet who was gathering sticks for a fire. The piglet didn't know he was being stalked by the wolf.

*Why would I think of such a horrible thing on my wedding day?* Visibly Samantha shook her head to clear the thought away.

"You okay, Baby," Waylon asked in his gentlest tone.

"Yeah. Just wishing Mama and Papa and my sisters were here, I guess. It's my wedding day and not a single soul that I love to witness it."

"You love me and I'm here. That's what is important. Now don't start saying that again. We talked about this on the drive here. Remember, you are saving your parents a lot of worry and money doing it this way. They love you so they will love whoever you marry. Don't worry, Sam. In less than an hour we will be married and tucked away in a hotel somewhere and--"

"Way! Not in public.....people are listening to us."

"Oh, don't be such a fuddy-duddy, Sam—"

"Mr. Graves." A woman in a grey wool suit called his name. "You're up next."

Taking her by the hand, Waylon had to nearly pull Samantha to her feet.

Leaning close to her ear, Waylon said, "That's us, Sam. It's time."

Again, the wolf image came to her mind followed by another shudder coursing through her young body. Swallowing loudly, Samantha mustered up the courage to answer her soon-to-be husband. "Yes, Way. It's time."

Plastering a smile on her face, Samantha tried to look older than her fourteen years and determined to carry herself as a woman would. She had applied enough make-up on the trip here from her purse's cosmetic bag and freshened her hair hoping she looked old enough to marry. Oh how she wished for curly hair instead of the straight tresses she had. Curls would have made her look much more grown up.

They were led into a small room covered in dark paneling, the source of the cigar smell that had lingered in the waiting room. Samantha covered her mouth and coughed once receiving a disapproving glance from Waylon.

"Come in, Mr. Graves. You have your future bride and my money, I assume?"

"Of course, Sir." Waylon rummaged nervously in his coat pocket and withdrew a wad of rolled up bills.

The man's name plate stationed on his desk read simply "*E. H. Hendershot.*" Opening a concealed drawer in his desk, Mr. Hendershot crammed the bills in and shut it with a resounding thud.

Samantha made a mental note to ask Waylon who this man was, a justice of the peace, a minister? And just how much money did he have to pay him? And come to think of it, why wasn't she asked for her birth certificate or to fill out any paperwork before marrying Waylon? She remembered the week long hunt for her sister's birth certificate before she got married. Finally they discovered it had fallen somehow underneath the drawer of the dresser and was lodged in the back.

Something just wasn't right to Samantha, but Waylon had assured her everything would be fine. And she had promised to trust him, which is what women did with their husbands, she reasoned.

"Mr. Graves, step forward with your lady there. What's her name?"

Samantha opened her mouth to respond but Waylon interrupted her. "Sam. Samantha Owens, Sir."

"Fine. Then let's carry on. There's lots of others waiting to stand in your spot before sundown." The man rubbed his hands greedily together and stood to his feet, producing a belly the size of the biggest watermelon Samantha had ever seen her Daddy grow in the backyard garden.

"So, just repeat these lines after me, you two." Lifting a sheet of paper from his messy desk, Hendershot began what was to be Samantha's wedding ceremony.

Her empty hands trembled for lack of a bouquet of bridal flowers that should have been in place.

Her face felt exposed to this man's scrutiny for lack of a white veil that should have placed its lacy cover over her eyes.

Her mouth felt dry for lack of words that should have tasted sweet to her tongue while loved ones would have been craning their necks to hear her choked out responses.

Before Samantha knew it, she heard herself saying two last words. "I do."

And it was over.

A ceremony she couldn't even remember.

Waylon glanced at her from the corner of his eye. "Sam, we did it."

Hendershot gave one last command. "You may kiss your bride."

Fearing fangs could come from Waylon's once sweet kisses, Samantha quickly closed her eyes and went through the motions of their first kiss as man and wife.

~~~~~~~~~~

A light rap on the screened door brought Sylvia from her dinner preparations. Wiping her hands on a towel, she shoved tendrils of her hair back off of her perspiring face.

"Claudia! Can you get the door?"

Giggles from the open window signaled to her that Claudia and little Geoffrey were in the backyard. They wouldn't hear her calls from there.

Sighing at the interruption, she headed to the front screened door. Peering through the tightly woven screen, Sylvia was surprised to see two of Samantha Jean's friends standing on the front porch.

"Girls, what brings you by?"

"Is—is Samantha home?"

Glancing down in one of the girl's hands, Sylvia noticed Samantha's book bag. A weight the size of the giant sand bags used to stop the floodwaters of the Mississippi River hit her with a thud in the chest. Sylvia stepped out on the porch. She reached down and grabbed her daughter's book bag. "What do you mean, 'is Samantha home'?"

The other girl spoke up. "We took another way home from school today to deliver some homework papers to a sick friend for Teacher. And.....I saw something lying under a tree so I went to see what it was and it was Samantha's book bag. I thought maybe she dropped it? So, she's not home yet?"

Fear clutched Sylvia's heart. She looked to see Henry striding up the dirt road toward their home. Relief overwhelmed her. She knew Henry would have an answer to this ridiculous riddle.

Addressing the girls, Sylvia senselessly questioned them in rapid fire. "Did you not walk home with her as you always do? Did Samantha seem okay at school? Was she feeling well?"

"No ma'am. I mean, no she wasn't okay at school. She didn't come to school today. I thought she was sick and then I saw her bag—" Tears choked the young girl's voice.

Sylvia called to Henry as he turned to head to the backyard and Little Geoffrey. "Henry! Come quick."

Knowing something was wrong, Henry went immediately to Sylvia. He took in her red flowered print dress, the one she wore most days for housework. He noted the wringing of her hands as she twisted the handle of a cloth bag of sorts. And mostly he saw the look of absolute fear on his wife's face that urged him into a run.

"Girls, run on home. I will call your mamas as soon as I find out about Samantha Jean. And thanks for...."

In unison the two answered Sylvia. "Yes ma'am!" They tore down the sidewalk as quickly as they could, terror and uncertainty about their friend chasing the girls home to safety.

Grabbing her by the shoulders, Henry erupted, "Syl, what is it? What's wrong?"

Unable to form words, Sylvia just stared at Henry trying to wrap her mind around what she had just learned from Samantha's friends.

Shaking her gently, Henry continued, "Tell me, woman....what happened?" He led her to a cushioned porch chair, the plastic cover making a crinkling sound underneath their combined weight as the two sat.

"It's Samantha Jean. Something's happened." She glanced at the book bag belonging to their daughter. "Lois and Margie brought Samantha's book bag by the house. They found it under a tree and wondered if she was alright. She's *not* alright, Henry....." Fear turned to anger, which she loosed on Henry's chest. Sylvia shoved him with both hands in his chest and continued in a terror-tinged pitch. "I *told* you something wasn't right with Samantha. See?"

Henry grabbed her by the wrists and brought her head to his shoulder and let her regain her composure. Though about to burst with his own fears, Henry remained calm. "Sylvie, start at the beginning."

Pulling back, Sylvia looked down the sidewalk's cracks filled with lime green moss. "The girls said she wasn't at school today. They found her bag on a different route home than they usually take so they came to see if she was okay. She's *not* okay, Henry; I just know it. Something horrible's happened to our girl. She—" Sylvia's voice broke with tears.

"Now don't rush to conclusions. Let's go in the house so we can talk this out and make a plan. Maybe she went home with another friend. Maybe she—" Not sure what else to say, Henry guided Sylvia to the kitchen table.

Pulling out a chair for her, Henry shoved Sylvia to sit down before she collapsed in the floor. Heading to the always ready coffee pot he poured them each a cup.

Starting to rise, Sylvia burst out. "We can't just sit here! We have to do something!"

Henry placed a hand on her shoulder. "Something, yes. But we need to think this through and not run off halfcocked. She may walk through those doors any second."

Wrapping her hands around the chipped, pale blue, coffee cup, Sylvia took a grateful sip. The heated liquid warmed and calmed her for a second. "Where could she be? And why wouldn't she go to school?"

"You saw her off this morning?" Henry asked.

"Yes, as usual. She helped Claudia with Geoffrey, ate her oatmeal, complained because I hitched her skirt down an extra inch….you know the usual morning routine. I watched her walk off down the sidewalk to go meet her friends…..and then they bring her book bag home and tell me she wasn't at school today!!" Near hysteria caused Sylvia to raise her voice. Shaking she spilled some coffee on her hand and wiped it on her apron. "Ouch! Oh, why, Henry? Where did she go? Has she been kidnapped, hurt?"

Henry rose from his chair and went to her side. Pulling Sylvia up, Henry embraced her and rubbed her back. "Sylvie, she's fine. I know in my gut she's ok. No one has hurt our girl."

Pushing away, Sylvia shouted, "How could you possibly know that, Henry??"

The back screened door screeched in protest as Claudia and Geoffrey entered.

Looking from one parent to the other, Claudia demanded an explanation. "Whatever is going on in here? We heard you two hollerin'." Not receiving an answer, Claudia watched Sylvia's face turn an ashen gray. "Mama, what's wrong?" Claudia rushed to Sylvia's side.

Henry took over. "Sammie-girl didn't go to school today but her friends found her book bag and brought it to your mother a while ago. We don't know where she is."

"What?? Daddy, why are you still standing here? She could be hurt and alone and you should be—" Helplessly, Claudia broke off her sentence.

Feeling the weight of the world on his shoulders, Henry Owens stood and faced his little family, one of them now missing as words, plans, and any reasonable thought escaped him. His mind felt like yesterday's jell-o they had for dessert.

*Dear God, help us all,* was all his mind could muster up.

# chapter 4

Leaving the smoky building that had served as her momentary wedding chapel, Samantha inhaled deeply of the fresh spring air. Finally she felt her lungs could fully take in a breath. Again she breathed deeply and slowly, trying desperately to exhale the misgivings and nervousness she was feeling.

As soon as she and Waylon had said their *I do's,* Waylon practically drug her out of the small building and straight towards the car. She wondered why he was in such a hurry. Besides, she was starving. A picture flashed across her mind as she suddenly realized where her afternoon lunch had been abandoned.

Her book bag. Her lunch. Both left under the tree.

Her friends and parents!

Panic filled her chest and she stopped dead in her tracks causing Waylon to lose his tight grip on her arm.

"Sam, what's the matter with you? You look as pale as a ghost." A smirk spread across Waylon's face as he continued. "You're not nervous about what comes next are you?"

Another rush of panic filled her trembling body as she fought the taste of bile rising in her throat when the reality of Waylon's words hit her full force. *Oh goodness! I hadn't thought....*

Bending close to her ear, Waylon hissed, "Sam! What is it? What's gotten into you? Now you are acting like you're fourteen! Have I just made the biggest mistake of my life marrying you? Come on! Let's get to the car."

Unable to form words, Samantha Jean Owens Graves forced her feet to walk to Waylon's car mostly so she could get him out of her ear. Reaching her car door before she did, Waylon jerked the door open and slammed it shut with a loud thud that threatened to shatter the window.

*Get yourself together, Samantha Jean!* The scared young thing fought another wave of nausea that threatened to empty her stomach.

"I'm sorry, Waylon. I just got too hot and stuffy and maybe I had a case of the pre-wedding jitters in that room. But—but I'm okay now. Don't worry about me. I just need to eat. I haven't had anything since breakfast. Neither have you for that matter. Let's find a diner and get some supper. How does that sound?" As she spoke she gently rubbed Waylon's arm and tried her best to sound calm.

"Eat—right now? Baby, we just got married and you know what happens next!" Waylon leaned in to kiss her but without thinking she leaned away.

Quickly realizing this was a very stupid move on her part, Samantha said the first thing that came to mind. "Waylon, please let me call Mama and Daddy and tell them the good news....they will be so excited and will be wondering if I am okay since I didn't come home from school by now. It's late and I don't want them to worry. Please? It would mean the world to me, and then we will eat supper after.....you know....."

Softening slowly before her pretty batting eyes, Waylon sighed deeply. "Sam, you have a way with me, you know that? Okay, let's find a phone and call your parents then there's a bed calling our names right over there in that hotel.....what do you think?"

Following Waylon's pointing finger across the street to the hotel, Samantha nearly gasped at the run-down condition of the dump where she would spend her honeymoon night. Watching disappointment flit across her face, Waylon responded, "What? You think you're too good to stay there? You know I don't have much money and I paid for the ceremony and now the hotel and supper!"

"No—no, it's just fine. I'm sure it will be wonderful." Again the plastered-on smile appeared on Samantha's face. "Now, let's find that phone and get that behind us."

Before Waylon changed his mind, Sam reached for the door handle of the car and bolted out before the crushing emotions caved in on her and smothered her to death.

"I'm going to the police, Syl—" Interrupting Henry midsentence, the jangling black telephone perched on the wooden maple telephone table nearly rattled off the tiny rounded surface.

Grabbing the phone off its base, Henry quickly answered. "Hello? Sammie-girl! It's you! Thank the Good Lord!" Pausing and listening Henry ran a hand through his graying hair.

Sylvia rushed to his side and gripped his forearm, tears springing to her eyes. A choked sob escaped between her pale lips. Pressing her fingers to her mouth, she waited.

Henry resumed the questions. "Where are you? Are you okay?" Another pause. "What?!?!"

Again he listened. "Samantha Jean, I'm coming to get you.....Honey, listen. Are you safe?.....I just don't understand. How could you do this without even—Sammie-girl, I love you and all you have to do is call me and I will come—Yes, I'll tell your Mama and sister. You swear you're okay? When will you be home? Sammie—Sammie, wait! I love you too, girl. 'Bye."

Phone still dangling in his hand, Henry turned to his little family who stood wide-eyed before him awaiting an explanation he had yet to understand himself. Henry just stood speechless.

Claudia broke the unbearable silence. "For goodness sake, Daddy, tell us what is wrong! Is Samantha okay?"

Henry visibly aged ten years before their eyes. The death grip Sylvia had on his arm, the pleading in her eyes, and the constant buzz of the disconnected phone receiver still in his hand brought him back to the present.

Shaking her husband, Sylvia shouted, "Henry, say something! Is she hurt?"

Dropping the phone into the cradle, Henry plopped down onto the telephone table's connected seat, suddenly looking and feeling very small. Quietly he finally was able to mumble a response. "No, Syl. Sammie's not *hurt*. She's *married*."

In unison, Sylvia and Claudia chorused in astonishment, "Married?!?!" Then they all three erupted into a volley of questions that began to muffle and mingle in Henry's head. His vision blurred and he felt the floor trying to pull him to his knees.

Forcibly pulling himself together, Henry stood to his feet and raised both hands to quiet them down. "I need some air. Let's go to the front porch and I'll explain." Holding the wall to steady himself, Henry led them outside.

They all trooped to the tiny house's front screened porch and found a chair. Even little Geoffrey felt the solemnity of the moment and stuck his thumb in his mouth as he too sat down in his little wooden rocker.

"Samantha Jean's gone and got married."

Sylvia's hand flew to her mouth as she tried to stifle the second round of tears.

Claudia asked the question for them. "Married to who? That's impossible! She's fourteen!"

Henry continued. "To a boy named Waylon Graves. That's all I know. She's not hurt and doesn't want me to come get her. She wouldn't stay on the phone long but said she would call back tomorrow. It doesn't sound like she wants us to know right now any more than that. My gut tells me she's okay and unharmed, but I just don't understand—" For the first time since this whole event began, Henry's voice cracked and his green eyes misted with tears.

Geoffrey watched as Henry withdrew his handkerchief from his overalls pocket and swiped at his eyes. His little legs reached for the floor from his rocker and he paddled over to Henry. "We go catch lit'n bugs, Pops, then you feel better."

It took all of Henry's energy to not burst into a torrent of tears, but he didn't want to scare his little buddy. "You're right, Little Man. That will make me feel better. How about you play under the big tree with your trucks for a bit and then we will go get us a glass of lemonade and find that pickle jar, okay?"

"Okay, Pops." Geoffrey headed to his trucks and was immediately lost in the fun of the moment while the adults discussed things further.

Sylvia finally spoke. "What do we do now? I can't believe this! Our little girl has run off with a boy we don't even know and got herself married—" Silent tears poured down her cheeks as words halted in her dry throat.

"There's not anything we can do at the moment. She won't tell me where she is. She said she was happy and wanted this, so she wanted us to be happy too. Well, I can't do that just now. I'm *not* happy one bit! I'm mad as a hornet! And scared all at the same time...."

Claudia reached for her father's shoulder. "Me too, Daddy. If she walked up on this porch right now I would hug her first, then choke the life out of her."

"So we just sit and wait. That's it."

"Yes, Sylvie. That's it for now." Reaching for his wife's hand, Henry squeezed it tightly then went indoors for Geoffrey's pickle jar.

"I need to go call Samantha's friends, Lois and Margie. They will be worried sick." Claudia rose to follow her husband inside.

Laying a hand on her mother's arm, Claudia took over. "Let me do it, Mama. I will just tell them she called and is okay and we will give them more details later. That will have to be enough for now. That's all any of us can manage at this point."

Lying in the musty hotel room on the hard mattress, Samantha Jean Owens Graves watched silently as a long brown roach skittered up the wall of the tiny room. It didn't even seem to faze her as she was accustomed to such critters in the mining camp homes. Her Mama kept a spotless home to discourage any such bugs and varmints from entering her house but she had seen plenty in friends' homes that weren't as clean as where she lived.

*Mama, oh Mama. What you and Daddy must think of me now. At least I married first before letting a man take me to bed…..and I am happy.*

The lie tasted less sweet the second time around. It was a lie and she knew it. She *wanted* to be happy with her decision to marry Waylon. Clearly, in the moonlight's stark beam she could see what she hadn't seen the past weeks and months after meeting Waylon.

After Samantha had called home, thankfully Waylon's stomach encouraged him to take her to eat before taking her to bed. His aggressiveness that she had overlooked in the past reared its ugly head in full force after they ate dinner and checked into the hotel room. Love wasn't supposed to be like this. Demanding, rough, selfish. All along she believed that Waylon would be different and like the man of her dreams. He was pushy because he wanted to be with her and she wanted to wait for marriage. And before she knew what was happening, he had convinced her that this was the best decision.

She lie still and listened to his loud snoring. *Have I married a grizzly bear instead of a man?*

She glanced at the night table and saw the bottle he had produced from a bag in his car. She knew what it was. Her daddy drank the very same stuff, only a very small mason jar not even half filled was his preferred amount. Waylon had swigged away nearly the entire bottle before they went to bed. She definitely didn't like this about him. Drinking made men mean. She had seen it happen before and knew the results. Her daddy drank too much one time and that was all Mama would put up with. She nearly kicked him to the curb that night and threatened to leave if he ever drank more than what she deemed acceptable, and never could Daddy drink on Sundays.

*I should be happy right now,* Samantha chided herself. *This is supposed to be beautiful. This is…..my life now.*

Reality wormed its way into her mind and heart.

*Why didn't I insist we wait? Why did I get so caught up in the moment under the tree not even 24 hours ago and run off and do something foolish? I wanted my family and friends there when…..*Samantha allowed her thoughts to hit a dead end. She couldn't change things now.

A loud snort came from the man who slept next to her. Waylon rolled over in his sleep, threw an arm atop Samantha, and facing her, breathed a rancid huff of stale, alcohol-laced, breath into her face. Quickly she rolled the opposite direction never causing him to stir.

*I just want peace. Like at home with my family when I lay in bed at night, peace and quiet at the end of the day.*

But peace seemed elusive at that very moment, something she would not be able to find. Funny, she had never thought much about peace before until then, when she didn't have it.

Samantha looked around the dimly lit room. She had tried her hardest to fall asleep but her mind wouldn't allow such a thing at this point. She glanced at her surroundings as Waylon continued his loud snoring behind her. In the corner of her eye, she caught a glimpse of something rectangular shaped and white. She stared at it a moment longer trying to determine what was lying on the open shelf of the night table. Curiosity got the best of her; besides, she needed to use the bathroom.

Easing out from under Waylon's arm so she didn't wake him, Samantha crept as slowly and soundlessly as she could out of the bed. She glanced back at her snoring husband, the man she should be thrilled to be lying beside, not trying to escape from. Sadness stole around her heart and tears came to her violet blue eyes.

Reaching for the white rectangle, Samantha lifted it from the table. It felt like a cloth-covered book of some description. She tucked it under her arm and with one more glance to ensure Waylon was still asleep, she crept to the bathroom and shut the door with the tiniest sound.

Sitting on the toilet, Samantha waited to make sure she hadn't wakened Waylon. Still snoring.

She eased the object from the white cloth and found it was a book. Glancing at the cover, Samantha read *Holy Bible* in gold letters on a black cover. A twinge of disappointment coursed through her young mind. Then a moment of remorse followed. Sure she had heard the Bible read from the pastor, and at church had memorized a few verses or two in Sunday School, had prayed the prayer of salvation with her friends a few summers ago, but she had never made it a part of her daily life to actually read the sacred Book. Only preachers and Sunday School teachers did that sort of thing.

*Have I ever opened a Bible before?* The thought startled her a moment.

Then she realized that, no, she had never chosen to pick up a Bible and read it. Her parents had one that sat on the bottom shelf of the coffee table but they were never allowed to touch it. The only thing Samantha had heard her parents read from the book was from the Birth and Death Records page in the family Bible.

A slim golden ribbon was tucked in the pages of the Bible. Samantha flipped to where the gold strand rested. Reverently she whispered the words that were underlined with a red pencil, "Psalm 29:11. The Lord will give strength unto his people; the Lord will bless his people with peace."

Quickly she closed the book and sat in stunned silence at the words she had read. Snoring continued from the next room as she remained seated on the toilet seat of the tiny bathroom.

Flipping the Bible back open to the marked page, she read the verse again silently. *The Lord will give strength unto his people; the Lord will bless his people with peace.*

It really did say that. Peace, the one thing she longed for not ten minutes ago. This black book just told her where it could come from. From the Lord.

Other than the mealtime prayer, talking to God was unfamiliar to Samantha. Oh, she believed in Him and knew Jesus had died on a cross and rose from the grave for her sins and she would one day go to heaven where other believers went after death, but *talking* to God here on earth was so very foreign to her.

Except when Little Geoffrey was sick and almost died. Samantha recalled the fact that she had stormed out of the house after her Mama had told her how sick he really was. The screened door slammed and she flew down the back steps to the trees behind their house. There she fell on her knees, face to the moist soil, and wept, cried, prayed, and begged for God to heal Geoff.

The very next day, his dangerously high temperature broke and he quickly recovered from the illness he suffered. Samantha had always wondered since that day if God really had heard her prayers or if he just got unexplainably better to the surprise of the doctors.

*Maybe You did hear me. If it was You that answered my prayer for Geoff, please hear me now and give me peace. I may have made a mistake marrying Waylon, God. Please help me and give me the strength I need to make it.....Amen.*

Like a silken robe placed on her slim shoulders, peace settled about her. She could actually take a deep unforced breath. Her heart returned to a normal rhythm. Samantha felt God's hand on her.

Even though down deep she knew she had committed an enormous error by marrying Waylon.

## chapter 5

The sun rose in all its blessed brilliance, bringing the start to a new day and a reason to leave the hotel room, the room that should grace her thoughts with pleasant honeymoon memories in the days to come. But the fourteen year old bride knew that wasn't the way it would be. This room would hold no sweet memories for Samantha.

Right now she wanted a shower, her own bed, her Mama's cooking, and her family around her. After the sun came up and woke the sleeping bear, he clearly had two things on his mind. Waylon wanted his sweet young wife and a hot meal. The wife came first since she was the first available.

After leaving the hotel and eating at a greasy diner, Waylon turned the car towards Wataker so Samantha braved a few questions. "So now what? Where do we go? We haven't talked about *anything*, Way. Where will we live?"

"Look, don't start acting like a scared child, Sam! I told you yesterday to trust me." Waylon's words were harsh and stung his new bride.

"But, Way—" An intense pain in her left arm stopped her words immediately. "Ow!! You're hurting me. Let go of my arm." The more she tried to pull away the tighter Waylon increased his grip. "Waylon! Stop it!!"

"I told you not to bother me with your childish questions! Now hush up, Sam!"

She pressed him anyway. "Why are you treating me this way? I'm your wife--"

Through gritted teeth, he snarled back at her. "Don't act like a child and I won't treat you like one. You want to be treated like my wife then don't whine like a brat!"

Stunned at the difference in the man under the tree she had been secretly meeting compared to this person, Samantha got the message and was actually afraid not to be quiet.

He continued. "Let me think some things through while I drive." Reaching over into the back seat of the car, Waylon brought out another brown bottle of whiskey.

Opening her mouth to protest, Samantha quickly clamped her lips shut at the look of warning Waylon shot her. "If you'd take a swig, you might loosen up a bit too. But, no, I up and married a Miss Goodie Two Shoes! Geez!"

Waylon's comment hurt her young heart more than words could describe. None of this was supposed to be happening this way. Maybe he was just upset and needed to think and when they settled down somewhere he would calm down.

Fear began working its way into Samantha's heart. She had never felt such insecurity and uncertainty in all her life. Her daddy was a good man and provided a safe place for them to live. It wasn't much but it was theirs and she knew she would have food, a home, and a loving family. Tears pooled in her eyes and she quickly looked out the window trying to hide them from Waylon. She wouldn't let him see how he had upset her. Suddenly she was afraid of him. Afraid of how little she knew about him and who he was. Afraid of what he would say or do or how she might set him off again.

Determined to keep calm, Samantha did what she always did; she looked for the beautiful.

She searched out the car's dirty windshield and finally saw it, a puffy cloud in the brilliant blue sky overhead shaped like a duck. In a matter of seconds, the duck turned into a boot, and just as quickly the boot-shaped cloud morphed into…..a perfect, puffy, white heart. And for about the span of two minutes, the heart stayed in the sky, making sure she saw it and realized it was just for her. She believed with every ounce of her being that God had shaped that cloud to get her attention.

To remind her that He loved her and always would.

No matter what kind of a mess she had gotten herself into.

And to remind her where her peace came from. Pulling her purse close to her side, Samantha reached inside and placed her hand on the cloth-covered Bible. After reading a little more in the wee hours of the morning, she had returned the Bible to the white pouch and gently placed it in her purse to take with her. She just *knew* the Bible was meant for her, so she took it hoping stealing a Bible wasn't a sin. There was no name in the front or anywhere between the pages, only red penciled marks that underscored verses throughout the sacred book. She believed the treasure was meant for her.

Her trembling hand sought the comfort of the Bible's hard surface. Miraculously stilling her mind and heart, Samantha sat with one hand resting on the outside of her purse where the Bible lay snuggled deep within. Oh to be able to open the pages and read some more, but she dared not risk letting Waylon know she had it.

An hour of silence had settled between the couple making the drive awkward and uncomfortable for Samantha. She had so many questions left unanswered.

Getting closer to town, Waylon finally spoke to her. "Look, doll. It's Saturday so you don't have to worry about school and I don't have to go to work until Monday. Let's just go crash at my dad's place for the weekend until I sort through some ideas."

Another thought hit Samantha and she dared voice her question. "Way, I don't even know where you work. Tell me about your job and your home. We really know so little about each other." She ended the shaky sentence with a faltering laugh.

"Well, I work at the Shell gas station about a mile from town. The one between Wataker and Mills End. You know the one."

"Oh, sure. I know that one. What do you do there?"

"What do you mean 'what do I do?' I pump gas, clean windshields, air up tires, you know, run the place. I'm important there. They couldn't keep the place open without me….heck, maybe one day, I'll even own the joint."

*A gas station attendant? Not that anything's wrong with the job, I just expected Waylon to do something else with his life.* Samantha kept her thoughts to herself.

"As far as *home* goes," Waylon laced the word 'home' with a sneer, "you'll meet the old geezer soon enough."

"You mean your Dad?" Samantha pressed.

"No, I mean the old geezer. And before you ask any other questions, my Ma's dead. I never knew her. Died right after I was born from an infection." Waylon rubbed a hand over his eyes and continued to drive.

"So just you and your dad live together….at home?"

"Yeah."

That was all she got out of Waylon on that subject which left her with more fear than before. She would have to spend the weekend at Waylon and his dad's place. Two men she barely knew and herself, one young woman. *Oh God, what have I gotten myself into?*

Tears threatened to spill over her eyelids, but she refused them. What good would they do anyway?

Waylon made a quick left turn down a pothole filled dirt road. He jerked the car to a sudden stop in front of a ramshackle house that looked more like it came off the pages of a comic book she had once seen passed around class. The only thing missing on this house before her eyes was a thick layer of cobwebs blanketing the windows and shutters that the comic book's house wore like a worn out bridal veil.

Reaching for the car's door handle, Waylon stopped her. "Let me go in first. You sit here until I come get you. Understand?"

"Ye—yes, Waylon."

Ten minutes later, Samantha sat in the car and began sweating from the hot temperature beating down on her. She had to get out and at least move around behind the car. Slowly she eased the door open and tried to not make a sound. Leaving the door ajar, she stepped to the back of the old rusty car and surveyed her surroundings.

Other cars in worse shape than the one Waylon drove sat in a graveyard of sorts for dead automobiles. Bags of trash, boxes, old clothes, a lone shoe, a few pieces of broken furniture were scattered across the yard.

*What a horrible place to live,* Samantha thought.

Despair and sadness like she had never felt before stole away her remnant of peace and became her new cloak. *In the middle of all this ugly, find the beautiful, Samantha Jean,* she reminded herself.

She looked. She looked long and hard. Finally turning away from the house she walked towards a clearing to her right. Pink and yellow primroses lifted their pale faces to hers. There it was. Hundreds of the little beauties surrounded her feet. She bent to pick a few needing to hold something beautiful in her hands and close to her heart.

"What are you doing, Sam?"

Nearly jumping out of her skin, she turned to see Waylon behind her. Without thinking, she spoke, "Finding the beautiful."

"What the—you stupid girl! I told you to stay in the car, not run off picking flowers."

Grabbing her forcefully by the arm, the same arm that already blued with this morning's bruise, he jerked her towards him and whispered in her face. "If I tell you to stay put, you do it! Do you hear me, Sam? And stop talking nonsense!"

Releasing his grip on her arm, she held tightly to the primroses clutched in her fingers. "Is your dad home? Can I meet him now?"

"He's here, but he's sound asleep. Usually what he does all weekend anyway. Let's go take in a movie at the Majestic." Nervously he glanced back at the house, the brief look of fear not missed by Samantha.

"A movie? That would be great, Waylon! Our first real date as man and wife!" The excitement of the moment overtook her and she reached up and planted a kiss firmly on his lips. Samantha laid the delicate flowers on the car's dashboard and settled in by Waylon.

A soft smile touched his rough, handsome face. One of those rare moments when Waylon showed a tender side, he replied, "You know I do love you, Samantha."

Rarely did he call her by her full name and it touched Samantha deeply. He *loved* her! Maybe they would work things out after all.

## chapter 6

Samantha snuggled underneath Waylon's arm during the film. She hardly knew what movie was playing because she was giddy with excitement that he had taken her on her first real date, though she would never tell him that. Always before she was with her girlfriends or a mixed group of boys and girls and they would escape the small mining town and see a show. But today was different. She was in the presence of her *husband*. Throughout the movie, nervousness occasionally gripped her as she wondered if she saw some of her friends how she would explain herself in the presence of a man none of them knew. But thankfully, the crowd was thin during the time they went and neither of them saw anyone they knew.

They had each other all to themselves.

On the way out of the theater, Samantha quizzed Waylon about dinner. "Should I cook us some supper tonight? What does your dad like to eat? I can cook most anything you know."

Waylon's face darkened noticeably at the mention of his father. Samantha tucked that in the recesses of her mind for future reference.

"I don't know. Let's go to the grocery store and we'll figure it out there."

Another first that thrilled Samantha. Their first grocery store trip together, picking out dinner, walking the aisles hand in hand. Knowing her train of thought was silly, Samantha indulged her daydream all the way to the grocery store.

But once inside, Samantha saw the other side of Waylon that she didn't like.

When she reached for his hand, Waylon instantly pulled away. "Don't hang on me, Sam. I hate that," he spoke quietly but gruffly for her ears only.

"Oh, okay. I—I didn't mean—"

"Hush up, okay? Stop sniveling like a brat, Sam!"

Her mind clouded with the pain of his words once again. How was she supposed to know what would upset him? And she *wasn't* a brat! Wanting to retaliate, Samantha bit her lip knowing she wasn't about to make a scene in the store.

"Samantha!" She turned to see Lois and her mother enter the grocery store.

*Oh, no, not now,* she inwardly groaned.

"Hey, Lois!" Samantha froze in her tracks, words unable to form in her throat with Waylon standing right by her.

Lois and her mother glanced at Samantha then at Waylon waiting for Samantha to introduce them to the mysterious man.

Lois broke the awkward silence. "So…..how are you Samantha? We have been worried sick about you since Friday when you didn't come to school."

"Oh—I didn't mean to scare you. I just, just got sick on the way to school and—"

Waylon interrupted her and held out his hand to the two before him. His quickly devised scheme would work since he didn't know these two standing before him. "Hey, Ladies. I'm Waylon, a friend of Samantha's family. Just got into town and thought I would run a few errands with her and catch up."

Samantha opened her mouth, but again she was wordless. *How dare he??*

"Well, nice to meet you, Waylon." Lois battered her long black eyelashes in his direction while Waylon gave Lois a once-over with his eyes.

Finding her voice, Samantha interrupted them. "Mama's probably waiting on the groceries so we better hurry. Talk to you soon, Lois." Grabbing Waylon's arm and leaving Lois and her mother no time to respond, Samantha nearly drug her husband up another aisle away from her friend.

Under her breath, Samantha whispered, "How could you do that to me? Why did you lie about who you are? I don't believe this!"

"Sam, are you really ready to let your little friends know that you're married? That you just up and ran off without telling anyone? I'm not ready to spread the news yet, so let's just keep this to ourselves until the time is right. You hear me?"

Seeing he had a point, Samantha quieted. "I guess you're right. Mama and Daddy haven't even met you yet."

Under his breath, Waylon muttered, "And my old man hasn't met you either."

Disappointment clouded her thinking as she followed Waylon around the aisles of the grocery store. Before she knew it, Waylon had placed a can of pork and beans, a package of wieners, and a pound of coffee on the cashier's counter to be checked out. It was not the first meal she had imagined herself cooking for her new little family; nor had she imagined any of this working out the way it had. Samantha felt like she was sleepwalking in someone else's nightmare and none of this was made of the stuff of her girlish daydreams.

Silence filled the car on the way back to Waylon's father's house. Samantha noticed the tension that had eased its way into Waylon's shoulders, the constant drumming of his fingers on the steering wheel, and the clenching of his jaw.

Then it finally hit her. Waylon was uncomfortable about her meeting his father. He didn't want to introduce his wife to anyone, much less his own flesh and blood. A deep sense of sadness consumed her being. How could things be turning out like this?

At the house, Waylon grabbed the sack of groceries and turned to face Samantha. "Now listen, Samantha. Let me do the talking when we get in the house. The old geezer may be in a good mood or he may not. So don't say anything, you hear me?"

"Okay. I'm sure it won't be as bad as you think, Waylon. Like you told me, our parents will be happy if we are happy. Right?"

Cussing under his breath, Waylon just looked at Samantha and shook his head like she was such a foolish child without a lick of sense in her head. Silently, Waylon got out of the car and Samantha followed. Once on the porch he reminded her, "Not a word."

Eyes the size of saucers, Samantha quietly followed him in the house. Never before had Samantha seen such a mess. A radio's static filled the room with its ceaseless noise. She looked around and spotted a man lying on a sagging sofa, arm over his eyes, feet propped up on the other end of the brown stained couch. Waylon placed the sack of groceries on a table with two unmatching chairs pushed underneath. The table had a surface but for all of the clutter, she couldn't tell if it was oak, painted, or metal. Shoving a spot clear, Waylon knocked over an empty beer bottle. That was all it took to wake the sleeping man.

Disoriented for a moment, Waylon's father grumbled at the disruption in his sleep. He sat up and looked around the room and scratched his exposed belly. Squinting in Waylon's direction, his eyes fell on Samantha. A look of sheer hatred and anger caused her to back up a step or two.

"What the—"

"Dad, hey, sorry I woke you. I brought dinner home to cook." Waylon's voice literally shook with fear which caused Samantha's knees to begin trembling with anxiety.

"Looks like you brought home more than dinner. Who is *that*?"

Samantha found her voice. "Hello, Mr.—"

Waylon immediately interrupted her. "Dad, this is Samantha. She—she's my...."

The man swayed to his feet and Waylon took a step back as well unable to finish his sentence. "Speak up, boy. Your what? Your whore? Your—"

"Dad! She's my girl. My wife. I wanted you to meet her—"

Stepping towards the end table, Waylon's father reached for a beer bottle and hurled it at the wall behind Waylon's head. He immediately erupted in a string of curses that set Samantha's teeth on edge and her ears to buzzing. Her mouth fell open and she began backing slowing for the front door. The last words she heard rung in her ears for years. "I told you never to bring a woman in this house, much less a snot-nosed kid! How dare you…..what did you do? Get her pregnant? Get out of here and never show your face in my house again—I mean it! I don't need another mouth to feed! Get out!!!!"

Samantha ran to Waylon's car, got in, and slammed the door to drown out any further words his father was spewing in their direction. Covering her ears with both hands, she never knew if Waylon responded to his father, nor did she want to know what he said. Shortly he came out to the car with their grocery sack and a duffel bag he had thrown together.

Seething with embarrassment and anger, Waylon put the car in reverse, sending dirt flying up behind as he backed out full force. Whipping the wheel sharply to the left, Waylon straightened the car and careened down the road. Fear and confusion were becoming Samantha's constant unwanted companions. They settled into the car seat beside and behind her as her mind fought to figure out what their next move would be.

Part of her was grateful they weren't staying in the stinking rundown house; the other part was in shock as she realized within two days of being married, she and her new husband were now homeless. Numb with shock and fear, Samantha sank into the worn seat and stared hopelessly out the window as the world whizzed by them.

Something pink, yellow, and green caught her eye on the dashboard. Her wildflowers she had picked earlier. They were her moment of beautiful earlier. Dried up. Shriveled from the heat. Flattened from the lack of connection to their life source.

There was nothing beautiful to see.

The last two nights blurred into one long, ugly streak of sleeping at Waylon's friend Lenny's house and one night sleeping in his car in a park. Anger seemed to be settling in around the edges of Samantha's periphery. The center of her being was soaked with disbelief, fear, uncertainty, and misgivings while anger seemed to tinge the edges of her mind and heart.

Over and over, Samantha found herself thinking, *I can't believe this is my life. I just can't believe it has turned out this way. This is not what I dreamed of.*

And over and over she found herself doing what she did best, looking for the beautiful in every situation. Most of the time she found it, even during the long, hot nights sleeping on the floor of a stranger's house and spending what was supposed to be her honeymoon week with one of them in the back of a car seat and the other in the front. Samantha had never existed on such little sleep and it was taking its toll on her.

Sitting in the darkening, dank-smelling car, finally unable to take any of it a second longer, she resorted to begging and pleading. "Waylon—look, I know I am not making you happy...." Her voice choked with tears and Samantha paused to gather her courage to continue. "Maybe—maybe you shouldn't have married me, maybe I am too young to be a good wife. If you want to, just let me go. I won't tell anyone we got married if you want to change your mind. I'm no good for you. I'll let you pretend you never married me and we can just go on—"

A resounding smack across her cheek stopped her abruptly. Darkness and evil filled Waylon's eyes as he unleashed a torrent of curses on her. "Don't you ever say something like that again, you hear me, Sam? You're mine now and you will do what I say! Act like an adult and not a kid and *then* I might be happy."

Glancing down at his hand, Waylon realized he had smacked Samantha across the cheek. He watched as tears mingled with fear on her young, pretty face. She backed herself into a corner of the car as far from him as she could possibly get in the confined, cramped space. The face he once longed to see every day he had just hurt. Regret smoldered in his eyes as images of his old man slapping him around darted before his vision. He *wouldn't* be like his no-good father. He *wouldn't.*

"Sam, I'm sorry. I really am. I won't hit you again, I swear it! You just have to quit acting that way and making me so angry! We'll figure things out. Okay?"

Reaching for her, Waylon watched Samantha flinch when he got close. "Come here, Baby."

Reluctantly, Samantha scooted over in the car seat towards her husband. Finally she found the courage again to speak, choosing her words a little better this time. "Waylon, *please* just let me call home. It's been three days since I talked to Daddy and I know my family's worried to death about me. Let me call them and see if we can stay there until we figure out something, please. We can't live like vagrants any longer. This is not how marriage is supposed to be. And now you lost your job so we *have* to do something until you can work again. They will help us, I just know it."

Their situation pushed Samantha to press Waylon even though she could see the muscles of his jaw flex and his fingers begin drumming. She was afraid he would hit her again as he showed signs of his increasing anger, but she could take it no longer. It was worth the risk.

Taking a shuddering breath, Waylon stared out the window wordlessly for what seemed to Samantha an eternity. Thankfully she saw him calm down even more as he raked his fingers through his hair.

Laying his hands in his lap, Waylon spoke so quietly Samantha had to strain to listen. "I don't want you to fear me, Sam. I don't mean to hurt you. It's just sometimes…..sometimes my temper gets the best of me. I don't mean it."

"I know, Way. I know."

Waylon started the car and pulled from their hiding spot behind a tree in the park. "Let's go find a phone."

Hope surged through Samantha as she thought about hearing her Daddy's voice. And Waylon had apologized, sort of. Maybe he realized what he was doing and would be nicer now. He was stressed and worried just like she was.

It was time to go home.

Samantha knew she wouldn't have to look far after she arrived back home to find what was good and right and true and beautiful.

## chapter 7

Watching his sweet Sylvia continue her relentless pacing was about to do Henry in. He couldn't take much more of it. The past few days blurred into the same. Crying, pacing, yelling, worrying. Afraid his wife was on the verge of a nervous break-down, Henry gave it one more try.

"Syl, please. Listen to me. I am as upset about Sammie-girl being gone as you are. But all this pacing and fretting won't bring her home. We just need to trust the Good Lord and keep our eyes and ears open for anything at all...." This is where Henry's words fell short yet again. With each passing hour, the mantra was beginning to sound like nothing more than that, an empty chant resounding with dull tones that faded even more each time the words were uttered.

"Stop; just stop, Henry!" Spinning on her heels, Sylvia looked like a mad woman, her hair shooting out in all directions, her wrinkled dress and rumpled apron creased from wiping the tears that stained Sylvia's face and the constant twisting of the worn fabric between her shaking hands.

The rest of the household had done all they could to comfort and calm her, even Little Geoffrey. Henry knew the little guy sensed something was wrong, terribly wrong with their family. Unknowingly he would set his "Gamma" off into another torrent of tears with his innocent question of "Where is 'Mantha, Gamma?"

Claudia did her best to help around the house with meals and cleaning while Henry left for work each morning and came home to the same pacing and fretting. Her tears mixed with anger and frustration as the sheer helplessness of their situation was too much for all of them.

Three days of this was just about to send Henry over the edge as well. He didn't dare let Sylvia know how terribly worried he was about Samantha. How certain she had sounded on the phone about her decision to....to *marry* someone he had yet to meet. This was not how things were supposed to play out.

Henry walked out the front door to the porch and saw the pickle jar for bug-catching perched on the railing. Maybe a walk in the dusk looking for his grandson's favorite bugs would take his mind off things.

Sticking his head back indoor, Henry called to his little buddy, "Geoffie-boy? How about you helping your Pops put some light in this empty jar?"

A squeal resounded through the house along with the stomping of little feet. Henry heard the phone jangle indoors and left it to someone else to answer. The soft tread of Sylvia's footfalls came closer as she headed to the telephone table.

"Okay, Pops, let's go get 'em!"

The beautiful trill of a three-year-old's giggle filled the Mississippi dusk. As if cued up and waiting, the cicadas chimed in instantly with Geoffrey and added to the music of the evening's waning light.

Henry reached down and rebuttoned one of Geoffrey's plaid romper straps. Immediately the boy reached both sticky, chubby, hands up and placed his palms against his grandfather's stubbly jaws. "Pops, 'Mantha will be home soon."

Kneeling down in front of the boy, Henry looked deeply into his brown eyes. "Geoffie-boy, how do you know that?"

"A girl telled me. A girl with a white dress and wings. She said 'Mantha will be home soon." Grabbing Henry's hand, he said, "There's one! A lit'n bug! Get it, Pops!"

And with that, the moment ended, but the lingering sense of wonder and awe and peace settled gently over Henry. A whiff of honeysuckle filled the air around him and he breathed it in deeply, feeling calmed for the first time in days. As several more minutes passed, Henry felt as if with each capture of the shining bugs he was capturing another glimmer of peace.

The squeak of the screen door resounded in the recesses of his mind. Looking up he saw Sylvia standing on the porch's top step. She swiped at a tear with her apron.

"Everything okay, Sylvie?"

"Yes—yes, Henry. She will be home soon. Samantha Jean called and she will be home soon. Today." Her voice cracked with emotion and Henry rushed to her side.

The voice of his grandson followed in his wake. "See, Pops. I tol' you! 'Mantha will be home soon!"

"Yes, buddy. You told me."

Finally, unchecked and unashamedly, the tears fell freely down Henry Owens' face.

~~~~~~~~~~

"Sam, are you sure this is a good idea?" Waylon flexed the muscles in his jaw repeatedly.

Placing a reassuring hand on his arm, Samantha could feel the muscles taut underneath her small hand. Gently rubbing Waylon's forearm, she did her best to reassure him. "Yes, Way. I'm sure. Mama said to come on, there's plenty of room for us. I told her it won't be permanent, just until we figure some things out. Look, I'm real sorry your Daddy—"

"Shut up about him, Sam!! Just shut up!!"

Samantha jumped so violently at the sound of his shout. Never had she been spoken to like Waylon spoke to her. A vision of a neighbor shouting curses at his barking dog flashed through her mind. Was that all she was to her husband? A dog to shout commands at?

"Don't ever mention him again! He's dead as far as I'm concerned." Waylon ground out the last words through gritted teeth. His eyes bulged until Samantha thought they would pop out of his skull. Anger and fierce wrath filled his face while he waited on her to agree with his demand.

Swallowing twice, she finally found the words to answer. "Okay, Waylon. I won't. I swear it." Reaching a trembling hand to her throat, Samantha unconsciously pulled the neck of her blouse closed, trying to guard her wounded heart.

Glancing out the window, she continued to direct him to her home in Wataker and the small mining town community. Her voice barely above a whisper, she said, "It's up on your left after the yellow house. The one with white trim is ours. You can just park under that tree to the left."

Samantha dared not move until Waylon had put the car in park. She wanted things to be okay between the two of them before they got out of the car to see her parents, but for the life of her, Samantha didn't have a clue what to say or do.

Glancing at Waylon, she saw the nervousness in his body movements. Neither of them reached to open their car door. Samantha glanced at motions coming from the front window as the curtain opened and closed. Instantly she saw her mother come to the screen door and push it open. Her Daddy was right on Sylvia's heels and placed a stilling hand on her shoulder to stop mother from running to daughter. Samantha knew her Daddy understood she needed a moment before getting out of the car.

"Let's go meet them." Samantha laughed nervously and tried to ease the tension in the car, "I promise they don't bite."

Without another word, Waylon opened his car door and Samantha followed him.

Seeing her parents' worried faces, she couldn't have stopped her feet from running if she tried. Samantha and Sylvia reached each other and embraced instantly, Sylvia's tears falling on her daughter's head.

"Oh, honey!" That was all the words Sylvia could utter in the moment of relief at seeing her girl was unharmed and well.

Henry glanced at the man standing a few feet away giving them the space they needed. Then he grabbed Samantha tightly and did his best not to squeeze the life out of her. Whispering words only she could hear, he spoke close to his daughter's ear and straight to her heart, "Sammie-girl, I was so worried. You should have let me come get you."

Pushing back gently, Samantha looked into the eyes of the man she vowed never to hurt or displease. She saw deep hurt there which only further instilled in her young mind to show her Daddy she was fine and had made the right choice. She wouldn't let him know how much she had needed him and had missed him, afraid to cause her precious Daddy further pain. Samantha had to prove to her Daddy she was okay, unharmed in any way, and able to handle her choices.

"No, Daddy. That wasn't necessary. I'm sorry I worried you, but I am happy." Unshed tears threatened to spill over in her violet eyes, but she refused them.

Glancing behind Henry's shoulder, she heard the screen door open again.

"'Mantha! 'Mantha! You are home! Wanna see my lit'n bugs?" As little ones do so well, Geoffrey was ready to pick right back up with her as if she had never left. Samantha only wished the others could do the same and they could all put this messy ordeal behind them.

But she knew better.

Geoffrey ran to her and grabbed her legs giving them a big hug. She stooped down to his level and returned his hug. "Sure, Geoff. Go get me your bug jar. I would love to see them."

Standing, she walked the few steps to Claudia and hugged her sister close.

Claudia whispered in her ear, "What have you gone and done, you big oaf? You had me so worried."

Samantha chuckled under her breath, squeezed Claudia tighter, and replied sarcastically. "I love you too, Sis."

Clearing her throat, Samantha walked back over to Waylon's side. She took his hand and led him to her family. "Daddy. Mama. This is Waylon Graves. My.....my husband." Plastering an overly large smile on her face, Samantha continued. "Waylon, meet Mama and Daddy. This is my sister Claudia and little Geoffrey was the cutie out here a minute ago. Claudia's husband Mel is in the Navy."

Waylon worked the muscles of his jaw, extended a hand to the man before him and firmly shook it, then nodded a greeting at each woman in turn. "Nice to meet you all."

Samantha linked her hand in Waylon's arm and looked around the awkward group. "Well, Waylon. Let's go get our things and Mama will show us where to get settled."

Henry spoke next. "Sammie, how 'bout you go with your Mama and see what the plan is and I will help Waylon with your things."

"Sam can help me, Sir," Waylon challenged. The slight lift of his set jaw was all the challenge anyone needed to see.

Glancing at her father then her husband, Samantha knew she had a decision to make. Looking back at Waylon, she took Sylvia's hand and walked slowly to the house and away from her husband.

# chapter 8

Though the curtains stirred with the late evening air, it was humid like always for a spring Mississippi night. Sylvia tried not to touch Henry while they lie side by side in their bed, both stripped down to nearly nothing, trying to keep as cool as possible and to prevent sticking to each other from the thick humidity. But she couldn't help herself another minute.

Rolling to her side, Sylvia loosely placed her arm across her husband's midsection, needing the feel of his skin for comfort and reassurance. He didn't stir so she remained still at Henry's side. Finally she had to know.

Softly, Sylvia whispered into the night. "You awake?"

"Not after the events of the day and this oppressive heat. Can't imagine what summer will feel like. What's on your mind, Sylvie?" Henry rolled to face her in the dark.

"Nothing and everything all at once. What did you say to Waylon after Samantha left you two at the boy's car?"

Offering a humorless laugh, Henry thought a moment before answering. "The long and short of it was this. I told Mr. Graves he had a lot of proving to do. And I would have my eye on him."

"Sounds like you, Henry." Giving a mirthless laugh of her own, Sylvia continued. "What did he have to say to that?"

"Not much. Not much at all. He just looked at me and I thought for a minute he was about to blow a gasket. He didn't say anything but, 'Well, I guess time will tell, won't it, Sir.'"

Sylvia propped up on one elbow. "I asked Samantha if she was alright, if she wanted to stay married or if she needed us to help get her out of this crazy arrangement, but she wouldn't have it any other way. Said she was *happy*. I don't believe it for a minute. Told me I would like him once I got to know him. I asked her *why*—why on earth she just up and ran off and married a boy we didn't know—" Sylvia's voice cracked and she didn't continue.

Henry kissed her on the forehead and took Sylvia in his arms and just held her.

He had no words of comfort to offer.

The bed squeaked under her weight as Samantha turned over as gently as possible. Grateful for the old bed, the metal frame was far from quiet. And she did not want to waken her husband.

Happy to be home, she was slightly embarrassed to have had her mother suggest she and Waylon take over the screened porch as their bedroom! Never in her girlish dreams did Samantha picture her first bedroom as a married woman would be on her Mama's screened-in side porch.

But it was better than Lenny's house or Waylon's car with no place to shower or get comfortable.

Settling herself under the loose sheet, she gazed out the screen and into the starry sky. Samantha needed this time in the middle of the night to think. It's how she had spent the last few nights as a new bride. As soon as she offered herself to her husband when he demanded her body, she lay still until he surrendered to sleep and snoring.

And she thought.

The night was her time. Her time where no one could intrude and ask questions or make demands. It was her time to list what was beautiful and right and good and maintain her grasp on her sanity. Something down deep she had never been able to identify called to Samantha Jean Owens Graves. That something had always been there, calling, whispering, bidding to her.

She had always believed it was her conscience. Like the little cricket in the movie *Pinocchio* she and her friends had seen a few years back at the *Majestic*.

Jiminy Cricket had been the wooden boy's conscience and spoke to Pinocchio about what was right and good and true and how to be a good boy. Maybe that was what she had been hearing all these years whispering to her. Her own Jiminy Cricket.

But since finding the Bible at the hotel, Samantha was starting to second-guess that theory. Maybe, just maybe, it was something more than her conscience. Maybe it was an angel or maybe even God or His Son, Jesus.

She believed in God and Jesus and even the Holy Ghost that the preacher and her Sunday School teachers had talked about over the years. She knew the Bible stories and that God spoke to people through angels and burning bushes and even donkeys. But dare she believe He was speaking to her, a girl living in Wataker, Missisisppi, in a mining town?

She could stand it no longer. Samantha reached under the bed for the flashlight her mother had given her to use. Clicking the clunky light on, she eased out of bed and pointed the beam at her bag underneath. Instantly her hand found the precious Bible still wrapped in its sacred white cloth. Samantha froze in her tracks as Waylon rolled over and snorted loudly in his sleep. He didn't waken so she moved to the farthest corner of the porch with her back to him.

Shielding herself, the light, and the Bible with her body, she perched on a ladder-back wooden chair and cracked the book open. Laying it on her lap, Samantha held the flashlight in one hand and searched for another underlined verse with the other. The Bible had been marked up with red pencil by some loving hand, the lines drawn carefully, straight and true.

Her eye falling on an underlined verse, Samantha read it silently to herself.

*Isaiah 26:3. Thou wilt keep him in perfect peace, whose mind is stayed on thee: because he trusteth in thee.*

She reread the precious words. Once. Then twice.

*Perfect peace.* Could it be hers? Maybe she had to do something to get it. Something she had never even tried to do before. Samantha had to figure out how to make her straying mind *stay* in one spot for more than five minutes. She needed to learn to keep her mind stayed on God. And another thing too. She needed to trust Him.

These were both very new concepts to Samantha, but that night, she knew she needed to learn to do both. This would be her sanity, her peace.

If she could only trust and keep her mind on God, no matter what happened.

Samantha woke to the sound of birds chirping in the overhead trees and the blinding morning sun glaring in her eyes. It took her a moment to realize where she was and what day it was. Slowly reality set in. She was sleeping on her Mama and Daddy's side porch with her husband who was waking up beside her causing the metal bed to squawk under his weight as he stood to put his pants on.

"Sam, get up. These blasted birds won't let anybody sleep around here." Uttering a curse under his breath, Waylon continued grumbling. "Sleeping on a porch! Whoever heard of such a thing. I should have—"

Reaching for him, she playfully pulled Waylon back down on the protesting bed. "Oh, Way! It's better than your old car to sleep in. At least we're side by side." Releasing him she kissed his neck and waited for a reaction.

Melting at her touch, Waylon rubbed his bleary eyes. "I guess you have a point there, Baby."

"Know what today is?" Batting long eyelashes over her purple eyes only warmed Waylon further.

Laying back down beside her, Waylon tucked his arms underneath his head and watched Samantha get herself dressed. "It's Sunday. A day to rest or play or whatever we want to do."

"It's my birthday!" Samantha couldn't hide the girlish lilt in her voice if she tried. "I'm fifteen!"

"Fifteen….that you are, Sam. That you are." The smile slowly melted off Waylon's stubbled face.

"So what are you getting me for my birthday? Diamonds…..furs…..a Rolls Royce?"

"Hey, you got *me*. What more could a girl need for her birthday?" Waylon laughed at his own joke.

Stooping to kiss him on the nose, she replied, "You're exactly right, Waylon. You are all I need." For a moment it felt like old times to Samantha and she didn't want to break the spell of the moment. Reaching for his hand, she tugged Waylon to his feet. "Let's go see what Mama made for breakfast. It smells wonderful."

Sniffing the air appreciatively, Waylon followed Samantha and his nose into the connecting entrance of the house. Sylvia was indeed at the stove cooking breakfast while Henry topped off his coffee.

Looking up when Samantha and Waylon entered, neither Sylvia nor Henry said a word. Both were too taken aback to see their young daughter enter the room with a man's arms wrapped around her waist planting a kiss on her neck.

Samantha caught their discomfort and wriggled out of Waylon's arms. Heading to each of her parents, she kissed Henry first on the cheek, then Sylvia. "What's for breakfast, Mama? It sure smells good."

"A little bird told me it was somebody's birthday. So I made pancakes and sausage for my birthday girl. Happy birthday, honey."

"Thanks, Mama. My favorite! Waylon, you want coffee or juice? You can have a seat at the table by Daddy if you want."

Waylon looked at both Henry and Sylvia and uttered, "Morning. Uh—coffee's fine, Sam."

"Sammie-girl, how 'bout you sit here with your *husband* and let me get those drinks. It's your birthday after all and a girl shouldn't have to wait on herself on her special day."

"Oh, sit, Daddy. I can pour coffee as long as you promise to make me your special yellow cake with chocolate icing."

Laughter rang from Henry's throat. "You don't want much, do you girl? I *guess* I will make you a cake. Truth be told, didn't know if you would be here on your birthday, but I sure am glad you are. Mama's making a special lunch for the family after church so you can see Bernice and Frank and you can call Lois and Margie too if you want."

A cloud passed over Samantha's face briefly. "Okay, Daddy. I will think about calling them."

"Your choice. People are gonna find out sooner or later."

Waylon cleared his throat and loudly slurped his coffee. His face turned beet red at Henry's comment.

Sylvia arrived just in time with a plate of piping hot pancakes and sausage. Forgetting his manners, Waylon reached for the fork to spear a couple pancakes. Samantha cleared her throat and got his attention. She bowed her head and glanced at her parents. Waylon got the message and quickly set the fork down and bowed his head as well.

Henry said the morning blessing. "Father in heaven, we thank thee for this day and this food. We thank thee that our Sammie-girl is home safe and sound and that she is with us on her birthday. Bless this food to the good of our bodies. In Your Son's name. Amen."

Sylvia and Samantha echoed their *Amen's* then Sylvia started passing plates of food, butter, and syrup. The four ate mostly in uncomfortable silence with Waylon uttering a quick *Thanks for the food* in Sylvia's direction before leaving the kitchen. His empty plate, coffee cup, and chair stared back at Samantha.

The three left at the table heard his car start up and leave the yard. Unconsciously, Samantha uttered a sigh of relief that was noticed by both Henry and Sylvia.

"Mama, what time will everyone be here for dinner? Do you think I should invite Lois and Margie?"

"Samantha Jean! I'm surprised at you! Those two are your best friends. You would never have not considered inviting them to your fifteenth birthday. Until now—"

"Mama, things are different."

"You don't have to tell your Daddy and me that." Spoken kindly, the words still smarted.

Henry spoke next. "Call your friends, Sammie. They know when your birthday is and will be hurt if they aren't invited. Lois and Margie haven't done anything to cause you not to invite them to your party. All they have done is worry and call and check on you, their close friend."

"I think I'll go move some of my things to the porch. Mama, why can't Waylon and I have my bedroom instead of the porch? Geoffrey can sleep with Claudia."

Sylvia's face clouded with the look that dared anyone to question her further. "Samantha Jean, it's just not right. You're not bringing a man into your bedroom in my house. Even if you are married. Your daddy and I think it best if you two have the porch. Claudia needs her own space so Geoffrey can have your old room to himself. You don't need to move everything out to the porch. You can still leave what you don't readily need in your old room. We can change things up later if needed. Let's just see how you and this new husband work out before I rearrange my entire house. Now that's that."

Sylvia kissed Samantha on the temple and left the room.

"Yes, ma'am," Samantha replied under her breath. "I guess that's that."

# chapter 9

*April 28, 1942*

Glancing up the road for the hundredth time, Samantha kept looking for Waylon's car to pull back under the old tree out front. When he quickly left after breakfast, her parents went to church without her. Samantha couldn't remember the last time she had missed church.

Longing for the days of sitting on the scarred, darkened wood pews, third row from the back on the left side of the sanctuary, normally Lois would have been seated to her left and Margie to Samantha's right. All three girls would have been wearing their "Sunday best," until they out grew the one nice dress they owned and then received another hand-me-down. Elbowing each other and whispering how handsome Ellis Burton or Harold Stapleton looked that morning. Or snubbing their noses at the twelve-year-old boys who kept stealing glances at Samantha and her friends. Lois would maddeningly, shamelessly flirt with the poor younger boys until they blushed the color of her Mama's roses in the summer sun.

But those days were over for Samantha. No more flirting or sitting with her girlfriends in church.

A thought she had never before considered nudged for attention.

*I wonder if Waylon goes to church,* she pondered. So far there were no indications he had ever been in church in his life. All of a sudden, this troubled Samantha.

A car door slammed in the front yard, bringing her back to the present. Looking for Waylon, instead Samantha saw her sister Bernice and her new husband Frank exiting their newly purchased 1941 Chrysler New Yorker. The startling reality of the differences between her husband Waylon and her sister's husband made Samantha's breath catch. The scene that played out before her caused her to stop in her tracks and take it all in.

*This* was what she had dreamed of.

Frank exited his driver's side door and hustled to Bernice's side of the car. Opening the door for his wife, Frank held out his hand to her, planted a soft kiss on her upturned lips, then securely tucked Bernice's hand in the crook of his arm. Bernice looked lovingly into Frank's eyes as they headed for the front porch.

Samantha's young heart demanded she notice that this was *not* how her dreams were playing out. Momentary sadness swallowed her up in the face of her unmet longings.

Seeing Samantha in the window, Bernice waved. Instantly the happy couple began an uproarious rendition of *Happy Birthday* out in the front lawn ending on the porch steps while they enfolded Samantha in a warm embrace as she slipped out to meet them.

"Happpppyyy birrrth-daaaayyy, Dear Samantha Jean! Happy birthday to you!"

Laughter and another round of hugs enveloped Samantha and she felt at home for the first time that day, on her special fifteenth birthday. Tears pricked at her eyes and Samantha blinked them away, confused at their solemn intrusion in such a happy moment.

*Tears! I should be happy; it's my birthday after all*, Samantha reprimanded herself.

Noticing a pale blue box with a pink ribbon peeking out of Bernice's purse, Samantha couldn't contain her excitement.

"Is that for me?" Like a little girl, she clasped her hands to her heart and smiled eagerly.

Tapping her sister on the nose, Bernice said, "Silly. You have to wait until after the cake! Now, let's go get a glass of tea. I'm scorched! And *we* need to talk. Are you alone? Everybody still at church?"

"Yes, they won't be home for another half hour or so."

Frank took the hint and said, "If I can get a glass of that tea too, I hear a porch rocker and the Sunday newspaper calling my name."

"Coming up!" Bernice's love of life and peppy enthusiasm was a shot in the arm for Samantha. Bernice whizzed around the kitchen getting three teas ready. As soon as Frank was settled, Bernice turned to Samantha and pointed a perfectly painted fingernail at her and authoritatively commanded, "Me. You. Tree."

Her finger then directed Samantha to the giant of an ancient willow that invitingly hung its canopy of wispy branches nearly to the ground. The curtain of willow leaves gently parted here and there creating breezy entrances to the setting of chairs and a table underneath.

Henry and Sylvia Owens had the best "spot" in the entire mining camp town, the envy of all of Wataker's other inhabitants. At the end of the row of cookie cutter houses, theirs backed up to an open field and this God-send of a willow. Bernice felt like she had left one world of apartment buildings and city life and entered another entirely when she walked out the back door of her parents' modest home.

"Green or yellow," Bernice asked in her usual jovial way indicating Samantha choose a chair of her liking.

"Oh, I don't care," Samantha replied.

"Pick the yellow one. You need it to lift your spirits, Sis."

Samantha rolled her eyes at Bernice, plopped down in the yellow chair, and sipped her tea. She knew what was coming.

"You have about twenty-five minutes to explain to your Big Sis what you were thinking by going off and getting married. So tell me. I'm listening." Crossing her legs daintily, Bernice settled herself as she tugged the floral skirt of her shirt-waist dress over her knees, ready to hear Samantha's story.

Bernice had never made Samantha feel stupid, nor insignificant, nor ridiculous. She just accepted her no matter what. And that open, straightforward care and love Samantha saw in Bernice's eyes caused Samantha to be completely undone.

Like turning on a faucet, tears poured down Samantha's cheeks. Silent, slow, steady streams of tears. She neither sobbed nor made a noise. After a minute of this unstoppable flood, Bernice pulled her chair up next to Samantha's and wrapped her arm around her little sister's shoulders.

"Oh, honey. Is it that bad?"

Sniffling loudly, Samantha blew her nose on a flowered handkerchief. "I'm sorry Bernie. I guess it's just all so.....so new and—unexpected....I just wish for one day, for today--I could go back to being Samantha Owens and not be Samantha Graves."

Visibly, Bernice watched Samantha take a deep breath and look into her eyes. A shudder passed over her sister's small frame. Then, Samantha straightened her shoulders and squared her jaw.

"You will like him once you get to know him. I promise. He really is a great guy," Samantha reassured both herself and her sister.

Bernice had seen this set of shoulders and jaw on her sister before and knew she would get no further. But Samantha's tears had been very telling, though her words lacked the information Bernice wanted.

Today was her little sister's birthday after all, so Bernice chose not to press her any further. Instead she would do her best to make sure Samantha had a wonderful day full of love and presents and cake.

But in the future, the very near future, Bernice vowed to have a nice long talk with Samantha.

With the instant flurry of activity coming from several directions, Samantha knew her reprieve under the oversized willow's safe canopy of branches was now over. It was time to be the birthday girl, the fifteen year old new wife, the errant daughter and sister, the misunderstood friend.

How quickly one decision could change a person and their world. Samantha felt it to the marrow of her bones, the change and the reality it was bringing. What she once deemed *beautiful*, the man she thought would bring constant beauty into her little world was now the source of a thick fog of confusion and darkness. Samantha briefly wondered if she had forgotten what true beauty was.

Bernice broke the silence that had settled between them. "I'll go distract the others while you pull yourself together. It's your birthday, Little Sis. This will be a good day. I promise." Planting a swift kiss on Samantha's tear-stained cheek, Bernice took her tea glass and headed for the group of family. "See you in a bit."

A nod was all Samantha could manage. Reaching for her tea, Samantha pressed the sweating, cold, glass to her cheeks, hoping to cool them off and bring some color back to her face. Wiping the refreshing water droplets over her skin with her handkerchief did much to cool her down.

*Now, what to do about my heart and emotions,* she wondered.

Without warning, snippets of a passage she voraciously devoured this morning returned like a gentle breeze to her soul.

*The Spirit of the Lord God is upon me…..he hath sent me to bind up the brokenhearted…..to comfort all that mourn…..to give unto them beauty for ashes.*

*Would God do that for someone like me,* Samantha pondered.

The words were like poetry to her ears and a healing balm to her heart. Thankful she had a gift to memorize words with ease, Samantha repeated the sections over and over until she settled down. Could she really have what the Bible she had found promised?

*Beauty for ashes.* The promise of these three words stayed with her as she got up from her yellow chair and knew it was time to walk out of the tree's shelter into the rest of the day.

Lifting violet eyes to the world outside of the bright green branches, to her left Samantha watched as her two best friends approached, each with a gift under an arm, skirts swishing, laughter pouring from their girlish faces. To her right Samantha watched as Waylon pulled his old car back under the waiting tree, stepped out of it and walked towards her too, a paper sack tucked in the crook of one arm with a brown bottle peeking out of the top and a smaller sack in his other hand.

Wanting to intercept her new husband and two friends from meeting awkwardly for the first time, Samantha remembered the chance meeting with Lois and her mother in the grocery store. Her stomach flipped and she felt the bile rise to her throat knowing this would get very tricky. Quickly she stepped in front of Waylon with a smile plastered on her face.

Placing a swift kiss on his lips, Samantha said, "Hey, I missed you. Where'd you take off too?"

"Had a couple errands to run. But I'm back. Wouldn't miss your big day for anything."

A whiff of liquor passed before Samantha along with twinges of disappointment and a trace of fear.

"Can you leave this in the car?" She placed a hand over the bottle in the paper sack and looked bravely into his face. "Until later?"

Frowning but without saying a word, Waylon returned to the car and put the bottle in the back seat. Instead of immediately returning to her side, he took a pack of cigarettes from his pocket and stood by the car to smoke.

Divided between Waylon and her girlfriends, Samantha was elated to see them. She wanted to explain to them the new events in her life without Waylon standing there so she left him with his cigarette and turned back to Margie and Lois. Giving a little squeal she daintily ran over to her waiting friends. The three hugged and laughed as if they hadn't seen each other in years.

Lois broke the ice. "Samantha, we have missed you so much! I hope you are feeling better. Your mother wouldn't let us come near the house, afraid we would catch some mystery disease you had! Is that the same handsome friend I saw you with in the store the other day? He's still in town? You have to introduce me!"

Samantha stopped both girls in their tracks before they could get any closer to the house or Waylon. "Wait....."

Margie's young face creased with confusion. "Samantha, what ever is going on with you? You're acting odd."

Seeing the look on her face her two friends awaited an explanation. "I know you won't understand what I am about to say, and if you decide you never want to be my friend, I will accept that."

"Sammie, you're scaring us. What gives?"

"He's not a family friend. He's—he's my.....husband. I am married. That is my husband. Waylon Graves." Samantha felt the blood drain from her face as she struggled to tell her girlfriends the news.

Watching both of her friends' jaws drop in complete surprise, Samantha felt worse than ever. Images of long-ago daydreams with her two best friends standing on her left as she stood in a dazzling white gown and spoke her marriage vows dissolved into a mist of pain.

Speechless, the girls waited for her to continue. "Girls, all those mornings I couldn't walk to school with you, I—I was meeting up with Waylon. And…..he was so sweet and handsome and then he just asked me to marry him…..so we ran off and got married. Please don't hate me, not today on my birthday. Please."

Margie, always the peacemaker, reached for Samantha and hugged her tight. "We don't hate you. We sure don't understand, but we don't hate you. I just can't believe we never knew—"

Waylon chose that moment to approach the three. "Ladies, I'm Waylon."

Samantha jumped in to introduce them. "This is my husband, Waylon Graves." Samantha placed an arm around his waist. "Waylon, these are my best friends, Margie and Lois. You met Lois the other day, remember?"

Eyeballing both girls, Waylon drawled, "How could a man forget two pretty faces like these?"

Nausea swept over Samantha once again. "Let's—let's get inside out of this heat. Mama's got some sandwiches prepared and Daddy's cake is just crying to be eaten!"

The rest of Samantha's party went by in a blur. Unable to focus on much more than the constant question of *'What have I done,'* Samantha walked through the next few hours as if sleepwalking, conscious of what was going on around her but completely detached. Her cheeks hurt from too much smiling, the kind of smile you kept plastered in place to hide your pain or discomfort.

As soon as the chocolate-frosted cake was eaten and the plates returned to the sink, Bernice followed through with her promise. Producing the blue box with the pink ribbon, she placed it on a side table by Samantha.

"Open mine last," Bernice instructed.

Lois and Margie each handed her their small boxes. One contained a tiny bottle of cheap perfume and the other an embroidered set of handkerchiefs with scented stationery. Samantha gratefully hugged her friends and thanked them for the gifts.

Next her parents produced a hidden box from behind the couch. Inside was the prettiest scarf and brooch she had ever laid eyes on.

Sylvia spoke quietly from beside her daughter. "The pin was my Mother's. I think you will get more wear out of it than I have. I don't need a trinket such as that. And the purple stones will bring out the color of your eyes."

Standing to her feet, Samantha threw her arms around her mother's neck and gasped, "Oh, Mama!"

Though she loved the beautiful gift, she loved even more the fact that her mother wouldn't have given her such a treasure if she was not still accepting of her daughter and her decision. Things felt right again.

Even beautiful.

Geoffrey ran up to Samantha clutching a small box between his hands. "Me next! Happy birf'day, 'Mantha!" The little smear of chocolate frosting on his nose only endeared her nephew to her even more.

"From you, Geoffie? Oh, I can't wait to see what it is!"

Inside was a box that held eight chocolates, not the expensive ones, but eight glorious chocolates none the less. All her own.

"My favorites! Thank you, Claudia and Geoff! If you're a good boy, I might share one with you!" Samantha gave him a quick wink.

Glancing at Waylon, Samantha noticed the small paper sack tucked in his hand. Crossing his arms to conceal it, he waited for her to continue to open her last gift.

"Enough of the blubbering. Open mine now," Bernice commanded.

Gently removing the bow, Samantha lifted the blue box and the tiny card announcing where the gift came from. "*Harringtons!* Bernice, you shouldn't have!"

"Of course I should have! It's my baby sister's fifteenth birthday."

Lifting the white tissue paper, Samantha lifted out a sparkling, silver bracelet that was surrounded by jangling charms. One was a shiny "S," another was a pink embossed tiny birthday cake, a miniscule shoe and purse, and lastly a little Scottie dog completed the circle. Samantha's breath caught in her throat. Never had she seen anything so delicate and beautiful! She would be the envy of every girl in town!

Glancing up at Waylon, she watched him tuck the paper sack into his pants' pocket. Looking her way, he silently exited the room as she heard the screen door squeak behind him.

"Bernice, I can't believe you got me a charm bracelet. Thank you and Frank so much." Hugging her sister and brother-in-law tightly, she looked around the room. "Thank you all for making my birthday so special."

Lois and Margie said their good-byes. "We should be going. Thanks for inviting us, Samantha. See you at school?"

Taken aback at their innocent question, Samantha replied, "Umm, sure. Yes. Thank you both so much for coming and for my gifts!"

Hugging her friends tightly, Samantha felt something different in their embrace. Hesitation? Confusion? She couldn't put her finger on it at the moment.

"Bye, girls. See you later."

Something shifted in Samantha's soul. A change took place that was of her own making and decision and now she would have to deal with the consequences as they came. Never would she have imagined her relationship with her two best friends suffering from her relationship with a man. The reality of it settled around Samantha and smothered her like the heavy Mississippi air. Surely her friends wouldn't turn their backs on her. How would the future play out with school and life in general?

A question she never thought she would be pondering on her fifteenth birthday.

But amazingly, her heart whispered louder than the question that had rocked her momentarily.

*Beauty from ashes. Beauty from ashes.*

The gift wrapping all tossed in the trash, cake plates and coffee cups washed up and drying in the dish rack, Samantha glanced out the back window for the hundredth time looking for Waylon's car to be parked back under the oak tree.

It still wasn't there.

Henry broke into Samantha's thoughts. "Samantha, your mother and I want to talk to you."

Quickly she glanced around the room and realized she wasn't alone in the kitchen. Her parents stood quietly in the door. She heard Geoffrey's delighted squeals coming from the tree swing out back and heard her sisters and Frank laughing along with the child.

Knowing she couldn't escape, she coldly replied, "Sure."

Sylvia motioned to the kitchen table. "Let's sit. Everyone's outside in the back."

Scraping the metal chair on the wood flooring, Samantha seated herself in front of her parents. She was feeling like a twelve-year-old again and not a woman.

Henry started the dreaded conversation. "Honey, look. Your mother and I are worried sick about you. I know you say you are fine and you love this man—"

"*Waylon*, Daddy. His name is *Waylon*. And he's my husband, not just a man." A defensive tone edged her words. Samantha wished everyone would just accept the truth.

She was married.

Holding up his hands in defense, Henry began again. "We know you say you love Waylon. But….you don't seem happy or like you really think this was the best idea after all. Samantha, we want to help you get out of this marriage if you want to. It's okay if you do."

Aghast at her father's suggestion, Samantha quickly stood from her seated position. "Daddy! How dare you? I never asked for you to *get me out* of anything! I can't believe you would say that!"

Sylvia came to Henry's aid. "Samantha Jean. Calm down and listen to your father. We are still your parents and you are still under our roof. Just listen a minute and sit back down."

Nostrils flaring, Samantha crossed her arms across her chest as she used to as a small child. She obediently sat down again, but stared across the room refusing to make eye contact with her parents. Her foot jiggled underneath the table against its leg creating a monotonous tapping.

Without their knowledge, her two sisters heard the commotion from outside and snuck in the side door to listen in on their baby sister and parents' heated conversation. Heads bent together just off the kitchen, Claudia and Bernice held their breath and waited.

"We just want to see you happy and not forced into being with someone who—" Henry broke off here.

"Someone who *what*, Daddy? *Loves* me, *wants* to be with me, *cares* about me?" The lies sounded hollow even to Samantha's ears.

Now Henry stood over the two women before him. He could contain his frustration no longer. "Cares about you? Samantha where did you two live before coming here? From the looks of it, in the back of his car? And a man doesn't swig liquor like he does if he plans to care for a family! His trunk is full of empty bottles! I smelled it on him today, on a Sunday and on your birthday for crying out loud!"

"Oh, like you have any room to talk! Daddy, we all know you drink liquor too! So don't judge Waylon for the same thing you do!"

The sisters heard another chair scrape across the floor.

Claudia whispered, "Oh Samantha, you shouldn't have said that."

"Shush up so I can hear the rest," Bernice whispered in reprimand.

"Samantha, you know that's not true! I only take a sip now and again and never on Sunday. Your mother doesn't allow it." Shifting the focus back to Waylon, Henry continued, "He doesn't even have a job, Samantha! How's the man going to care for you?"

"How do you know so much about my husband? You have barely spoken two words to him!" Anger flushed her cheeks as she waited for her father's answer.

Sylvia stood this time. "Samantha, you will watch your tone with your father. He knows only what Waylon has told him."

"I asked him where he worked and he told me he didn't have a job at the moment. I told him there was a new opening at the mine, housing included. Didn't seem the least interested in the prospect of a job and a house. You would think a man would want to take any job out there especially if he's newly married."

Defeat deflated Samantha. The day, though meant to be special, had left its mark on her, and now this. Raising her chin, she looked squarely at her parents and spoke in a hushed but firm tone. "I will say this one time and one time only. I *chose* to marry Waylon Graves. You don't have to like my decision. That's your choice. He *will* get a job and we *will* leave here as soon as we can. I promise you that."

With that Samantha breezed out of the kitchen, nearly knocking her sisters over in the adjoining room. Allowing the screened door to slam after her, she headed for the willow tree and privacy at the edge of the property.

## chapter 10

Quickly stuffing her and Waylon's belongings into boxes and bags, Samantha allowed her mind to wander over the last week. She stood to her full height and stretched her arms over her head. Samantha felt the ache in both body and heart. Walking to the screened wall of her and Waylon's "bedroom," she longed for a place of their own with real walls and privacy.

And finally it was becoming a reality.

The past week had been full of sweet moments and heart wrenching conversations if you could call them that. Mostly all of the words spoken between Samantha and her parents or between Waylon and herself had been arguments and clipped sentences. And then in the blink of an eye, Waylon could turn into a man who only had eyes for her and sweep her off her feet reminding her of why she fell for him in the first place.

While continuing to pack, she recalled the day Waylon had found a job.

*After Waylon had spent the better part of the week job hunting with no success, he finally had given in to Samantha's pleas to go talk to the mine about employment. Against his own wishes, he gave in and went in search of a job in the dark, dirty, hole of the coal mine. Waylon returned back to her parents' house with an announcement the day before that he served up at dinner right along side Sylvia's mashed potatoes.*

"I got a job at the mine so Sam and I will be leaving tomorrow and moving into our own place down the road."

Looks of surprise filled each face around the table as all forks and knives stilled.

Samantha broke the uncomfortable silence. "Way....that's wonderful news!"

Henry spoke next. "What changed your mind? I thought you were dead set against the mine."

"Seeing as Sam and I want out from under your roof, I guess that was motivation enough." Waylon laced his words lightly with enough venom to make his point.

Trying to keep the peace, Samantha interjected, "But we really appreciate you both letting us live here. Right, Waylon?" She smiled sweetly up at her husband giving him a discreet nudge.

"Yeah. Thanks," Waylon replied without feeling.

Sylvia stood from the table quickly. Samantha caught the unshed tears glimmering in her mother's eyes as she turned to the sink to begin washing dishes.

As the others cleared out after the meal, Samantha stayed to help her mother in the kitchen. "You okay, Mama?"

Sylvia sniffed once. "Fine, Samantha. I'm fine."

"Well, you don't look fine to me." Samantha nudged her mother playfully.

Lowering her hands into the sudsy water, Sylvia quietly spoke. "Honestly, I was hoping you would stay. It's been good having you home."

Samantha brightened. "See, Mama. I told you that you would get used to the idea of me and Waylon."

Almost imperceptibly, Sylvia murmured, "That's not what I said."

Not daring her mother to repeat her words, Samantha quietly finished drying the dishes.

"'Mantha! Where are you, 'Mantha?" Geoffrey's voice brought Samantha out of her reverie.

"In my room, buddy!" The clomp of little feet reached Samantha on the porch-turned-bedroom for her and Waylon.

"This not your room, 'Mantha. This a porch."

Ruffling his blond curls, Samantha couldn't help but laugh at the ridiculousness of the situation. "You're right. This is a porch. It was 'Mantha and Waylon's room, but now it's the porch again."

"Where's your room now?" Geoffrey couldn't get things sorted out in his mind.

"Waylon and I will move to a new house down the street today. It's just a few doors down so you can come visit me anytime. How does that sound?"

Throwing his chubby arms around her legs, he begged, "Don't go, 'Mantha....pwease."

"I have to, Sweetie."

"But why?" He pressed her further.

"Because I am married to Waylon now and that's what you do when you get married. You live with the person you marry." Samantha did her best to explain.

"But why you married now?"

Her heart quickened its beating at his innocent question. Quietly she answered, "That seems to be everyone's question lately. Even mine. Hey, why don't you go see if Grammie has some cookies for you? I have to finish up here, okay?"

Forgetting everything but cookies, the three-year-old left Samantha to finish up her packing.

With more force than necessary, Samantha finished tossing the remaining items from their porch bedroom into the last box.

Bittersweet memories flooded her mind. Her first "bedroom" as a married woman. Laying with their bodies entwined under the damp sheets, listening to the last of the summer insects sing her and Waylon to sleep. Stormy fights after dark when Waylon was too drunk to make sense. Making up with him the next morning.

Looking down at her arm, Samantha pulled her sleeve down a bit lower to conceal the four finger-sized bruises that had formed on her flesh. *Waylon hadn't really meant to hurt me*, she told herself. The lie didn't sound any better the next day than it had the first time she chanted it to her fearful mind.

Samantha looked around the little room for anything she may have left behind. Peering under their bed, she saw her hidden Bible. Snatching it from the far corner against the wall, relief flooded Samantha as she held the white shrouded sacred book in her hands. She could never forgive herself if she lost the precious Bible, knowing she had been given a secret, wonderful, gift by a complete stranger.

Realizing she had a bit more time to herself, Samantha eased the Bible out of its covering and let it fall open on its own. Glancing down at the thin pages, there it was. Another verse underlined in red for her to read. It was from the book of Psalms, chapter 127.

*"Except the Lord build the house, they labour in vain that build it: except the Lord keep the city, the watchman waketh but in vain."*

It was like the words stood out in bold on the page from the rest of the other tiny letters.

*"Except the Lord build the house, they labour in vain that build it."*

Like a heavy quilt placed on her shoulders, Samantha felt the weight of the words wrap around her.

*"Except the Lord build the house...."*

She had both seen and heard these words before as her mind recalled them, like seeing someone you haven't been with in a long time. Stitched on a pillow at her Grandmother's house, Samantha never understood the words as a little girl. She asked her Grandmother what it meant one day and her response had stuck with Samantha all these years.

"A home built without God is just that. A house. A building. But a home built by God is so much more. It's love and peace and family. People should let God build their families and not do it without Him."

That explanation had been enough for her as a young girl.

But not enough for her fourteen-year-old heart when she chose to marry Waylon Graves.

And now it was too late to go back and change that. Oh, how she wished.....

Standing quickly, Samantha chided herself as she tucked the Bible into a safe spot in a box.

*Samantha Jean Graves! Stop it this instant. You're moving into your new house with your husband. This is your choice so make the best of it.*

And she knew she must since she hadn't asked God to build her house.

Swiping a silent tear from her cheek, Samantha began taking boxes and bags to the steps and then waited for Waylon to come for her.

As the hot sun was nearing the horizon, Samantha heard Waylon's car before she saw it as he pulled in to park in the usual spot. Slowly he lifted his frame from the car, black streaks smeared on his face, sweat marking his shirt. He looked bone-weary tired.

Compassion filled her heart as Samantha went to greet him. Smiling brightly at the prospect of moving into their new home, she moved to hug her dirty husband.

"Not now, Sam. I'm not in the mood. Let's get packed up and moved so I can get a shower and go to bed. I'm exhausted."

"Mama will let you shower here first. I left out a change of clothes and a towel and soap. I remember how Daddy always wants to clean up first thing after the mine." She took his hands in hers and looked up into his grimy face. "I love you, Waylon Graves."

Looking down at her hands in his, the purple dots on Samantha's forearm caught his eye. Frowning in confusion, Waylon glanced at Samantha. "What—"

Swallowing hard, she pulled him forward. "Let's get you inside and cleaned up."

*He doesn't remember,* she realized. *He didn't hurt me on purpose.*

The rest of the evening was spent unloading the boxes from Waylon's car and stacking them in a corner. Only their bare essentials were brought out for the night and the tired couple ate the ham sandwiches and potato salad Sylvia had sent with them.

Quickly Samantha spread clean sheets, also sent by Sylvia, over the bed that came with the house. The rest would wait til tomorrow. Not wanting to unpack their few things in the tiny house that needed a good scrubbing, Samantha couldn't wait to clean her first home and set up housekeeping there.

As soon as their meager dinner was cleaned up, Waylon reached for his now nightly brown bottle and poured his second glass of the evening. Wordlessly, Samantha glanced at his glass and looked away.

"Don't give me that look, Sam."

Clearing her throat nervously, Samantha tried not to look scared. She had seen a pattern in her husband. Liquor meant he was mean. If she could keep him from drinking so much then he was nicer to her and didn't hurt her. But if she ever said anything about his drinking it angered him greatly. Either way she would suffer his wrath, so Samantha decided to try to distract him from the idea.

Patting the clean sheets she murmured, "How about we break in our new bed in our new house, Way? What do you say? I can help you forget your bad day."

Her purred words had little effect on Waylon. He was cranky and tired. "You or nothing else can help me forget today or tomorrow or the next day that I'm stuck in that God-forsaken mine! Now just let me be. A man just wants to come home from a hard day and relax with a hot meal, in a quiet house, and have a glass of booze. Is that too much to ask for from my wife?" Downing his glass, Waylon reached to pour a third.

"No, that's not too much to ask. I promise to have a hot meal for you tomorrow and a clean house to come home to. You'll see, Waylon. I just wish you wouldn't drink so much, that's all." Samantha turned to her bag of clothes to find her nightgown and continued. "I was thinking today. I really want to go back to school in the fall and finish up my two years. You will be away at work all day so I just thought that would be a good idea. And I would like to go to church Sunday with the family and then eat dinner with them at Mama and Daddy's after—"

Waylon grabbed her forearm tightly and spun her around cutting off her words. "Sam! Shut up! You don't go ordering me around now that we aren't at *Mama and Daddy's house.*" The tone he took with her cut her to the bone. "This is *my* house. We will go where I say, when I say. You got that?" Squeezing her arm for emphasis, he shoved her away from him. "Now let me be."

Tears coursed down her face and she quickly turned away from him to wipe them away. Not sure if her arm or heart hurt the most, Samantha focused on getting herself ready for bed in the little bathroom and stuffing the tears once again. She pulled her gown over her head, brushed her teeth, and washed her face all the while reminding herself to find something beautiful.

*I will find the beautiful here in my own home. I will!*

Samantha let her mind drift to her plans to clean and set up their house, hoping to make it pleasing to Waylon and something she found joy in. That would be up to her. First thing tomorrow she would go pick some flowers then hang the curtains Mama sent.

Stepping out of the bathroom, Waylon had poured the end of the bottle into his glass. He slurred out the next words. "You can forget school. You are a married woman, not a school girl. And as far as church goes, I've never set foot in one and I never plan to."

Quietly, she answered, "Whatever you say, Waylon."

In three days' time, Samantha had her little house sparkling and set up how she wanted it. Sylvia, Claudia, and Geoffrey had carted over "leftovers" as Mama called them. She brought extra silverware, dishes, tablecloths, sheets, small furniture, and even pots and pans for Samantha to use. Many of the items were Samantha's grandmother's that had been stored away since her death years ago. It touched Samantha deeply for her mother to help her set up the house with so many essential items. She even brought a recipe book for Samantha to use along with some small portions of kitchen essentials like flour, sugar, and lard.

The days after her mother and sister left and the house was all in order, Samantha was faced with emotions she wasn't prepared for. Knowing she could walk the short distance to visit her family anytime she chose, Samantha was determined to prove she could make it on her own. The biggest battles she faced was with loneliness and quiet. Used to the hustle and bustle of her mother in the house and little Geoffrey under foot, or accustomed to her week days spent in a classroom with twenty other people her age, Samantha was about to go crazy in the tiny, still house.

As soon as Waylon left for work each day, she fell into her morning routine which lasted a total of an hour then she was confronted with the rest of the day staring her emptily in the face. There just wasn't enough to do to occupy her time and hands, much less her mind.

After two weeks of this quiet madness, Samantha gave in and went to her mother's house nearly every day for lunch, returning in time to prepare a meager dinner for Waylon and herself. Then an even more maddening routine began.

Her nights were either filled with silence between the two of them, heated arguments that always ended in him shoving or hitting or hurting her, or they were spent in the throes of love in their bed when Waylon dictated. Samantha longed for evenings like her family had always shared. At one time she thought they were boring and uneventful, but now she wished for just that.

Her young heart ached for peace and security, love and acceptance, quiet and laughter.

As reality settled in around her, Samantha knew that was not something she could or would have in her little house she shared with Waylon Graves.

# chapter 11

Weeks turned into the end of the first month in Samantha's new house with Waylon. She finally had settled into a routine that at least filled her days and made them as bright and beautiful as possible. A ritual she protected fiercely, Samantha waited patiently five days a week when Waylon would leave for work so she could have her time to herself. Finding she had begun to enjoy these couple of hours before heading to her Mama's house for lunch, Samantha spent each morning pouring over the Bible and looking for each red-marked verse she could find. Wanting to savor them all, Samantha allowed herself to read one verse a day, hoping they would never run out. Then she would head outdoors to a field edging the woods that backed up to Wataker's tiny mining town houses to slowly, carefully choose her prize for the day.

Something beautiful to take back to her little house, something to savor and remind her that outside the four faded walls containing her and Waylon's dark secrets, there really did exist goodness. The world did hold a measure of serenity and something lovely. So each day she would find it, hold it in her hands, press it to her heart, and collect its beauty within her soul.

Her mason jar sat ready and filled with fresh water for today's bouquet of wildflowers. Her windowsill perched ready and awaiting a new and interesting rock, a clump of emerald green moss, or an empty bird's nest. Today held new treasures for her and she was determined to find them.

Samantha saw her first sign of beauty, a little crop of upturned, yellow faces of miniature sunflowers. Just looking at them made her smile and forget the pain in her heart. Last night was one of silence. She felt unseen and unloved, but the smiling flower-faces reminded her to look up and do as they did; face the sun.

Gathering a small bouquet for her jar, Samantha heard the crunch of tires against the hard packed dirt road. Looking up she saw the familiar white, shiny Chrysler New Yorker.

Bernice!

Running the flowers to their waiting water, Samantha ran out the door and nearly tore the car's door from its frame as she pulled her sister from her car.

Laughter rang in the air as Bernice leaped out and hugged Samantha tightly. "Oh, how I have missed my little Sis! Look at you all grown up!"

"What are you doing here? I am so happy to see you, Bernie." Samantha hugged her again as her smiled continued to grow.

"Can't a girl come see how her little sister is getting along? I wanted to see your little bungalow too."

Samantha blushed and ducked her head. "Bernie, it's nothing compared to your apartment. Nothing shiny or fancy, but it's mine and that's what counts. Want some coffee? Oh, and I made biscuits this morning, but they are a little burnt...."

Stepping into the small house, Bernice exclaimed over everything before like she had never seen Mama's or Grandmother's things. Samantha appreciated her sister's kind words.

"Samantha, it's so darling! I love your collection of rocks and flowers in the window. Really brightens things up to bring the outdoors inside. I like that. It's you."

"Just makes my world a little brighter." Wishing she could retract those last words, Samantha busied herself with arranging the flowers.

"So tell me about your world. It's not very bright, Sis?"

"Oh, I didn't mean that. I'm just being silly."

"Hey, I have an idea! Let's get you dolled up and go out to lunch. I want to take you to *Harrington's* and buy you a little housewarming present too. What do you say?" With pure delight, Bernice watched her sister's face go from momentary melancholy to utter surprise.

"Really, Bernie? Oh, you don't mean it!"

"Yes, I do! Come on. Put on your best dress and let's do the town."

Samantha touched her hair. "Okay. I look a mess, Bernie. Just give me a minute and I will change."

Bernice looked around the tiny house for a moment gathering ideas of what Samantha might need to make her life easier. As in days long ago when the two shared a bedroom back home, she barged right in on Samantha as she was pulling on her dress. Bernice's eye didn't miss several bruises on her sister's upper arm and hip. Quickly looking away, Bernice fumbled with her purse while Samantha finished dressing.

"Here, let's add a touch of lipstick and swoop your hair up and we can go." Bernice spun Samantha around and within minutes she had her hair twisted up and applied a layer of pink lipstick to her sister's mouth. "Perfect! Here we come, *Harrington's*!"

Giggles spilled from Samantha as she was lost in the moment with Bernice, a welcome adventure to her day. "Let's go!"

The twenty minute ride to downtown's well-known department store was spent discussing some ideas of what Samantha would need for her house. New dishes, serving bowls, a vase, a new toaster? The girls laughed and talked of days long ago as children together. It was refreshing and much needed for Samantha.

Her head spinning with all of *Harrington's* expensive and shiny items to choose from, Samantha finally settled on a toaster since she hadn't gotten the hang of biscuits yet. It was a difficult decision between the toaster and a small cut glass vase with delicate flowers adorning the front.

Leaving the revolving doors of *Harrington's,* Bernice suggested they stop in for a bite of lunch at her favorite café. The two ate toasted sandwiches while they sipped lemonades at a leisurely pace. Samantha felt like she had died and gone to heaven.

Seated in a corner booth gave the two sisters some privacy, so Bernice took advantage of this. Leaning across the table from her sister, Bernice took both of Samantha's hands in hers and looked her in the eyes.

"Okay, enough of this. I've left you alone for a month. Tell me about you. Are you alright? I know all of this has been a big adjustment for you." Bernice sat in the surrounding silence as Samantha fiddled with her lemonade straw. "Samantha Jean, I'm your sister, for goodness sake! And I bought you a toaster, so you owe me *something*."

Sighing deeply, Samantha looked up at Bernice. "You're right, Sis. It's just hard to talk about. I don't even know what to say."

"Okay....this is a start. How about I ask questions and you answer them?"

Again, silence from across the table engulfed the two.

"Well, answer this one. Are you happy, Samantha? Truly happy?"

"Sometimes. I guess."

"Good. Tell me something great about your husband. Make me like him."

Samantha thought for a moment. "He takes care of me. He took a job he hates so we can have a home."

Bernice sipped her lemonade. "That's good. Is he nice to you? Do you two get along? Or is it all a life of work and no play?"

Samantha smiled at Bernice. "That's a lot of questions. Ummm.....yes, he can be nice, and no, we don't have a lot of fun. I guess we try to when Waylon's not tired, maybe on the weekends."

Unconvinced, Bernice pressed her further. "Tell me one fun thing you two have done since you got married."

"Waylon went and played poker with his buddies and I…..well, I went to Mama's and played hopscotch with Geoffrey." Samantha hated how pathetic she sounded. Balling up her napkin, she tossed in on the table. "Happy now, Bernie?"

Bernice watched Samantha in silence as her sister stared at her empty hands in her lap. "No, I'm not. Especially if you aren't. I'm not asking these questions to satisfy my own curiosity. I'm asking because I really care about you. Don't you know that, Little Sister?"

Secretly Bernice was Samantha's favorite sister and she instantly felt guilty for pushing her away since she married Waylon. Relaxing again, Samantha responded in a near whisper, "I know you do. I'm sorry, Bernie. I don't even know what's wrong with me."

Down deep Samantha knew, but she didn't know how to tell anyone. It was her choice to marry Waylon; it was her mess, not anyone else's.

Bernice's next question was spoken so quietly, Samantha could hardly hear her words. "Samantha. Tell me about the bruises. I saw them earlier when you were getting dressed. What happened?"

Silence.

Bernice fiercely whispered, "Samantha Jean. Tell me! You can trust me!"

"I fell, okay?"

Grabbing Samantha's arm that rested on the table between them, Bernice looked straight into Samantha's glistening eyes. "Do *not* lie to me. I know when you aren't being honest. Your lip twitches just like now," she continued in a whisper.

Samantha covered her mouth with a shaking hand and swiped at a stray tear with the other. Her next words stunned even herself. "It's okay, Bernie. He didn't mean it. I swear."

Bernice leaned back in her side of the booth, the air whooshing out of her lungs, and shook her head slowly. Finally she spoke. "I knew it. The booze, the fear I would see on your face, the bruises. Samantha, you can't live like this. You don't *have* to!"

"It's okay, Bernice. It's—okay. It's my choice."

"But it doesn't have to be. Let me help you. Please…."

Fear clouded Samantha's features. "No. And you can't tell *anyone!* I shouldn't have told you….I'm going to the ladies' room."

Bernice watched her emotionally and physically battered fifteen-year-old sister as she stalked off to the restroom. She sat in silence trying to put the pieces of her now burdened heart back together. She *had* to make Samantha listen to reason.

She just had to.

The ride back to Samantha's little house was mostly a silent one. Bernice could tell her sister's anger had diffused as she now sat still and stared out the window of the car.

At the house, Bernice retrieved the bag from *Harrington's* from her back seat and followed Samantha through the front door. Placing the bag on the small kitchen table, Bernice turned to Samantha. "Look, Sis. I'm not trying to pry or tell you what to do. I am worried about you *and* your future children. That's all."

A deep frown creased Samantha's young face. Letting down her strawberry blond tresses, she looked at Bernice. "What do you mean? My future children? I don't want children….not now, maybe not ever. Not here."

Bernice tugged on Samantha's arm and pulled her to a chair. "Sammie, sit."

Samantha sat in front of Bernice again. "Let's not do this anymore, Bernie. I will figure this out on my own."

"Okay, smarty pants. Then tell me how you are preventing from having these future children you don't want? Tell me that." Raising her perfectly shaped eyebrows, Bernice stared at Samantha.

Huffing in exasperation, Samantha said, "What do you mean? I don't know….."

Reality dawned on Bernice's face. "Mama didn't get to have *the talk* with you, did she? Of course not. You married a boy at fourteen. Samantha, what *do* you know about marriage and babies?"

Blushing furiously, Samantha knew she needed some more information but she didn't want to ask. "I know *how* it all happens and *how* you get pregnant. But that's about it. I know when you stop having your period that's a good sign you might be pregnant. But that hasn't happened to me yet…..so I'm not."

"Oh, honey. Let's make a pot of coffee. We need to talk some more."

Grateful for the distraction, Samantha set up the percolator. When she turned around the beautiful cut glass vase held her bouquet of sunflowers she had picked earlier. It took center stage on her scarred wooden table. "Oh, Bernie! You shouldn't have! You really bought that for me?"

"Of course. And now's a good time as any to give it to you. It will be perfect for your wildflowers. I could tell you were torn between the toaster and the vase. So…..now you have both. I *do* love you, Samantha Jean."

Throwing her arms around her sister's neck, Samantha held on and finally allowed a month's worth of tears to pour from her wounded, confused soul. The sound of the coffee bubbling in its metal pot roused her from her tears.

She retrieved two unmatching, chipped cups and poured them each a steaming cup of coffee. "Okay, wise sister. Tell me what I need to know about marriage and babies."

Bernice's laughter filled the small room and brought ease to a tense subject. For the next thirty minutes, Samantha found the courage to ask questions and receive information on the delicate subject of womanhood, something her mother was not given the privilege of telling her.

But that was fine with Samantha.

For in this moment with her sister, she found yet again what her heart constantly longed for.

Beauty.

## chapter 12

Surprisingly, for the last few months, Waylon had agreed for Samantha to attend church with her family then afterward he would meet them at Henry and Sylvia's house for the usual family lunch. They each had done their best to accept this strange marriage, one that the entire group hoped wouldn't have lasted past Samantha's fifteenth birthday party.

But somehow Samantha Jean Owens Graves had hung on and hoped on.

Sylvia and Henry had watched their daughter age right before their eyes, the days of lollipops, giggly girlfriends, and trips to the movies long gone. Those fleeting moments had been replaced with household chores, frugal meal planning, and occasional looks of longing mixed with a dose of reality that indeed those times were now over and done for Samantha.

Grateful to have her back in church with them, Samantha smiled more on Sundays than her parents could remember since the surprise marriage. She seemed to enjoy the quiet, still, peaceful moments in the lemon oil scented sanctuary. She would stare ahead at the cross that hung behind the preacher's head and listen intently to his words about hope and peace and joy. Sylvia watched her daughter accept her new seat in church beside her parents, away from her girlfriends who now spoke to Samantha only briefly like they would have spoken to a stranger.

Then afterwards, Samantha was another of the women in the kitchen cooking and cleaning, instead of one of the children playing in the yard awaiting the dinner hour. The changes had all been instantaneous and deliberate on Samantha's part, knowing she had chosen to be a "woman" so she needed to put away childish things and notions.

It both grieved and made Sylvia proud to watch Samantha transform from girl to woman. Grievous to Sylvia, because it was done too early in her young life with days unlived left behind. And a source of pride for the mother as she watched her daughter bravely face the unknowns of womanhood, though she knew down deep Samantha Jean occasionally longed for the olden days of girlhood.

Samantha interrupted Sylvia's thoughts. "Mama, don't let me burn the okra. You know it's my first time to fry it up and I don't want to ruin it."

"You're doing just fine, Samantha. Just fine. Don't stir it too much or the cornmeal will all fall off. That's right, keep your heat on medium and watch it carefully. It's almost done."

Samantha found herself enjoying the Sunday meal preparations and clean-up with her mother and sisters. Unexpectedly, she learned quickly and wanted to do something new in the kitchen each week.

So today was okra cooking lessons.

And it was a beautiful thing.

Not like a pretty rock or a brilliant sunset, but beautiful, like a shared moment, a refreshing glass of cool water, or a child's soft hand in hers.

It was acceptance and approval and beauty to her soul.

"Sam!" Waylon's voice startled her out of the moment.

"Hey, Way. I didn't know you were here." She moved from the stove to greet him, but stopped at his next words.

"Just get me a glass of tea. It's hotter than—"

Quickly interrupting his sentence, Samantha stopped him before he cursed in front of Mama. "Sure, Waylon. I'll bring it to you on the porch. Daddy and Frank's out back if you want to join them."

Geoffrey barged into the kitchen in between Waylon's legs. Lifting the little boy up into the air, Waylon swung him high until he squealed with laughter. "Hey, Little Man. I brought you something. Want to see?"

"Sure! What is it?"

Waylon produced a small, red, fire engine from his pocket and held it out to the boy.

Surprise flickered over Samantha's face. "That was nice, Waylon. What do you tell Uncle Way, Geoffrey?"

A huge smile was plastered across Geoffrey's face. "Thanks, Unk Way! Wanna play with me?"

"Sure, buddy." As Geoffrey headed outside, Waylon turned back to Samantha. "Make it quick, Sam. I'm thirsty." Without another word, he left the kitchen and let the screen door slam behind him.

"Oh, my okra!"

"Take Mr. Big his tea. I've got your okra," Bernice replied, not missing the small tremor in Samantha's hands as she fixed Waylon's tea.

"Thanks, Sis. See. He can be nice when he wants to be." Samantha headed out the porch with Waylon's drink.

Claudia lowered her voice for her mother and sister to hear. "I wish he could show an ounce of kindness to Samantha. I could choke the daylights out of that man if given the chance. Ohhhh!! He makes me so mad! How does she *sleep* with him at night?"

Bernice erupted into a fit of giggles. "Only you would think of that, Claude."

"Girls! Don't let Samantha hear you say things like that. I don't like him anymore than you do. Have you noticed—" Sylvia stopped short of what she was about to say.

"What, Mama? Noticed what?" Claudia pressed.

"Oh, nothing. Why don't you round Geoffrey and the men up after you get the dishes down and set the table? The rolls are just about done."

"Sure, Mama." Claudia went about setting the table and looking for Geoffrey.

"Between me and you, what have you noticed about Samantha, Mama? What were you going to say?" Bernice stood close to her mother's elbow and awaited her response.

"It's just—I don't know. Maybe it's me being overprotective because I don't like that boy, but...."

"Say it, Mama. What?"

"The bruises on her arm. Sometimes I see them when her sleeves creep up. She is wearing longer sleeves than usual in the summer. But sometimes, I just wonder, why does she have so many? Never you mind, Bernice. Forget I said that..."

Laying her hand on Sylvia's arm, quietly Bernice said, "I've seen them too."

The kitchen instantly filled with hungry people waiting on Sunday dinner. After the prayer, they passed steaming platters of fried chicken, okra, sliced garden tomatoes, rolls, mashed potatoes, and gravy. Sylvia took pride in her cooking and took pleasure in feeding her family. Sunday was her favorite day of the week.

She had prepared a wonderful meal somehow on their meager income. Her family was all together and the evening would be spent in the back yard with the men playing horseshoes and the women hidden under the great willow tree chatting away while everyone ate cherry pie or coconut cake or some other delicacy Bernice and Frank would bring from the city bakery.

Sylvia's life was pleasant. She had a roof over her head, food, and family. That was enough.

Only today, she couldn't get away from the uneasy sense that something more really was going on with Samantha. Maybe she had known it all along and was only trying to hope for the best.

But after today, she knew there was no longer any use in denying the truth.

Samantha was suffering; her daughter was suffering silently and alone.

Henry, Frank, Little Geoffrey, and Waylon went to their usual shade tree out back to play horseshoes as was their normal Sunday custom. Three months into the strange marriage between Samantha and Waylon, the family was doing their best to accept what their hearts wanted to reject.

For weeks they would politely ask for Waylon to join them. That didn't work, so Henry did what men do best with each other. He taunted Waylon until he agreed to play. Waylon had eventually agreed to a game of horseshoes with the other two men to prove he wasn't 'afraid of being beat,' as his father-in-law had suggested. And now they were engaged in the usual "friendly" game of horseshoes with the underlying current of competitiveness between men who really couldn't stand each other but had to for the women's sake.

Mostly they played peacefully. But today felt a bit different to Henry. More tension and less friendly competition.

And then Henry got a whiff of the reason Waylon was so uptight.

Booze.

He noticed the young man disappear to his car for a smoke and linger there a while longer than usual. Henry now knew what he had been up to. This was not a pattern he wanted to see take shape. Nothing good could come of this.

Frank threw the next horseshoe and accidentally took Waylon's turn.

Anger flaring up instantly, Waylon shouted, "Who do you think you are? Can't you keep track of whose turn it is? Or is cheating the only way you can win?"

"Settle down. I'll take my turn back. My mistake!" Frank went to retrieve his errantly thrown horseshoe. "And no, I don't *have* to cheat to win."

Henry didn't like Waylon's tone. "Take your turn, Waylon. It was an innocent mistake."

Waylon whirled to face Henry. "Always taking everyone else's side, aren't you, Henry?"

Geoffrey walked over to his grandfather, concern etching his brow. "Pops?"

"Geoffie, how about you go find your mama and see if that pie's ready?"

The instant Henry mentioned dessert the little boy raced off to see if he could get some.

"Look, Waylon, let's just get back to the game. I'm not taking any sides here. Now it's your throw." Henry pointed to the horseshoe pit to hopefully get Waylon interested again in the game. "You're winning anyway."

Waylon wouldn't let it go.

"Rich boy here thinks he can go and do whatever he wants. I don't think so!" Waylon shoved Frank in the chest. "I'll show you whose turn it is!"

"That's enough, Waylon! I think we're done here." Henry turned and began picking up the horseshoes and heard Frank's response.

"Rich boy? At least I don't put my hands on women like—"

Waylon lunged at Frank just as Henry turned to step in.

Instantly Henry's handful of horseshoes connected with Waylon's left cheekbone below his eye. Blood spurted from the cut and ran down the stunned man's cheek.

"Hey! Enough!" Frank stepped between Henry and Waylon to make sure Waylon didn't attack Henry.

The women and a hysterical Geoffrey surrounded the scuffling men.

"Stop it, all of you! Daddy, what did you do?" Samantha was as confused as the rest but Henry's fist and Waylon's bloody face told them something had happened.

"Let's get him inside," Sylvia said. Placing her hand on Waylon's back, she tried to usher him towards the house.

"Get off me! All of you!" Waylon's eyes told of his shock and hatred for the entire group. "Sam, let's go."

Without another word, Samantha ran to keep up with Waylon as they walked the short distance home. Inside, she got an ice pack and bandages then gently and deftly cleaned Waylon's wound. She didn't dare utter a word, afraid he would explode on her.

Once bandaged, Waylon shoved her aside and went to his car. Opening the trunk he withdrew a fresh bottle of booze, returned inside, poured glass after glass and never looked Samantha's way the remainder of the evening.

The sun was still setting when she heard the first snore come from Waylon. He had passed out on the couch shirtless and shoeless. Looking at his handsome, bruised face, Samantha could see the young man she had once fallen hopelessly in love with. His eye had already turned a purplish blue color from his cheek bone up into his lower eyelid.

*How did we end up like this, Waylon? What happened? Were you always like this and I was just too silly and blind to see past a handsome face?*

Grateful he was asleep, she crept out the front door and into the woods beyond her house, knowing instantly why she was headed there.

She had to find it. Anything to make things feel good and true and right.

But all she encountered in her usually brilliant, green world of nature and loveliness were shadows and growing darkness.

It wasn't here. Not tonight.
She couldn't find anything beautiful at all.

## chapter 13

With the next day being Monday, Waylon got up, looked in the cracked mirror that hung over their lopsided dresser, dressed for work and left without coffee or breakfast or a word to Samantha. Her heart broke with being ignored and shunned. She offered to change his bandage but received no answer in response, not even a look her way. Waylon ripped the bandage off his face and stormed out the door, leaving her standing there helpless.

Dressing quickly, Samantha didn't follow her usual morning routine of reading her Bible verse and wandering the back field. Instead she walked to her parents' house. Entering the front door without knocking, Samantha was surprised to see her Daddy standing in the kitchen getting a cup of coffee.

"Daddy, what are you doing here?"

"I could ask you the same question, Sammie-girl." Henry moved to hug his daughter. "I have to report in an hour at Doc Starnes' office for my work physical, then I go in for my shift."

"Oh. I guess it's that time of year again."

The owners of *Watson and Whitaker Mining Company* required every man in every position to pass a physical each year, and if for some reason they didn't pass it, they were no longer employed by the company. Each man signed an agreement to this policy when he was hired. Word had it that Mr. Watson and Mr. Whitaker didn't want any 'sickly' employees on their hands. Production was most important to them, not the health of their employees. Poor health meant poor production. So far Henry had passed every physical with flying colors; thus his job was secure.

"Why are you here so early, girl?"

"Honestly, Daddy, I don't even know myself why I am here. I just had to escape the quiet, I guess. May I?" Samantha pointed to the coffee pot.

"Of course. You know that whatever I have is yours……even my help if you ever want it."

Stirring sugar into her coffee, Samantha looked at Henry. "What does that mean?"

"Your husband—Samantha, he's not—"

"Daddy, don't! I didn't come here for this! Just leave *my husband* alone."

Holding his hands up, Henry looked at his daughter knowing she wouldn't admit to any problems they were having, though by now the whole family knew Waylon was abusing her. "How's his eye?"

Offering a humorless laugh, Samantha said, "Black and blue. But he went to work regardless."

"I'm sorry. It really was an accident. I moved to block him from coming at Frank right when Waylon lunged and my fist....and a couple of horseshoes....connected in the wrong place at the wrong time."

Muttering quietly, Samantha said, "He probably deserved it."

Lifting her chin so she looked at his face, Henry said quietly, "I have no doubt he did."

Tears unbidden spilled over her cheeks.

Gathering his youngest daughter in his arms, Samantha cried into her father's shirt. "Oh, Daddy....why is life so hard sometimes?"

Letting her cry a bit longer, Henry finally eased her back and said, "Samantha, I am here for you when you decide you need me. When you need me to step in, I will. But as long as you keep protecting—"

Pushing away, she replied, "It won't happen again. He swears it. He won't hurt me again. Just stay out of it for now. I will let you know if—I need to be going, Daddy."

Dropping his arms to his sides, Henry watched his daughter, his hurting and wounded Sammie-girl, leave through the front door.

Sylvia entered the kitchen tying an apron around her morning dress. "Did I hear Samantha?"

Henry blew his nose loudly on his handkerchief and tucked it back into his overalls pocket. "Yes, Sylvie, you did. But I scared her off. I mentioned trying to help her and hinted at Waylon's treatment of her....and she left. She won't listen to me! She just wants to protect that—that.....I can't even call him a *man* because real men don't hurt their women! We are going to have a talk today. As soon as I get to work after this doctor's appointment, we are gonna talk. And I do mean business this time! He's taken things too far."

"Henry—" Sylvia watched him rush out the same door where his daughter had stormed out earlier.

The lunch bell couldn't sound soon enough for Henry Owens. He had passed his physical and now it was time to deal with Waylon. All morning he replayed over in his mind what he would say to Waylon.

As soon as he saw Waylon emerge alone from the mine's warehouse, Henry walked quickly over to him. "I'll have a word with you now and I won't take no for an answer," Henry growled quietly to the stunned man.

Waylon began walking away from the other men and Henry followed beside him. "Listen to me and listen good. I am only going to say this once. I know you are laying your hands on my Samantha and leaving your mark on her. If you *ever* hurt her again, I will do the same and *worse* to you. She can't do anything about it and she hasn't got enough wits about her to leave your sorry butt. So don't you ever touch her in a hurtful way again or you *will* be sorry."

Spitting in the dirt beside him, Waylon stopped and faced Henry. Placing his face inches from Henry's, he spoke quietly through gritted teeth. "Old man, don't you *ever* threaten me. If she's got nothing to complain about, then neither do you. So you just stay out of our business. You hear?"

Waylon spun on his heel leaving Henry fuming. Henry knew this wasn't the time or place to discuss this any further and he knew Waylon wasn't the type you discussed matters with anyway. At least he had let the jerk know he was aware of what was going on with Samantha. For now that would have to be enough. His hands were tied unless Henry saw with his own eyes that she was being abused by Waylon. Especially if Samantha was still taking up for Waylon and covering his deeds, there wasn't much more to be done.

Ultimately it was her choice. Henry would never understand two things.

Why a man would hurt a woman, and why a woman would allow it.

The hardest part was that the woman was his own little girl.

It was several weeks before Waylon showed his face at Henry's house again. Samantha had begged him to come back for Sunday dinners and prove to her and her family that he was a decent man and that he loved her. Waylon always did his best to apologize, especially in the bedroom when he saw the bruises on her body. She believed he truly hated what he was doing but when he drank, he was senseless.

At least that was what Waylon told her. He promised to never hurt her again and that he would watch how much he drank, but that usually lasted a couple of weeks and then it all started over again.

Waylon appeared at Sunday dinner meek and mild and actually muttered an apology under his breath aimed towards Henry and Frank for his behavior last time. Warily, the men shook hands and played their usual round of horseshoes, only peacefully this time.

He even brought a bright yellow bouncy ball for Geoffrey and spent time teaching him how to catch it. With Mel in the Navy and away from Claudia and Geoffrey, Waylon told Samantha he felt sorry for the little tyke not having a daddy around to show him things.

Samantha continued to showcase each nicety Waylon displayed and pointed out to her family that he was really a good guy, just raised in a bad home and didn't know how to treat people, but he was learning. Henry still was unconvinced but kept his thoughts to himself.

Nearly each week they were together, Bernice would ask her discreet questions about how she and Waylon were doing and Samantha would go overboard trying to convince Bernie that all was well in her little home.

At least for a couple of weeks it would be.

That Sunday was especially nice. The weather was cooler and everyone was in a jovial mood. Frank and Bernice had brought a delicious pineapple upside down cake from their local bakery and Claudia had received another letter in the mail from Melvin.

All gathered around the table and listened in as she read excerpts from the letter as Melvin had written a couple of sentences to each person. This time he wrote a few lines to Waylon and Samantha.

"Oh, here's a paragraph for Samantha and Waylon. *'To Sammie and Waylon, Here's hoping you two make something special of your relationship like me and my Claudia have. When I return from the Navy, I look forward to meeting you, Waylon. Sammie, I would pinch your cheek if I was there like always but I guess you are getting too grown up for that now. Take care of yourself, my little sis.'"*

"Oh, I miss Mel! That was sweet of him to include a note to us, wasn't it Waylon?" Samantha turned to where Waylon had stood by the doorframe earlier and saw he was gone.

"Carry on, Claudia," Sylvia encouraged.

One by one, she read each excerpt from Melvin's letter to the person it was intended for. When she flipped the page over, she blushed sweetly and stopped reading. "The rest is for me to read in private." Tucking the letter in her skirt pocket, Claudia settled back with a satisfied smile on her face.

Samantha spent the next five minutes looking for Waylon but determined he had headed for home. Helping the women finish with the cleaning up, she quickly left, worried about Waylon's whereabouts.

Sylvia dried her hands on the dish towel exhausted but happy at the end of the day. "Claudia, will you and Geoffrey take this basket of food down the street to Sally's house? Her four babies are sick and I thought dinner might make things a bit easier for her. Besides, Geoffrey could stand to run off some energy before bedtime. You let that boy eat too much sugar at night."

"Sure, Mama. We will take it to her." Claudia gathered the basket and Geoffrey to make the short trek down the street to a house nearly identical to theirs.

Geoffrey insisted on bringing the ball Waylon had given him and every few seconds Claudia had to stop to let him run after it. "Come on, honey. Hold your ball so you don't lose it. Pops will play with you when we get back."

"Okay, Mommy."

Looking up, Geoffrey realized they were across the street from Samantha and Waylon's little home. "Mommy, can I go see 'Mantha and Unk Way? He will play ball."

Sighing deeply, Claudia relented. "Okay, but only for a minute. I will come get you as soon as I drop Sally's dinner off. Check around back first. I think I hear them in the backyard."

Galloping off to see Samantha and Waylon, Geoffrey rounded the house ready to find someone to play ball with him. Startled at the sound of Waylon's tone, Geoffrey stopped and peered around the side of the house. He didn't like the sound of Waylon's voice so he remained hidden before making his presence known. Peeking around the corner he watched a moment.

"You alright, Way?" Samantha asked.

Without answering, he lifted his eyes to hers. In their depths she saw a great mixture of anger, resentment, and hurt.

Her own chest filled with sympathy and fear. "What happened back there? Tell me."

Letting the chair return from two legs to four, Waylon stared at her a long minute. "You really want to know what a loser your husband is? Okay, I will tell you. Claudia's *precious* Melvin is in the Navy and I couldn't even get accepted into any branch of the military!" Standing to his full height, Waylon continued. "That's what kind of loser I am, Sam! A *reject*! Not fit to fight for this country!"

Full of confusion and caution, she questioned him, "What happened? What do you mean?"

Spinning to face her, Waylon looked like he had run a marathon, his face red and muscles bulging in his neck and chest. "I got rejected, Sam! *Rejected!* Back in January, on my 18th birthday no less!" He paused for another drink from the brown bottle. Cursing under his breath, Waylon paced the worn grass inwardly fuming and cursing the country he lived in.

It all made sense to her now, why he left when Claudia read the letter from Mel. A reminder of his own pain of not being able to serve in the military and a reminder of the rejection he still suffered from today.

"Why—why were you…."

"Does it even matter? I was rejected because I—I can't see *anything* out of my right eye!! Satisfied, Sam? I am partially blind! My old man never thought enough of me to have it checked out, said 'one eye was good enough.' Then the army said I was not *'physically fit'* to serve this country even though I have lived eighteen years of my life that way, they said I was *rejected, turned down……*"

Reaching for his arm, Samantha touched him gently to calm Waylon back down. "Waylon, that's *silly*—"

"Silly??? How dare you!"

Before she knew what was happening, the back side of Waylon's hand connected with her cheek, nearly knocking Samantha off her feet. "Ahhh! Way—"

Little Geoffrey's face turned ashen as he froze in place speechless. He didn't know what to make of what he had just witnessed. Fear ignited in his body as he dropped his new yellow ball and ran in the direction of his Mommy.

Claudia was handing the basket into the neighbor's door and was saying a quick good-bye when she heard her son's cries.

"Mommy, Mommy!" Tears poured down his dirty cheeks causing streaks to form on his face.

Claudia rushed to Geoffrey and picked him up. "What's wrong, honey? Did you fall?"

Chest heaving with sobs, the little boy could hardly speak, "N-n-n—no!"

"What happened? Oh, Geoffrey! I'm so sorry! Did something scare you?" Setting him down on the ground, she knelt down by Geoffrey placing both of her hands of his shaking shoulders and said, "Baby, tell me. Are you hurt?"

Grabbing his mother's hand, he began tugging her towards Henry and Sylvia's house. "Let's go to Pop's and Grammie's house, now! Let's go, Mommy!"

Confused at the fear on her son's face, Claudia stood and walked quickly with Geoffrey back to the house. Unable to get any other explanation from him, she was as disturbed as ever. Henry nor Sylvia could make sense of it either. Geoffrey refused to explain to the adults what had happened. The remainder of the evening he stayed close by Claudia and wouldn't let her out of his sight.

# chapter 14

Holding a cool cloth to her stinging cheek, Samantha tried her best to soothe her face and her heart. Watching Waylon storm into the house after his outburst and the smack that nearly landed her on her rear end in the dirt, she remained in the shadows of the trees at the back of their property in shock. All over a misunderstood word, when all she was trying to do was comfort him.

She had called the situation *silly*. And he had exploded.

*How stupid can I be,* Samantha questioned her actions for the millionth time. Knowing *silly* had indeed been a wrong choice of wording, she now wondered more at the reason why she actually thought she could comfort Waylon at all. *That* was what had been silly. Almost physically she could feel the walls go up around her heart where her husband was concerned. There was no reaching Waylon, no comforting him, no talking to him. Like the blinding sun that was now on the horizon's edge, reality screamed at Samantha that she had chosen a man she didn't even know, a drunk, mean man and was now in a mess.

And now those growing walls were offering her a semblance of comfort and protection. If she shut off her heart to Waylon, it seemed to hurt less. Pressing the cool cloth to her cheek, Samantha decided then and there she couldn't leave Waylon because she was the one to choose this man, this life for herself, but she could stop trying to fix his pain and focus on doing her duties as a wife, making him dinners, keeping the house clean, remaining quiet and behind the scenes unless he wanted her.

Yes, she could live like this. She *had* to live like this. It wasn't even remotely close to the fairy tale dream of her girlhood about marriage and life with a man. But it was her own fault for not getting to know Waylon Graves in the beginning and allowing her emotions to be swept away by his charm and handsome face in the early weeks she had met him.

All night Samantha's young mind replayed Bernice and her father's words. *"I'm here for you…..when you need me to step in, I will…..you don't have to live like this. Let me help you."*

And yet Samantha Jean Owens Graves knew she would never ask for their help. She couldn't let them see her pain and how difficult life was with this man. It would only hurt her family further, and besides she *wanted* this marriage to work, for them to be happy. She would just have to watch herself with Waylon, watch what she said and did, and not let him see any displeasure or disappointment from his actions.

*Maybe if I.....*

"Samantha! Where are you, Sam?"

Startled out of her skin, Samantha quickly removed the cloth from her face, checked the height of the walls around her heart, and croaked, "Here, Way." Clearing her throat, she tried her voice again. "Back here, Waylon."

Samantha walked toward the house, dreading each step as she drew nearer to the man who had smacked her in the face only half an hour ago. Like the crawling, coiling, choking kudzu vine that infested the Deep South, fear began its usual creeping around her throat and heart when he was in this uncertain of a mood.

She could see it on his face. His anger hadn't passed. She could see it in his walk. He was still on the verge of exploding. So she stood quietly and waited.

Waylon stood not two feet from her and stared. Samantha watched his gaze flick over her face; she saw him note the handprint that she knew blazed on her cheek. Quickly she ducked her head so he couldn't see the tears that threatened to spill over. Once he had been so very charming and handsome and.....

Waylon reached a finger under her chin and lifted her face. Closing her eyes, she feared what would come next. "Look at me, Sam. Look at me!"

Snapping her eyes open, the quietness of his tone unnerved Samantha. Normally he would be shouting, but now Waylon spoke in a hard, quiet, tone. "Listen to me good. Don't you *ever* tell anybody about this. If you would watch your mouth, I wouldn't have to hit you. I don't want to, Sam, but you give me no other choice sometimes." Moving his face within inches of her, Waylon's hot breath brushed her cheek as he whispered in her ear. "If you ever tell, I will hurt your precious family, starting with your *Daddy.*" Moving back to look in her eyes, Waylon saw the fear there that he was trying to instill.

Spilling over her lower lids, two streams of quiet tears coursed down Samantha's face. Wordlessly, Samantha shook her head in affirmation as a shaky tremor coursed down her spine.

Waylon released her chin and stepped back. "Just as long as we understand each other." Turning on his heel, Waylon headed for the car and left.

After Samantha heard the engine start and the car leave, she collapsed onto the ground where she stood and gave in to the torrent of tears. Afraid the neighbors would hear her, she muffled her cries in her wadded up skirt letting her heart weep for all it was worth. After ten minutes of the teary release, Samantha swiped the washcloth across her face. Slowly she stood to her full height, straightened her skirt, and walked into the tiny house knowing without a shadow of a doubt this was her life with Waylon.

Her future and her choice.

The day dawned bright and early as usual with no thought to Samantha Jean Graves' dark emotions. Sun shining brighter than normal, Samantha shielded her eyes as she took her first cup of coffee to the little porch off her house. She pulled her sweater tighter around her shoulders.

Waylon hadn't come home last night.

She glanced at the wall calendar and read that today was the last day of December and tomorrow would mark the New Year of 1943. This was not the first time in their first eight months of marriage he had not returned home. Surprisingly, Samantha wasn't worried. She knew he would come back when he wanted to and would act like things were normal with no thought or mention of hitting her nor of threatening her family if she told about his abuse.

The morning's cold was too much for her thin sweater so Samantha returned quickly indoors and reached for her Bible. As with each morning, she sought solace and comfort between the pages. Today's reading came from the book of Matthew, chapter 11, verse 28. The red, steady line underneath the verse showed her someone else had found help here too.

Samantha read the short verse aloud in the deathly quiet room. "Come unto me, all ye that labor and are heavy laden, and I will give you rest."

Leaning back in the kitchen chair, she rested her arms on the Bible's pages and repeated the verse over and over in her mind until she was certain it was locked there with all of the rest. Again thankful for her ability to memorize anything she put her mind to, Samantha knew the verse would be another gem in her treasure chest of beauty. Over the past few months, Samantha still sought her beautiful gifts from the Earth itself, a treasure trove of color, shape, and texture. But she was finding a far deeper beauty within the pages of a left behind Bible, words that captivated her heart and soul, that brought peace and loveliness to her difficult days.

*Rest.....that sounds wonderful,* Samantha mused. *This verse says I have to come to Jesus and He will give me rest. But even in* this *house,* this *marriage? It's promised to the ones that labor and are heavy laden.*

Her eyes scanned the next two verses that followed. Again she read aloud, "Take my yoke upon you, and learn of me; for I am meek and lowly in heart: and ye shall find rest unto your souls. For my yoke is easy, and my burden is light."

*Sounds like a mule team. Me and Jesus working together, yoked up with each other.*

The visual caused a slow smile to creep across Samantha's face. It brought a measure of peace to Samantha. Knowing Waylon would probably always be Waylon, she would try to work with Jesus to be the woman and wife she needed to be, like her mother who seemed to know how to make others happy and help them enjoy life.

Roused from her thoughts, Samantha heard Waylon's old car turn into the yard. The slam of the car door caused her to jump. She instantly closed the Bible and returned it to its hiding place.

Banging the screen door open, Waylon looked at Samantha. "Don't start on me, Sam. I need a bath and some breakfast then I have to get to work. Get me a cup of coffee."

"Sure, Waylon." Clamping her mouth closed before she said something she would regret later, Samantha did what was foreign to her. She prayed and asked God to help her right then and there. If the Bible said she needed to come to God, she would try it.

Throughout her days, Samantha *talked* to God, but she really hadn't thought about asking Him to *help* her deal with Waylon. Today she would see what happened.

Taking a fresh cup of coffee to the bedroom, Samantha handed it to Waylon. "Here's your coffee. Want me to get your clothes ready while you clean up?"

Taking the coffee, he sipped it noisily. Looking at her, Waylon eyed her warily, like she was a strange insect he had never seen before. "Okay? Sure, baby. But I have to hurry."

Samantha knew he expected her to ask a bunch of questions about his whereabouts and what he had been doing all night. But honestly, what good would it do her to know? It wouldn't stop his behavior or actions.

Within fifteen minutes, Waylon had dressed and eaten a piece of toast with a fried egg, then headed out the door for work. Grouchy about being late, he rushed out without telling her good-bye or thank you or anything. Stung by his easy dismissal, Samantha tidied up the house and went to her mama's house for the morning.

As soon as she entered the front door, Samantha was enfolded in love, hugs, and care, all of which were the reasons she came here each day she could. To receive these beautiful gifts from her family she couldn't find in her own home.

"Did Waylon decide if you two could come to Frank and Bernice's for the New Year's Eve party?" Sylvia looked at her daughter for an answer.

"No, Mama. He hasn't said."

"Did you not ask him last night like you said?"

"He didn't come—it didn't come up last night. Waylon was tired and we just didn't talk about it." Nearly confessing the truth about his absence last night, Samantha busied herself with fixing another cup of coffee.

Deciding to drop the subject, Sylvia said, "Well, I hope it works out for you to be there. It will be fun!"

"I really want to come but we will see. I'm sure Waylon will be fine with it."

The rest of the day was spent helping her mother with some household tasks. Samantha enjoyed the busyness and the hard work, then she returned to her house to prepare dinner for the two of them.

In her little kitchen dishing up the beans and ham, Samantha placed it on the table next to a small round tin pan of cornbread. She set the plates carefully on the table and poured each of them a glass of tea.

The banging back door announced Waylon's return from work. "Smells good. I'm starving. That mine will be the death of me, Sam."

"Hey, Way." Samantha kissed him on the cheek. "At least it's a job and you aren't in the belly of the mine like so many others. I'm glad you have the warehouse job instead of mining."

"Are you saying my job's not difficult? You have no idea of what I go through day in and day out!"

Quickly regretting her ill-chosen words, Samantha amended them as best she could. "No, not at all. I'm just glad you aren't in the heat and black coal dust. Now, how about a bowl of beans and ham? I made your favorite pie for dessert too."

Samantha had learned to do all of the things Waylon expected and liked to keep the peace, though often enough nothing worked on him. Today, things seemed to go in her favor.

Sitting at the table, Waylon dove into the hot meal. After eating in silence for a while, Samantha broached the subject of the New Year's party.

"What do you think about us taking the bus to Frank and Bernice's tonight for the New Year's party? It will be fun! We haven't done anything like that in a while. Want to?" Keeping her tone light, Samantha waited for him to quit chewing.

Laughing humorlessly, Waylon sneered, "And why do you think I would want to spend my New Year's Eve at your uppity sister and brother-in-law's house surrounded by all their wealth and snooty stares and mentions of getting a better job where Frank works? I've had about enough of that. So no, Sam, we aren't going. My buddies and their girls are having a poker party tonight so that's what I'm doing to ring in the New Year. With or without you, Sam, I'm going."

Sucking in her breath, she inwardly prayed, *Help me, God.* The mention of being with Waylon and his buddies made her shudder. All Samantha could respond with was a lingering, "Okay, if that's what you want to do."

"And I won't have my wife crossing town without me, so forget Bernice's party because I'm not going. You don't want to come with me, fine. But you're staying home, so suit yourself." Without another word, Waylon rose from the table and headed to their bedroom.

Quietly letting out her breath, Samantha answered, "Then I guess I will be staying home."

She had built her own house without any help of the Good Lord Above and she would do her best to stay in control making things as calm as she could. For Waylon and for her own sake. Learning the skill, if you could call it that, of keeping her husband calm and as happy as he could get, Samantha rose each morning weary of the previous day's and night's efforts of doing her best to please Waylon. It was a difficult task to try to please someone who could find little pleasure in anything. But she did her best.

This was the way her life was.

Dark, cold, lonely, and ugly.

Part Two: **Longing for Beauty**

*"Everything has beauty, but not everyone sees it."*
*--Confucius*

# chapter 15

*August, 1943*

Life has a way of blazing by, especially a life that has been lived in a long season filled with hiding one's pain, working to keep the peace, trying to maintain a sense of stability, and living in a state of numbness. Samantha Jean Owens Graves found her sixteen-year-old self right in the middle of such a season. Little did she know as she read her morning verse and saw her husband off to work, today's events would stir things up for her and create a whirlwind of change in her young world.

Two hours after listening to Waylon's car leave the yard for his mining job, Samantha stepped off the city bus and into the deserted park of the little town of Wills, Mississippi. A thirty minute bus ride from her hometown of Wataker, Wills was far enough away that she could feel brave enough to do what she needed to do.

Not able to exit the emptying bus quickly enough, Samantha got to the nearest park bench as quickly as her legs would take her. Fighting an overwhelming sense of nausea, Samantha reached in her handbag and retrieved a small embroidered handkerchief and pressed it to her forehead. Closing her violet eyes tightly against the churning in her stomach, she forced herself to take deep, cleansing breaths until the nausea passed.

*How could this have happened? I've been so careful. I can't be.....*Unable to complete her thought, Samantha slowly opened her eyes and looked around the park.

A path curved gently around the park's perimeter inviting its guests to walk among the canopy of huge magnolias and stately sycamores. The temperature was bearable here among the shade trees. An unusual light breeze and cloud cover announced the possibility of rain later in the day. It would be a welcome relief in the summer's heat.

The doctor had confirmed her worst fear.

She was indeed pregnant.

Remembering the doctor's long stare over the top of his glasses, he had declared in a condescending tone, "Nurse, mark in Ms. Graves' chart she will be a mother in April or May of next year. Hmmm....and she will barely be seventeen years old at that time. A very *young* mother. Do you have family to help you at home, Ms. Graves?"

Sitting taller than before, Samantha resented the doctor's comment. "Doctor, I am well suited for this. My family lives close to me and my husband."

Glancing back up at Samantha, the doctor's gray eyes showed obvious surprise at her pronouncement. "I see. Well. I will see you back in my office next month, *Mrs.* Graves," he said with emphasis. Without another word, the doctor left the stuffy little office that reeked of alcohol and bleach.

And Samantha was now seated in a park trying to absorb both the shock of the news and the reality that she had undeniably allowed the worst to happen. She couldn't possibly bring a baby into her and Waylon's life!

Placing a hand over her abdomen, Samantha felt hot tears pool in her eyes. This explained the nausea and vomiting. She told Waylon she was suffering from a stomach bug and would be fine soon. Never questioning her, Waylon believed what she said. Samantha did her best to hide the continuing nausea from her husband and had succeeded until she realized it was only increasing. Then after being one week late with her period, she feared the real reason for her nausea was pregnancy.

*A baby? How can I do this? I can't raise a baby in our home!* Samantha was in a whirlwind of mental turmoil when she suddenly heard a voice whisper to her heart, riding in on the gentle breeze that surrounded her.

*I will never leave you, nor forsake you.*

*Come to me.*

Peace. There it was. Something she was growing accustomed to lately. Even in the worst of the worst moments with Waylon. Even in the darkest of nights surrounded by fear and dread and worry. Like a stream of sunlight settling on her shoulders to warm her on a chilly day, it was there when she needed it the most. God's gentle touch that brought peace to her storm.

*Okay, God. Looks like we will have a baby on our hands soon. Me and You, we can do this, right?*

This time, she felt a deep sense of God's presence surround her, like He had sat down on the bench beside her and wrapped a strong arm around her shoulders. Samantha drank in the moment and pictured herself sitting, with God's arm around her.

Peace. It was hers. Even in this park she had never been to a day in her life, under trees she had never laid eyes on. God's peace would follow her anywhere.

And that would be enough for now.

That afternoon, Samantha was seated in one of the metal gliders in her Mama's backyard watching as Claudia and Mama hung clothes on the line. Geoffrey was beside Samantha, playing in the dirt with several cars and trucks.

Sylvia glanced over at Samantha and watched her daughter's face turn from pink to pale to a sickly green. "Honey, do you feel okay? You look a little under the weather today."

Guilt stole around the edges of her mind. Samantha had been there an hour and hadn't uttered a word about her news nor had she helped her mother with a single chore. She couldn't today, not with the sick feeling in her stomach or the churning emotions in her heart.

"No, Mama. I don't feel well. How about I get you and Claudia a glass of lemonade and y'all take a break for a while? This heat will make anyone feel ill."

"That sounds nice, Samantha. We are almost done with these sheets."

A moment later, Samantha returned with a tray of four lemonades. Sitting in the shade, the four of them gratefully sipped their lemonades. Little Geoffrey, now four years old, ran off to the tree swing, finally able to swing alone without much help.

Addressing her sister, Samantha stalled a few more minutes. "Claudia, have you heard from Melvin lately?"

A sad smile crossed her sister's face. "Yes, a letter came yesterday. I can't believe he's been gone two years. I don't know what we would do without the money he sends home each month, but I can't wait for him to get off that ship! He's been assigned to the *Battleship Nevada* for God knows how long. I know I don't sound like it, but I really am proud of my Mel. I just miss him terribly. What if Geoffrey forgets his Daddy? I show him pictures every day and talk about Melvin in hopes he won't forget—" Claudia broke off and swiped at a stray tear.

"I'm sorry, honey. I didn't mean to upset you." Samantha reached over and squeezed her sister's arm in comfort. "I can't imagine what you must be feeling."

"It's okay. I really appreciate Waylon trying to be so kind to Geoffrey. I don't know why Geoffrey won't have anything to do with Waylon anymore. He won't even play with the toys Waylon brings. Maybe missing Melvin makes him confused and he won't allow himself to get close to another man besides his Pops."

Sylvia changed the topic. "Samantha Jean, how are you feeling now? Better?"

Taking a deep breath, Samantha replied, "Not really, and I probably won't feel much better for several more months."

Frowns crossed Sylvia and Claudia's faces. "Mama, I'm pregnant. I'm going to have a baby. That's why I feel so sick lately."

Scooting to the edge of her chair, Sylvia nearly spilled her lemonade. "What!?!? Samantha, how do you know? Are you sure?" Joy mixed with shock flitted over Sylvia's face.

Claudia covered her mouth with her hand. "Oh, Sammie! A baby!"

Blushing sweetly, Samantha explained to the two women. "I suspected it might be so and I went to Wills to the doctor and he confirmed it this morning. Waylon doesn't know yet."

At the man's name, Sylvia and Claudia's faces lost some of the excitement from earlier. Sylvia asked the next question. "How do you think he will receive the news?"

Hesitating a moment, Samantha answered, "Honestly, I have no idea, Mama. I guess I will find out tonight."

Sylvia hugged her daughter tightly and glanced over Samantha's shoulder at Claudia. Claudia's face mirrored Sylvia's, a mixture of worry and excitement at this new announcement. Instantly the women erupted into fits of joy and chatted about the new baby to come.

"Oh, my girl! Married at fourteen and a mommy at seventeen. Samantha Jean, you sure have a way of keeping me on my toes, girl!"

"Samantha, what do you want to have? A boy or a girl?" Claudia was caught up in the moment, her sadness lifted over Melvin.

"I hardly know, Sis. I've barely accepted the news I'm having a baby! Hmmm.....I think I want a little boy, just like Geoffie."

Finding her nausea had been exchanged for a swarm of butterflies in her stomach, Samantha placed the last steaming dish on the table as she heard Waylon come through the door. She had pushed through her tiredness and nausea to fix him his favorite supper including mashed potatoes and gravy. Wanting everything to be perfect, Samantha breathed a silent prayer before speaking to Waylon.

"Hey, Way! How was your day? I fixed your favorite supper."

Reaching for the offered glass of sweet tea, Waylon downed the entire glass before answering her. "Same old grind, Sam."

"Are you hungry?"

"Yeah. I could eat now."

Dinner was silent with Waylon glancing up at her face repeatedly. Finally his brow creased with a deep frown as he leaned back in his chair after eating the last of his potatoes. "You look different today. Pretty."

Surprised at the compliment, Samantha blushed. She had taken the time to freshen up her face and put on a clean dress hoping it would help when she broke the news. "Thanks, Waylon. You look—" Unable to come up with the right words, she took on an amused look and finally said, "dirty, but handsome."

An unusual laugh came from her husband, something she had not heard in a long time. "Dirty, but handsome. I'll take that as a compliment."

Reaching across the table for his hand, Samantha felt her courage return. He was in a decent mood so maybe now was the right time to tell him about the baby. "Waylon, I have some news."

Quickly he glanced at her face, frowning at her.

Fear clutched her stomach, but she pressed on. "I-I-I'm pregnant. We're going to have a baby."

Blinking quickly several times, Waylon withdrew his hand from hers. He rubbed his face and finally rested both arms on the table in front of him. Whispering a response, Samantha strained to hear him. "A—a baby?"

"Yes, Way. You are going to be a father." A pretty smile settled on her lips.

"Really, Sam? Are you certain?"

"Completely positive. It's real. I'm pregnant."

"But—but, I can't be a *father*. I can't....." Running his hand back through his hair, Waylon stood and went to the front door and looked out.

Samantha let him absorb the news a bit longer and finally went to his side. Looking up at her husband, she saw something she had never seen before. Waylon had silent tears running down his cheeks. "Oh, Way! Aren't you happy? Don't be upset! I'm sorry—"

"Sam, it's okay. I'm just not sure....." Waylon trailed off and stopped short of saying what was on the tip of his tongue.

"Neither am I, honestly. I'm just not sure either, Waylon. It's our first time as parents, so it's scary. I'm terrified."

Turning to face her, Waylon wrapped his arms around her and Samantha instantly remembered all those days under the trees by the school house, at age fourteen, falling head over heels in love with him. "Sam, you will be a great mommy. I'm just not sure I will be—" Dropping his arms back to his sides, Waylon kissed her on the forehead and went out the back door without another word.

Despite the summer's heat, a shiver coursed its way down Samantha's spine as she watched Waylon walk away from her and the baby she carried.

# chapter 16

With the trees dropping the last of their orange, brown, and scarlet leaves, autumn gave way to winter in Wataker, Mississippi, leaving the mining town's inhabitants joyful that the hot summer months were over. Samantha was probably one of the happiest people in the little mining town. For several reasons, actually.

First of all, her mornings consumed with nausea had finally disappeared and were replaced with feelings of euphoria and hope as the little baby she carried nestled inside her grew. And because she had noticed a change in Waylon over the past few months. Though quieter, he was much calmer. Since he heard the news of her becoming pregnant, he hadn't laid a mean hand on her. To Samantha's pleasure, he had taken her out on a few dates to the movie theater or the ice cream parlor. He didn't say much to her, but he had definitely become more gentle than before and almost attentive. Not sure what to make of these changes except to think the baby had brought them on, Samantha was getting used to this new husband.

Samantha would catch Waylon looking at her growing belly that was just starting to show signs of pregnancy. No one else could really tell yet, but Waylon could.

He had stopped drinking as much too. And on the usual Sunday dinners at her parents', he was nicer to the family, though still not engaged like she wanted him to be. Remaining usually quiet during conversations, Waylon was at least pleasant now. Still refusing to attend church with her, she was happy with the changes that had been made.

Often she found herself believing that things would turn out alright for the two of them. Thanking God above for the little baby she carried, Samantha had overcome her initial misgivings of bringing a baby into their home. Maybe this baby was actually an angel in disguise, sent to right her upside down world.

With Christmas a week away, Samantha was working furiously to gather as many items as she could for the baby. Several mothers in the mining town had given her nearly everything they would need for the new addition. She spent her time washing, scrubbing, and setting in place each outfit, blanket, and baby bootie she received, longing for the day she would hold her little one in her arms.

Maybe it was the season and the message of the approaching holiday, but Samantha could feel it like never before. *Peace.* Like a fuzzy, puppy following her around, it seemed to be her constant companion. And she relished every second of its presence.

Samantha watched as Waylon left through the screened door that Sunday morning bundled up in his old coat and scarf. He told her he had an errand to run so she busied herself getting ready for the Christmas church service all the while keeping her thoughts at bay. Deep down she had hoped Waylon would attend the Christmas service with the family, but she didn't push him to do so.

Tying a red velvet ribbon in her hair, Samantha applied a dab of red lipstick to her lips. Truly she did feel and look different. Her face was a little fuller, her figure changing with the passing weeks. She really *did* glow. Yes, she could see what everyone kept saying to her.

"Samantha, you are glowing! You look beautiful!"

Blushing at her own reflection, Samantha quickly turned from the mirror and grabbed her purse, not wanting to keep the family waiting. Quickly she donned her coat and scarf and took the short walk to her parents' home.

The morning air held an invigorating chill, one that made you take notice of the season and that stirred a child-like excitement within your bones. Standing on her porch to breath in the fresh cool air, Samantha smiled. She had grown more excited about bringing a baby into the world and at the same time was still filled with concerns too.

Knowing the short walk would do her good, Samantha took the steps quickly to the path to her Mama and Daddy's house. Before arriving there, she knew the house would be filled with the scents of a freshly cut Christmas tree, coffee brewing, and some baked treat Mama had made.

A few steps into her trek, Samantha stopped suddenly and reached for her belly. She drew in a quick gasp of breath and felt it again.

There it was! Like a graceful butterfly inside of her, Samantha stilled to make sure she hadn't dreamed it.

Again, the tiniest of a flutter brushed her inside.

*Is that the baby? Did it just move?* Samantha stood in awe in the middle of the path with her hand gently placed on her stomach. Just like Mama and Claudia had described, the baby moved again to confirm its presence.

A tinkling of a giggle erupted from Samantha's lips. Like a sweet secret stored within the heart, Samantha held the reality of her baby's movements deep in her soul. For now she would enjoy this discovery and treasure it all to herself.

Continuing on to the house, Samantha couldn't erase the grin from her face if she tried. It was stuck in place and she was happy.

This moment with her baby held what she longed for. Beauty.

She had found the beautiful in carrying this baby of hers.

Nothing could have prepared Samantha for the Christmas church service. Never before had she seen the Christmas story through the eyes of the Baby Jesus' mother. Like Samantha, Mary had been a young mother, scared, uncertain, yet excited about the baby growing within her. The pastor had read from Luke's account of the conception and birth of Baby Jesus. One passage stuck in Samantha's mind and stayed with her through the day.

*But Mary kept all these things and pondered them in her heart.*

Samantha felt an instant drawing to Mary, almost like she had just met her twin sister. Someone Samantha felt she could share her soul with if she could have the opportunity. Like Samantha, Mary gathered treasures in her life and stored them deep within her heart and found something beautiful.

Mary pondered them in her heart. She too had found the beautiful.

Awestruck, Samantha noticed the family rising from their wooden pews ready to leave the service. She made her legs do the same though she wanted to sit on this pew for the rest of the day and think about Mary, the Baby Jesus, and His birth. She wanted to talk to the young mother and ask her the myriad of questions that rolled within her mind and heart. Samantha would have listened with rapt attention to Mary explain the glorious event and then the two of them would have compared their heart-treasures of beauty.

But it was time to leave, time for the Christmas feast that awaited the family.

Arriving at her parents' home, Samantha noticed Waylon standing on the porch sipping a cup of coffee. Surprised he was already there, she went to him and placed a kiss on his cheek.

"You look wonderful, Sam." A sad smile crinkled the corners of Waylon's eyes.

The family walked around the couple and entered the house to finalize the meal preparations leaving them alone for a moment on the porch.

"You okay, Waylon?"

"Sure."

That was all he would offer so Samantha let it drop. "Are you hungry for Mama's turkey and dressing?"

"Definitely. I've been tortured since I got here with the smells from her kitchen."

"Well, let's go see if they need help." Looping her arm through her husband's, Samantha vowed silently to soak up every ounce of this side of Waylon she could.

With the last dish washed and dried, Henry asked the family to move to the little living room. Everyone perched on the sofa and chairs, stood along the walls, or sat on the floor just to be together. The Christmas tree sparkled with shiny glass ornaments and cast off a heady scent of evergreen. It was perfect.

Henry donned a Santa's hat that Sylvia had fashioned for him to wear and began passing out the meager presents. Exclamations of joy over embroidered handkerchiefs, warm socks, little vials of inexpensive perfume, and several toys for Geoffrey quieted down as each thanked the giver for their gifts.

Waylon cleared his throat and got everyone's attention. "I have a special gift to give my wife if that's okay."

No one knew what to make of Waylon anymore. Quiet had been exchanged for harsh, calm for tension. But underlying this new personality was a sense of deep sadness. They could all see it in his eyes, but no one ever got the chance or invitation to discover its depths.

"I'll be right back." Within a few moments, he returned carrying a wooden cradle. Setting it before Samantha's feet, he uttered, "I made this for the baby."

Gasps erupted around the room at the simple beauty of the gleaming wooden cradle.

Samantha couldn't find words to express her thankfulness and surprise at such a beautiful and thoughtful gift from the man who had missed every birthday and anniversary they had shared. She could only cover her mouth and stare at the precious gift.

Henry broke the silence. "Waylon, that is incredible! What a wonderful gift!"

Finally Samantha stood and wrapped her arms around his neck and kissed him soundly on the lips.

"Ewww....'Mantha! That's yucky!" Geoffrey exclaimed his great distaste at her show of affection.

Laughter broke through the moment as everyone examined and praised Waylon's handiwork seen in the cradle. Turning back to ask Waylon a question about the cradle, Samantha looked around the room and noticed he was once again gone.

The front door closing confirmed her husband's escape yet again, as the tiny baby within her stirred along with its mother's skittering heart.

# chapter 17

Caressing her every-growing belly, Samantha glanced across the dining table at her husband. Waylon slurped his coffee and read the Sunday newspaper in silence. Sometimes she longed for him to just talk to her instead of the nearly constant quiet. Waylon always had some comment or remark to make about almost anything, though normally his comments were critical and harsh. But now, since the announcement of the baby, he was quiet for the most part. Even his tone of voice had been reduced to barely audible.

Samantha remembered going to the hospital once with her mother to visit an aunt to take her some flowers. The nurses, patients, and visitors all spoke in hushed, somber tones that brought a tinge of fear and uncertainty to Samantha's soul. She didn't like hospitals and how everyone behaved there, all waiting for the next bad thing to happen, walking around like the quiet would prevent the scary from appearing.

This was as close to describing Waylon's behavior as she could conjure up. Quiet and somber. Waiting for something unpleasant to happen. Even a bit timid and fearful.

But for the life of her she couldn't explain why this change had taken place.

Hoping to encourage him to talk to her, she spoke. "Have you thought about what you want our baby to be? A boy or a girl? What do you think, Waylon?"

Looking up from the paper, he folded it and set it aside before answering. "Hmmm.....I don't know. What about you, Sam?"

A sweet smile graced her lips. "A boy, I think. Like Geoffie. He's so much fun and sweet and rambunctious...."

Quickly Waylon stood and carried his empty coffee cup to the sink and began rinsing it out. After taking a couple of minutes to do a fifteen second task, Samantha walked up behind her husband, reached around him, and turned the faucet off. Gently she took the cup from him and turned Waylon to face her. "Honey, what's wrong? Tell me, please. You seem so sad and quiet. Is it the baby?"

Sighing heavily, Waylon stepped around her and walked to the screened door to peer out. "I think I would like a girl. It's too hard to be a man, a good man like your Daddy and like Frank. Sam, I don't know. No, it's not the baby. It's not, I swear it. It's me—"

"Waylon, you'll be just fine. I know you're nervous, but—"

Spinning on his heel, Waylon turned to face her. "Sam, you don't get it, do you?" His tone hardened with frustration. "I *can't* be a good father! I don't have it in me! Look at my old man....he's a sorry excuse for human flesh, he's a drunk, can't hold a job, he—he hates me! I don't want to be like that. And look at Geoffrey. He hardly even looks at me anymore ever since that day....I want to do this, Sam. I just *can't.* I'm afraid I will hurt you again or the baby—"

Grasping his forearms, Samantha stopped his flow of words. "Hush, Way. You *won't* hurt me or the baby. You've changed and you *are* a good man. You're not at all like your father. You're *not* that man!"

Jerking away from her, Waylon paced the room and said nothing more for a while. Finally, like a caged tiger, he stopped and poured himself a glass of water and muttered to himself, "It's just too hard."

Blinking back tears, Samantha watched as he stormed out onto the front porch and sat on the front step. Walking over to the wooden cradle her husband had made, Samantha ran her hands along its wooden sides and traced each detail. Instantly, she rubbed her belly where the baby pushed from the inside. Smiling at the little one's nearly constant activity, she longed for the day to hold the sweet bundle in her arms.

Fear tried to steal around the edges of her mind. *Will Waylon be a good daddy? Could he possibly return to his old ways and hurt me or....the baby? Surely not, after this long. He hurts so deeply on the inside.*

The sound of a car's engine followed by the slam of a car door brought her back to the present. Walking to the front door, she heard Waylon talking to someone.

"Lenny! What are you doing here? It's good to see you, buddy."

Samantha's heart sank as she peered out the window and saw Waylon's old friend striding up to him. Not wanting to talk to Lenny, she stayed inside and caught snatches of their conversation.

"—you been hiding—haven't seen you in months."

"Sam's pregnant—trying to be a good—need to be home with her."

"—play a round of poker with the boys—just one night—"

"I don't know, Lenny—"

*Oh, dear God, no,* Samantha silently prayed.

The door was pushed open and Waylon came in. "Sam, I'm going out for a bit."

Reaching for him, she whispered a plea, "Waylon, please don't go with Lenny. You know what happens...."

Waylon clenched his jaw. "Look, Sam. I'll be careful. I can't stay cooped up here another minute. I'm just going for a round or two of cards, no big deal." Quickly he kissed her forehead and exited the small house again without another word.

Samantha's stomach churned with dread and worry. Now it was her turn to pace the worn kitchen floor.

Rolling onto her side, Samantha heard the slam of a car door. Darkness covered her like a blanket. Sometime after dark she had gone to bed alone, mad, and worried. Listening to see if it was Waylon, she heard the front door open then Waylon's stumbling through the door and into a chair.

A tear leaked from the corner of her eye. These noises were all too familiar. She heard him curse under his breath as he tried to right the fallen chair then heard him collapse on the couch and mutter her name.

Not moving an inch, Samantha held her breath until Waylon's snores filled the small house.

Red hot anger coursed through her.

*How could he? I knew this would happen, I just knew it! The man can't stay away from booze and cards for more than a few months without returning. And I'm going to have his baby soon....*

As if in response to her thoughts, the little one twisted in her womb and got her attention. Breathing deeply, Samantha knew this anger would help nothing. Grabbing her flashlight and watch, she looked at the time.

4:20 a.m.

Despair and rejection flooded her being. She had truly believed that Waylon had turned a corner for the good, that he would never go back to heavy drinking and cards and all-nighters away from home. She thought he had accepted the fact he was now a husband and soon a father.

His drunken snores punctuated her emotions even more with a sense of loss. She was going to lose Waylon again if this all began to repeat itself.

The familiar gentle whisper of words from her Bible brought a measure of peace to her soul.

*I will never leave you nor forsake you.*

Silently crying into her pillow, Samantha dozed until sun up.

The rest of the week resumed a sense of normalcy; surely she had simply had a nightmare about Waylon leaving with Lenny, getting drunk, and not returning home till the wee hours of the morning. Since Waylon was ignoring that any of this had taken place, she tried to do the same. It would do no good to argue about it or try to discuss it with him. Maybe it really was a one-time event, like a terrifying thunderstorm with intense lightning and ear-splitting thunder that shook you to the core, then in an instant was over and the sweet smell of the rain-washed earth made you forget the horrible storm and its damage.

Samantha could only hope this was true.

Waylon spent the week in near silence. Her actions of kindness that she continued to show him only seemed to rub salt in his wounds so Samantha let him sit around in quiet humility. There was no bringing him out of this stupor for now, so she stopped trying.

As Friday came to its beginning, Samantha looked at the calendar and nearly laughed aloud.

*April 28, 1944.*

It was her birthday today. Her seventeenth birthday.

Were the numbers reversed, they would have been truer to how she physically felt. The lack of sleep from the baby's bulk and movements, the heartburn, and the constant back aches were all taking their toll on her young body, not to mention her concern over her husband. Samantha was ready for this baby to make its appearance.

Passing the day with laundry and a nap, Samantha tried to remind herself of the fact that Waylon would be oblivious to the date, much less that it was her birthday. She told herself not to expect anything from him but the usual silence and to just enjoy the day, just her baby and herself. Come Sunday, Mama and Daddy would have a celebration and cake for the family so she would put the notion of her birthday aside until then.

Sitting on the porch sipping a glass of tea, Samantha heard Waylon's car approach. Reaching into the back seat he lifted out a box tied with a pink ribbon. Looking up from the car, he tried to shove the box behind his back and exclaimed, "Sam! What are you doing out here?"

"Just having a glass of tea." She tried to hide the smirk that crept in place. *A present for me?*

Clearing his throat nervously, Waylon stammered, "Well....okay. How 'bout going in the house and get me one too?"

"Sure." Samantha set her glass on the porch table and went for Waylon's.

When she returned, he was sitting in a chair opposite the one where she had been moments before. Out of the corner of her eye she caught a glance of the pretty box tucked behind his porch chair. She would let Waylon keep his secret until he was ready to reveal it.

They went through the perfunctory list of questions and answers that occurred nearly every day when Waylon got home from work. Patiently she waited through moments of silence while Waylon finished his glass of tea. She could see the nervousness etched on his features. Finally he pulled the box from behind his chair.

"I got you a little something, Sam. You and the baby. I know it's your birthday and all, so I wanted to get you a present. To make up for....everything."

Two tears coursed down her cheeks. Swiping at them with the edge of her apron, Samantha reached for the beautiful box. "Oh, Way."

Savoring the moment, her mind took her on a short journey back to her fifteenth and sixteenth birthdays when Waylon never gave her the gift he had brought to her party. Never knowing what it was, she willed herself to forget he had ever bought anything in the first place, then on her sixteenth birthday, there simply was no gift. Their first and second anniversaries went unacknowledged as well. Overwhelmed in the moment, she could only sit and quietly cry. A small smile shone through the tears as Waylon sat silently watching her.

"Are you going to open it, Sam?"

Sniffing loudly, Samantha laughed at her tears. "Yes! I'm sorry. I'm just emotional lately."

Gently removing the pink and blue striped bow from the white box, Samantha peeled back the layers of white tissue paper and gasped at what lay beneath its folds. Lifting out a wispy pink nightgown, Samantha gazed at the delicate flowers that adorned the soft cuffs and neckline. It was the most beautiful piece of clothing she had ever seen, much less owned.

"I thought you needed a pretty gown for after the baby is born."

Wordlessly, she peered into the box and removed a white blanket trimmed in pastel yellow, green, pink, and blue. Like a puffy cloud, the blanket felt as soft as anything she had ever touched before. Holding it to her face, Samantha looked up at Waylon and shook her head slowly. "How did you—"

"Let's just say I had a little help from your sisters. They knew what you would want better than I could ever guess. And I saved a little money here and there to get you and the baby something." Raking a hand back through his hair, Waylon looked at her intently. "I'm trying, Sam. I really am."

"I know you are. Waylon, you don't know what this means to me. The gown. The blanket. You. I don't even know what to say."

"Well, that's a first." An unusual smile tinged with a hint of sadness briefly lit Waylon's face.

"Oh, stop it!" Samantha playfully slapped his knee and gathered the gift to her chest and held it there for a moment. "Thank you, Way. I love you."

Wordlessly he rose from the chair and kissed the top of Samantha's head and went inside.

# chapter 18

*May 6, 1944*

Groaning quietly, Samantha rolled to her side in the lumpy bed. She reached for Waylon and realized he had already left for work. Her night's sleep had been fitful so she must have slept soundly as he readied for work not waking her. Easing her body to a sitting position, Samantha felt a deep ache in her lower back. Standing and stretching her arms overhead, she walked carefully to the kitchen and poured herself a glass of water. Her watch read 9:30 in the morning so she must have slept the last few hours without waking.

Letting out a quick gasp, Samantha felt her stomach muscles tighten with a sharp stab of pain in her lower back. After a few moments the sensation left her.

*I must have slept in one position for too long.*

Gently she stretched as much as she could and felt her muscles ease from the tension that seemed to swallow her from the base of her neck to her thighs. Easing her body into the kitchen chair, Samantha knew she needed to eat something but nothing sounded very appealing. Finishing the water, Samantha felt another ripple of tightness across her abdomen coupled with pain. Standing to her feet, Samantha decided to get dressed for the day and at least brush her teeth, even if that was all she felt like doing.

Taking longer than usual to get dressed, Samantha felt increasing tension spread over her lower back. Like a bolt of electricity, a shot of fear brought her to reality. *Was it time for the baby to come?*

Quickening her pace, Samantha finished her tasks and fought the pain that continued to come in spasms over her abdomen.

"Okay, Little One. Let's get to Mama's house first before you do much more."

Weeks ago, Samantha and her mother had planned out what would happen when her day came to deliver. She had taken the necessary items for her and the baby to her parents' home so she wouldn't have to think about that when she went into labor. Over and over again, Samantha had drilled Waylon on what would happen when she thought her time had come if he wasn't home. She would get to her mother and they would call the midwife and deliver at her parents'; then she, Waylon, and the baby would stay there for several weeks until Samantha could get back on her feet.

Another stab of pain sliced through Samantha taking her breath away. "Okay, Baby. We're going. You gotta wait till we get to Mama's, got it?"

Immediately, Samantha turned back to her bedroom and gathered up the present Waylon had given her last week on her birthday. She wanted the pretty pink gown and the baby's new blanket with her. Clinging to the box like a life-line, Samantha was now ready to go.

Grabbing her sides, Samantha waited until the pain subsided then headed as quickly as she could to her mother. Breathing through the pain, she continued to the house, grateful it was a five minute walk and no longer. Once she stopped in her tracks and waited for her breathing to return to normal after the contraction ended then hurried the rest of the way as much as her burden would allow.

As her foot reached the bottom step of her parents' welcoming porch, Samantha cried out. "Mama! Ohhhh!!!" The next contraction brought a wave of fear with it as it stole the air from her lungs. Slowly she eased down on the closest step. "Ma-Mama!!"

Sylvia instantly went to the door and found her daughter sitting on the steps holding her abdomen. "Samantha Jean! Let's get you indoors! Oh my goodness, it's time, isn't it, honey? Everything's going to be okay. Just breathe and we will get you up in a minute."

The comfort of her mother's arms and voice allowed Samantha to give way to the tears that now surfaced. "It hurts, Mama."

"I know, Baby. Tell me when you can stand and I will get you inside. Claudia!! Quick, call the midwife. The baby's coming! Can you stand now, Samantha?"

"I think so." Samantha wiped the sweat and tears from her face and allowed Sylvia to help her stand.

"Let's get you into the bed in your old room. I already got Geoffrey in with his mama last week and I'm glad I did. It's going to be okay. I promise. Just breathe through the pain and before you know it, you will meet your sweet baby." Sylvia got Samantha settled just as another contraction made its way over her belly.

"Oh, Mama....I can't do this! It hurts too much! Where's Way?" Samantha lay her head back on the pillows and tears ran down her cheeks.

Claudia ran into the room. "I called the midwife and she will be here any minute. What can I do, Mama? Sammie, are you alright? Do you need anything?" Claudia didn't know what to do with herself.

Sylvia looked at Claudia. "I can tell you won't be much help. You would think you had never given birth before. Watch for the midwife and send her back here then keep Geoffrey occupied. And get me some cool cloths for her face. Then you can send a neighbor to the mine for the men. I don't think it will be long."

Glad to have something to do, Claudia set about doing all Sylvia had instructed. Taking Geoffrey by the hand, she took him outside to play while her little sister labored in the house to bring her baby into the world.

Tears of joy mingled with Waylon's as Samantha stared into the white cloud of a blanket that held their new born daughter. "What do you think, Waylon? Isn't she beautiful? Oh, I can't believe she is finally here. You got a daughter, just like you wanted."

Waylon swiped at a tear as he stared in awe at the tiny bundle. "You did so good, Sam. I can't believe she's here either. What are we going to name her? It needs to be a pretty name, just like her."

Timidly, Samantha looked at Waylon. "I've had nine long months to think about names for a boy or a girl. I just knew we would have a boy but never could settle on a boy name. I did pick out a girl name just in case."

"What is it?" Waylon peeked under the blanket's folds to admire the baby's long fingers.

"What about Lily Ruth? Lily Ruth Graves. I like it. She's perfect like a freshly bloomed lily. And I like the name Ruth too." Keeping a precious secret to herself, Samantha had chosen the name Ruth only a month ago after reading the story of Ruth in her beloved Bible. She liked the sound of the simple name of the woman she now admired from the Book.

Waylon repeated the name aloud. "Lily Ruth. That's pretty. We'll name her that. I like it."

"Hello, sweet Lily Ruth. Welcome to the world. Your Mommy and Daddy love you and will be the best parents in the world to you," Samantha cooed to the little violet-eyed baby. Her tuft of reddish-blond hair that stood straight up on top of her little head perfectly matched Samantha's tresses.

A light knock sounded on the door frame to the bedroom. Henry stood in the doorway. "Can the new Grandpa come in and see your little one?"

Holding a hand out to him, Samantha beckoned Henry to come in. "Of course, Daddy." Samantha pulled the blanket down from her baby and let Henry see the little beauty.

"Oh my goodness, Sammie-girl. She looks just like you when you were born. What's her name?" Henry stroked the tiny hand with his large finger.

"Lily Ruth. What do you think, Daddy?" Joy tinged with contented weariness filled her eyes as she watched her father look her baby over from head to toe.

"I am so proud of you, Sammie. She's perfect....just like you." Turning to Waylon, Henry patted him on the back. "Congratulations, Waylon. I'm happy for you two."

Waylon looked into the expectant eyes of his father-in-law and saw within their depths what it meant to be a man and a father. He knew he could never measure up to Henry Owens. Not in a thousand lifetimes could he do it. Without a word, Waylon left his wife and baby and walked back to their tiny house down the street.

It was too much for him.

It was all too much.

Henry looked at his daughter as she wiped a tear from her face. "Give him time, Samantha. It's a lot to absorb. Just give him time. I will keep a distant eye on Waylon. Now you rest and don't you worry your pretty self about anything. Your Daddy's here. You and your beautiful daughter sleep. I sure love you, girls." Henry stooped and kissed Samantha and Lily on their cheeks and eased the blankets back around them both, then exited the room silently.

Her body taking command of her senses and emotions, Samantha's weary eyes closed as one thought flitted through her head.

*I have found the most beautiful thing in my life today.*

Waylon paced the small house until he was afraid he would wear a hole in the wooden floors. He had to get out of there. His mind was filled with pictures of his past, his childhood, his failures.

He couldn't do this *father* business. It was impossible.

First of all, he had never seen it done right, until he had met Henry Owens, a man he could never measure up too. Waylon knew his own mistakes and ways were so very opposite of Henry. But how did a man change who he was and how he was raised in an instant? And that's what needed to happen to him. Instantaneous change from the man he was into a father he could never be.

Like a magic show Waylon had watched when he was a small boy, the magician could make a rabbit appear from a hat, read his mind to know which card Waylon had picked, and turn a silver coin into a dollar bill. But that kind of magic wouldn't work on him, though down deep he believed it would take a magician to change him instantly into Henry Owens, a good husband and father.

It was too late. The demons of alcohol and cards and meanness had lived within Waylon's soul for far too long, until he believed there was no way to be free. No way he could be what Sam needed and wanted in a husband and now be a father to their baby. Sure he loved Samantha and Lily Ruth, though he had only just met the baby an hour ago. Waylon held anyone he loved at arm's length, knowing what darkness resided in his heart, believing he would be hurt by them or worse yet, he would hurt them. Love made him hold them away from himself. Love kept him from getting too close. Waylon *knew* himself and what he was capable of.

It was too late.

Reaching for the bottle on the top shelf of the cupboard, Waylon convinced himself he was due a celebratory drink. After all, his buddy at the mine had given him the bottle as a gift when he learned Waylon was to become a daddy. So he would use it for that.

To celebrate.

He was now a daddy.

And he couldn't be one.

# chapter 19

The past two weeks were simply heaven on earth for Samantha. Staying at her parents' home until she recovered enough to take care of her little family on her own had been a slice of heaven. Sylvia had spoiled Samantha with her favorite meals, pampered her and allowed her to get the much needed rest her body longed for, taught her how to diaper, bathe, feed, and comfort Lily Ruth until Samantha had gained enough confidence to do it on her own.

And today she felt a rush of excitement and alarm as the three women packed Samantha's, Waylon's, and the baby's things to move them back to their little house down the street.

Placing the last of Lily's blankets and diapers into a used cardboard vegetable box Sylvia had lined with newspaper, Geoffrey did his part of helping the women load up his red wagon to get Samantha's belongings home. Her thoughts ran rampant while she looked around the room to make sure she didn't leave anything.

*Can I do this....be a mommy alone without Mama's help? Will I be able to take care of a baby and a home and a husband by myself? What if Lily gets sick....will I know what to do?*

Startling Samantha out of her troubling thoughts, Sylvia stuck her head in the doorway. "Are you about ready?"

Turning to face her mother, tears threatened to spill over Samantha's eyes.

"What is it, Samantha?" Placing her hands on her daughter's shoulders, Sylvia looked into the depths of Samantha's soul.

"Oh, Mama.....I don't know if I can do this. How will I take care of Lily, cook meals, be a wife, clean a house, and keep us in clean clothes? What if my baby is sick? I won't know what to do!"

Understanding dawned on Sylvia's face. "Honey, you have what every new mother gets. 'Mommy anxiety' is what I call it. It happens every time. Facing new things and new ways of life is a challenge, but learning to care for a new little person can be really scary. But you have the same God-given instinct every woman has when she gives birth to a baby. Your senses and emotions and mind are all in tune with your baby and you will mostly know what to do. To comfort, feed, care for, and raise this baby, you have been *chosen* to be that mother. *Lily's mother.* And no one else on this earth can do that job better than you. If you get confused or don't have a clue what to do, I will help you. You know that, right?"

Hugging her mother, Samantha replied, "Thanks, Mama. I needed to hear that. Okay, let's go show Lily Ruth her new home."

Samantha's days and nights finally fell into a routine of sorts. Nights straightened themselves out once Lily was nearly a month old. Lily hardly cried unless she was hungry or needed a clean diaper. She smiled, cooed like a dove, and stole her mother's heart from the very beginning.

One thing that truly troubled Samantha was the lack of attention and bond that Waylon had with the baby. Of course, he held Lily, loved her, and fed her a bottle while Samantha finished dinner preparations. But there was never that attachment she longed to see between father and daughter. Maybe Waylon just needed more time to adjust to being a daddy. He admired the baby and helped when he was needed. Samantha didn't doubt that Waylon loved Lily; he just didn't seem to connect with her.

The other troubling thing was that Waylon had begun drinking again, not a lot but nearly nightly. She had broached the subject with him once and was surprised at his instantaneous outburst of anger, though deep inside she knew it should have been expected.

His tone of voice and hurtful words still rang in her ears several days later.

*"You may be Lily's mother, but for God's sake, Sam, you're not my mother. So back off, okay? Don't start in on me about having a glass of whiskey every now and then! I don't need this from you!"*

Vowing then and there, Samantha decided she would remain quiet about the matter. Waylon's outburst had sent the sleeping Lily into a fit of crying that took Samantha a half hour to calm her down. After ten minutes of the baby's screams, Waylon jumped in his car and left for several hours. Thankfully he returned sober and before midnight. That night was something Samantha did not care to repeat.

Flipping the calendar each month, the young mother saw with ever-increasing discomfort the old patterns returning with her husband. Their first Thanksgiving and Christmas with Lily had felt like ones in the very beginning of their tumultuous relationship, Waylon barely acknowledging it was a holiday and saying there wasn't enough money for presents for Christmas that year. He did buy Lily a stuffed doll with yellow yarn hair wearing a pink gingham checked dress. Though Waylon had forbade Samantha from spending any money for "senseless presents," he had bought his daughter something.

Usually in the past, Waylon's occasional displays of kindness in words or gifts would help temporarily shore up Samantha's heart and remind her that maybe he really was a good man down deep. Normally she would convince herself that he just didn't know how to show someone he cared.

But lately, Samantha felt dulled and hardened to the brief and rare acts of kindness Waylon would produce. She feared she was closing her heart off from her husband, but was helpless to do anything about it. Still willing to love and serve him in whatever capacity Waylon would allow, Samantha felt she was living with a stranger, instead of a husband.

The rumble of distant thunder and the howl of the increasing winds pierced its way into her thoughts. Shivering involuntarily, Samantha felt a sense of foreboding creep up her arms and down her spine. Uneasiness chilled the blood in her veins, a feeling she woke up with in the wee hours of the morning and still curled around her senses like briars growing at the base of a tall tree.

Reaching for the coffee pot, Samantha poured herself her first cup for the day and shoved the offending feelings away as she pinned back the calendar's page for the new month. Today marked the first day of February, 1945. Lily would be nine months old in a few short days.

"Mama." The sweetest sound to her ears, Samantha heard her daughter's sleepy voice call out her name.

Unable to stop it if she wanted to, a smile spread over Samantha's features at the sound of Lily's voice. "Mama's coming, Baby. Did you sleep well? I bet you are ready for a diaper and breakfast." Lifting the curly headed, sleepy faced, beauty from her bed, Samantha breathed in the scent of Lily Ruth. Her nose tickled Lily's neck and the little girl let out a burst of giggles that caused Samantha to nuzzle even closer.

Lily wrapped her chubby arms around her Mama's neck and snuggled into Samantha.

"Whew! Somebody needs a clean diaper."

"Shew," Lily mimicked. "Stinky."

"Yes, stinky!" Samantha made quick work of cleaning her baby and placing the smelly diaper in a bin to wash later. The biggest part of her days involved feeding, cleaning, washing dirty laundry, folding, and doing it all over again, but Samantha had never been happier in her life than she was as a mother.

Again thunder sounded from outside, this time only louder. The thin glass windows shook from the noise; a storm was brewing outdoors.

"Bobble, Mama." Lily Ruth tugged on Samantha's dress front as she carried the little one to the kitchen.

Only a few weeks ago, she had weaned her baby and now had her taking a bottle or cup instead. Lily liked her 'bobble' first thing in the morning and before naps or bedtime.

"Mama's going to fix you a bobble, Sweetie." Glancing out the window at the darkening sky, she placed a few toys on the seat of a dining room chair. Samantha stood Lily in front of the chair to occupy herself while the baby waited on her bottle.

Lily's usually happy demeanor surfaced and she played with the toys contentedly. With Samantha busily preparing the milk, she let the baby play a moment while she gathered her Bible and refilled coffee cup and brought them to the worn couch. Her morning custom was to read aloud from the Bible to Lily while she drank her bottle.

Turning to scoop up her baby, Samantha watched in shock as Lily took two tentative steps away from the chair towards the middle of the kitchen. Taking in a quick breath, Samantha watched Lily take two more shaky steps and squeal with glee at her accomplishment. Plopping down on her bottom, Lily burst into a fit of giggles.

Swinging Lily up into the air, Samantha laughed along with her. "Lily! Look at you! Oh my gracious, your Mama's going to have her hands full now! Walking at almost nine months. You're a big girl!"

Ready for her bottle, Lily settled by Samantha on the couch for their usual routine. Contentedly the baby took her bottle and nestled up against Samantha as she reached for the precious Bible. Holding Lily with one arm, Samantha rested the Bible next to her on the couch. It flipped open to a page that contained the familiar red pencil markings denoting the original owner's underlined verse.

"Let's see what the Good Book will tell us today, Lily Ruth. John 14:27 says this: 'Peace I leave with you, my peace I give unto you: not as the world giveth, give I unto you. Let not your heart be troubled, neither let it be afraid.'"

Lily reached a hand up and touched Samantha's cheek. She stopped drinking long enough to address Samantha, "Wead, Mama."

"Okay, I will read it again to us, Lily." Again Samantha slowly, deliberately read the verses aloud to them. "'Peace I leave with you, my peace I give unto you: not as the world giveth, give I unto you. Let not your heart be troubled, neither let it be afraid.'"

The words washed over Samantha's soul as she peered into the contented, quiet face of her daughter while the thunder rumbled outside her cozy little home. The noise didn't faze the happy baby; Samantha longed for that kind of peace that she saw on her daughter's face. A thought whispered across Samantha's troubled mind.

*She's at peace because she feels safe and trusts her Mama. That's what I need to do. Trust. Trust God.*

Again, Samantha's gut tightened as the thunder rumbled outside. For some reason, she couldn't shake the sense of fear and worry that kept working its way to the surface of her troubled soul. She felt an undercurrent of dread, yet had no real explanation for it. It just simply was there.

The remainder of Samantha's day was spent listening to the howling wind, the fiercely pounding rains, and crashing thunder. Wataker, Mississippi hadn't seen a storm like this in quite some time. Not once did the sun make an appearance. Steel gray skies interspersed with charcoal black clouds hovered throughout the day and into the evening. The kitchen clock was the only way Samantha knew what time of day it was, since the sky held no hint of sunshine.

A chill crept up Samantha's spine even though the temperatures hovered in the 80's. Shivering involuntarily, Samantha peeked in on her sleeping daughter. Somehow the day hadn't fazed little Lily.

A crash sounded from the front yard that startled Samantha nearly out of her skin. She made her way quickly to the front screen door and peered out into the slashing rain.

Waylon had arrived home.

The look on his face was enough to cause Samantha to shrink back into the house. Waylon's countenance had merged with the weather, dark and threatening.

Tremulously, Samantha greeted her husband. "Hey, Way."

Shoving her aside, Waylon stormed into the kitchen. Leaning over the sink, he took deep breaths, each threatening to burst his shirt wide open.

Placing a hand on his shoulder, Samantha asked, "What happened?"

Spinning to face her, Waylon's voice thundered as loud as the gray sky. "What happened? I'll tell you what happened! I got laid off from the mine! I've worked my—"

Their baby's startled scream erupted from the next room. "Mama...."

"Waylon, you have to hold it down. Lily's sleeping—"

The backside of Waylon's large hand collided with Samantha's face, causing her to stagger back a couple of steps. Reaching for her cheek, Samantha ran for Lily's room and shut the door behind her.

Leaning against the closed door, Samantha struggled to regain her composure and hide her anger and fear from Lily. A lone tear made its way down her stinging cheek. Lily's screams brought her to her senses. "Baby, it's alright. Mama's here." Picking up the crying child, Samantha did her best to calm Lily when all she wanted to do was scream and cry with her.

Cradling Lily's head on her shoulder, Samantha listened as Waylon slammed cabinet doors in the kitchen. She knew what he was doing. She knew every move by heart. First he opened the door that held the glasses, then he slammed it shut. Next Waylon found his bottle of booze from the top shelf, slammed that door shut, poured a glass, drank it quickly, poured another, and cursed under his breath the entire time.

"Samantha! Sam! Get out here!"

Lily began crying again. "Hush, Baby. It's okay. How about a cracker? Does that sound good?" Desperately trying to distract Lily before she went to Waylon, Samantha did her best to settle the little girl.

Opening the door, she said, "I'm here, Waylon."

"Where's dinner? You know I want a hot meal when I get home! What have you done all day?" In between sentences, Waylon gulped down another glass of whiskey. "I guess I will have to start making my own meals around here now, huh?"

"No, honey. It's been a difficult day with the storms—"

"Shut up! I'm done with your excuses! You never listen anyway. I lose my job and you would think the least I would get from you is a hot meal! Forget it—I'm leaving!"

Again, Lily began crying as Waylon's temper continued to flare.

"Way, just give me a minute, okay? I will have dinner done before—"

Uttering a string of curses under his breath, Waylon grabbed the bottle, climbed back into his car, and left before Samantha could even ask about his job.

Much less tell him his daughter had taken her first steps that day.

Sitting down on the couch with Lily, Samantha knew. She finally understood the reason behind the uneasiness she had battled all day.

Just like the little town of Wataker was struggling under the fury of a thunderstorm, Samantha knew the storm had returned to her life in full force.

## chapter 20

Today felt like the worst day of Samantha's seventeen years of living. Tightening her hold on her baby's hand, Samantha repeated, "Hold tight to Mama's hand, Lily."

"Owww. Hurts Lily." The strawberry blond one year old struggled to keep up with her mother.

Stooping down to lift Lily off her short, chubby legs, Samantha swung her purse over one shoulder and placed Lily on her opposite hip. "Oh, Baby. I'm sorry. I didn't mean to hurt you. Mama's just in a hurry. I can't expect your little legs to keep up now, can I? We've gotta get you to Grammie and Pop's so Mama can—"

Tears choked off the last of Samantha's sentence. Blinking rapidly, she continued on the short walk to her parents' home to see if Sylvia and Claudia could watch Lily for the morning.

*I can't believe him! Waylon makes me furious. How am I supposed to leave my baby and get a job and run a house too? He's supposed to be the one to take care of us, not the other way around. I want to* raise *Lily....I don't want to leave* her.

A stray tear trekked down her face. Lily reached a small hand up and wiped it away. "Mama cry," she asked.

Taking a shuddering breath, Samantha answered the little girl, "No, Mama *won't* cry. It's just the wind, Honey. It made my eyes water, that's all. How about we sing?"

Clapping her hands together, Lily Ruth wiggled in Samantha's arms. "Sing, Mama. Sing sunshine!"

"Ok, but hold my hand tight and I will let you walk while we sing sunshine. Ready? "

"Weady!" Lily punctuated the word with a quick hop.

The two broke into a mother-daughter rendition of *You are My Sunshine* that made the song birds of the tiny mining camp stop and take notice. Lily made up her own words to the song and sang as loudly as she could. Ending in their usual way, the two sweet voices finished the song out. *"Please don't take my sunshine awaaayyyy."*

Lily finished with her usual round of applause and an excited, "Yaaayyy! More, Mama!"

"That's all for now. It's time for you to play with Geoffrey a while. Doesn't that sound fun?"

"Geoff-weee!" Lily shouted loud enough for her cousin to hear as the two entered the house. Instantly the little girl was rewarded with the sound of Geoffrey's running feet and then a hug from her cousin.

"Hey, Aunt 'Mantha! Lily Ruth, I missed you!" Geoffrey loved his baby cousin. He enjoyed having a playmate even though they were several years apart. Lily adored Geoffrey and followed in his every footstep.

Hearing her daughter and granddaughter enter the house, Sylvia dried her hands on her apron and hugged Samantha. Instantly Sylvia noticed Samantha's countenance. "Good morning, girls! Honey, what's wrong? You look upset."

Plopping down on the worn couch, Samantha buried her face in her hands. "I am upset." She pushed back her straying strands of hair as her mother sat down beside her.

Sylvia noticed yet another bruise on Samantha's forearm. She gently touched it and looked at her daughter. Gently, she asked, "Samantha Jean, did Waylon do this to you again?"

Pulling her arm away, Samantha evaded the question. "Mama, he's making me get a job! A job, for crying out loud! How am I supposed to care for Lily and work a job? He can't keep steady work since the mine laid him off so now *I have to*!" Anger tinged her tone and she made herself quiet down.

"Oh, Samantha. I was afraid this would happen. Is Waylon back home or still gone? Why can't he get a good job?" Sylvia was nearly as frustrated as Samantha was.

Emitting a humorless laugh, Samantha just shook her head. "Oh, there's work. He just can't *keep* a job. There's always a good reason he had to quit. And he spends all of his money on—never mind Waylon. All I know is that if I am going to be able to feed the three of us, I have to work too. Waylon's really giving me no other choice."

"What are you planning on doing? You know Claudia and I will keep Lily for you during the days you work. Maybe your sister can get you a job at the department store she works at." Sylvia stroked Samantha's arm in reassurance.

"That's what I am hoping, Mama. I wanted to see if Lily could stay here this morning while I take the bus into town and look for work."

"Of course she can. Here, let's get you some breakfast and maybe a scarf to hide the stain on your dress. You need to look your best when you look for a job. We will help you, Samantha. You're not alone in this." Taking her by the hand, Sylvia pulled Samantha to her feet and towards the kitchen.

"Thanks, Mama."

Stepping off the smelly bus, Samantha breathed a sigh of relief as she took the last of the leg on foot back to her parents' home.

Quietly she repeated aloud yesterday's Bible verse to herself as the truth of it slowly hit home. "'Philippians 4:19. But my God shall supply all your need according to his riches in glory by Christ Jesus.' Thank you, God, for supplying my need of a job today. And me, a school drop-out."

Nearing the house, she heard giggles come from the backyard so she walked around the side and found Lily, Claudia, and Geoffrey. "Hey, Lily! Mama's back."

Lily ran to her mother, arms outstretched. "Mama, Mama!"

Swinging Lily up into her arms, Samantha breathed in the scent of outdoors that lingered on her daughter. She smelled of sunshine and dirt and all things sweet. "Oh, Baby, I missed you."

Claudia laughed at Samantha. "Oh, what I wouldn't give to have a few hours away. But I get it, Sis. It's hard to be gone from our babies. So, did you find a job? Tell me." Claudia patted the chair next to her and Samantha took a seat.

"I did. I got a job at *Steadman's* downtown." Samantha grinned sheepishly.

"*Steadman's*? Wow, Sammie! That's great! Surrounded by all of those fancy clothes and shoes and finery! What will you be doing?"

Taking a deep breath, Samantha answered under her breath. "Well, I shouldn't be complaining but I will be in the *back* of the store, not really *in* the store. I will be 'behind the scenes' as Ms. Covington so *sweetly* called it." Samantha's voice dripped with sarcasm. "Without saying it, she let me know I wasn't *presentable* enough for the store front but 'if I could count and tally' then I was good enough for the *back of the store*." Using her best haughty, uppity sounding tone, Samantha perfectly mimicked her new employer until she and Claudia dissolved in a fit of laughter.

Coming up for air, Claudia wiped a tear from her eye. "Oh, Samantha, I'm so sorry you have to work, but I am also happy you found a job."

"Yeah, me too, Claudia. Me too. I just can't imagine leaving my Lily for eight hours a day, five days a week. It makes me so sad—and mad!! Ughhh!! I could choke Waylon for making me do this!"

"Then *leave* his sorry self. It won't keep you from having to work, but it would at least remove a very big headache from your life. He's no good for you, Sammie. He's....mean." Glancing at the obvious bruise on Samantha's arm, Claudia stopped there.

"Claudia, he's *my husband* and Lily's *father*."

"I love you, Samantha Jean Owens, but no good man hurts their woman and leaves for days without a word and doesn't hold down a decent job. It's just not right."

"It's not right, but it's my life, Sis. It was my choice and that's just the way it is. Now enough about Waylon. Have you heard from Melvin?" Samantha changed the subject and waited for Claudia to follow her lead.

Her face brighter than the noonday sun, Claudia beamed in response. "Yes, I did!" Reaching for Samantha's hand, Claudia continued. "Sammie, Mel will be home in October! Two more months! Can you believe it???"

Hugging her sister, Samantha couldn't have been happier for her. "Oh, Sis! That's the best news I've heard in a long time! Geoffrey will be so excited to see his daddy. I'm sure *you're* not that excited though," Samantha teased and patted her sister's knee.

Blushing furiously, Claudia squealed with delight. "You have no idea! I miss him so much!"

Even if the beauty seemed to be waning from Samantha's life with each passing day, it was good to see it return to her sister's life.

# chapter 21

Nothing seemed to make sense to Samantha anymore. Sipping her morning coffee, she thought back over the last three years. Life felt more and more like a jigsaw puzzle than anything. Thinking back to when she was fourteen, Samantha's world had resembled a lovely painting. She had her friends, school, family, a new boyfriend, and things were easy, even living in a mining town.

But now, her life felt more like a jumbled up pile of disconnected pieces that fit nowhere. Her fairy tale marriage was non-existent. Her life as a mommy had been brutally interrupted by a job; leaving her daughter each morning was one of the hardest things she had ever done. And to top it off, Waylon didn't appreciate the fact that she was working and bringing home a meager pay check that barely helped out at all. He seemed to resent the fact that she worked, even though it had been his idea. Scoffing and complaining about the laundry or dirty house made her feel worse than ever and less than a wife and mother since she couldn't take care of everything that he demanded.

It all just didn't make sense anymore.

And his abuse had increased. The harder she worked the more resentful he was. It wasn't her fault Waylon didn't hold on to a job for long. Nor was it her fault that he had taken to drinking too much again.

No longer bitter at him for being gone several days at a time, Samantha now secretly relished the days Waylon was away. It afforded Lily and Samantha the peace they both needed and craved. There was a marked difference in Lily's demeanor when Waylon was home. The little girl sucked her thumb almost constantly when Waylon was around which annoyed him greatly. When he was away, Lily hardly ever sucked her thumb. Lily cried more and clung to Samantha's skirt until she put her to bed for the evening. Sadly, Samantha had begun to see Lily as her guardian angel of sorts. When Lily was attached to Samantha, Waylon hardly came near her. He was less abusive when his daughter was nearby, but as soon as Lily was away from Samantha, Waylon was either grabbing her arm too tightly, shoving Samantha, or cursing her under his breath and berating everything she did.

He could stay away for all Samantha cared.

Though it sounded crazy even to her own heart, she still loved Waylon, but all hope that he would ever change was gone forever. She had chosen this man, and this was who he was. Samantha knew she desperately had to hang on to the Bible and her hope in God to survive.

The rumble of thunder announced the coming of another storm. Samantha's nerves already on edge, the loud noise did nothing to calm her. Applying extra make-up to the remainder of Waylon's handprint on her left cheek and the dark circles ever-present under her eyes, she deftly covered the mark he left. It was not the first time she had to do this before going to work or church or her parents' home.

Lily had spent the night for the second time with her grandparents; Samantha both loathed and deeply appreciated this. For the second time she had been asked to go in for an early shift to cover for another employee who was out sick, so Sylvia told Samantha to let Lily spend the night instead of having to get her up in the wee hours of the morning and then bring her to Sylvia to keep. Reluctantly Samantha had agreed.

Waylon's loud snores in the next room reminded her of all the reasons she had begun to resent her husband. All he had to do was just work a job and love her and Lily. Why was that so difficult for him?

Staring at her face in the mirror, Samantha faced the cold hard facts that she had chosen a man at age fourteen based on the surface only. What Waylon had shown her of himself those several years back had been just that, the surface. Now she saw the man for what he really was. Waylon Graves was nothing but a shallow mud puddle, not a deep well to draw from, though her soul ached for the latter.

Unbidden, an image flashed across the screen of her mind. Waylon's own father crashed out on his couch, drunk, snoring. It was the first time Samantha had met the man and it would be the last she would ever lay eyes on him. Reality hit Samantha head long. Waylon was repeating the same habits his father had cultivated years before. This was what Waylon had seen as normal. He'd been raised unloved, undisciplined, unwanted. Though Samantha had tried, she now saw that there was no way she could change her husband. It was up to him to make changes; she couldn't do it for him.

Sympathy for him was a new emotion for Samantha. Chiding herself for feeling sorry for Waylon, she just couldn't help herself. The man he was today had evolved from the boy he once was, a boy who had never been offered a drink from a deep well. The only resource Waylon had ever drawn from was obviously very similar to himself, another shallow mud hole. She knew that was the case with her husband's father and with his friend Lenny.

Samantha believed or at least wanted to believe that Waylon had been a deep well for her, but now she finally faced the truth.

He was the furthest thing from it.

Tucking her Bible in her purse, Samantha needed its presence to comfort her whether she could find the time to read it today or not. She just needed it near.

Without a word to Waylon, she left the sleeping man to his fitful dreams as the crashing thunder left him undisturbed.

Letting her precious Bible lay open on her lap, Samantha gazed out the grimy bus window knowing she had another twenty minutes to herself. Under the streetlight at the last bus stop, she had opened it to John and her eyes fell on a verse in chapter four.

Repeating the words over and over in her mind, she thought of Waylon.

*'But whosoever drinketh of the water that I shall give him shall never thirst; but the water that I shall give him shall be in him a well of water springing up into everlasting life.'*

Samantha knew these were the very words Jesus had spoken to a woman such as herself, a woman who had many lovers but was dying of thirst on the inside. Samantha had loved only one man, but all she was left with from that choice was what resembled an inner death. She read that Jesus tells the woman He will quench her thirst with water that He offers, not a drink from a muddy puddle like she was used to, but a thirst-quenching drink from a deep well.

Silently, Samantha prayed as she traced a trail in the clinging moisture on the bus window.

*Oh God, I am so thirsty. Like this woman, I need a drink from the well of life. Please fill my need. I long for You.*

Slowly, yet instantly, peace and joy and love poured over Samantha starting with the top of her head and ending with her feet. She felt it on the inside and knew God had heard her prayer. She needed *Him*, not Waylon, to make her feel loved and cared for.

She *needed* God.

Gathering her things, Samantha entered the day, a new day. The job was the same, the situation at home was the same, Waylon was the same.

But she wasn't.

Samantha was *loved*, and she knew it.

God loved her. And that's all she needed to know, no matter what today or tomorrow held, storm or calm, Samantha Jean Owens Graves *knew* she would be alright because God loved her.

Pulling her sweater tighter around her shoulders, Samantha entered her parents' home for what seemed like the millionth time to pick up her daughter and take her home for a couple of hours before Lily's bedtime. Geoffrey's laughter, cheerful chatter, and a new voice greeted her ears as she pushed the door open.

Melvin! It had to be him!

The kitchen bustled with her family and yes, there in the center was Melvin.

"Oh my goodness! Melvin!" Samantha ran to her brother-in-law. Throwing her arms around his neck, Samantha was delighted to see him. Since he and Claudia had begun dating when Samantha was a young girl, Melvin had been her big brother, protector, and biggest tease. He would bring her lollipops or gumballs and often allowed her to go on an ice cream date with him and Claudia.

"There's my grown up little sister! Look at you, all married and a mother since I left! And you had the audacity to do all of this without *my* approval." A look of mock consternation touched Melvin's features briefly then quickly gave way to his usual jovial smile. "I missed you, Sammie."

"I guess I sort of missed you too," she teased. "When did you get here?"

"Right after lunch I surprised my Claudia and little man."

Claudia wrapped her arms around Melvin's waist and gazed up at him. "It was the best surprise of my life. At first I was furious with him for not letting me know he was coming. I looked a mess! I had curlers in my hair and my old dress on helping Mama hang clothes on the line."

"And you were the prettiest sight I had ever laid eyes on." Melvin kissed Claudia soundly and clung to her like a lifeline. "I couldn't believe how much my little man has grown. Six years old and nearly sporting a beard!" Despite his laughter, tears collected in Melvin's eyes. "I missed so much when I was gone—"

Samantha took up where Melvin left off. "But you're back and that's what counts! You have your family around you and you're healthy and well and home!"

Sylvia interrupted their chatter. "Chocolate cake and coffee! Any takers?"

"Music to my ears, Mama Sylvia," Melvin answered.

After each of them had settled at the table with cake and coffee, Melvin turned to Samantha. "So when do I get to meet this man of yours, Little Sis? I've already met your beautiful daughter who looks just like her mother."

A cloud passed over Samantha's face as she reached and wiped a spot of chocolate off Lily's face. "Soon, I'm sure. Maybe Sunday at dinner after church. So tell me about you, Melvin. It's been years."

Allowing her to redirect the conversation, Melvin glanced at Claudia with a knowing look. He saw the dark circles and how much Samantha had aged since he was gone that confirmed all that Claudia had told him. Determined to do what he could to help Samantha, Melvin was glad he was home for several reasons. He wouldn't sit by and watch her get hurt anymore. Samantha was eighteen years old. What did she know about life and love and how to handle men like the one she had married? Though Claudia had told him of her family's involvement in Samantha's and Waylon's marriage struggles, he determined to do something to get rid of the pain he saw in her eyes.

And the sooner the better.

# chapter 22

*July 1946*

"Sammie-girl....let me help....you can't....no!!"

The sound of his own voice and the rapid beating of his heart was enough to bring Henry Owens out of a deep sleep fraught with troubling dreams. Dreams where his youngest daughter was crying out for help, but when he reached her side, Samantha wouldn't let him help her. She kept pushing Henry away as he watched her scream.

Wiping the sweat from his face, Henry noiselessly rose from Sylvia's side trying not to waken her. He went into the kitchen and poured himself a glass of water. Easing the dining chair away from the table, Henry sat down wearily. This was not the first of these recurring dreams.

For the past few weeks he had dreamt of Samantha. Always the same theme, she was in pain or scared and crying out for help but when he would reach out for her, she would push him away. What did it all mean? Sure, he knew Samantha and Waylon were in trouble. He had even threatened Waylon harm if he ever laid a hand on his daughter again. For every mark on Samantha's body, she had a well-crafted, even believable excuse.

Not long ago, Henry had confided in Sylvia that he hoped and believed that Waylon would just leave Sammie and Silly Lily, as he called his granddaughter. He said it would be best for all of them if Waylon would just leave. For the life of him, Henry couldn't understand why Waylon stayed. Clearly he didn't love his wife or daughter, or at least he didn't know how to show it. At first Henry thought Waylon would change. Oh, he had been different for a few months, but then he'd returned to his old ways with a new vengeance.

And what made him the angriest was that Samantha always defended Waylon or excused his behavior. Oh, that made Henry so mad!

Now these dreams kept returning and he was beginning to wonder if there was something to them. The preacher had read in the Good Book about old men dreaming dreams. Maybe this was God making him have dreams to let him know his daughter really needed help.

But Samantha had just announced at Sunday dinner that Waylon had come home from a week of work with a handful of cash and a promise to take her and Lily to the coast for their first family vacation. It had sounded fishy to Henry but the starry-eyed look his daughter wore kept him from asking any questions or raining on her parade. Samantha told them Waylon said he was "making up for all of the missed birthdays and anniversaries and lost time with his girls." She was happy so Henry had determined to be happy for her.

The dreams rushed back in full force. Rising from his chair, Henry decided that as soon as Samantha and Waylon returned from their trip to the coast, it was time for him to intervene.

Grabbing her arm, Samantha's co-worker and friend pulled her into the ladies' room as soon as Samantha entered the back door at *Steadman's*. Freeing herself from her friend's grasp, Samantha sounded irritated even to her own ears. "Heavens, Gloria! You're about to pull my arm off! What gives?"

Gloria stared at Samantha, the hurt on her face causing Samantha to feel instant remorse at her tone. "Samantha, what happened to you? Your face!"

Turning away, Samantha pushed her way into a stall for privacy. She had tried her best to cover up the mark Waylon had left on her face yet again but obviously she hadn't tried hard enough. "Nothing, Gloria. I'm fine."

"Samantha, get out here. I'm your friend. Come on. You can't hide in there all day. We've got work to do. Now come here this instant." Spoken firmly, but with compassion, Gloria coaxed Samantha out of the stall.

"Gloria, just--don't, okay? Not today. I leave tomorrow on vacation with my husband and daughter and I don't need this today." Pushing past Gloria, Samantha caught sight of her reflection in the cracked mirror. Reaching a hand to her bluing eye, Samantha gasped, "Oh, dear God. I had no idea...."

"Come here, Samantha. Let me help you." Gloria's eyes and tone softened as she saw the surprised look on her friend's face. Samantha was truly unaware of her black eye.

"Glo, what am I going to do? This is bad!" Tears pricked her eyes when she caught another glimpse of her face.

"Honey, I can help you. I've got my make-up bag with me. We have ten minutes for me to work my magic and before our shift starts. So….I promise to be gentle. I've done this kind of work before." Reaching into her bag, Gloria found what she was looking for and began to deftly apply foundation on Samantha's black eye.

Samantha propped against the restroom's sink and closed her eyes trying to relax. Tension coiled itself in the pit of her stomach. Quietly she ventured, "What do you mean you've done this before?"

"Let's just say my Dad wasn't always the nicest to my Mom. We kept her looking her best for her job at the diner when I was growing up. Sometimes she just couldn't do it herself….you know, cover up her own bruises, so she taught me how. Okay, now why don't you tell your friend what happened? Your secret's safe with me."

Taking in a shuddering breath, Samantha said, "Your mother's story is a little like mine. My husband can be a real jerk sometimes. He doesn't mean it….it just—"

"Stop right there. Don't ever tell me a man doesn't *mean* to hurt a woman. It's his choice if he treats her good or bad." Seeing tears collect in Samantha's eyes, Gloria hugged her friend briefly. "I won't stand by and act like I don't see you being hurt, Sammie. I won't. And I know for a fact it *will* escalate. You think he doesn't *mean to* now? One day it will be your daughter, Samantha."

Blocking out the images Gloria had conjured up, Samantha covered her face with both hands. She drew in a shaky breath. "Stop, Gloria. Please. I have to work in a minute. Look, I know what it—"

"No, you don't. If you're still with this loser after all these years, you're crazy. Now you have a daughter in the equation. You need to leave him before it gets worse. I'm only trying to help you, Samantha. You've got to listen to me." Gloria stuffed her make-up into her cosmetic bag.

Hugging her friend, Samantha gently pushed past her. "Come on, we have work to do. And thanks for helping me with my face, but I promise things will get better with me and Waylon."

Shaking her head in disbelief, Gloria opened her mouth to say more to Samantha's retreating back. But what more could she say? Gloria wordlessly followed Samantha out of the restroom.

~~~~~~~~~~

*July, 1946*

*Mississippi Coast*

Waylon's day trip he had planned for himself, Sam, and Lily was going all wrong. The little family depicted on the poster that hung taped to the drug store's front window was nothing like what he was experiencing today. A month ago Waylon had spotted the poster displaying the announcement for a *Carnival on the Coast: Where Memories are Made!*

That's all he wanted. Memories. *Good* memories to share with Samantha and his daughter. But with each passing day, Waylon felt the chasm grow wider between them as a family. Watching how close Samantha and Lily were upset Waylon more than he wanted to admit. Since Lily was old enough to recognize him as her daddy, all he had done was manage to cause the little girl to flinch when he spoke or to hide in her mother's skirts and suck her thumb when he was around. For the past two years of Lily Ruth's life, Waylon had tried to get her to like him, but even the dolls and small toys he could afford did nothing to make her want to be near him for more than a few seconds.

Waylon's conscience told him it was really his own fault. He was loud and gruff most of the time and he knew his fuse was short when it came to Sam. All he seemed to do was make the baby cry and run to her mother. And Samantha was always holding Lily or letting the girl hang onto her legs or making Lily hold her hand like he was going to grab her and make a run for it.

Hoping this day trip would give them a chance to start over or at least make a few good memories that would hopefully overshadow the bad, Waylon was seeing it was futile. He tried to coax Lily to share some cotton candy with him to no avail. After he noticed she was interested in the pony rides, Waylon had taken her hand and wanted to help her pet the pony and maybe ride it, but Lily only hid deeper in Samantha's skirt and stuck her thumb in her mouth.

Frustrated, he suggested they take a walk on the beach and look for shells. At the sandy beach, Lily saw the ocean and waves, she squealed with delight.

Reaching for Lily, Samantha took hold of her hand. "Hold Mama's hand tight, Lily Ruth."

"Let her be, Sam. She just wants to run and play. I'm right here. She won't get hurt. You never let her be a kid."

Samantha released Lily's hand when she saw the stern look on Waylon's face.

"Look, Sam. I'm really sorry about your eye. I didn't mean to—"

Breaking in on his sentence, Samantha said, "I know. You never *mean* to, Way." Brushing past him, Samantha headed for Lily. "Baby, let's find some shells to take home with us and show Grammie and Pop."

He stood and watched them collect shells and when he tried to add to Lily's collection, the little girl stuck her dirty thumb into her mouth and looked away. This infuriated Waylon to be ignored by a baby, his baby.

Stooping down to her level, Waylon grabbed Lily's wrist and pulled her thumb out of her mouth. "Look at me, Lily. Quit ignoring me! Now stop sucking your dang thumb and acting like a baby."

Lily's eyes pooled with tears and her bottom lip quivered. She tried to place her thumb in her mouth again, but Waylon squeezed her wrist and hand in his larger one. Instantly Lily let out a wail and tried to get away from Waylon.

Samantha instantly reacted. Grabbing Waylon's forearm, Samantha yelled at him. "Stop it! You're hurting her. Come here, Lily."

Fury etched itself over Waylon's features. He drew his hand away from Lily as Samantha lifted her up into her arms. Reaching back, Waylon prepared to smack Samantha across the face. Lily wrapped her arms around Samantha's neck and covered her mother's face with her little body. His hand freezing in mid-air, Waylon cursed under his breath and quickly looked around them. No one seemed to have seen what had taken place.

Instantly, all the families around Waylon seemed to move in slow motion as he looked around. He saw a couple sharing a large bag of popcorn sitting on a blue and yellow striped blanket. A little girl with pink ribbons in her hair chased a black puppy over the sandy shore. A family of four played with a brightly colored beach ball up ahead of them as the dad's laughter rang loud and true.

Everyone was oblivious to the storm that raged within the man not far up the beach from their perfect moments. Everyone but Samantha and Waylon.

Overcome with an inner strength she had never known before, Samantha looked Waylon in the eyes, and spoke through clenched teeth. In a hardened tone she barely recognized as her own, she said quietly but firmly, "Take us home, *now*."

Never before had Samantha dared to speak to Waylon in such a manner. He was caught off guard at his raised hand, ready to strike his wife and possibly his child. And never before had he seen such a look in Samantha's eyes, something that would take him days to identify and years to forget.

Whispering to the crying child, she replied, "Everything's okay. Hold onto Mama, Lily."

To Waylon, she muttered, "We'll be in the car."

The hour's drive home was made in complete silence. Thankfully Lily quickly fell asleep in her mother's arms. Their little house was a most welcome sight as the car's headlights turned down their dirt road. Lifting the sleeping child out of the car, Samantha couldn't get in the house quick enough and away from Waylon soon enough.

*How dare he hurt Lily! He has no right to treat her like he did. She's a defenseless child. Gloria was right.....*

Placing the baby in her bed, Samantha turned from the room and went in search for a bag. Finding one, she quickly began stuffing clothes, baby toys, diapers, and anything else she readily saw that she and Lily would need in the near future. She stilled when she heard Waylon slam into the house.

As soon as he saw her, he began ranting. "What are you doing, Sam? What do you think you're trying to pull here? You're not going anywhere!" Jerking the bag from her hands, Waylon dumped the contents on the bed.

"Waylon, stop it! Leave me alone! Just leave—"

His hand connected with her face stopping the flow of words.

This only added to Samantha's fury. She grabbed the bag and began repacking their things in it. Waylon shoved her hard against the door frame. But like a mother bear defending her cub, Samantha rose to her full height. "If you lay another hand on me, I'll scream bloody murder, Waylon Graves," she bit out.

Running to the kitchen, Samantha looked around for what she would need from there. Waylon roughly grabbed her arm and spun her around to face him. It felt as if her arm had been ripped from its socked. Pain shot through Samantha's body, infuriating her further.

Waylon pulled Samantha closer until her face was within inches of his. "Sam, what do you—"

A sound Samantha had no idea she could make rose from her belly and erupted from her usually closed lips. "Ahhhh!! Help!! Somebody help me! Get out of here—"

Eyes as big as saucers, Waylon stared at her in disbelief as Samantha jerked free and stood on the porch screaming for the neighbors to hear. Grabbing his car keys from the dining table, Waylon headed out the front door and got in his car as several neighbors came out onto their porches.

Samantha continued to scream as she watched Waylon fumble to get in the car. Finally on the third try, the engine turned over as he gunned the car spraying the porch with dirt and rocks.

Collapsing onto the porch, Samantha gave way to the months of tears she had kept pent up inside.

Feeling a hand on her shoulder, Samantha looked up into the face of her neighbor. "Honey, let's get you and little Lily to your Mama and Daddy's. Come on, now. My husband's got his gun out and ready if that man of yours decides to come back. Let's go get your things."

The next twenty minutes went by in a blur. The kind neighbors helped Samantha pack and got her and the still sleeping Lily to her parents safe and sound. Thankfully the day had worn her daughter out, so Samantha gladly let Lily sleep through all of it. Speaking in hushed tones with her parents, Samantha dissolved into another round of tears as her brother-in-law Melvin wrapped his strong arms around her in comfort.

The only thing Samantha remembered was Melvin's words whispered against her hair. "You don't ever have to lay eyes on that man again, Sammie. It's over, girl. I promise. It's over."

Part Three: **Searching for Beauty**

*"Though we travel the world over to find the beautiful, we must carry it with us, or we find it not."*
-Ralph Waldo Emerson

# chapter 23

Utter darkness enfolded the young, lone mother as she placed a hand on her sleeping daughter's head. Stroking the reddish-blond hair from the two year old's face, Samantha felt the hot streak of a tear run down her own pale cheeks. Involuntarily, a shudder passed over her small bruised frame. Samantha gathered the collar of her plaid dress as tightly as she possibly could against her neck, clinging to the false sense of security. The brush of the scratchy fabric brought another stream of tears as the smell of the Mississippi sun and wind reached her nose. Leaning her head close to the folds of her dress, Samantha inhaled her home, her world, her life.

But with each turn of the bus's wheels and with every jar from the metal entrapment of bouncy seats, snoring passengers, and intermittent street lights that blurred by, the very young nineteen-year-old mother of an innocent daughter, knew her old life was now completely gone. Nothing would or could ever be the same again.

Unbidden images flashed before her eyes as quickly as the street lights flicked by.

....Her arms tightly enfolding the crying Lily, Samantha walked as quickly as her legs would take her. The only comfort was the neighbor's hand encircling her arm pulling her forward to her unaware parents. Her neighbor's husband walked behind them, gun in hand, ready to defend Samantha and Lily if Waylon returned for them....

....Her parents' household awakened from sleep at the pounding on the front door alerting them to her arrival. Quickly Samantha, Lily, and the few belongings she had haphazardly packed were thrust at Sylvia while the neighbor pulled Henry and Melvin outside to fill them in on the earlier events....

....Everyone was finally settled in bed, Lily sleeping as soundly as if nothing had happened hours before. Samantha was just drifting off to sleep when she heard Waylon outside. Hoping to get him to leave, she rushed out onto her parents' porch to plead with him to go; Waylon grabbed Samantha by the throat, his hot, booze-laced, breath blasting in her face as his heaving chest announced an anger so vile and palpable. Just as she nearly passed out from lack of air as his grip on her throat continued to tighten, the sound of her Daddy's voice and the rasp of a bullet being loaded into the gun's chamber caused Waylon to release her....

....Waylon ran to his car at the sound of Henry's gun being fired into the air. Amid shouts of murderous threats towards Samantha and her family, threats to come back for his wife and daughter, the drunk man drove away into the night as his wife collapsed to the hard porch floor....

....Samantha read and re-read the name plate of the lawyer seated behind his stately desk. Sounds buzzed in her head, voices of Mr. Zuckermann, Henry, and Frank, each discussing her and Lily and Waylon. Samantha knew it had to be done. Somehow she saw the pen in her hand through the tears that pooled in her eyes as she scribbled her name on the appropriate lines that began the divorce proceedings. Refusing to press charges against Waylon, Samantha was willing to sign the divorce papers. Mr. Zuckermann advised Samantha to get as far away from Waylon as she possibly could due to his threats to her and her family....

....Samantha snuck in the back door at work the next day to find Gloria. Immediately her friend saw the ugly marks on Samantha's neck and knew she needed help. Giving Samantha her promise of a safe haven at her beloved aunt's home, she made arrangements for Samantha to escape as soon as she could....

The images only solidified all the more the most difficult decision she had ever made in her life. Knowing there was no other way to protect herself and her two-year-old, Samantha agreed to move with Lily Ruth to Big Bend, Wisconsin to an unknown state, an unknown home, to unknown people.

The deep yearning stirred within Samantha to fiercely protect Lily. Anger combined with fear and what she imagined a mother bear felt when her cubs were threatened rose up in Samantha as she willed the wheels of the bus to turn faster, quickly whisking her and Lily away from the danger that had surrounded them for months. Her gut churned with anxiety and uncertainty until she thought her last meal from hours ago would lurch from her with the bus's next lunge.

*Deep breaths, Samantha. You have to stay calm.* Forcing the slow intake and release of air from her lungs, she felt her stomach settle again. She looked around the bus, scanning her surroundings desperate to find something beautiful. Anything that would soothe her soul. *God help us,* she silently prayed over and over with each expel of breath.

Like the gentle touch of Lily's hand in hers, words caressed her heart, treasures she had buried deep within its recesses for when she needed them most. Now was one of those moments.

*He that dwelleth in the secret place of the most High shall abide under the shadow of the Almighty....I will say of the Lord, He is my refuge and my fortress: my God; in him will I trust....Thou shalt not be afraid for the terror by night; nor for the arrow that flieth by day....For he shall give his angels charge over thee, to keep thee in all thy ways.*

Akin to a drowning person grasping for a life-line, Samantha clutched tightly to the words from her Bible. Having read Psalm 91 every evening since the horrific night with Waylon, she had most of this chapter committed to memory. Shutting her eyes against the dark sky, Samantha repeated the lines over and over until peace crept in and settled her down.

Her mind unable to settle down, Samantha wondered for the hundredth time if she had made the right decision to just up and move to Wisconsin. But that was as far away as she was able to get from Waylon where she could immediately find refuge. Much to her parents' concern, they knew they had to trust God with their two girls and let them go. Samantha swore she would leave with or without their blessing because she had no other choice. Henry and Sylvia knew she would, just as she had left before. Stubborn and set in her ways, Samantha Jean would no doubt go. Knowing it was equally difficult for her Mama and Daddy, Samantha had made up her mind to do the unthinkable.

The only one in the family who saw her reasoning was Melvin. He supported her decision completely just to know she and Lily would be safe away from Waylon. With the promise to return as soon as she could, they all kissed their girls' cheeks and reluctantly let them leave. It was out of their hands.

Now Samantha faced the last few hours of the leg of her eternal bus trip. It both terrified and relieved her. Big Bend, Wisconsin would now be home for her and Lily. But how could you call a place *home* that you had never seen before, surrounded by people you had never laid eyes on or spoken to before?

Her friend Gloria had made all of the pertinent phone calls to the aunt and the necessary information was scrawled on a scrap of paper which Samantha had reluctantly handed over to her sister Bernice. Frank and Bernie had insisted on paying the bus fair and had forced a wad of bills in Samantha's purse before she left.

Tears threatened to spill again from her eyes, but she wouldn't allow them to show their presence the rest of the day at least. The bus driver had just announced she had an hour left until her drop off spot where she would be met by Robert and Mildred Stockton, Gloria's family and owners of *Hidden Lake Hunting and Fishing Resort* in Big Bend.

How on earth was she supposed to *do* this horrible thing of leaving those she loved the most and join a bunch of strangers in an alien world all the while dragging her child with her into this foreign realm? How would Lily Ruth take to being away from Geoffrey and the rest of the family? Would she adapt well to these sudden and swift changes that lay unknown to the sleeping child?

But there was no other choice, no other way. Again Samantha reached for her neck as she tried to forget the feel of her husband's hands around her throat. No longer could she deny the obvious. Waylon Graves was a sick, disturbed man who could very possibly cause great harm to his wife and child, who *had caused* them harm.

And she no longer was willing to run such a great risk.

So, Wisconsin-bound she was.

Whimpering in her confusion, Lily Ruth stirred as she woke to find herself in a strange place surrounded by unfamiliar sights and sounds. Letting out a frightened, sleepy wail, the two year old was instantly gathered up in her mother's arms and comforted until she quieted.

"Hush, Baby. It's okay. Mommy's got you. We are going on an adventure. Shhhh….everything's alright. How about a cracker? Are you hungry, Lily?" Samantha distracted the child by offering her the last of the crackers she had packed in her bag.

Reaching into the bottom of the huge tote, Samantha produced the yellow-haired doll Waylon had given Lily. Holding the cracker in one hand and the doll in her other, Lily stuck her thumb in her mouth and tucked her doll tightly against her chest while she gazed wide-eyed around her at the bus's interior. The bus was nearly empty at this point, leaving Lily and Samantha aboard with an elderly couple seated two rows up.

Thankfully the sun had made an appearance warming Samantha up as it did. She had noticed the change in temperature as the hours ticked by and the closer north they reached.

The older lady turned around and addressed Samantha, "Your baby is really good. She slept most of the night. Such a pretty girl. What's her name?"

"L—Ruth. Her name's Ruth." Afraid to give her daughter's real name, Samantha did her best to steady her voice. Glancing around the bus as if Waylon was behind her, she chided herself yet again for the fear.

"And your name, dear? I'm Bea. From Peoria, Illinois headed to see my sister in Milwaukee."

"I'm Jean. It's nice to meet you Bea." Again, she lied about their names. At least it wasn't an all-out lie; she *had* given their middle names.

Shifting in her seat, Samantha struggled to hide the tremor that started in her legs and arms. She was nearing exhaustion from the lack of sleep during the night and the travel the day before. She needed good food, a bed, and somewhere she felt safe.

The woman's husband got Bea's attention so Samantha didn't feel the need to talk further with her.

"Mommy, bite?" Lily held the cracker to Samantha lips.

"You can eat it. I will get my own." Snacking on crackers with her daughter quelled the nausea in Samantha's stomach. A dull headache was her constant companion along with knifing tension in her shoulders and neck.

*God, give me the strength to get through the next few hours. Please. I can't do this on my own.*

Stirring restlessly, Lily wanted to get down from the seat and move around. Samantha scooted to the end of the row and placed Lily on the cushioned seat so she could stand and look out the window. "What do you see, Lily? Trees? Birdies? Let's look for something beautiful, okay? Let's play our game and see who finds it first."

Lily loved to play their game of who could spot the beautiful thing first. They called it *I Spy Something Beautiful,* an altered version of the game *I Spy;* Samantha had taught her this early on, something she knew would serve her daughter well throughout life. Today it was doing just that.

"Cloud, Mommy? Beau-ful! Beau-ful!"

Samantha loved the way Lily said the world *beautiful.* She was close but always left out the "ti" in the middle so it became their own silly word.

"Yes, Lily! Those clouds are beau-ful! Okay, what's next? Oh, I spy something beautiful! I see a cow! She's black and white. See it?" Wrapping her arm around Lily's waist to steady her, unconsciously Samantha muttered to the child. "Hold tight to Mommy's hand, Lily."

And unconsciously the little girl obeyed as she clasped Samantha's hand, her link to her daughter, her security that she was indeed by her side and safe.

Standing on the sidewalk beside her suitcase, bag clutched tightly in one hand, Lily's hand equally grasped in the other, the brief touch of a hand on Samantha's shoulder caused her to startle noticeably as she gasped aloud. Wheeling around, she was face to face with a woman in her mid to late forties, smiling as broadly as the wide girth of her ample hips.

"Samantha Graves?"

"Oh! Y-yes, I'm Samantha. I'm sorry, but you scared the life out of me." Setting her bag at her feet, Samantha extended her hand in greeting. "You're Mildred Stockton, right?"

"I am. And I'm sorry I scared you. Your red hair caught my eye. My Gloria described it to a tee so I knew it was you and your little one. You must be exhausted, dear. Let me help you to my car."

"Yes, ma'am. I am. Thank you so much for—for...."

"Samantha, don't you think about 'thank yous' at a time like this. You think about a hot meal and a comfortable bed, then we will talk about the particulars of everything. Understand? Rest first; talk later." Taking Samantha's suitcase, the woman led the girls to her waiting car.

Seated comfortably inside, Samantha leaned her head back on the seat and breathed. "Oh, I never thought we would get off that bus. It's so good to be away from the cramped quarters."

"Well, I promise in twenty minutes you will be in a spot of your own where you can stretch your legs, shower, eat, sleep, whatever you need, dear." Mildred reached a plump hand and placed it tenderly on Samantha's shoulder.

Instantly liking the woman, Samantha settled herself for the remainder of the car ride and listened to Mildred talk a blue streak from the front seat. Lily quietly took in the sights around them. Reaching for Samantha's hand, the little girl said quietly, "Hold tight, Mommy."

Knowing Lily must be feeling uncertainty and confusion, Samantha did her best to reassure the girl. "I've got you, Lily. I'm holding tight."

Turning down a dirt road lined with the tallest, white-barked trees Samantha had ever seen, Mildred continued her discourse. "Just so you know the plan, I'm putting you and Lily in one of our vacant hunting cabins. It's small but plenty big for you two. My husband Robert, my son William—oh, he's four—and I live in the main lodge not a hundred yards from your little cabin. So if you need anything, we are close by. We just updated some of the hunting cabins including yours so you have a shower and running water and indoor facilities. We left it rustic for years and the hunters began asking when we would have indoor plumbing so we decided to update a few and leave the others as is for those that enjoyed roughing it. Now, I know what you're thinking. How will you pay for your room and board? Give it no thought. Gloria and I discussed everything and she said she would tell you about the arrangements. Did she? I'm not sure what you even know."

When Mildred took a breath for air, Samantha saw the opportunity to jump in the conversation. "Yes, ma'am. Gloria said I would have room and board and maybe a meal a day in exchange for me watching William and helping you clean the cabins, cook, do laundry, or whatever else you needed. I hope that's still the arrangement...."

"Oh child, yes! That's exactly what I want if you are agreeable to that."

"Most definitely, Mrs. Stockton—"

Mildred interrupted her with a raised hand. "Now there will be none of that *'Mrs. Stockton,'* young lady. It's Mildred to you."

Laughing despite her tiredness, Samantha replied, "Yes ma'am, Mildred. And please call me Sammie. My family called me that more than Samantha and it will make me feel at home to hear it."

"Well then, Sammie it is....so as soon as we get home, I have potato soup and bread ready for you and your little one to eat, then you can have a shower with clean towels, a bed with clean sheets—though there's only a full sized bed so you and your daughter will have to sleep together—and tomorrow we will go over everything else. Today is eat and rest day. In the morning if you want to join us for church, we will leave at 9:00 so if you're interested, be waiting on your porch and you can ride with us. Then there's mashed potatoes, peas, deer roast and gravy, rolls, and wild berry pie for Sunday lunch that you *must* come for. Oh, I'm sorry. I'm doing it again. My Robert says I talk entirely too much when I get excited. I apologize. You must think me awful to prattle on so."

"No, Mildred. I am rather enjoying myself for a change. You are making me feel most welcome. And yes, church would be wonderful in the morning." Tires crunching on rock caused Samantha to look to her right as Mildred eased the car down a driveway.

A dark green sign with brick red letters announced an entrance surrounded with smooth, large, gray-speckled rocks stacked to perfection creating an appealing setting for the entry. *Hidden Lake Hunting and Fishing Resort.*

And here she was. Her new home.

# chapter 24

Mildred Stockton had indeed delivered on every one of her promises. The little cabin, though nearly as big as Samantha's tiny mining town house, was perfection. If she could have dreamed up a cabin, this would have been the stuff of Samantha's dreams. Enfolded in walls of log, stone, and mortar, the cabin was snug and tight, blocking out the cooler temperatures. There was a small fireplace in one corner of the living room and kitchen that contained a gently blazing fire when she had arrived yesterday, a pot of potato soup with pieces of ham and carrots simmering in the rich broth, a generous chunk of golden wheat bread and yellow butter, matching bowls and silverware with perfect, unchipped cups and saucers for coffee and hot tea. It was stocked with pillows and blankets, rugs and woodsy décor. There was even a set of fluffy bath robes for Samantha and Lily. In another corner was a beautifully hand-woven basket with matching lid full of stuffed toys, wooden blocks, a ball, a doll with red hair and blue dress, all nestled among various toys that would delight any toddler for hours.

Mildred quickly walked Samantha through the cabin upon their arrival, showed her how the fireplace worked, the shower was operated, how to use the stove, where the towels and extra blankets were stored, then breezed out the door with the command to enjoy the food and rest since 'tomorrow was soon enough to discuss their arrangements then.' She handed Samantha the door key and asked her to stay close to the house if she went outside until she had been shown the grounds properly and to lock up at night if she felt safer that way.

In awe, Samantha and Lily spent the remainder of the day exploring the house, playing with the new toys, eating the luscious food, showering and lounging in their bath robes by the warm fire while they took in their new surroundings. Tears would surprisingly spring to Samantha's eyes unbidden and without warning while she stared in awe and thanksgiving at the little cabin in the woods designed for her safety and enjoyment. She felt as if God had hand-picked this *gift* for her and Lily, feeling overwhelmed with His great provision. Never could she have dreamed of such a place for them to call their refuge and haven.

Nearing 7:00 that first evening, after second bowls of reheated soup and bread, Lily and Samantha both began yawing and struggling to stay awake. Not remembering a night when she had ever gone to bed that early, Samantha scooped up her daughter and the precious Bible then piled up in bed surrounded by enough pillows and blankets to keep a family of eight warm.

Flipping open the book, her eyes landed on the familiar, straight, red lines that called her attention to a verse.

"Wead, Mommy." Popping her thumb in her mouth, Lily settled under Samantha's arm to listen to the sacred words.

"Ok, what will we read tonight, Lily?" Tracing a finger under the words, she read aloud. *"Come unto me, all ye that labour and are heavy laden, and I will give you rest."* Samantha read the next couple of verses to herself then returned to these precious, timely words. She read them aloud again, then yet again as the words settled around her shoulders. "Rest, Lily. That's what we are going to do. Rest and trust God. And thank Him for this little house and food and safety. What do you think?"

No answer came from her daughter. Samantha looked down at Lily's closed eyes and sleeping face. A smile crept over her lips as she noticed something else about Lily. There was no frown creasing her baby-like brow. She was at peace. Completely at rest.

Reaching for the lamp's switch, Samantha turned off the light and rolled to her side to wrap Lily in the cocoon of her arms. Praying quietly in her heart, Samantha was consumed by the same peace and rest as her daughter as she lay nestled in the warm bed imagining God's arms surrounding them as they slept soundly, silently, peacefully for the first time in ages.

An unfamiliar *thunk, thunk, thunk* awakened Samantha as the sun streamed through slightly parted curtains brushing over her face all the while bringing her out of the deepest sleep she had ever known. Stretching to her full length, Samantha opened her eyes and took in the room around her. Sleeping contentedly beside her Mommy, Lily stirred slightly in her sleep. Pulling the heavy star-patterned quilt up around her daughter's shoulder, Samantha eased herself up into a seated position pushing down-filled pillows around her neck and shoulders to create a comfortable nest.

*Thunk, thunk.*

Creeping reluctantly from the warm bed, Samantha grabbed the robe and wrapped it around her frame. She felt the chill of the room as she noticed the fire was now reduced to a few coals. Shivering involuntarily, Samantha reached for the tea kettle sitting on the stove. Filling it with water, she turned on the burner to get hot water ready for tea.

*Plunk, thunk.*

The continuing noise led her to the nearest window. Parting the curtains, Samantha's breath caught in her throat. She saw the backside of a man in a heavy coat and leather gloves stacking firewood between two trees, much too near for her comfort. Pulling back from the window, Samantha hastened to get dressed then remembered it was Sunday. Glancing at her wrist watch, she saw it was shortly after seven in the morning.

*I slept nearly twelve hours! How on earth did that happen?*

In the past three years with Waylon, Samantha had slept no more than five or six hours at a time due to Waylon's unstable patterns and her worrying. No wonder she felt so refreshed this morning.

She had two hours to prepare for church if she decided to go with Mildred and her family. That was plenty of time to get the rest of her bag unpacked and determine what to wear.

Turning back to the window, Samantha glanced out and saw the man was gone. Opening the door a crack, she looked out both ways then snatched the few sticks of firewood from the porch and rekindled the fire. Warmth filled the room as the tea kettle whistled on the stove. Retrieving a mug and tea bag, she went back to the bedroom while her tea steeped.

Lily was still sleeping so Samantha brought the over-sized suitcase into the living area and tossed it on the couch. Quickly she withdrew their two dresses, rummaged through a closet, and found a few hangers to use. Samantha then placed the hangers' hooks on the mantle near the heat of the fire to hopefully release the wrinkles. If they were going to church their dresses would be as wrinkle-free as possible.

Turning back to her suitcase, Samantha withdrew the remainder of her and Lily's clothes. Refolding them, Samantha found the paper-lined drawers of the little dresser awaiting their clothing. In the bottom of the suitcase, Samantha withdrew a cigar box and a cloth wrapped item. Unwinding the cloth, she produced her precious vase that Bernie had given her for the wildflowers she loved to pick. Placing the vase center stage on the round dining table, Samantha couldn't wait to get her hands on something to fill the vase. But that would have to wait until later.

Next she opened the cigar box and took out all of her treasures she dared bring from home, a handful of colorful rocks, a patch of lime green moss, the brooch and scarf her mother had given Samantha on her sixteenth birthday, the sparkling charm bracelet from Bernie that had hardly graced her wrist due to Waylon's disapproval of such an expensive gift, and lastly a drawing from Geoffie of two stick people, one her and the other Geoffie, depicting in little boy art the both of them catching lightning bugs in the yard.

Grief as heavy as a wet blanket settled over Samantha and caused her to sit on the couch before she could continue the unpacking. Giving into a few tears, she let the sadness and loss of her family give way for a moment. Steeling herself for the morning, Samantha swiped away her tears, placed her treasures in special spots, then poured herself a hot cup of tea.

"Mommy!! Mom-my!" Lily's cries broke Samantha's heart at their fear-laced sound.

Running to the next room, Samantha cradled Lily until she calmed. "It's okay, Baby. You are in your new bed! Want to see your new toys? Let's get you some milk and breakfast. My girl slept a long time last night."

Wriggling out of her Mommy's arms, Lily dashed for the new toys in the pretty basket. Squeals of delight filled the room as Lily was lost in the fun of blocks and dolls. While she played contentedly, Samantha fixed them both a breakfast of milk, bread, jam, and eggs. Mildred had stocked the cabinets and small refrigerator with the necessities for several meals, another blessing Samantha noticed and inwardly thanked God for.

Nearing time for church, Samantha quickly washed off Lily's breakfast remains and cleaned her up in the little bathroom. Next she did her best to smooth the wrinkles out of their toasty warm dresses, pulled on tights and shoes, did their hair and applied a little make-up on her cheeks and lips, took her Bible from its protective shroud, and grabbed her purse. In record time the two girls were sitting on the porch's swing made perfectly for two awaiting a ride to church.

Coats buttoned tightly to their chins, they provided enough warmth for the August morning. Mildred had warned Samantha to expect chilly mornings and evenings with pleasant afternoons. She was right about the chilly part. Samantha was going to have to allow herself time to acclimate from the muggy, hot Augusts of Mississippi to this different weather of Wisconsin.

Tires crunching on gravel alerted her to the arriving car. Mr. Stockton, Mildred, and their son William all perched in the front seat allowing room for Samantha and Lily to have the back of the car to themselves. As pleasant as his wife was, Robert Stockton made Samantha feel like family instead of a stranger almost instantly. They did feel like an aunt and uncle to her, as if Gloria's family had always been her family only she hadn't seen them in a long time. Conversation flowed easily on the short drive to church. William and Lily remained silent as they stole shy glances at each other all the while Lily constantly sucked her thumb, a battle Samantha determined to fight later.

Samantha worried how these sudden changes would affect her daughter. So far she had taken everything in stride, but Samantha was worried a melt-down was in the near future for Lily when she realized her Grammie, Pops, Geoffie, and the rest wouldn't be in her life for a long time. This thought saddened Samantha greatly so she shoved it aside as quickly as her tender heart would allow.

The tall white spire pierced the clear sapphire sky ahead announcing their arrival at church. The sign proclaimed for her the church's name and denomination. *Big Bend Baptist Church.*

Parishioners were getting out of their cars, walking into the open oak doors that were centered between two mosaic stained-glass windows of crimson, emerald, gold, and cobalt blue hues. The tall white building seemed to swallow the people whole and smile during the process. The hum of *Good morning, Reverend* and *Hello, isn't it a lovely day* along with various other greetings spoken in a different accent Samantha had never heard before all buzzed in her ears like a swarm of bees high in the trees. She enjoyed the sound of their happy greetings.

At the door, the Reverend introduced himself to Samantha and asked how she knew the Stocktons. Mildred intervened with an answer before Samantha could find the words to respond. "Oh, Reverend Hill, this is my niece's friend who now works for us at the resort. Samantha and her daughter Lily."

That simplified things for Samantha and the explanation required no further details to the hearer. "Welcome to Big Bend, Samantha. I hope you enjoy it here."

"Thank you, Reverend Hill. I'm sure we will."

Samantha and Lily were ushered into the row of wooden pews where she guessed the Stocktons usually sat. She glanced around her admiring the polished woodwork and glittering stained glass picture windows. The large empty cross at the back of the stage held Samantha's attention until the organist struck the first keys to a hymn she knew by heart. Knowing the dear words since childhood, today they took on an entirely new and fresh meaning.

*To God be the glory, great things he hath done;*
*so loved he the world that he gave us his Son,*
*who yielded his life an atonement for sin,*
*and opened the life-gate that all may go in.*

*Praise the Lord, praise the Lord; let the earth hear his voice!*
*Praise the Lord, praise the Lord; let the people rejoice!*
*O come to the Father through Jesus the Son,*
*and give him the glory; great things he hath done.*

*O perfect redemption, the purchase of blood,*
*to every believer the promise of God;*
*the vilest offender who truly believes,*
*that moment from Jesus a pardon receives.*

*Great things he hath taught us, great things he hath done,*
*and great our rejoicing through Jesus the Son;*
*but purer and higher and greater will be*
*our wonder, our transport, when Jesus we see.*

*Praise the Lord, praise the Lord; let the earth hear his voice!*
*Praise the Lord, praise the Lord; let the people rejoice!*
*O come to the Father through Jesus the Son,*
*and give him the glory; great things he hath done.*

Throughout the song Samantha had to fight two things: she fought the tears that clogged her voice at the very thought of all of the great things God had done for her in the last two days, and she fought the desperate urge to turn around and see who sang in such an incredible baritone voice behind her. When the hymn ended she settled back in her seat and gave Lily a pencil and scrap of paper from her purse to keep the child still during the sermon. Samantha listened intently then found herself conjuring up the face of the owner of the deep voice behind her. Her mind's eye saw a robust, slightly balding, barrel-chested, man seated with an arm across the back of the pew encircling his wife and two children aged ten and eleven who he kept in order throughout the service with nothing more than a stern look or tap on the head. Nearly giggling at her imaginings, Samantha refocused as the service was winding to a close.

Unable to stand it another second longer, she stood to follow the Stocktons out of church and peered behind her at the gentleman who had the wonderful voice. Face etched in shock, Samantha uttered a small gasp at what she saw.

This was no balding man in his mid-forties with wife and two children in tow. This was a man in his mid-twenties, a thick shock of sandy blond hair, and bold green eyes talking to an elderly woman seated near him. His deep voice betrayed his looks and age, but Samantha knew he was the owner of the distracting, sonorous voice. Casting a curious glance her way, Samantha quickly broke eye contact with the man, turned away, and lifted Lily onto her hip.

"You girls ready?" Mildred looked her way indicating it was time to leave.

"Oh—um, yes ma'am. We are ready."

"Alright then, roast and potatoes are calling Robert's name so we better hurry." The twinkle in Mildred's eye only endeared her more to Samantha. She was like a plump fairy sent to earth to make Samantha's world easier and safer.

Samantha paused to reflect once more on God's goodness in her life. The Stocktons were truly a blessing and gift.

An unexpected source of beauty and hope for Samantha and her daughter.

# chapter 25

After speaking to a few more people on the way out, the Stocktons and their newest family members got in the car and headed home. Before pulling into the driveway, Mildred turned to Samantha, "Dear, would you like to change clothes before lunch? If so, we will drop you off at your cabin and you and Lily can join us when you're ready."

"Yes, that would be nice. I don't want Lily to ruin her only nice dress. Is your house the large one on the path down from our cabin?"

"It sure is. Just follow the path from your back door and you will run into us. The day is nice enough for the walk, don't you think? Oh, and I have ice cream for the pie for dessert. So the sooner you return the sooner we can get to the pie."

An unusual giggle escaped from Samantha's lips. "Yes, ma'am. We will definitely hurry for pie and ice cream."

Within minutes, Samantha had changed Lily into play clothes and had donned a pair of slacks and button-up blouse with a cardigan. Looking in the mirror, Samantha saw the marks on her neck that were still slightly noticeable. "Oh that will never do!"

Anger threatened to push into her soul, but she refused it. Taking a deep breath, Samantha refocused on something more pleasant. Looking out the window she saw two chipmunks dart from tree trunk to tree trunk and nearly squealed with delight. She watched the little furry creatures and made a mental note to visit them later. Grabbing a matching mock turtle-necked sweater and jacket in a deep turquoise, she silently thanked Bernice for the beautiful set. Perfect. The sweater covered her neck and made her feel more secure. Little did she know the color enhanced the violet in her eyes until they looked like stunning amethyst gemstones.

"Lily Ruth, are you ready for lunch? Let's go for a walk. How does that sound?" Samantha decided against their coats since the day was warming up nicely and put a light sweater on her daughter. "Hold Mommy's hand tight."

Obediently Lily reached for Samantha's hand and they stepped outside into the lovely day. "Sing, Mommy. Sing star song, Mommy."

"Okay, let's sing the star song." Clearing her throat, Samantha launched into the lyrical melody with Lily singing every other word that she could pick up, complete with animal motions a bit off timing. The two belted it out beautifully on their walk to the Stocktons' home.

*"Would you like to swing on a star*

*Carry moonbeams home in a jar*
*And be better off than you are*
*Or would you rather be a mule*

*A mule is an animal with long funny ears*
*Kicks up at anything he hears*
*His back is brawny but his brain is weak*
*He's just plain stupid with a stubborn streak*
*And by the way, if you hate to go to school*
*You may grow up to be a mule*

*Or would you like to swing on a star*
*Carry moonbeams home in a jar*
*And be better off than you are*
*Or would you rather be a pig—"*

Abruptly Samantha's song came to an end when she rounded a bend in the path and heard someone whistling the tune along with their singing. Looking around cautiously, Samantha saw him. There he was not ten feet away standing on the Stockton's front porch like he was waiting for her and Lily to catch up with him.

"Oh, don't stop on my account! You sounded better than Bing Crosby any day. Please continue."

Samantha looked into the greenest eyes she had ever seen. Blushing furiously, she tried to regain her composure before speaking. It *was* him, the man from church with the wonderful voice. What was he doing here of all places?

"Um—excuse me, but Mrs. Stockton is expecting us for lunch."

"Well that makes two of us." Extending his hand, the man replied in his deep voice, "I'm Benjamin Wright. Most call me Ben. I've never seen you around here before."

Quickly, so as not to be rude, Samantha shook his hand and said, "I'm new here. My name is Samantha Gr—Owens. This is my daughter Lily. Lily, say hi to Mr. Wright."

Stuffing her thumb in her mouth, Lily hid behind Samantha's legs. "I'm sorry; she's shy and it's all new and strange for her. Well, for both of us...." *Oh, why did I say that,* Samantha chided inwardly.

"I hope you will like it here and find it less strange soon. Here, let me get the door." Ben opened the door wide for the two girls to pass. Samantha noticed he didn't knock or ring the bell. He simply let himself in. *Who is this person to just barge into someone's home like that?*

"Hello, Mildred! It's just me and I found two lovely ladies singing their way up your front walkway." Ben extended his hand to the left indicating the way Samantha should go.

"Hello, Ben!" Mildred planted a quick kiss on his cheek which surprised Samantha even more. "Come in, girls. I'm so glad you're here! Would you like to see Willie's toys, Lily?" Mildred bent down to address Lily and the little girl tentatively took her hand following the woman into a room off the kitchen where William sat playing.

Samantha watched in awe as Lily went with Mildred while she introduced her son to Lily and showed Lily a few toys that immediately caught her interest. Standing in the doorway for a moment, Samantha watched as Lily interacted with Willie slowly at first then comfortably. *Of course she likes William. He reminds her of Geoffrey.*

Turning back to the kitchen, Samantha's jaw dropped in amazement again at the man named Ben. Like a strange Mississippi bug in her parents' yard, she eyeballed him until she realized she was staring. The man had both sleeves rolled up to the elbows and was chopping carrots then dropping them into a steaming pot of water on the stove. Quickly she turned her attention to Mildred. "How can I help?"

"Do you know how to slice a roast, Sammie? I hope it's okay to call you that."

Oh, it was so good to hear her nickname again! Joyful tears sprang to the surface but she swallowed them down. Clearing her throat, she replied, "Yes, ma'am. I do know how. Where is your carving knife?"

Ben addressed Samantha with his back to her still cutting carrots. "Sammie? That's cute. Is that a nickname?"

"Yes. My family called me all variations of Samantha. Sammie-girl, Sammie, Samantha Jean, Sambo, Sister Sam. The only one I don't care for is just plain old Sam. It's too harsh." Never again did she want to hear the name 'Sam.' It reminded her of Waylon and his severe treatment.

The roast nearly fell off the knife's blade; it was so tender. Her mouth watered at all of the delicacies and aromas in the kitchen. For the next fifteen minutes, she mostly listened to the light-hearted banter in the kitchen as they all finished the lunch preparations. Finding she enjoyed these strangers' company, Samantha determined to take each moment in and savor it. It was beauty she wanted to capture and behold on the days she would need it most when she would be missing her Mississippi life terribly.

After the family was seated around the dining table, Mr. Stockton broke the silence. "Before we eat, I would like to say something. Samantha, I want you to know how grateful we are to have you with us. I know we are strangers but I hope you will be able to call us family soon enough. We want to help you in any way we can, so don't hesitate to ask. Just know you and Lily are welcome here for as long as you wish to stay."

A lone tear ran down Samantha's cheek. Quickly she swiped it away.

Mildred rose to the occasion and saved Samantha from needing to reply to the kind words in her emotional state. "I agree whole-heartedly, Robert. Now, Ben, would you say grace?"

"Of course. Dear Heavenly Father, we thank You for this bountiful feast You provided for us to enjoy. Help us to walk in Your ways and not miss the path You set before us. Thank You for these dear friends, both old and new, and for leading Samantha and Lily to us. In Your Son's name I pray, Amen."

After a round of *amens,* Mildred began passing platters and dishes of hot rolls, roast, potatoes, carrots, and gravy. The distraction gave Samantha time to compose herself after Mr. Stockton's gracious words and after Ben's prayer. Running over the details she had gained, Samantha mused, *Ben referred to them as friends, not family. I thought he must be related to the Stocktons. That's odd. Maybe he is right.* God *did choose this path for me to take, to this place, to these wonderful people.*

As Samantha ate, she watched Lily and William carry on in their two and four-year-old chatter. Surprisingly Lily had quickly warmed up to him. Placing her tiny hand on Samantha's arm, Lily said, "Geoffie funny, Mommy. No—not Geoffie...." Confused the little girl frowned and pursed her pink lips then popped her thumb in her mouth signaling her uncertainty.

"Baby, that's Willie. He's your new friend."

Tears pooled in Lily's violet eyes. Quietly she said, "I want Geoffie and Grammie and Pops." Her little throat clogged with tears as a stifled cry emerged; Samantha could see the inevitable melt-down coming.

Standing from the table, Samantha lifted Lily into her arms saying, "I'm so sorry. We will be right back." She scurried from the dining room and took the front door since it was the first route of escape she could find.

The last words she heard when she left was sweet Mildred. "Oh, poor dears. I know they miss home and their family something fierce."

Collapsing into the nearest porch chair, Lily and Samantha's tears mingled with each other's. Having held her emotions in check for so long, Samantha had not the willpower nor the energy to keep them at bay. Amidst her sobbing, she tried to soothe Lily. "It's okay, honey. We will see Grammie and Pops and Geoffie soon….We have some new friends now and this is our new home, okay?..... We're going to have fun and play with your new toys…." The words of comfort sounded empty to her own ears but Samantha had to try. Slowly Lily calmed down.

Samantha felt a hand on her shoulder. In the midst of their tears, she hadn't heard the front door open. It was Ben, standing with a floppy-eared bunny in one hand and a sheepish smile on his face. "May I?"

Samantha's tear-stained smile answered for her.

Kneeling down at Samantha's feet, he rubbed a hand over his blond hair and looked at Lily. "Hey, Lily. Look who I found in the house. Mr. Floppy loves carrots and wants you to help him eat his lunch. Then he wants to play with you and William. And then, you know the best part? Mr. Floppy loves pie and ice cream, but he knows you have to eat carrots first. Want to go with me and Mr. Floppy to eat our carrots?"

Surprisingly the little girl leaned towards Ben's out stretched arms and the floppy bunny. Without a word, she let him lift her from Samantha's arms and stand.

Whispering to Samantha, Ben said, "Take all the time you need, Sammie."

A new rush of emotion hit her at the man's kindness. She tried to choke out an answer but covered her mouth with her hand to stifle the next wave of tears, so she only shook her head in affirmation as she watched him take Lily inside. Her heart ached with the pain of her destroyed marriage, with missing her family, and with feeling so very inadequate to protect Lily from further pain.

Retrieving a handkerchief from her pants pocket, Samantha blew her nose and took several cleansing breaths. Then she stood to her full height, straightened her shoulders, and went back inside determined to eat the bountiful food and enjoy the delightful company of new found friends.

## chapter 26

"Mama, come quick! I've got a letter from Samantha Jean! It arrived today and I came right over after work to show you." Bernice had just nearly busted down the front door of Sylvia's house with her excitement.

Hand to her mouth, Sylvia intercepted her daughter in the living room and pulled her down on the couch beside her. "From Samantha? Oh, I've been worried sick these past few weeks! Well hurry and read it to me!"

"I will, Mama, as soon as you hush....okay, let's see....it's dated August 20 so she's been there about 3 weeks now....

*Dear family,*

*I don't even know where to begin. I know I will probably ramble so bear with me as I write this. I've been in Big Bend, Wisconsin for what seems an eternity now but it's only been weeks.*

*I know Mama and Daddy want to know one thing right up front. LILY AND I ARE DOING FINE. Though we both miss you terribly and all of the others until I think I may just hop on the next bus and come back home.*

*And then I remember why I am here in the first place. I hope there haven't been any incidents with you-know-who since I left. I don't care to ever utter the man's name again so I won't. I pray for y'all every night and for your protection. I figure between God's angels and Daddy's gun you will be alright.*

*I know without a doubt that I made the right decision by leaving but that doesn't make it any easier. I just miss seeing you all so much!*

*Okay enough of that or I will cry the ink off the paper.*

*Lily is doing very well. She has a new friend, a four year old boy named William. He is perfect for her since she misses Geoffrey so much. They get along great and he is as patient with her as her cousin was. She enjoys the tall, tall trees, the chipmunks that play in the woods around our cabin, and the lake near the resort.*

*We live in a tiny cabin that is made of the stuff of dreams. It has a fireplace, a shower, a big bed that we share, even toys for Lily. Mama, you would love it! I get to live here free, can you believe that? The arrangement I have with the Stocktons (remember they're the family who own the resort and Gloria's aunt and uncle she connected me with) is that I help clean the hunting cabins, do laundry, help Mrs. Stockton with baking and any other chore she comes up with. Actually I love the work and the location. It's simply beautiful. God is so good to put me here since I had to leave. I feel safe and hidden away.*

*I promise one day to come home soon, but it has to be when I know it's safe. I can't thank all of you enough for helping me leave the way you did though none of us wanted that to happen.*

*Oh, I found a nice church to attend with the Stocktons. It's a Baptist church but I don't think God really cares what kind of church I go to, just that I worship Him and read my Bible and talk to Him. That's all that matters.*

*I will keep sending my letters to Frank and Bernice's house like Mr. Zuckermann suggested so you-know-who can't go through the mail trying to find me and Lily. Please write soon to the address on this envelope. I can't wait to hear from you all.*

*Love,*
*Samantha Jean Owens*

Wiping tears away with her apron's edge, Sylvia sat in silence a moment before she spoke. "My little girl. Samantha Jean *Owens* was always strong and brave. She still is after all she's been through. Strong, not broken down. Oh, I miss her...." Sylvia's shoulders shook with silent sobs.

Wrapping a comforting arm around her mother's thinning frame, Bernice said, "Mama, why don't you write her back this afternoon and I will pick up your letter Sunday after church to mail it for you? You'll feel better if you can communicate with her."

"That's a good idea, Bernie. Thank you." Sylvia kissed Bernice's cheek and stood. "I think I'll put the kettle on for a cup of tea. Want to stay?"

"I have to get home to Frank. I'll leave Sammie's letter for you to share with Daddy and the others. See you Sunday." With that Bernice left as quickly as she came.

Picking the letter up off the table where Bernice placed it, Sylvia brought the envelope to her nose and inhaled trying to catch a scent of her daughter and granddaughter. Closing her eyes, she tried to imagine where Samantha lived, what her cabin looked like, if she was happy, if Lily was growing faster than a dandelion. Her mother's heart ached for her daughter.

Yes. Life came with the good and the bad, the right and the wrong, the fair and the unjust. In that moment, Sylvia could only see the bad, the wrong, and the unjust where this was concerned. A deep hatred for *you-know-who*, as her daughter called him, swirled within her chest.

Needing a distraction, Sylvia poured herself a cup of tea, squeezed a lemon slice in the steaming brew, and stirred in a spoonful of sugar. She grabbed a pencil and her stationery set then sat down at the scarred table to write a letter to Samantha.

*Dear Samantha Jean,*

*You have no idea what your letter meant to me. (I haven't even read it to your Daddy yet and here I am writing you back already.) It was a soothing balm to my soul.*

*I hope and pray you two really are as good as you say and you're not just trying to make your parents feel better about you leaving. I do understand but that doesn't ease the pain of it. I just miss you both so very much.*

*I'm so glad to hear the Stocktons are nice, respectable people. It sounds like a perfect arrangement that you have. Don't work too hard and make sure you stay warm in the cold north. I can't imagine living there! It must be so different from Mississippi.*

*Well, I have some news for you too. The mine has had rumors of it shutting down this fall and you know your Daddy. He won't sit around to wait for something to happen so he decided to look for a new job and a new place for us to live. I do think that's smart so we "won't get caught with our pants around our ankles" as he said. So we are moving the end of this month, which all things considered, may be the best decision ever since you-know-who won't know where we end up. We are keeping it hush-hush around here for that reason.*

*My sister Hazel knew of an apartment in her building that was vacant with more room than this little shoe box we live in now so your Daddy began looking for work in Godley and found a warehouse spot open. The best part is he will make a few dollars more a month than he does now and Melvin got on there too! Mel will be working as a delivery driver for the warehouse and he gets to bring home the delivery truck each night. He gets a job and our family has a vehicle as long as he stays employed there. Of course we can't just go gallivanting around but if we had a need for wheels, we have them. He only has to clear it with the boss each time he uses the truck that isn't for work purposes.*

*As our preacher would say, God always shows up when we least expect Him too. I guess that's what He's done now with these jobs and apartment and truck.*

*I forgot to tell you that Claudia, Geoffrey, and Melvin will still live with us when we move to the apartment. It has two bedrooms but there's a little alcove off one of the bedrooms that's big enough for Geoffrey to have his own little "room."*

*Well, I guess I better close this letter for now. I will send you our new address after we get settled so in the meantime keep those letters coming to Bernice's address.*

*Oh how I love and miss you both!*
*Mama*

Knowing she could have penned her heart out all day to her daughter, Sylvia stood slowly from the table and folded the precious correspondence and gently placed it in an envelope to be mailed to Samantha. A deep, longing, pain pressed so heavily on her heart until Sylvia had to sit back in the chair to keep her legs from buckling. Her heart hurt so deep and raw she thought she would die from the pain. And again that sharp-edged ache turned to a burning hate for the man she detested for stealing her fourteen-year-old daughter away years ago and now he had done it again. Waylon Graves had made Samantha and now her granddaughter leave *again*.

Except this time it was worse than the first. She couldn't get to the girls or see them even occasionally to make sure they were okay. The man's hateful, evil ways had interrupted Sylvia's life until she thought she could kill him if given the chance. He had stolen her two precious ones from her.

And she hated him for it.

Henry walked in the front door and sniffed the air. His stomach growled something fierce as he had missed lunch. Sylvia hadn't come to the mine with his afternoon meal that he looked forward to each day. All day he had worried she was sick or maybe Geoffie-boy or Claudia was ill. Again he tried the air, his nose looking for promises of dinner cooking. Nothing.

"Sylvie! Syl...." Henry entered the kitchen noticing it looked just as it had that morning when he left for work. Clean, everything in order, no dinner sizzling in skillets on the stove. "Where are you, woman?" She wasn't in the house; that much was certain.

Claudia stuck her head out of her bedroom with a finger placed on her lips. She closed the door quietly behind her. "Shhhhh, Daddy. Geoffrey is asleep. I want him to finish his nap before dinner. He didn't sleep well last night and he's all tuckered out."

"Where's your Mama?"

"I don't know; maybe she's getting clothes off the line." Claudia seemed unconcerned so that eased Henry's worry.

"Okay, I'll go see." Henry went out the back door and saw the empty clothesline as answer to his question. Standing in the small yard he looked around for his wife but didn't see her. A flash of blue caught his eye to the left. He looked at the old willow tree and sure enough, there was Sylvia in her blue house dress. Not where he expected to find her, Henry made his way to his wife.

Parting the green leafy overhang, Henry found her sitting with her back to him in one of the metal chairs. "Sylvie?"

She didn't move a muscle.

Henry approached her and placed a hand on her shoulder. "Syl...."

Instantly she shot up out of the chair, wheeled to face him, her hand to her mouth. "Ohhh! Henry! You scared the daylights out of me! Don't you ever sneak up on me that way again." Anger clouded her face as she tried to brush past him.

Grabbing her wrist, he pulled her close. "Honey, what's wrong? Are you alright? I didn't mean to scare you, I swear."

Jerking away, she frowned. "I'm *fine*," Sylvia ground out. Reaching a trembling hand to her hair, she effortlessly tried to smooth the strays back into her bun at her neck. "What time is it anyway? Why are you home so early?"

Panic tightened Henry's chest. "Sylvia, it's 5:30. I always get home at this hour. Do you feel okay? Are you sick?"

Harshly, she retorted, "I *said* I'm fine." This time she pushed past him and into the house leaving Henry baffled at her response.

In the kitchen, Sylvia began taking her frustrations out on dinner preparations. She banged and clanged the skillets and pots so loudly it awakened Geoffrey. Chopping the potatoes sounded louder than Henry when he split logs for their firewood stash. Feeling the anger fuel her every movement, Sylvia used its power to get dinner on the table in record time. Jerking the oven door open, she cried out in frustration as she peered in at the biscuits with burned tops.

"Mama, what's burning? It smells like something's on fire!" Claudia rushed into the over-heated kitchen to see what was wrong. She couldn't remember the last time her mother had burned anything.

"Claudia, if you're going to criticize, just leave me be! Round up everybody. Dinner's ready. Now hurry up before it gets cold!"

"Yes, Mama."

Henry took in the entire scene as he entered the back door just in time to see the biscuits burned and Sylvia's outburst. Leaning to Claudia, he whispered, "Do as your Mama says. She's not feeling well."

All gathered round the table. Everyone except Sylvia. She left the kitchen as soon as she had set the table with no more than, "I'm not hungry. You all go ahead."

Frowning, Claudia stood to follow her as Henry reached a hand out and placed it on his daughter's arm. "Let her be for now. Let's eat."

Dinner was a silent, somber meal. The peas were under-cooked, the biscuits burned, and the potatoes tasted scorched. This alone was enough of a clue that something wasn't right with his Sylvia. Henry had never tasted a meal his wife had prepared that wasn't ambrosia to his taste buds.

Something was wrong. Very wrong.

# chapter 27

*October, 1946*

Settling into a comfortable routine, Samantha and Lily worked together to hang the sheets on the line. Today she had cleaned three cabins getting them ready for the next group of hunters. Lily had turned into a surprisingly pleasant helper. Samantha had worried the job would be too much for her since she had a two-year-old in tow, but quickly she found what worked great for them. A basket of Lily's favorite toys and snacks was what kept the little girl occupied while Samantha scrubbed and shined each used cabin. Having a great love of the outdoors like her Mommy, Lily willingly 'helped' Samantha with the laundry by handing her clothes pins while they sung their favorite songs.

On days when she could, Mildred would bring Lily to the house to play with William and 'help' Mildred bake or work on her own chores to keep the resort up and running. Just last week Samantha had reluctantly allowed Ben Wright to take Lily with him as he went from cabin to cabin at the resort checking pipes, electricity, restacking firewood, and various other maintenance jobs for the onslaught of winter's hunters. Ben had suggested he could help Samantha by taking Lily off her hands for a couple of hours to be his handyman and companion.

As a hunting and fishing guide plus maintenance man at the resort, Ben was there daily. Quickly he proved to be a friend to Samantha and Lily. The more she was around him, the more she was astonished of how caring he was to others. So even though it was hard to let Lily out of her sight, Samantha allowed her new friend to let Lily 'help' him.

And it was help. Samantha was able to finish her chores in a fraction of the time. Ben was always thinking of others. He was just as attentive to the Stocktons' and the resorts' guests; he wasn't treating her any differently than he treated others. That's just who Ben Wright was.

Kind, caring, considerate, helpful, and of course, handsome.

*Now where did that come from,* Samantha chided herself for daydreaming and focused on hanging the last of the sheets to dry in the cool, crisp air. *Don't you dare even think about a man in any way except as a friend. They are trouble! You and Lily are just fine alone. Besides, home will be in Mississippi again soon enough.*

The self-dialogue continued as Samantha finished up the list of chores for the cabin until it was as welcoming and clean as she could make it for the next men ready to take over.

Pressing a hand to her right side, Samantha fought the stab of pain that had interrupted her activities more than once that day. Nausea was the next culprit as she leaned into the pain and sat on the nearby stump from a fallen tree. Breathing through the discomfort that seemed to increase minute by minute, finally it eased up enough for Samantha to gather the basket so she and Lily could stop for lunch.

Unable to eat, Samantha fixed her a cup of hot tea and sat with Lily while she ate. *I must have eaten something that didn't agree with me. Think I'll stick with crackers and tea for today and tomorrow be as good as new.*

The last cabin on the list was within walking distance. Nearing the brick red, story-book house, Samantha and Lily went inside to get started. Within minutes the pain started up again in her right side with increasing intensity. Unable to ignore it, Samantha sat on the couch and leaned her head in her hands.

"Mama sick?" Lily asked.

"No, baby. I'm okay. How about a story? Get me your books and we will sit and read a bit."

Nausea again assaulted Samantha as she watched Lily toddle over to her basket that was always with them on their cleaning rounds. "Pigs, Mama. Wead pigs!"

*The Three Little Pigs* was one of Lily's favorite stories. Having read it so many times, Samantha had it memorized. "Come sit by me and we will read pigs."

Again the knifing pain caught Samantha off guard.

The sound of an engine approaching sent Lily running for the window. "Ben-Ben-Ben!!"

Trying to stand, Samantha couldn't move from her spot. Sweat beaded on her forehead as another wave of nausea hit her full force.

A gentle knock sounded on the door. "Come in," Samantha weakly called.

Turning the doorknob, Ben stuck his head in and said, "Did I hear a 'come in'?" Looking in the room, Ben saw Samantha sitting with her head in her hands and walked over to her. "You alright, Samantha? You don't look so good."

Moaning slightly, Samantha said, "No, I'm not alright. I am sick I think." Her green tint and sweaty face instinctively sent Ben for the nearest trash can. He thrust it under her chin just in time. "Ohhhh....that hurt!" Grabbing her side, Samantha wretched into the trash can again.

"Mommy sick." Lily looked worried as her mother continued to relieve her stomach of its contents.

Ben went to the bathroom for a wet washcloth and brought it to her. Gently he held back her hair and bathed her face. "Sammie, where do you hurt? Is it your stomach?"

"No, it's my right side. It hurts very...." Unbidden, tears ran down both cheeks.

"Okay. Lie back on the couch. I'm going to take Lily to Mildred then get you to a doctor." Instantly Ben began gathering Lily's things.

Protesting, Samantha tried to stop him. "Ben, it's just a bug or something. I'll be okay in a minute. You go. I'm okay now—ohhhh!" Again she grabbed her side.

"Don't move, Samantha. I'll be right back."

Within what seemed like seconds, Ben raced back to her side. "Mildred will keep Lily and she insisted I take you to see the doctor. No arguing!" Retrieving the washcloth, trash can, and a bent over Samantha, Ben guided her to his waiting truck. "Okay, be careful getting in. Keep this trash can handy. It's going to be ok, I promise."

Fear and near panic clutched her chest at the thought of being sick and in a man's truck who was taking her to God-only-knew-where. "Ben, wait—" Pain silenced her protests as he got in the driver's seat and took the shortest route to town.

Glancing over at her, Ben watched as Samantha's eyes rolled back in her head and she fell against the door. She had passed out. Bypassing the doctor's office, he drove the next block over to the hospital. Shaking her shoulder, Ben couldn't rouse the sick woman. "Samantha! Sammie!"

Tires squealing to a stop, Ben jumped out of his truck, ran to Samantha's door and flung it open. Lifting her from the seat, he walked as quickly as he dared into the emergency room. The sight of a limp girl in a man's arms caused the medical staff to spring into action.

All he was able to choke out when asked what was wrong with her was, "It's her right side. She's in a lot of pain." One nurse directed him to a waiting room with a promise to update him as soon as possible on her condition while the rest whisked Samantha out of sight.

Thankfully the waiting room was empty at the moment so Benjamin Wright took full advantage of the open, secluded space. Pacing, he prayed aloud. "God, please be with Samantha. Please, God. She needs you right now. She's so sick and helpless. Help the doctors find out what's wrong and get her well fast. Please God. She's so innocent and alone. Samantha and Lily need Your help in the worst kind of way. Be with her….I love her, God. I need her to be okay."

Like he had run into a plate-glass window, Ben stopped in his tracks as the words he had just prayed aloud rang in his ears. *I love her, God. I need her to be okay.*

Knees wobbly from the stress of the last half hour, Ben sat in the closest chair. Running his hands through his hair, he then covered his face and sat silent and still for a minute as the words bounced around in his heart and mind.

*I love her? This girl I barely know? How and when? God, help me. I can't get too attached here….but I can't deny that I care for her and Lily. Be with her now. Help me see the truth about my feelings and not be an idiot with my heart and hers. Heal her, please.*

Again he paced. The smell of freshly brewed coffee reached his nose. Ben headed toward the smell as his stomach reminded him he had missed lunch. Around the corner was a coffee pot and a box of half-day old doughnuts. That would have to do. Quickly pouring a cup of the black brew, Ben grabbed two doughnuts and returned to the waiting room for any news from the doctor.

Within seconds, a doctor in a white coat carrying a clipboard approached him. "Sir, did you bring in a woman who was unconscious with pain in her right side?"

"Yes, I did. Is she okay? Can I see her?"

The doctor's coat had the name *Doctor Harris* stitched in black over his heart. "What is your name and relationship to the patient?"

"I'm Ben Wright, a friend and co-worker."

Doctor Harris scribbled on the clipboard. "Can you tell me the patient's name and age? Anything else you know about her? Medical history? Allergies?"

The reality that he truly knew next to nothing about Samantha Owens hit home. "Uh….her name is Samantha Owens. I honestly don't know her age or medical history. She's a mother of a two-year-old daughter who moved to Wisconsin in August so, no, I have very little helpful information."

"How can I contact her next of kin?"

"I have no idea. Doctor Harris, why do you need her next of kin? She just had some pain in her right side—"

Holding up his hand to interrupt Ben, the doctor replied, "Sir, this is very serious. She needs surgery. She's unconscious still with occasional wakeful though confused moments. She's very sick. I think it is her appendix and the sooner I get it out, the better. Ms. Owens is unable to consent to surgery on her own but it must be done immediately. Now, I need someone to sign for surgery. Can that be you if there is no next of kin to contact? There must be someone, if possible, to consent or at the very least acknowledge responsibility for the patient and her procedure."

Stunned, Ben held out his hand for the clipboard. "I will sign for surgery." Quickly Ben scrawled his name on the line.

"I will have an update for you as soon as I know anything. Will you be here?"

"I won't leave this spot, Doctor."

With that, the grim-faced Doctor Harris turned on his heels and rushed away from Ben leaving him alone in the waiting room to face his fears and doubts about signing his name to a document with two seconds to think about his decision. Inhaling deep breaths, he focused on trying to calm down. *What have I just done? I should have called Mildred first to see if there were next of kin to contact. Oh, God! I pray that was the best decision.*

Spotting a telephone in the waiting area, Ben grabbed for it as he would have a lifesaver. Quickly dialing Mildred's number, she answered almost immediately. "Mildred, it's Ben. They just took Samantha back for surgery. The doctor thinks it is her appendix."

"Ben, oh my goodness! I'm so glad you took her in. That could be very dangerous if it ruptured. You did well, Son. What else do you know? Are you staying there?"

"Yes, I am staying. Unless you need me to come back for Lily. The doctor had me sign for surgery because Samantha wasn't able to. She's in and out of consciousness. He asked for next of kin. I didn't know of anyone. Do you? But someone had to sign. So I did. I hope I did the right thing, Mildred—"

"Ben, stop! You did right. And no, there's no next of kin who would need contacting at this point. Samantha can make that decision later. You did the right thing so don't worry. Lily is just fine here. Stay as long as you need to. Call me after surgery when you have an update on our girl."

"I will, Mildred. And thanks. I'll call soon."

Ben hung up the receiver with Mildred's last words resonating in his chest.

*Our girl.*
He wasn't the only one attached to the mysterious woman and her daughter. Mildred cared for her too.
But not as much as he did.

# chapter 28

The next few hours Ben spent in prayer and reflection. And he realized one thing.

He loved her.

Looking back over the last two months since Samantha Owens had invaded his world, Ben had been content to work out his days as hunting and fishing guide with maintenance work on the list for the Stockton's resort. Each day was filled with different duties and challenges, all of which he enjoyed immensely.

But since August, Ben's daily routine had been altered. Now it involved checking in on two strawberry blonds with the prettiest, purple eyes he had ever seen. Unconsciously Ben had added the job of 'protector' and 'overseer' to his list. Faithfully his truck would turn down the path where Samantha would be working. Ben would take care of any jobs near her that needed to be done then carry on about his day after he had seen she was safe and going about her daily tasks.

And now, here he was sitting in an emergency waiting room hoping she was going to make it. That the surgery would fix her. That she would be okay in a few days and he would be dropping by to replenish firewood while she hung sheets in the yard.

But would Samantha be alright? He couldn't get the image of her lying limply in his arms looking as if death had stolen her from him within a split second.

The sound of shoes squeaking on the polished floors startled Ben out of his musings. Looking up, he saw Doctor Harris approaching. Quickly standing, Ben met him halfway to get any news on Samantha.

"How is she, Doctor? Can I see her?"

Breathing heavily, the doctor hesitated. "You saved her life, young man. If you had waited another hour, she probably wouldn't have made it."

Ben bent over his knees and placed his hands on his thighs expelling his pent up breath.

"She's not awake yet, but you can sit with her if you like. I will come explain things later when she wakes up. The girl needs rest. Follow me."

Not having to be told twice, Ben followed the doctor to Samantha's room. "She should wake soon, in an hour or so. Let her sleep until the anesthesia wears off. Then we will go over her surgery."

Nodding mutely, Ben could only stare at Samantha. Lying pale and unmoving with sheets pulled up to her chin, her face matched the stiff white sheets. Her mass of red hair was in a heap on her pillow. Tentatively, Ben pulled a chair up near her and sat silently staring at her face for several minutes.

Yes, he loved her. He knew it without a doubt. He loved Samantha.

A nurse came in to check on her. She uncovered one of Samantha's arms to check her blood pressure then simply replied, "Good."

"When will she wake up?" Ben's voice sounded small even to his own hearing.

"Not sure. But you let me know as soon as she does. I'm just down the hall at the nurse's desk if you need anything. Your wife will be fine, sir. She needs rest for now."

Ben opened his mouth to correct the nurse but she was already gone before he uttered a sound. Rubbing his face with both hands, Ben sat motionless for a while. Hearing the sheets rustle, he looked up as Samantha moved her legs a bit. Reaching for her exposed hand, he tenderly held it in his warm one. She stirred some more then stilled again.

Ben couldn't let go. So he sat and held on to her small hand wishing her to wake up and look at him. Before long, she did just that.

Stirring slightly, Samantha moaned softly. "Waylon—Way!" She spoke hoarsely through parched lips. "Mama, get Daddy. I need....Waylon."

Speaking softly to her, Ben tried to calm her as she continued to stir in the bed. "Samantha, it's okay. It's Ben. I'm with you."

Again she stilled. Another fifteen minutes ticked off on the wall clock.

A little louder, Samantha spoke, "No....Waylon, no. Get away....Daddy!"

"Samantha, you're okay. It's Ben. Can you hear me? No one is going to hurt you. You're okay." Ben stroked the back of her hand and pushed her hair from her face.

Slowly, Samantha tried several times to open her eyes. Finally she could crack them open with effort. Ben could tell she was struggling to focus on the room, his face, her whereabouts. She croaked out the next words. "Where's Lily? Where's my daughter?" Panic filled her face.

"Samantha, look at me. It's Ben Wright. Lily is with Mildred. She's playing with Willie. Lily is fine. Samantha, can you hear me?" Ben continued to rub her hand until she could focus on him.

"Ben?? Where am I? I don't feel so good. Something's wrong with me...."

"Sammie, you were very sick, remember? I found you throwing up and in pain. Then I took Lily to Mildred and brought you to the hospital. Do you remember?"

Surprisingly, Samantha looked down at her hand in his and didn't pull away. "Yes—I remember being sick. But Lily's safe? Mildred has her?"

Knowing this was the most important thing to her, he quickly reassured Samantha, "Yes, Lily's with Mildred and William. She's just fine. I promise. Now you need to rest and get well so you can go home and see your daughter."

Raising her head off the pillow, Samantha tried to get up. "Help me up. I need to get out of here. Lily needs me."

Placing a firm hand on her shoulder, Ben gently pushed her back to the pillow as she winced in pain. "Young lady, you're not going anywhere. Listen to me. You had to have surgery. That's why you feel so rotten right now. The doctor will be in here soon to explain. I'm staying right here with you until you can leave, okay?"

"Wait....surgery? What?"

Doctor Harris entered just at the right moment. "Well, little lady, it's good to see you awake. Better than when this man brought you in to me in his arms. You owe him. He saved your life, Ms. Owens."

Frowning, Samantha looked at Ben and then Doctor Harris. "What do you mean? Saved my life? I only have a stomach bug...."

"I wish it had been that simple. You had much more than a bug." Doctor Harris pulled the extra chair up to her bedside stalling a minute.

"What was wrong, Doctor Harris?" Ben wanted to know.

"Samantha had to have a hysterectomy. I thought you had appendicitis but when my team and I got in there we found more than that. Samantha, are you comfortable with me explaining this in the presence of your friend?"

"I guess so." Glancing at Ben, he quickly nodded his head indicating for the doctor to carry on.

"Your right ovary was the size of a grapefruit and about to burst. I had to remove it and your other female organs. Neither ovary was healthy so I did what was best in this condition and did a complete hysterectomy. Otherwise you would have had a repeat surgery within months."

Samantha tried to sit up again but pain forced her back on the pillow. "I'm sorry....a hysterectomy? What does that mean?"

"Simply put, it saved your life. But....you won't be able to have children ever again. I'm sorry Ms. Owens, but there was no other choice."

Ben interrupted. "You didn't explain that to me, Doctor Harris. You said her appendix needed removing. I didn't sign for that decision."

Samantha's face twisted in confusion.

Doctor Harris explained further. "I had to have someone's consent for surgery, Samantha, and you were unconscious. There was no next of kin to contact according to Mr. Wright. He signed for surgery. I did what needed to be done to save your life. I'm sorry, but you were very, very sick. The right decision was made today or your little girl would be motherless."

Lying silent for a minute trying to take it all in, Samantha finally responded. "Thank you, Doctor. So now what?"

"Rest for at least six weeks. Bed rest for the first three. Light activity for the last three. I will see you in a few days and then we will remove stitches after the six weeks are up if all has healed well. You will be fine, Ms. Owens. This room will be home for the first week or so then we will talk about sending you home with someone caring for you. Eat. Drink. Rest. That's your prescription. I will talk to you soon." With that, he was gone.

Pulling her hand from Ben's, Samantha covered her face for a moment hoping to block out this event. "I can't believe this....surgery....and now—"

"Samantha, I'm so sorry. I only thought you were having your appendix removed according to what Doctor Harris told me. Please...." Ben broke off there not knowing how to even finish the sentence. A weight of responsibility so heavy fell on Ben, he felt as if he would be crushed under its mass. Standing to his feet, Ben said, "I need to call Mildred and let her know you are alright. If you want I will come back and sit with you. Or if you prefer, I can leave; I would understand."

Shaking her head wordlessly, Samantha turned her face to the wall.

"Ben, you go back in that room and ask her who Waylon is! We have to know if he should be contacted. See if we need to call her parents too. Do you want me to come talk to her?" Mildred was trying to convince him to do what Ben knew was inevitable.

"No, Mildred. You take care of Lily. I will handle things here."

Walking to Samantha's room, Ben felt the weight of the world on his shoulders. He both wanted answers yet was afraid to hear them. He had to do this. *God, help me,* he silently prayed.

Sipping a glass of apple juice, Samantha looked up as Ben entered.

"Is it okay?" Sheepishly, Ben asked her permission before assuming Samantha wanted him there.

"Ben, sit, please. Yes, it's okay for you to be here."

"Sammie, we need to talk. I need to ask you some questions."

Nodding her assent, Ben began with the dreaded conversation, struggling with the idea of prying into Samantha's life since he had known her for such a short time. But the circumstances left him little choice. "Can you tell me who Waylon is? You cried out for him after surgery. Do I need to call him and let him know you had surgery? What about your Mom and Dad? You asked for them too."

Her face paled at the mention of Waylon's name. Tears pooled in Samantha's eyes and slid silently down her white cheeks. Not bothering to wipe them, she sat as they flowed unchecked. "Waylon is my—*was* my husband. I got a letter last week that our divorce is final." Ben handed her a tissue. Wiping her face and blowing her nose, Samantha then continued. "I will let my parents know later what happened. Thanks, but no, you don't need to contact them."

Samantha continued, "Waylon was a drunk, and a mean one. He wasn't always that way – or I didn't think he was. He used to....I was scared for Lily, for my whole family. We had to leave Mississippi, and go somewhere he couldn't find us. My friend that I used to work with back in Mississippi is Mildred's niece. She was the one who helped me escape, who got me a job with the Stockton's and a safe place for Lily and I to live."

Relieved that Ben knew the truth, Samantha couldn't help feeling ashamed and once again, so vulnerable. What would Ben think of her? Between the revelation of her mysterious past and the fact that she was now totally helpless and in need of care, Ben might want her to go back to Mississippi so her parents could take care of her.

Samantha finally found the courage to look at Ben, desperately trying to read his thoughts.

Quietly Ben asked the burning question. "Will you go back? When you think it's safe?"

"I honestly don't know. I just don't know what to do."

Reaching for her hand, Ben looked in her eyes. "Samantha, can you ever forgive me?"

"Forgive you? Forgive you for what, Ben?"

"For signing for the surgery. I didn't know...." He ducked his head but still clung to Samantha's hand.

"Look at me, Ben. How could I ever hold that against you? You saved my life according to the doctor. I am still here for Lily because of you. I will always be indebted to you for that! But can you still look at me the same way, knowing about my past – and my future?"

Sighing deeply, Ben exclaimed, "Sammie, I am just so relieved you are okay. I was so worried. Worried about you, worried I had done the wrong thing. I didn't want you to hate me."

Squeezing his hand with the last bit of strength she had, Samantha then released it, liking the feel of the source of comfort and warmth in this man. Trying to hold her eyes open, Samantha whispered, "How could I hate you? You are a good man, Ben Wright. Good men are hard to come by."

And then she surrendered to sleep.

# chapter 29

*Thanksgiving, 1946*

Samantha sat at the table in Mildred's kitchen forming rolls from the mound of yeasty dough. Finally out of bed, stitches removed, and a clear bill of health from Doctor Harris, she was overwhelmed with gratitude to perform the simple task before her.

"Dear, how are you doing? Any discomfort? Is that too much for you?" Mildred doted over Samantha like she was her very own daughter.

Laughing light-heartedly, Samantha replied, "Mildred, this is the best medicine for me right here. Making rolls in your kitchen, feeling almost normal again, with Thanksgiving to look forward to."

Shoving the image of her Mama's golden brown turkey and cornbread dressing from her mind, Samantha focused on the upcoming northern Thanksgiving dishes they would feast on that evening. Mildred had white bread dressing and pheasants in the oven, neither of which Samantha had heard of nor tasted before. Instead of pumpkin pie, there was wild berry pie for dessert. Determined to enjoy the difference in cultures from the north to the south, Samantha focused on the beautiful blessings in front of her.

Busting through the side door with an arm load of wood, Ben stooped to kiss Lily on the cheek as he stoked the fire in the fireplace. Whistling happily, Ben entered the kitchen and quickly planted a kiss on Mildred's cheek as well and then one on Samantha's unsuspecting face.

"You're in a good mood, Sir. Now get in here and make your famous gravy, Ben. Robert's about to wither away to nothing at the looks of things. He went to cut down a tree so we can decorate it tonight. I've got popcorn and cranberries so you all keep your evening free. There's work to be done and we can't break tradition. Samantha, as soon as the last Thanksgiving dinner plate is washed and put away, we put the tree up and string popcorn and cranberries. Will you help us this year?" Mildred looked like a schoolgirl bursting with excitement.

Laughter escaped Samantha's lips. "Of course, I will. There's nothing else on my calendar tonight." She reached a hand up and touched the spot on her face where Ben had lightly kissed her. She shouldn't make too much out of it since he had soundly kissed Mildred and Lily. Still her cheek tingled just at the thought of his lips on her face.

"Samantha....earth to Sammie....can you hear me? You look completely lost over there. I asked you how the rolls were coming and if you needed my help?" Ben's amused look made her blush crimson.

"No—yes, umm....I'm good over here. Almost done." *Get ahold of yourself, Samantha.*

"If you handle that ball of dough anymore, it will be as hard as a brick when it's baked. Let me help you finish, Sammie." Ben pulled a chair up next to her, his leg brushing against Samantha's. Neither of them moved away from the other as they worked to finish up the batch of dough. When their rolls were ready, Samantha stood to carry a pan to the waiting oven.

"You sit, I've got these," Ben protested.

"But I'm tired of sitting. That's all I have done for six weeks. Besides the doctor released me to normal life. No more being spoon-fed and pampered. It's time to get back to normal."

"Okay, smarty pants. No more sitting, huh? Then how about we take a walk? Go for a run? Dance? What will it be? Your pleasure." Ben stood with his hands outstretched awaiting her answer.

When she was lost for words, he took the pan of rolls from Samantha, reached for her hand and twirled her in a simple dance step. She laughed as Ben spun her again and brought her into a couple's dancing pose. Humming *Would You Like to Swing on a Star*, he led her in a few dance steps. "Not bad for a patient."

"Oh, you two get out of my kitchen and let me cook or we will never eat our Thanksgiving Dinner. You have half an hour to dance all you want and then we eat." Mildred waved them out while she finished up.

Not sure what just happened, Ben grabbed Samantha's hand and pulled her towards the front porch. "I want to show you something. Grab your coat and gloves."

"What about Lily?" Samantha hesitated.

"She's fine. Won't even know we are gone. Hurry, we only have thirty minutes or Mildred will send out a search party." Ben threw on his coat and gloves then helped Samantha into hers.

Putting her gloved hands in her pockets, Samantha looked at Ben. "Ok, Ben Wright. Where are we going?"

Looping his arm in hers, Ben led the way. He liked the fact that Samantha didn't pull away from him. The last six weeks had allowed him to gently, carefully, slowly, ease into her life and heart without it being too obvious he hoped. Their relationship had turned quickly into a deep wonderful friendship.

"Follow me and I'll show you something unbelievable."

"*Unbelievable*? This had better be good. You've got my hopes up pretty high." Samantha loved that they were comfortable with each other.

Within a few minutes more of walking, they were nearing Hidden Lake. "Okay, stop here. I want you to trust me. I'm going to blind-fold you with my scarf just for a bit then guide you to the surprise. Trust me?" Ben withdrew a plaid scarf from his pocket and held it out to Samantha.

Turning around she said, "Okay, blind-fold me."

Securely tying the scarf around her eyes, he made a few silly faces to see if she could see anything. When she didn't laugh, he said, "Take my hand and trust me. I won't let you trip or fall. I promise. It will take us about a minute to get to the spot."

A sense of peace settled over her. She was walking blindly by a man who promised to protect her. Promised to show her something that was going to make her happy. A man who guided her and held her hand tightly. All of this felt so foreign but so right all at the same time.

"Almost there. A few more steps." Ben continued to lead her.

Samantha could hear the lake very close by. The leaves overhead stirred in the trees sounding like they were clapping for her, cheering her on.

"Okay, stop. I'm going to take the blind-fold off now." Gently he reached around her and untied the scarf from Samantha's face.

She slowly opened her eyes, intrigued at his surprise. Instantly the darkness of the inside of the scarf was transformed. Before her eyes was a myriad of colors she had never seen in such vibrant hues. Across the lake on the opposite shoreline stood stately trees of so many varieties and colors it took her breath away. Reaching both hands to her mouth, Samantha gasped and stood speechless. The late autumn colors were breath-taking. Golden yellow birches, dark green junipers, orange sugar maples, and nutty brown oaks all vied for her attention. To Samantha's delight, this beauty was perfectly reflected in the still waters of the lake giving her a double view of the trees' magnificence.

She simply had no words to utter. It was the most gorgeous sight she had ever seen.

Ben broke the silence. "Autumn was mild enough this year that the trees turned colors later and held on to their leaves longer. I thought you would like it, Sammie."

Lowering her hands, she finally could speak. "This is the most glorious, beautiful thing I have ever laid eyes on. Ben, thank you!" She flung her arms around his neck and gave him a long hug.

"Thank *you*. Wow, if I had known this would be the response I would get, I would have shown this to you days ago!"

Samantha pulled back from the hug and looked into his eyes. "I have never had anyone show me something so beautiful before. This will stay with me even after every tree has dropped its leaves." She turned back to the trees and stared longer. "Unbelievable beauty."

Reaching for her hand, Ben said, "I have learned how much beauty means to you, Samantha. Thank you for letting me help take care of you these past few weeks. I want to bring beauty to your life if you will let me."

Smiling shyly, she ducked her head. "Well you can try, but I don't know how you will ever top this!"

An easy laugh resounded from his chest. "We better get back to Mildred's or she will come looking for us."

Hand in hand the two walked as slowly as they dared back to the waiting Thanksgiving dinner, hearts full with promises of things to come.

# chapter 30

*December 1946*

    The ache in her heart was almost more than Sylvia could bear. She had missed her daughter so very much, her Samantha Jean. And words could hardly describe the constant pain Sylvia endured with her granddaughter so far way. Unable to contain herself another second, the woman tore into the envelope that contained just what her soul longed for, words from her daughter.

    *Dear Mama and Daddy,*
    *Some days I just have to sit and write so that I feel closer to each of you. This is one of those days. I miss you all terribly, but otherwise I am fine.*
    *Lily is doing well though she asks for everyone by name. I know her little two year old mind doesn't understand all of these big changes in her life, but she seems happy. And she's stopped sucking her thumb so that's an improvement.*
    *Last month had its challenges. I don't want you to be mad at me, but I need to tell you this. I had to have surgery. The doctor thought it was my appendix but it ended up being female problems. He had to do a hysterectomy. Mama, you know what that means. I guess the Good Lord knew one child was enough of a handful for me. It's okay. I could never be happier with another child as I am with Lily Ruth. She's enough for me.*
    *I know I should have told you sooner, but I didn't really feel like writing for several weeks when I was on bedrest. And I don't know if you have a telephone number at your new place or not. Since all worked out just fine, I thought it best to write after I had fully recovered and the doctor gave me a clean bill of health. I know this must be difficult news for you, Mama. I am sorry to have to tell you this way.*
    *I hope you all had a wonderful Thanksgiving. Lily and I spent Thanksgiving with the Stocktons. We ate pheasant and white bread dressing. Can you believe people don't use cornbread in their dressing? And I never knew you could eat a bird that wasn't a turkey for Thanksgiving! It was all so good, but strange. Then the Stocktons and Ben (he works at the resort too) showed me how to string cranberries and popcorn for the Christmas tree. It was such fun! I missed our family traditions and wondered what each of you were doing during the Thanksgiving season.*

*You wouldn't believe how beautiful the autumn colors are here! I have never laid eyes on such a rainbow of fall leaves. It is unbelievable. I wish I could mail you some leaves but I know they would be brown and crunchy if I tried.*

*With Christmas right around the corner, I wanted to let you know I will miss you terribly but will think of you daily. I pray for every one of you by name and can't wait to lay my eyes on your faces again.*

*Pass hugs around from me to you.*

*Merry Christmas to my family!*

*Love,*

*Samantha*

Flinging the letter aside as if it had turned to a snake, Sylvia abruptly stood to her feet, knocking the chair backwards in her effort to get away from her daughter's words. Uttering a never-before spoken curse word, Sylvia clapped a hand over her mouth to stop a string of them from spewing forth. Boiling to a dangerous level in her heaving chest, anger threatened to consume whatever was in the way. Grabbing the broom, Sylvia attacked the floor with a vengeance as she swept the house from corner to corner and silently fumed.

Next she grabbed a scrub brush and bucket from the back porch and filled it with water. On hands and knees, she scrubbed and scoured every speck of dirt from each floor in the house. Two hours passed and Sylvia still scrubbed.

"Sylvie, what are you doing, woman? Trying to scrub the grain off the wood floors?"

Startled, Sylvia tried to rise from her kneeling position but her aching back and knees wouldn't allow it. "Ohhh!" Grabbing her back Sylvia tried again.

Reaching for her elbow, Henry tried to assist his wife. Roughly she shoved his hand away.

"I can get up off the floor, Henry, without you. I've done it all my life." Finally she was able to rise to a standing position.

"How long have you been down there?" He reached to tuck a stray piece of hair back from her face and she jerked away. Hurt clouded Henry's face.

"Obviously long enough to miss getting supper on. Now let me dump this bucket and start dinner." Trying to brush past him, Sylvia impatiently sloshed water on her feet. "Now look what you made me do!"

Taking the bucket and scrub brush from Sylvia, Henry asked, "Where's Claudia, Mel, and Geoffrey?"

"The park."

"Good. Then we are going to have ourselves a talk. Me and you, Syl."

"Henry, I don't want to talk. I need to cook."

Ignoring her, Henry tossed the bucket's contents out the back door and pulled his wife to their bedroom. Once inside, he shut the door and sat her down on the bed. "Now Sylvia, you listen to me and you listen good. I am sick and tired of you working yourself to death around here. What is going on with you? You have to talk to me, honey. I'm worried about you. You're wasting away to nothing. Look at you, all skin and bones. You are either staring off into space or working like a mad woman. Tell me what has you so torn up. Please."

Silence met him head on. For several ticks of the clock, he watched her face go from mad to furious. Still no words were spoken. Henry had had enough of this.

Placing his hands on her shoulders, he bent down eye level with Sylvia. "Talk to me, woman! You are ignoring everyone's concern and closing yourself off from us. Even Geoffrey. Talk to me, Sylvie!"

Last week, Henry had walked into the kitchen just as a pot of water full of potatoes boiled over and onto the stove. Sylvia stood motionless and oblivious to the mess staring out the window not five feet away. Today, she erupted like the starchy boiling water that spilled over the pot's edge.

Rising to her feet, Sylvia shoved Henry in the chest. "It's your fault, Henry! You! You did this to us!! I told you right before Samantha ran off with Waylon that something was wrong, but no! You said she was fine. Then I tried to get you to help her when he started drinking and hurting her, but you said Samantha had to *choose* help! It's your fault! She left because of *you*!"

Grabbing her by the arms, Henry watched her angry pent-up words turn to a flood of tears. Regardless of her protests, he enfolded his wife in his arms against his chest and let her cry until she had no more tears to shed. Finally her sobs turned to quiet sniffling and he released her.

"Sylvia, I did all I could. All Samantha would let me do. I am as upset about this as you are. I can't believe our girls are gone—" Henry's weary voice broke so he stopped to compose himself. "I want them back as much as you do. It's *not* my fault, Sylvia. I *tried*. I swear it." Henry handed her his over-sized bandana to mop her face with.

"I'm sorry, Henry. That was unfair of me. I know you tried. I do. It just feels like we missed something." She stopped and blew her nose. "I'll tell you this....If Waylon Graves ever shows his face here again I will *kill* him with my bare hands, Henry. I *will*! I hate that man! I *hate* him! He can go to hell for all I care! He took my daughter not once, but twice from me, and now my grand baby! I hate him—" Sylvia began shaking with the intense anger she felt. Nostrils flaring, she brought fear to Henry's heart. Never before had he seen her in such a state.

"Sylvia, you're going to kill yourself if you keep this up. That man isn't worth this! I can't stand him either. But, honey....look what's happening. *Hate* is ruining your life. It's robbing you of any good you could have. Hate is stealing you away from me and your family. Even little Geoffie. You *can't* hang onto this hate, Sylvia. You have to forgive him. You have to set yourself free from this hate and forgive the man."

"But what he did was *wrong*, Henry! You should hate him too!"

"Trust me. I did for a long time. You're right; what he did was very, very wrong. I still have to forgive him almost daily. But I can't live my life in a prison of hate for a man who has done our girls and us wrong. I can't. It keeps me in knots and unable to enjoy what I do have. That's what is happening to you, Syl. It is locking you away from us, the ones that love you. You have to choose freedom over this inner prison you're locked up in. It's tearing you up. Don't you see?" Henry drew her to his chest again and felt her breathing return to normal.

"I can't let it go, Henry. It's with me every time I take a breath. It hurts so bad."

"I know it hurts. I'm so sorry. But you have to get rid of the hate. God can do that for you." Holding Sylvia at arm's length, Henry looked into the depths of her soul. "Remember those crab apples we picked last year for your jelly? We had four bushel baskets full. You got your jelly made from two of the baskets and by the time you got to the third basket the next day, they were stinking something fierce. Remember? Right in the very middle, there was one rotten crab apple. And it destroyed all of the ones it touched. We had to throw out half of that basket of apples, all because of that rotten one. Syl, hate is doing that to you. It does it to all of us. If it stays, we rot."

A single humorless laugh escaped her. "I was so mad about those wasted apples. All from a single rotten one. What if I can't get rid of it—this hate? What if it has caused too much damage already?"

"Sylvia, there's no damage so great that God can't undo. It's what He does and who He is. He will heal you. All you have to do is ask." Kissing her forehead, Henry hugged her once more.

"Mind waiting a little longer on dinner? I think I need to go have a talk with God."

"A ham and tomato sandwich will do me just fine. Forget cooking tonight. You take care of your heart. I miss you, Sylvia. I want my wife back. Now you go pray and I will fix sandwiches for supper. Deal?"

"You've got yourself a deal, Henry."

While Henry was slicing tomatoes and chunks of ham, he did all he knew to do at that moment. He prayed while he watched his hurting wife pace beneath the willow tree's branches. Henry knew she was walking out her prayers, as he called it. He knew she was wrestling with letting it go too.

Pouring his heart out to God, the man prayed for his wife and daughter. He pled for Lily and Sammie-girl's safety. He begged God for answers.

For resolution.

For justice.

~~~~~~~~~

"You is nice, Ben." Lily batted her eyelashes at the man. He had brought her a new story book. It told the story of a little squirrel who lived in a tall tree with his family. They ate berries right off the bushes and drank water from giant leaves. She loved the colorful pictures and animated woodland creatures. "Wead again. Wead skwolls."

*Squirrels* was too difficult for the little girl to say so she did her best.

"Lily, how about you tell Ben good night. It's your bedtime."

"Skwolls, Mommy!"

Kissing her lightly on the top of her head, Ben lifted Lily into his arms. "Better mind your Mommy, right? I promise to read squirrels to you tomorrow. How is that?"

Pouting a moment longer, Lily thought about what Ben said. "Okay. Night-night, Ben."

"I'll be right back. Let me tuck Lily in." Samantha gathered her yawning daughter from Ben's arms.

"Mind if I put on a pot of coffee?"

"Sounds good. Thanks."

Samantha had decided weeks ago that she may as well give up on keeping Ben Wright at arm's length. It was impossible. She liked the man. She *really* liked him. And she could get used to this.

Returning from tucking Lily in bed, she found Ben on his knees stoking the fire for her comfort. Coffee brewing filled the little room with its aroma. He looked so comfortable in her cabin and Samantha loved having him there. Each night he came by, it was more difficult to watch him leave when the time came for him to go.

"Want some chocolate cake? Mildred sent some home last night with us and I have just enough for two."

"Perfect." Standing from the fireplace, Ben came to help Samantha get out plates for cake and coffee cups. They moved around the miniscule kitchen with ease, occasionally bumping into each other.

"It's kind of cramped in here for two, huh?" Samantha said.

Both turned to move to another spot out of the other's way and collided. Laughing easily, Ben instantly wrapped Samantha in a gentle hug and pulled her close. Inhaling her shampoo, he whispered close to her ear. "I like it this way."

Samantha didn't answer him. Instead she gently eased out of his embrace and turned to pour coffee. Getting her signal, Ben fixed plates of cake. "Want to eat by the fire?"

"Sure." Samantha withdrew into herself even further.

Troubled, Ben let her settle on the couch while they ate quietly for a minute. "I'm not one to beat around the bush, Sammie. So....I'm sorry if I made you uncomfortable in the kitchen. I shouldn't have."

Taking her time to respond, Samantha replied, "I'm not very good at beating around the bush either. I prefer honesty and openness. You did *not* make me uncomfortable. I am just trying to...."

Letting her think through her next words, Ben waited patiently. After a few more minutes, he prodded, "Trying to what? You can tell me."

Glancing at the little end table next to her side of the couch, Samantha silently fingered a collection of 'beautiful things' that sat there. Some were items she had found back home and others were forest trinkets Ben had collected for her when she was sick and recovering. During her bed rest, he checked on her daily and often would come in with a treasure for her collection. Picking up a golden birch leaf, Samantha twirled its stem between her fingers. Taking a deep breath, Samantha continued. "I guess I'm trying to not get too used to you."

Confused, Ben set his empty plate on the table and asked, "Will you explain that?"

"Ben, you hardly know me or anything about me. I know that's my fault because I haven't given you too many details. I like you. I really do. I'm just afraid if you find out more about me, you won't like what you find out. I'm a mess. My past is a mess. And honestly, I don't know how long I will be in Wisconsin. My family is in Mississippi. I miss them so much. My heart's desire is to return when I can. Only you're making that very, very difficult for me to even think about." Nervously, Samantha pushed a wayward strand of hair from her eyes.

"Why don't you let me decide if I like you or not. And I've known from the beginning that you were here temporarily. *And* I plan to continue to make it very, very difficult for you to be away from me." Reaching for her hand, Ben said, "Now how about you start from the beginning and tell me whatever you're comfortable with about Samantha Owens. I've got all night." His green eyes lit up with an endearing twinkle that the firelight set off magically.

Drawn into his kind, warm, gaze, Samantha began her story. The story of Samantha Jean Owens Graves.

Just like Ben, she had all night too.

# chapter 31

*Christmas, 1946*

Mildred's toasty kitchen was filled with the scents of gingerbread men baking, hot apple cider brewing on the back burner, and spicy mincemeat pies cooling on the counter. The ever-present percolator bubbled with the promise of hot, strong coffee while the prized radio blared out crackly tunes that added to the Christmas Eve atmosphere.

"Do 'nother, Mommy!" Clapping her hands together, Lily Ruth watched as Samantha deftly cut out another half dozen gingerbread men and placed them on a baking sheet. Lily and William shared the job of decorating the men with red cinnamon candies and raisins, Lily placing the red buttons down the center of the cookies while William carefully placed raisin eyes and smiles in their correct spot. Occasionally when Lily wasn't looking William would rearrange some of her misplaced cinnamon candies so the buttons lined up in perfect order. Samantha laughed easily at their excitement while she worked to swiftly keep the pans full of brown dough-men for the children to decorate.

William burst into singing with the radio. *"Santa Claus is comin' to town!"*

Constantly imitating everything William did, Lily sang too, though her version was endearingly misconstrued. "Sannie Kwaus is tumm'n a town!"

"That's good, Lily!" Willie was always quick to encourage the girl. Her vocabulary had expounded incredibly since moving to Wisconsin and being around a five year old daily.

Robert entered the kitchen and swiped a few cinnamon candies from the bowl beside Lily and popped them in his mouth. "Lily Ruth, your men look good enough to eat," he teased. Hugging the little girl, he turned to Mildred. "What time is the caroling tonight? I want to have the sleigh ready to go."

"I think everyone will be ready by 6:00. Then afterwards we will have the goodies the kids are working on while you read the Christmas story to us. Sound good, Robert?"

Kissing Mildred on the cheek, Robert said, "Perfect, Mrs. Claus!"

Samantha heard an incessant *bump, bump, bump* coming from the back door off the den. She went to see the cause of the noise and found Ben kicking the door with his boot. Loaded to his chest with firewood, his arms were full and about to overflow.

"Oh, Ben! I'm sorry I didn't hear you sooner. Need some help?"

Entering with his load, Ben unloaded by the fireplace and sat on the hearth to warm up. Strains of *"I'll Be Home for Christmas"* floated in the air around the couple. "Care to sit with me a minute? It's freezing out there. We need to take plenty of extra blankets when we go caroling or we will all turn to snow people. Smells wonderful in the kitchen. What are you baking?"

Samantha stared across the room without answering.

*"Christmas Eve will find me*
*Where the love light gleams*
*I'll be home for Christmas*
*If only in my dreams*
*If only in my dreams...."*

The song came to a close as a single tear dropped from Samantha's lashes.

Standing to his feet, Ben went immediately to her side. Taking her hand he pulled Samantha to the couch. "Sammie, what's wrong? Did something happen?"

Sniffling loudly, she replied, "I-I'm sorry. That song....it made me think of home and my family. Don't get me wrong. I'm happy here. I guess it just hit me. I *won't* be home for Christmas. For some reason, I have kept it in the back of my mind that I would be home before Christmas. Even though I knew down deep I wouldn't, I coaxed myself to believe that."

Drawing her into a gentle hug, Ben simply said, "I'm so sorry. I should have known it would be hard."

Laughing quietly, Samantha sat back. "But the funny thing is, there's not another place I would want to be right now. Tonight. Here with you and the Stocktons making cookies and later going caroling. It's perfect. I apologize for my silliness. Forgive me?"

"How can I forgive you for having honest, heartfelt feelings? Of course you miss home and family. I would too. But it makes me very happy to say you want to be here." Reaching for his handkerchief, Ben dried her tears. "Better?"

Placing a light kiss on his cheek, Samantha whispered, "Much. Thank you for caring."

The remainder of Samantha's Christmas Eve in Wisconsin felt like she was living in a dream. Taking in each detail to savor later, she snuggled closer to Ben Wright on her left while she tucked the plaid wool blankets tighter around her laughing daughter. The hour long sleigh ride and caroling were the perfect way to spend her first Christmas Eve here. Under the canopy of stars that lit the coal black sky, Samantha sang every carol with renewed meaning and gusto.

Just that morning she had read from the book of Luke about the birth of Jesus. Wondering if the sky looked like this one, full of stars and promises, she thought about the shepherds, the angels, and the star in the sky that later guided the wise men to the Christ Child. She wondered if on the night of Jesus' birth everyone could feel the difference in the air because of the Baby's arrival. Tonight she felt an almost tangible difference in the air, thick with promises of good things to come, of life and love.

Noticing a change in herself, Samantha pondered what she was sensing. Something was different. *Good. No, better.* No longer did she feel apprehension and fear. No longer did dread or anxiety follow her around. No longer did a heaviness drape itself over her shoulders wearing her down. Tonight, Samantha noticed she felt light, free, and loved. She relished the peace and security, the anticipation of good and not evil.

And it was beautiful to her soul.

*Thank You, God, for taking my messes and mistakes and turning them into something good. I never dreamed life could be like this. Especially away from my family. I had no idea You could turn things around so quickly. Thank You,* Samantha silently prayed as she gazed into the starry sky.

Ben wrapped his arm around her shoulders and pulled her closer. "Are you warm enough? And how's my Lily?" The deep care and concern for the girls was palpable. The two red-haired girls smiled identically at Ben in affirmation of their comfort and happiness.

Leaning close to Samantha's ear, he whispered, "Is your Christmas a happy one, Samantha?"

"Better than I could have ever dreamed possible. Thanks to you."

"Oh, remind me when we get back to the house, you got a letter in the mail. I left it in my truck to bring in but I forgot to get it after I brought in the wood."

The sleigh pulled into the driveway and unloaded its passengers. Samantha scooped Lily up into her arms and followed Mildred into the warm house.

"Don't take too long with the horses, Robert. We have refreshments and the Christmas story awaiting us." Mildred bustled about the kitchen getting everything just right for the remainder of the evening.

"I'll go get your letter." Ben headed to his truck and quickly returned with the promised mail.

Samantha looked at the envelope. It was from home. But it wasn't her mother's or sisters' handwriting. This was a manly script. Instantly she knew it was from her Daddy. *Why would Daddy write me? He never has before.*

Watching her face, Ben leaned in close. "Why don't you take a minute to read your letter alone? I will help Mildred with the children and whatever she needs in the kitchen."

"Thanks." Quietly, Samantha went down the hall to an empty bedroom. Perching on the quilted bedspread, she slowly opened the letter and withdrew a single sheet of paper.

*My dear Sammie-girl,*

Instantly tears clouded her vision at her father's words. *Oh, Daddy. I miss you so much.* Blinking rapidly, she did her best to clear her eyes.

*I've got some news for you. Waylon's been arrested and put in jail. Sammie, he killed a man. Supposed to be self-defense, I really don't know. It's his word against a dead man's. But he will be in jail for a very, very long time.*

Samantha's hand started trembling. Reality slowly set in as the actions of a man she had chosen to marry hit her full force. Releasing a shaking breath, Samantha continued to read.

*The good news is you and Lily are free to come home and you will be safe. But before you go buy a bus ticket for home, I need to say some things. Things your Mama won't be able to say, so hear me out.*

*I want you home more than anything. But I know the last few years have messed up home for you and left you with a bad taste in your mouth. If Wisconsin and the people there are good to you and Lily, then stay put. Do what's best for you two girls. Think about things, Samantha, before you make any decisions. More than having you back home, I want what's best for you and Lily.*

*Love,*

*Daddy*

Samantha let the tears fall freely. The intensity of her Daddy's love and sacrifice swallowed her whole for several minutes. Folding the letter, she placed it gently back in the envelope then in her pants pocket.

She truly had a lot to think about now. But it would have to wait.

Gingerbread men, coffee, and the Christmas story were calling her name.

And Ben Wright was calling her heart.

# chapter 32

Never could Samantha think of a happier, busier season in her life. Having spent the last two months in a whirlwind of endless mopping, cooking, dusting, sweeping, washing, and mothering, she flopped down on the couch in her cozy cabin exhausted. She had just tucked Lily in for a nap and planned to settle down with a cup of hot tea and a borrowed copy of last month's *Woman's Own* magazine. Mildred was good to send the magazines Samantha's way after she was finished with them.

Pulling a wool blanket over her legs, Samantha perched her tea cup on the table's edge to cool while she glanced at the cover. The picture and words that blazed on the front cover caught her attention. *'May 1947 be a prosperous and happy New Year for you!'*

*Goodness, 1947 already. How does time fly by so quickly,* Samantha mused. She gazed at the male and female cardinals hovering between a couple surrounded in warm coats and scarves walking arm and arm beneath a gently falling snow. The artist's illustration was eye-catching to any reader as it depicted two people full of joy and expectation for the new year ahead.

*This could nearly be a drawing of Ben and me. Makes me wonder what is ahead of us or if I need to make plans to go back home to Mississippi.* Samantha's mind wondered from the magazine to the letter she had shoved way back in the recesses of her thoughts. The letter from her Daddy telling her to do what was best for Lily, to consider what would make them both happy before running home too soon. He was right about one thing. In the few short months in Wisconsin, she had become attached to the people here and this new life of hers. One so very different from life in Mississippi. Samantha knew she needed to write her Daddy back soon with her decision.

Samantha sipped her tea, forgetting the unread magazine as her mind strayed like a kite in the wind-blown sky. For now, she needed to stay put in Wisconsin. For Lily and for herself. Not only did she *need* to stay where she was, she *wanted* to.

And today only served to cement that decision firmly in her heart and mind. Today was February 14th, Valentine's Day, and she had a date tonight with Ben Wright. This was their first official date. Sure they had run errands together, gone to church together, cooked meals, worked, and taken long walks. But this was the first time he had asked her to be his date, his Valentine, as he so sweetly worded it.

And it would be one of the few times Lily wouldn't be with them. Ben had already arranged for Mildred to watch Lily for the evening while they went on their first date.

Glancing at the creamy off-white dress and jacket with lush red-velvet trim, Samantha silently thanked Bernice yet again for the beautiful outfit. Bernice had mailed nearly matching mother and daughter dresses in off-white and red. Lily's was red with white trim, just the opposite of Samantha's with a little hat that tied under the chin. The girls had received the unexpected presents for Christmas and hadn't had a chance to wear them yet. Though a bit too big for Lily, Mildred promised to alter the dress as soon as hunting season had ended and time allowed so the girls would have matching church dresses.

Tonight, Samantha would debut her gorgeous outfit for Ben on their Valentine's date.

Nervousness eased its way into her soul. Along with it came a rush of giddiness just thinking about going on a date with Ben. *Stop it, Silly. You've been a married woman before so there's no reason for first-date jitters. It's not like you've never spent time with a man before.* Sipping the remainder of her tea from the cup, Samantha flipped unseeingly through the pages of the magazine. Finally she gave up all hope of concentrating and glanced at the clock. Two hours until Ben would pick her up.

The contrast between her time spent dating Waylon before they hurriedly married, if you could call that 'dating,' to the evening she and Ben would have together as her first real 'date' with a man didn't go unnoticed with Samantha. This time there was no sneaking around and hiding out, nor was there any guilt associated with her decision. Two things defined her choice to be with Ben, joy and peace, something due to her own making that was lacking most of her life since she had met Waylon Graves. This time would be different.

While Lily snored softly in the next room, Samantha enjoyed the peace and quiet with time to reflect on how different life was now. As she painted her nails, rolled and styled her hair, brushed her dress off for the hundredth time, and retouched her make-up yet again, Samantha was overwhelmed with the wonder of God's grace and mercy. She didn't deserve all of this goodness and beauty. But she determined to never take it for granted and to relish every moment of it.

Finally she donned the gorgeous dress and jacket. Strapping on her shoes, Samantha gathered her purse and lipstick. A knock on the door roused her from her deep thoughts. Knowing she had another quarter of an hour to finish preparing for her date, she peeked out the curtains and was surprised to see Robert Stockton standing on her doorstep.

"Robert! Come in." Samantha held the door for him.

"Samantha, you look stunning. Ben will have the prettiest Valentine in all of Wisconsin as his date tonight." Robert placed a fatherly kiss on her cheek and continued with the reason of his visit. "Your gentleman caller asked me to pick up Lily before he arrives to get you. So, I am here for your daughter."

"Goodness, he thinks of everything. Let me get Lily for you. She just woke up from her nap and will be happy to find out she's going to your house to play with William." Samantha went to gather Lily and her things for her time at the Stocktons' home.

Waving her daughter and Robert off, she returned to the house to wait for Ben. Rechecking her lipstick, Samantha chided herself for worrying over her appearance as if she and Ben had never met before. Within moments another knock sounded at her door causing her heart to skitter like a scared chipmunk.

Placing a steadying hand over her heart, Samantha took a deep breath and released it slowly. Opening the door, she gasped in surprise at what stood before her. There was Ben, face covered by a dozen pink rosebuds wearing a gray suit and pink tie, the color of the flowers. His usual loosely styled hair was slicked back and perfectly in place. Lowering the roses, his gasp matched Samantha's as he took in her beauty. Never had he seen her looking so absolutely gorgeous as she did in that moment.

Each stood in silence until Samantha finally came to her senses. "Hello, Ben. Come in; I'm sorry to leave you standing on the porch." Blushing furiously, she continued, "Those roses are breath-taking! And you look so very handsome….I've never seen you in a suit before."

Ben still hadn't uttered a word. He entered her kitchen and placed the roses in the vase Samantha found. She quickly added water and set them in the center of her dining table. "Well…." Samantha began uncomfortably as she smoothed her hands down her dress.

Finally able to speak, Ben gently placed both hands on her arms and eased them down to Samantha's hands. "Samantha, I don't remember ever being speechless until right now. You look so—so pretty and lovely and…."

Giggling at his discomfort, Samantha planted a quick kiss on his cheek. "Why, thank you, Ben Wright. You look wonderful as well. We've never seen each other so dressed up before except for church clothes."

Regaining his composure, Ben laughed at her comment. "You're right. We are usually in flannel shirts and work pants. You know our entire relationship has been a bit backwards. After six months of meeting you, I finally get to take you out on a real date, just the two of us, dressed up and alone. We've done everything opposite of what most couples do. Usually you dress up and date first, then you get comfortable enough with each other to not have to dress up, then you go on long walks and sleigh rides, and later comes the difficult medical decisions complete with taking care of the bedridden until they recover. Not us. We reversed all of it."

"So true, Ben. Well, if backwards has worked so well for us up until now, let's not change a thing."

"Deal. Ready to go? I assume Robert came for Lily already?"

"Yes, he did. And thank you for thinking of that little detail. So, mystery man, where are we going on our first date? You've left me in the dark for a week."

Wrapping her coat around her shoulders, Ben led Samantha to his truck. "I'm sorry, but this is my only vehicle, but I brought this." With a flourish he opened the passenger side door and produced a stool from the front floor board. Setting it on the ground, he bowed low at the waist, kissed the top of Samantha's hand and replied, "Your carriage awaits, my lady."

Overcome with giggles, Samantha stepped up onto the low stool and into the waiting truck. "Thank you, kind sir."

Before long, Ben directed the truck down a gravel road she had never seen before. Turning into a driveway, Ben shut the engine off in front of a one-story white painted house with black shutters. The house spoke of care and neatness. A few potted evergreens perched on the porch and by the black front door creating a welcoming entrance. The gently curved, smooth, stone path led from the driveway all the way to the three steps that welcomed you to the front porch with a matching black swing for two. Ben exited his side of the truck and came around to Samantha's. He retrieved the stool from the bed of the truck and placed it at Samantha's feet again then helped her to the ground.

"Where are we, Ben? This is beautiful!"

"I hope you won't be disappointed but we are having dinner here and maybe we will go dancing in town later. This is my home."

"*You're* home?"

Leading Samantha to the front door, Ben laughed at her surprise. "Yes. Where did you think I lived? In the woods behind the Stocktons with the bears and squirrels?"

Slapping him playfully on the arm, she responded, "Maybe I did. Honestly, I assumed you lived in town or in a cabin at the resort close to your work like I do. I guess I never gave it much thought. Do you live here alone? Or with your parents or another relative?"

"I promise, we will get to that later. Like I said, you and I obviously do things backwards. So tonight, on our first date after knowing each other six months, I will tell you about me. But first, how about dinner?"

"Sounds great! What restaurant do you have in mind?"

Holding his arm out with a flourish, Ben directed her to a dining room that led to a quaint kitchen. In the kitchen she saw a cloth-covered basket, a green salad, and a steaming dish sitting on the stove. "We are dining at Ben's Kitchen this evening. I hope you aren't disappointed."

"What? You made all of this?" Samantha lifted the foil edge of the casserole dish and discovered a piping hot lasagna underneath. Inhaling deeply, she peeked under the cloth and found crusty French bread already buttered and still warm. "Who cooked this for us? This looks incredible!"

Wrapping both arms around her waist, Ben pulled Samantha in close. "Your mystery man is full of surprises. *I* cooked all of this. Only I can't take credit for dessert. Mildred contributed to that part of our meal." He kissed her lightly on the nose and reluctantly released her.

"You did all of this for me?"

"Yes. Now are we going to gawk at it or eat? I haven't had anything all day and I'm starving! Here's the plates and glasses for drinks. I'll be right back." Leaving her in the kitchen, Ben quickly went into the dining room to light the tall red candles on brass candlesticks. He checked to make sure the salt and pepper shakers were full.

In the kitchen, Ben retrieved a chilled bottle of wine from the refrigerator and poured them each a glass. "Ready to eat?"

"Absolutely." Samantha placed a serving of the lasagna on each of their plates while Ben added bread and salad. She followed him into the candle lit dining room. "It's perfect, Ben! You've put so much thought into this meal."

"I won't deny that. I wanted it to be special. Since we've waited six months for this." He laughed easily with her as they ate and talked casually of their day. Ben would touch Samantha on the arm as he spoke to her or offered her more bread.

Nothing felt more right and complete to her. Never had she felt so cherished and cared for, except for when her Daddy was around. But another man had never made her feel so wonderfully, perfectly at home.

The two quickly washed the dishes and put away the leftover food. Coffee brewed while they worked. Neither was in a rush to speed the evening along. Just being together without interruption was heavenly.

"Want to sit in the living room by the fire while our dinner settles?"

"Sure. And I want to hear all about you, this house, and whatever else you want to tell me."

Removing her shoes, Samantha tucked her feet under her skirt and leaned against the couch's cushions. Coffee in hand, she settled in beside Ben facing him while they talked.

Sipping his coffee in silence, Ben turned to face Samantha. "So you want to hear the Ben Wright story? Okay. Where should I start? There's not a lot to tell really. I'm am from Wisconsin, have lived here my entire life with my family. When I was little, my parents owned and operated a restaurant. Mostly home style cooking. Thus my incredible cooking abilities." He paused and laughed at his own joke. A sadness passed over his face before he continued. "My mother and father both could cook anything you could name. They taught me everything they knew about cooking and running a restaurant. I basically grew up in an over-sized kitchen wearing an apron with a menu in hand. I loved people and food so it was a happy childhood." Again he paused in this story. "More coffee? I need a refill."

"No, I'm fine." Samantha watched his retreating back as Ben went for a refill.

Quickly he returned. "This is the part of my story I don't like to tell, so bear with me."

Samantha reached a hand over to his and gave it a squeeze. "I don't want to pressure you, Ben, if you would rather talk about something else."

"You were kind enough to tell me about you so I want to do the same." Clearing his throat, Ben continued. "When I was fifteen, my parents left me to manage the restaurant after the lunch rush. They needed to go to town for some grocery items for that evening's dinner menu. The only stragglers that came in after lunch were patrons wanting coffee and pie or a soda. Nothing I couldn't handle. Four o'clock rolled around and....my parents weren't back. I got concerned because we always began dinner preparations then and the evening crew had already come in to start the prep work. Five o'clock and still they didn't show. I panicked. The employees began panicking. Patrons started filtering in for dinner. Finally at six o'clock I knew something was wrong. They never would have stayed gone so long without having car trouble or—" Ben sipped his coffee a minute in silence.

Samantha's gut tightened at what he would say next.

"The employees stayed at the restaurant to handle the dinner crowd and I went to the police station. I knew them all by name since they were regulars at our restaurant. When I ran in the station, they knew something was wrong. I told them what had happened and immediately a patrol car was sent on Mom and Dad's route. The police knew....that my parents should have come back for the dinner rush. They tried to stay calm in front of me but I could read it in their eyes. One officer took me to my grandmother's house to wait for them to bring back any news. Around ten that night they showed up. Mom and Dad were gone. Their car had somehow not made it around a sharp bend in the road and careened over a steep hill. They were both dead when the police arrived. There was nothing anyone could do at that point." Twirling his empty coffee cup in his hand, Ben glanced up at Samantha. "I know this wasn't the best choice of nights to spill my past on you, but we really haven't had much time to sit alone like this and talk."

"I'm so sorry you had to go through the death of your parents. I can't imagine losing them both. And I'm sorry to upset you by having you tell me about yourself. I feel bad that I asked."

Placing a hand on her arm, Ben stopped her flow of words. "Sammie, this is who I am. I can't separate my past from me anymore than you could separate yours from who you are . God has been good to heal me and bring wonderful people in my life who have helped along the way. It's okay. I want to finish the rest of my story."

Taking a deep breath, he continued. "After the death of my parents, I moved in with my grandparents and finished high school. It was too difficult for me to continue working at the restaurant so I found a job with the Stocktons on weekends and it eventually turned into the job I have now. They have played a huge part in my healing. I wouldn't be where I am today without them. My grandparents did their best. They were hurting just as much as I was. My parents willed the restaurant to me so when I turned eighteen, I decided to sell it. And I bought this house. For a while I toyed with moving away from the area and all of the memories but I didn't want to leave the two people who felt like parents to me. So here I am…..sitting across from the lovely Samantha Owens….in my own home….and loving the feeling of having you here by my side. That's the part of my story I love. You. And Lily. If I had moved away from here, I would never have met you." Ben reached across the couch and pulled her to him. They hugged for a moment before either spoke.

"Ben, I can't imagine my life at this stage without you. Thank you for staying. I know I wasn't in the picture then, but thank you for not leaving this area." Pulling away from him, she looked into Ben's eyes. "So are we still doing things backwards in this relationship?"

Laughing lightly, Ben replied, "Sure, why not? It's worked well so far."

Boldly, Samantha wrapped her arms around Ben's neck and planted soft lips on his unsuspecting ones. She kissed him lightly again, only this time he was prepared. Easing away, she looked at the handsome man in front of her. "I hope that was okay, Ben Wright."

"It was more than okay, Samantha Owens. I've wanted to do that since…...let me think….August! So does that mean you might stay around for a little while longer?"

"Definitely! I'm not going anywhere right now. I won't promise that I'll never go home to see my family, but right now, I am here. With you."

Pulling her to her feet, Ben kissed her first this time. Lost in each other's embrace and kiss, Samantha wanted to stay this way forever. Protected, safe, loved.

Stepping back to look in her eyes, a serious look crossed Ben's face. "Can I tell you the truth about something?"

"Of course." A swirl of fear darkened the special moment. Samantha fought to push it away.

"Sammie, I need you to know something. I don't want to pretend or act like it's not real or ignore my feelings for you. I hope that's okay. Remember how we both decided to be open and honest? Well, I have to do just that. I need you to know this….I love you." At the look of shock on her face, he gently laughed and brought his hand to her face. "Samantha, I *love* you. I've known it since the day I carried you limp into the hospital. I don't want to live another day without you knowing that. *I love you*, and I want to be with you for the rest of my life. I want to be the one to love you every day we have together whether that's fifty days or fifty years. I want to be the one."

A tear streaked down her face. Those were the sweetest words Samantha had ever heard. "Ben, I love you too. And I've know it for a while myself. Thank you for telling me so I could have the courage to be honest with you. You love me! That's the most beautiful thing I have ever heard in my life." Another moment of silence followed. Samantha lay her head on Ben's chest and listened to his heart beat. She couldn't believe what he had just told her. He *loved* her and wanted to spend his life with *her*.

Reality struck her immediately.

"Wait….Ben, if you want to be with me for the rest of your life, does this mean you want to marry me? Does this mean we should get marr—" Samantha stopped short of finishing her sentence.

Laughter erupted from Ben like a free-flowing well. "In the spirit of doing things backwards, I would say you just proposed to me, Samantha!"

"What!! No, I didn't! I just meant that if you wanted to spend your life with me that it must mean that we—you—I mean, I should…."

"Oh, yes! That's definitely a marriage proposal, though backwards in nature. And I accept. I *will* marry you, Samantha Owens."

Overcome with giddy joy, Samantha collapsed into the most beautiful heap of laughter Ben had ever seen. Unable to control herself, she laughed until tears ran down her cheeks. This time they were tears of pure joy with the reality that she indeed had proposed to the man she loved with all of her heart.

# chapter 33

*March 1, 1947*

Two weeks had scarcely passed since Samantha had "proposed" to Ben, as he liked to refer to it. Their Valentine's Day, their first date, had been memorable at least. And now Samantha stood in the little church's Sunday school room just off the stain-glass shrouded sanctuary and straightened her wedding veil; actually it was Mildred Stockton's veil.

"Oh, honey! You look radiant!" Unable to stop the flow of constant words, Mildred prattled on adding further exclamations and comments that linked to the last thirty minutes of her incessant chatter. Samantha only smiled as the older woman continued to fuss and fret over her dress, veil, and flowers. Lily had grown tired of the woman's adjusting of bows and collars and found something to amuse herself with while she watched her Mommy and Mildred carry on in a flurry. "This color of blue in these flowers brings out your eyes beautifully, Sammie! I'm so honored you and Ben chose Robert and I to stand up with you when you say your vows. I know you wish your family was here, but we will have to do. Oh, let me see your skirt. There's a bit of lint on the back." Mildred brushed at the back of Samantha's skirt for a moment.

Laughing easily, Samantha chided the woman. "Mildred, you would think your own daughter was getting married the way you are carrying on. And yes, you and Robert will more than 'do' as my attendants. You have taken me and Lily in as your own and I wouldn't have it any other way if my own family couldn't be here. But let's not dwell on that. I've shed my tears and that's all there is to do about it." She burst into a fit of giggles again.

"What's so funny?" Mildred questioned as she was unable to contain her own smile.

"I can't believe that just two weeks ago Ben and I were on our first date, then I proposed to him as he says, and in such a short time you helped me put together my wedding day! I never could have dreamed this up in a million years when I left home…..it's all happened so fast and so perfectly. I just know God is in this, Mildred." Samantha turned to face the older woman as Mildred spun her around to adjust her hair under the veil.

"Samantha, you look stunning! Ben will not be able to wait until the *I do's* to whisk you out of here. We have two minutes, girls. Lily, let me see your dress, sweetie. Oh, you look so pretty in your matching wedding dresses!" Mildred stood back to admire Samantha and Lily in their coordinating dresses. She had talked Samantha into letting her buy the dresses for the special day. Samantha's was a subtle pale blue suit that made her look like a violet ready to bloom. A few shades darker, Lily wore a matching dress with a sweater jacket with hand-embroidered pale blue flowers across the shoulders that matched her Mommy's suit. The girls' violet eyes and strawberry blond hair set off with the blues in their dresses made them both look like angels sent straight from heaven.

Lily did a quick spin in her twirling skirt and laughed at the flutter of material that gathered around her short legs. Readjusting Lily's bow in her hair, Mildred replied, "Alright, girls. This is your hour to shine. Your prince awaits." With that, she opened the door and led Samantha and Lily to the back of the church. An organist hit the deep quiet notes on the instrument and began playing the tune chosen by Samantha and Ben, *To God Be the Glory*.

This was their cue for the simple ceremony to begin. Mildred took Lily by the hand and walked slowly to the front of the stage and stood opposite of the waiting, handsome, Ben and her husband Robert. William stood beside his father tugging on the neck of his shirt. She hoped her son would make it through the wedding without busting the buttons off of his collar.

Samantha heard nothing but the sweet refrain of the first line of the song. In her mind she sang along with the words, "To God be the glory, great things He hath done…." She got no further with the song's lyrics. Like a lightning flash, Samantha saw the hard-lived, bittersweet, nineteen years of her life burst before her vision. Her family and home in the mining camp, the willow tree's sheltering branches that held all of her girlhood secrets, her sisters and brothers-in-law, little Geoffrey, her girlfriends, Waylon, laughter and joy, tears and sorrow, Lily's birth, the Mississippi beach….all of it flashed before her, threatening to cause her feet to stumble as they slowly made their way to the front of the church.

And then she glanced up and caught the emerald eyes of Benjamin Wright.

The lightning flash stopped and the sun shone instead. Peace, love, and beauty surrounded Samantha as she saw the man she loved with all of her heart, the man God had sent to be her husband and Lily's daddy. Love filled her chest and moved her feet a bit faster to his outstretched hand. As she stepped up beside Ben and took his hand, the organist played the last refrain to the hymn, "and give Him the glory, great things He hath done."

Surrounded by the few she had grown to love, Samantha listened to the preacher's words from I Corinthians about love and what God's love looked like. How it was kind, just, patient, all the things she had never known in a marriage and looked forward to learning with Ben, how to really love someone the right way. God had helped her make the choice in her spouse this time around and Samantha knew it would be wonderful, no....*beautiful.*

As she and Ben exchanged vows, Samantha felt his eyes on hers. Looking into their depths, she knew this man loved her, for the right reasons. She didn't doubt for a moment that he would give his life for her if needed. And she knew he loved her Lily Ruth as his own child.

Without a second's hesitation after the preacher's directing, Ben kissed his new wife soundly on the lips. Samantha couldn't have stopped the laughter that bubbled up in her throat if she tried. Sometimes joy is uncontainable and shouldn't be held back. Ben scooped Lily up in his arms and hugged them both tightly to his chest. Then he uttered the sweetest words in Samantha's ear, "Thank You, God, for my girls."

Lily, caught up in the moment of love and joy, placed her little hands on Samantha's cheeks and kissed her Mommy on the end of her nose. She then repeated the same with Ben then wrapped her arms around his neck, giving it a big squeeze. Samantha's heart melted at her daughter's love and acceptance of the man, another God-given blessing.

With congratulations and hugs abounding, Mildred reminded the couple they had a weekend honeymoon awaiting them and that Lily Ruth would be just fine for a couple nights without Samantha. Robert had insisted on the newlyweds taking the weekend off from the resort for their honeymoon so he sent them to a lovely cottage in the woods an hour away from the resort.

Bags already packed and in Ben's awaiting truck, the couple waved at their friends, kissed Lily's cheeks, and left for a weekend to be alone with each other.

In the truck, Ben reached for Samantha again before driving off. "Mrs. Wright, have I told you that I am so glad you proposed to me?"

Laughter filled the truck. "Every day for the last two weeks if I recall. And I am so glad you said 'yes.'" Kissing her husband on the lips, Samantha replied, "Now let's be on our way before we fog up these windows. We have the whole weekend in front of us, just the two of us."

Eyes full of hope and love, Ben turned to the road and drove his wife to their honeymoon.

Opening her eyes slowly, Samantha looked around the bedroom of the honeymoon bungalow. It was her first night with Ben Wright. She snuggled closer into the arms of her husband. Never had Samantha felt so honored, cherished, and loved in all her life. And she hadn't even been married to Ben for one full day.

Samantha had to say that Robert Stockton had chosen well. Their honeymoon hideaway was perfect. Perched high on the edge of a cliff, the cottage overlooked a valley of evergreens cut through the middle by a winding stream. The view from the porch off the back of the cottage was breath-taking to say the least. For two days they wouldn't have to leave the place unless they chose to. With a fully stocked kitchen, firewood, and all the amenities anyone would need for a romantic weekend, Samantha determined to thank Robert profusely when they returned.

Lying still and content in Ben's arms, Samantha listened to his heart beat in his chest. Unwilling to move from the spot, she sighed deeply, perfectly at ease and at peace. Never before had she felt such wonderful emotions and deep feelings for a man, nor did she know such a reality was even possible.

Real, true love had cast out all remaining demons from her first relationship with Waylon. Ben and Samantha's first time together as a married couple, Samantha had to fight the images and negative emotions that Waylon had ushered into her mind and heart with their tumultuous marriage and choose not to see or relate to Ben in that light. Ben was *not* Waylon; Samantha determined to put the past behind her and trust this man God had chosen for her. Ben had proven himself to be patient, loving, kind, and unselfish.

Not knowing he was awake, Ben startled her from her thoughts. "What are you thinking, Mrs. Wright?"

Loving the sound of her new nickname, Samantha giggled and kissed Ben on the cheek. "You'll laugh at me, but I was thinking about Ruth in the Bible. I read her story the night before our wedding and wondered if she felt as if I do right now. She sort of proposed to Boaz, in her own way. Boaz was her second husband and also her rescuer. He saved her from being alone and without protection and provision. And I believe he really loved her. I don't know about her first experience, but I like to think that her second one was absolute perfection for her, full of love and beauty and goodness. I guess I was comparing you to Boaz and me to Ruth. I know that sounds silly, but you asked."

"There's nothing silly about you seeing me as someone who wants to love and protect and rescue you, Samantha. That's my heart for you. And I'm glad you know my heart so well already." Full of passion and the love he professed, Ben kissed his new wife yet again. After a moment, he looked into the deepest places of her soul. "I don't know all of your past experiences, but I plan on replacing each bad experience you had in your life with something good and wonderful because that's what you deserve." He reached a finger to her cheek and wiped at the tear that slowly made its way down her face.

Whispering her response, Samantha placed her hand over his. "You have no idea how much that means to me, Ben. And I must say, so far your track record has been perfect." Placing a quick kiss on his lips, she said, "How about we get dressed and find something to eat? That view is calling my name. I want to sit and stare at it for hours!"

Jerking the covers off of her body, Ben teased, "I will agree to clothes and food for a little while, but we are *not* staring at *any* view for hours. We will get dressed and eat and stare at the view for fifteen minutes tops! This bed and you are calling my name!"

Jumping up from the bed, Samantha raced for her clothes to cover her freezing body. Laughter and joy like she had never experienced coursed through her veins. The joy of having a man who loved her unselfishly eased all of her fears and settled her soul to its depths.

Life was indeed beautiful. Samantha Jean Wright knew she didn't have far to look as long as Ben was in her life. It would always be right in front of her face.

# chapter 34

"Syl!! Sylvie! Where are you, woman?" Henry burst through the front door of their apartment in search of his wife. "Honey, are you in here?"

Heading to the back of their little apartment, Henry found his wife sitting in the bathroom with a washcloth pressed to her flushed face. "Are you alright, Sylvie?"

A slow smile turned up the corners of her mouth. No one had ever called her by that name except her Henry. *Sylvie.* She loved the way it sounded coming from his booming voice. Blinking a few times, she looked up at her husband. "Henry, I didn't hear you come in."

"Are you feeling poorly again? What's wrong? Where do you hurt?"

"Oh, calm down you old hen. It's just like the last times….my heart's racing and I feel flushed. I probably worked too hard around here this afternoon. I'm fine, Henry. Just needed to sit a spell and cool down."

Concern etched the lines even deeper on Henry's face. "That's it. You are going to see the doctor next week if I have to drag you there myself, woman. This has gone on too long and these spells are more frequent than ever. I'm taking you in next week. And don't argue with me about it anymore."

"Okay, okay. But just to prove to you this is nothing more than old age setting in so you'll leave me alone. I'll call Monday morning. Now what was all of the fuss about when you charged in the house?" Sylvia drug the washcloth across the back of her neck and inhaled deeply. "Let's go into the kitchen for some tea and you can tell me what's going on."

Helping her stand to her feet, Henry led Sylvia to the kitchen, his news nearly forgotten with worry over Sylvia. "We got a letter from Samantha Jean."

"What? Then stop fussing over me and read it to us! I'll get the tea."

Placing a firm hand on her shoulder, Henry led his wife to the table. "No, you won't. You will sit while I pour the drinks. I'm capable of fixing tea, Syl. When did this last spell start today?"

"I don't know—after breakfast, I guess. I was washing the dishes and I just felt really flushed and my heart started racing again. Like the other day when I was sweeping the floor, remember?"

Setting their tea glasses on the table, Henry sat down in front of Sylvia. "Yes, I remember. Nearly made me have a heart attack watching you like that. You work too hard, Honey. This has gone on for nearly two months and it's time we get you seen to by the doctor. Drink your tea and maybe that will help. Want me to read the letter now?"

"Of course, I do. I'm dying to hear from our girls." Sylvia pressed the cool glass to her flushed cheeks. She slowly sipped the cold liquid and waited.

"Okay, here goes." Henry gulped down half of his tea before beginning the letter.

"'Dear Mama and Daddy,

*I'm sorry it has taken me so long to write you again. My hands have been very full at the resort and with Lily Ruth. Can you believe she is three years old? Life has been busy, but good. Very good. Which leads me to my news.*

*I can just picture Mama's face when she hears about this, but Mama, please know what I am about to say is so different from last time. I promise you that.*"

Henry glanced up at his wife before continuing.

"What have you done now, Samantha Jean?" Sylvia sat up straighter in her chair steeling herself for Samantha's news.

Henry continued. "*I got married a few weeks ago! Please don't worry! I promise this time is different. My husband's name is Ben Wright. Mama, you would adore him! He's a God-fearing man, hard working, is gentle and kind, and doesn't drink anything but milk, water, and unsweet tea. Ben is so good to me and Lily. She has taken to him like nothing I have ever seen before. They both love each other and have so much fun together.*

*We want to plan a trip back home as soon as we've saved the money to do so and when it's a good time to leave the resort. I will let you know as soon as we have something planned. The end of summer will be best before fall sets in with all of its extra duties for us here.*

*I just wanted to tell you both and ask that you trust me with this decision. If God ever brought anything good into my life, it is Ben Wright. Please pass this news on to everyone and let them know of our upcoming visit.*

*I am sending a photo of Ben, me, and Lily taken on her third birthday. At least you can see how happy we truly are.*

*Love to each of you,*
*Samantha Jean Wright*"

Grabbing for the envelope, Sylvia opened it wide to retrieve the photograph Samantha mentioned. Her hand flew to her mouth, stifling a sob. "Oh....." She handed the picture to her husband.

Taking the photo from Sylvia, Henry stared into the faces of his girls. They looked so happy and healthy. His Sammie-girl was beautiful. Her eyes shone even in the black and white picture, no traces of dark circles underneath. The once-present haunted look in his granddaughter's eyes was gone. She stood on a chair in front of a birthday cake with lit candles, her little hands clasped to her chest, no thumb in her mouth. The man, Ben Wright, stood with one hand placed on Samantha's hip and one hand on Lily's shoulder. He wore the same expression as the girls, one of sheer joy and contentment.

Placing the photo on the table, Henry smoothed the single sheet of paper in front of him. He reached in his overalls' pocket, withdrew a large handkerchief, and unashamedly wiped at the tears that gathered in his eyes. "Our baby's done it again. She sounds and looks happy though." Reaching across the table, he clasped Sylvia's hands and felt a slight tremor in them. "Honey, it will be okay. We've prayed about this many times and just have to trust the Good Lord that He got some sense into our girl with her choice of a man."

Giving a slight nod of her head, Sylvia reached for the picture and stared into their faces once more, then rose from the table and silently began dinner preparations. Her back to her husband, she stood at the sink and began viciously scrubbing a half dozen potatoes.

Sylvia silently prayed for the ability to accept this news, this startling announcement from Samantha of yet again another wedding she, as the mother, had been unable to attend. And yet again, her daughter had chosen a man that Samantha hadn't even introduced to them.

Quickly she chopped the potatoes and tossed them into the waiting pot of water. With each strike of the knife's blade, Sylvia felt the subtle stabs in her mother's-heart. Her baby girl had left her out of another important decision that would influence the rest of her life. All their lives.

Last time was such a disaster with Waylon, Sylvia could only beg God that this was truly as the letter and picture said. Different. That this Ben Wright was a good, Godly man and not some no good drunk. *Oh please, God. Let it be so.*

Henry watched silently as Sylvia continued to chop vegetables. His heart felt the news like a blow. The girls were so far away. The reality that, as Samantha's father and Lily's grandfather, he could do nothing to protect them from this strange man was hard to swallow. Waylon Graves had been such a horrible man to his girls. Deep down after Samantha and Waylon's divorce was final, Henry had vowed that the next go-round would look entirely different. When Samantha returned home safe and sound, Henry had decided to have a long talk with her and ask her to let him meet any future prospects that came her way to help protect her and Lily.

But today, those vows vanished like the steam rising from Sylvia's simmering pot.

"Hen—Henry….help—"

His wife's broken cry startled Henry from his thoughts. Looking her way, Henry watched as Sylvia swayed and grabbed the sink's edge. Rushing to her side, Henry reached Sylvia as her knees buckled. Catching her in his arms, Henry lifted her off her feet as she grabbed for her chest. A strangled cry escaped her lips as he eased her to the sofa.

"Sylvie, talk to me! What's wrong, Honey?"

"My chest—it hurts so bad!" Sylvia's face paled as she grimaced in pain.

"We're getting you to the doctor now!"

Thankful for his new job, Henry had transportation sitting outside their apartment. The delivery truck he used for work would have to do. Grabbing the keys, Henry reached for Sylvia and lifted her in his arms again. Adrenaline coursed through his body, giving him an unnatural strength and ability to make the flight of stairs with his wife in his embrace. Placing her gently in the front seat, Henry repeatedly honked the horn of the truck at other drivers to get them to move over and drove as swiftly as he dared to the hospital.

The next few hours flew by in a blur. Somehow, without much thought to the tasks, Henry called his adult children and had them gathered by his side as they awaited the results of tests done on Sylvia. Claudia paced the small waiting room wringing her hands and swiping frequent tears while Bernice kept full cups of coffee in each of their hands and nearly drove Henry mad fussing over him.

A white cloaked doctor stepped into the room and instantly all eyes were on the man. "Are you the family of Sylvia Owens?" After receiving affirmation, he continued. "Have a seat please." Everyone sat as soon as the doctor did. "I'm Doctor Wilson. I examined Mrs. Owens and just viewed her tests. Mr. Owens, you were right in rushing her to us. We gave her medication to slow the heart's racing and possible onset of a heart attack then ran necessary tests. She did not have a heart attack so there is not any damage to her heart. That's great news."

He paused as the family breathed sighs of relief and refocused on the rest of his words. "She does have a weak heart, which is leading to the chest pain, flushing, dizziness, and erratic heart beats. I understand Mrs. Owens is a hard working woman after asking her a lot of questions. She admitted to worrying about a family member for the past year and noticed her symptoms begin soon after that. Stress and worry are also playing a huge role in the health of her heart, that coupled with physical exertion. I would recommend rest and stress reduction for now and I will keep a close eye on her over the coming weeks as I determine a course of treatment."

Bernice broke through the doctor's speech. "Will she get better with these recommendations? Can you give her medication? When will she make a full recovery?"

Taking a deep breath, the doctor hesitated a moment before answering. "From what the tests show and having dealt with patients over the years with these same symptoms, Mrs. Owens' condition won't go away or heal itself. Honestly, you need to keep her from exerting herself as much as you can, limiting her activity, keeping her calm. Sadly, there's not anything we can do but maintain her condition as best as we can. We want to prevent future flare ups and keep her heart as calm as possible. Over time, the symptoms will increase and affect her overall health. I know that's not what you want to hear, but I must tell you the truth."

Henry was the next to speak. "So you're saying this will slowly get worse and we need to keep her calm and resting? How soon can we expect things to worsen?"

"Yes, in a nutshell, that is what I am saying. Only Mrs. Owens' heart can answer that last question. I've seen patients follow all the rules and their hearts last for years. And I've seen patients follow the rules and they may make it a few months before things worsen. It goes either way. But every patient that ignores my suggestions suffer more chest pain and heart damage, inevitably shortening their life. It is up to the heart and the patient."

Standing to his feet, Doctor Wilson shook Henry's hand. "We will see you in a few weeks in the office for your wife's check-up."

Wordlessly Henry stood and shook the doctor's hand. Watching his retreating back, Henry ran a hand through his gray hair. "My Sylvie."

The family surrounded him with hugs. Claudia and Bernice assured Henry they would do all they could to help in Sylvia's recovery, as they called it.

Henry knew there would be no recovery. He heard what the doctor had said, but didn't have the heart to say it again to his family.

# chapter 35

*End of May, 1947*

Throwing the last of the folded clothing into the second suitcase, Samantha wiped a fresh course of tears from her cheeks. Not three days had passed since she received a phone call from her Daddy about her mother's visit to the hospital a couple weeks ago. Henry had explained as much as he could what the doctor had said and had been very honest with her when she probed with further questions.

His last words rang in her ears still. *"We don't know how long your Mama's heart will hold up, but after the first doctor visit last week his news was slightly worse than in the hospital. Sammie-girl, I wish I could answer your questions but it's all really up in the air. Her heart is weak. She has chest pains and dizziness and her heart races often which leaves her exhausted and irritable. Will you try to come home sooner than you planned for that visit?"*

And that's just what she was doing.

Ben had been instantly compassionate and understanding. After talking to the Stocktons about their jobs and the timing of the trip to Mississippi, things were set in motion for them to leave as soon as possible. Bus fare was purchased, plans were made, and Samantha couldn't get home fast enough. They received the blessing from Mildred and Robert to stay for an entire month if needed, knowing they would be needed back at the resort to prepare the cabins for cold weather and the arrival of hunting season.

For the thousandth time, Samantha checked and re-checked their suitcases making sure she had enough clothes for them yet keeping their bags as light as possible. And for the thousandth time she prayed for her Mama.

*God, please be with Mama. Make her heart strong and healthy. Give her the peace she needs and help her slow down. Help Daddy be what she needs and to be patient with her. Please, heal her.*

"Lily help Mama?" Her daughter's voice stirred Samantha from her prayers. Entering the bedroom with an arm load of toys, Lily placed her pile on top of the open suitcase. The past few days Samantha had tried to prepare Lily for the upcoming trip and talked often about seeing the family.

"We can't take all of these toys, Honey. Choose three, okay?" Removing the excess toys from her over-stuffed suitcase, Samantha sat on the edge of the bed and lifted Lily to her lap. "Your cousin Geoffrey will have plenty of toys for you to play with. Remember Geoffie and Grammie and Pops? We are going on a trip in a big bus to see them! Won't that be fun?"

Confusion clouded Lily's face. "Can Daddy Ben come too?"

Hugging her daughter tightly, Samantha relished the fact that Lily instantly bonded with Ben. They had referred to him as 'Daddy' but Lily had been unable to drop his name from the new title. Thus the name 'Daddy Ben.' Leaning back to look in her daughter's eyes, Samantha answered her, "Yes! Of course Daddy Ben will come. He's part of me and you, Lily. We both want Daddy Ben to come."

Clapping her little chubby hands, Lily bounced down from Samantha's lap and danced the dance of a three year old girl at her Mommy's pronouncement. "I love Daddy Ben!"

Laughter bubbled from Samantha. "Me too, Sweetie! Me too."

Entering the bedroom then, Ben asked, "What's the celebration about? Did I miss something?"

"Only that your two girls love you very, very much! Lily is excited you are going with us. I wonder what her little mind still struggles with after—well, you know."

"More than we can probably comprehend. She needs reassurance and time that I'm not going anywhere! I will prove it to her, Sammie, I swear it." Ben wrapped his arms around Samantha and kissed his wife on the forehead. "Now, how can I help? All of my duties are done. Robert is comfortable with us being gone for a month. I wanted to set that up before we left so we can spend time with your family and not have to rush back or worry about this place."

"Thank you, Ben. You are wonderful. So….I guess we need to eat a quick breakfast and get Robert to take us to the bus station then we will be Mississippi bound. I'm nervous and excited about seeing my family. These butterflies in my stomach are getting the best of me." Zipping the final bag, Samantha headed to the kitchen to prepare a simple breakfast for the three of them.

Within the next two hours, the little family found themselves seated in a bus headed to Mississippi and Samantha's waiting family.

"Daddy! Mama! Oh, I've missed you!!" Joy, laughter, and tears all combined as Samantha greeted her parents. Ben stood back a few steps holding Lily in his arms with their suitcases at his feet giving his wife a moment with her parents.

Lily wriggled in Ben's arms at the sight of her grandparents. Recognition dawned on her face as she took in her Mommy's excitement.

Turning to Lily, Samantha said, "Lily, look! It's Grammie and Pops!"

A smile spread across Lily's face as she ran into Henry's outstretched arms. Lifting her high in the air, she squealed with delight as Henry brought her into a warm hug. Sylvia reached to brush a strand of Lily's long hair from her face and placed a kiss on her cheek.

"Do you remember your Grammie, Lily? We have missed you so much!" Tears choked off Sylvia's words. "I have something for you." Sylvia pulled a stuffed pink lamb from her purse and held it out to Lily who instantly pulled the lamb into a tight hug.

"Thank you, Grammie!"

"Mama. Daddy. I want you to meet my husband, Ben Wright." Samantha reached for Ben's hand and pulled him to her side.

Ben extended his other hand to Henry and shook it heartily. "Mr. and Mrs. Owens, it's great to finally meet you. Samantha talks about you both so much, I feel like I already know you."

A kind smile spread over Henry's face. "Henry and Sylvia will do, Ben. We look forward to getting to know you, Son. Samantha speaks highly of you in her letters. We are so glad you three are finally here!"

"Enough gushing! Can we go home? I'm exhausted and I need some of Mama's cooking and sweet tea." Sheer joy settled around Samantha's heart. This was indeed beautiful. To have her parents meet the man she loved, the man God hand-picked for her and Lily. She looked forward to the days ahead.

Henry helped with the suitcases while Samantha linked arms with Sylvia and walked to the car. He noticed that Lily reached for Ben's hand as comfortably as she would have held onto Samantha's. That spoke volumes to Henry Owens concerning Ben Wright. Maybe the man was alright after all.

~~~~~~~~~~

The past few weeks were jam-packed with family, food, and reuniting with each other. Samantha couldn't believe how quickly the time had flown by. She sat in the still dark living room on her Mama's couch waiting for the sun to come up. Ben and Lily were still asleep so she snuck out to be alone for a minute.

Taking her precious Bible from its cover, Samantha turned to a verse that caught her eye with straight, red lines underneath. Quietly she read the verse to herself in the growing morning light. "Return unto thy rest, O my soul; for the Lord hath dealt bountifully with thee."

Yesterday, Samantha was struck with a new emotion. Something she hadn't felt around her family in some time. Due to her own choices and mistakes, Samantha realized that for the last several years she had been around her family, her insides were normally tied in knots of fear and dread over what Waylon would say or do, or what lie she needed to fabricate to cover up for his abuse. These few weeks allowed her to see that her wrong choices had influenced the entire family, creating a cesspool of dread, fear, and anxiety. They had all felt it, until now. It was gone, and in the place of the stinking cesspool there was now a crystal clear lake.

This verse spoke straight to what had happened in her life: *the Lord had dealt bountifully with her, so her soul could now rest.*

Thanksgiving and peace settled around Samantha like a light summer rain, refreshing and reviving her soul. God had been so good, so very good to her and Lily. She had more than the blessings of His goodness; she had the rest and peace that comes with it.

Her thoughts turned to her Mama yet again. Since their arrival, Sylvia had suffered with two spells and had gone to see the doctor. He hadn't offered any good news about Sylvia's condition. Guilt plagued Samantha about having to leave by week's end to return to Wisconsin. Maybe she needed to consider staying longer and letting Ben return. No, she couldn't bear the thought of being away from him for any length of time.

*God, show me what to do. If Mama is really very sick, should I come back home? Would Ben consider moving here and leaving Wisconsin? He doesn't have family there and You have caused Ben and my family to bond very quickly. Thank You that they all accepted him so well and that they seem to love each other already. You have dealt bountifully with me, even being back home and giving us all peace and making us a family again. Thank You.*

Samantha thought back to the weeks since they had returned to Mississippi. Geoffrey and Lily simply picked right back up where they had left off. The park across the street from her parents' apartment had afforded the children many hours to play together. Frank and Bernice, Melvin and Claudia, all readily embraced Ben as her husband within a few hours of being around him. Ben openly showed his love for Lily and herself in his usual selfless manner which endeared him all the more to the family. Instead of rowdy games of horseshoes, the men had taken to playing cards and Ben fit right in with a great sense of sportsmanship whether he won or lost.

Serenity.

That was the one word Samantha felt when she remembered the family's interaction with her new husband.

Life would nearly be perfect if her Mama was healthy and there were no concerns over her future. But that wasn't the case and Samantha left the option open in the back of her mind of one day returning to be near the ones she loved. It was something she would definitely have to talk to Ben about after they returned to Wisconsin.

Part Four: **Beauty Found**

*"A thing of beauty is a joy forever."*
                                             --John Keats

# chapter 36

*Big Bend, Wisconsin*
*September, 1949*

"Higher, Daddy!!" Squeals of delight erupted from her five year old daughter. Over the past two years since Samantha and Ben had married, Lily had finally begun referring to Ben as 'Daddy' instead of 'Daddy Ben.' Samantha enjoyed the beautiful sound of her daughter's voice as she laughed and shouted with glee while Ben continued to push her on the back yard swing. Hating to interrupt the moment, Samantha started to go back inside and share her news with Ben later.

"Sammie, it's your turn! Want me to push you?" Ben loved to tease her and she couldn't resist laughing at his offer.

"I want to play in the sandbox now, Daddy. Thanks for the pushes!!" Lily allowed the swing to slow enough for her to jump off and run to her waiting sandbox.

Samantha eased herself into the swing in front of her husband. "This will be the last month for enjoying the outdoors before cooler weather hits."

Ben began gently pushing Samantha in the swing. She lifted her legs and enjoyed the moment closing her eyes as the sun warmed her face. Wordlessly she allowed her husband to gently push her in the swing.

"Penny for your thoughts," Ben pried.

"Hmmm....I wish I wasn't thinking, honestly. It usually gets me in trouble."

"Talk to me. I'm all ears."

Dragging her feet to stop the swing, Samantha reached back for Ben's hand and pulled him around to the swing dangling beside hers. "Sit with me?"

Ben did as she asked, concern etching his handsome features. "What's wrong, Honey?"

Taking a deep breath, Samantha started. "It's Mama. She's had two good years, Ben. Her spells nearly disappeared after we left and now they have come back with a vengeance. Daddy called a bit ago and told me she had been in the hospital last week for a few days. Thankfully she didn't have a heart attack, only chest pains again but worse than ever. The doctor says this may be the onset of her heart getting worse. I honestly thought she would continue to get better over the last two years and was hoping she was healing....I know that's not the case with her condition, but you know how you trick yourself into believing that things are different than they really are?"

"I lived that way for years after my parents died. It took me nearly two years to accept they were gone. I forced myself to believe they were on vacation or were just going to return any minute with some grand excuse as to why they had been away so long. But that didn't help me at all; it only made healing worse. So, yeah. I understand that. I'm sorry about your mother. What can we do?" Ben's honest concern was a soothing balm to Samantha's soul.

"I don't know, Ben. We are so far away. There's not really anything to be done from here. I can pray and keep in touch, but that's about it." A single tear streaked down her cheek.

Ben reached a hand over and brushed the tear away with his finger. "Honey, I'm so sorry. I know this is difficult for you. I know what it's like to be away from your family. Whether they are in heaven or Mississippi, sometimes it feels just as far away."

They sat in silence a moment watching Lily build sand castles, oblivious to their conversation.

Interrupting the silence, Ben said, "Have you ever thought about moving back to Mississippi?"

"What? I can't leave you, Ben! I could never—"

Placing a hand on her arm, Ben stopped Samantha. "No, Sammie. Not *move without* me, but *with* me! Us….me, you, Lily. We can live wherever we want to, you know."

A fresh bout of tears flooded her face. "You would do that? Leave Wisconsin, the Stocktons, the resort….and move to Mississippi so I could be by my family?"

"Of course. It wouldn't be easy, but I would do that for you. *You and Lily* are my life, Samantha Wright. Not this place or even these people. I would do that for you."

Covering her face with both hands, Samantha wept unashamedly. Ben eased his swing over to hers and wrapped an arm around her shoulders. "Honey, don't you know how much I love you?"

Retrieving a handkerchief from her pocket, Samantha blew her nose and dried her tears. "I do, Ben. It's just something I am still getting used to. And I love it!" Breathing a huge sigh of relief, she continued. "Let's not jump to any quick decisions now. Can we think and pray about this a few days and then talk about it again? This would really affect the Stocktons. I want to think about every angle and then make our decision."

Kissing the top of her hand, Ben said, "You've got yourself a deal."

Samantha rolled her neck first to one side and then the other as she reached a hand up to her left temple and massaged it.

"Headache again?" Ben gently rubbed her shoulders to help ease the tension and pain.

"Yeah, I guess that's what crying gets me. Another headache." Taking a deep sigh as she enjoyed her neck rub, Samantha willed herself to calm down.

"Mommy! Mommy! I found it! It's beautiful. A rainbow shell!" Breathless, Lily held a shell the size of a half dollar up to Samantha, its center radiating pearly rainbows. "It was in my sand. I found something beautiful today, just like you do!"

"Oh, that's so pretty, Lily! Make sure you add it to your collection."

"I will, Mommy!"

Pride rose slowly in Samantha's chest as she watched Lily skip towards the back door to put her treasure away in a special box. Her little girl was paying attention to all she said and did. Lily had learned one of life's greatest lessons just by observing her Mommy's actions. She too had found something priceless and worthy of notice.

Little Lily Ruth had found the beautiful in her small world.

~~~~~~~~~~

Heaving the heavy trunk over the side of his truck, Ben surveyed the house he had grown to love. But this was just four wall with no soul or heart. He had found his home and it was much more than walls. His home was beside two girls who had stolen his heart. That's what made it easy for Ben Wright to consider leaving Wisconsin, his job, and the Stocktons. Though he would greatly miss this place and these people, Ben vowed to bring his little family back for a visit one day. For now, they needed to be beside Samantha's family. She needed to be close to her people and he was doing all he could to make that happen.

Two arms wrapped around his waist bringing him back to the present. Ben turned to face Samantha. She reached up to brush a section of blond bangs away from his forehead. "Are you sure you're okay with this decision? I never want you to regret what we are doing."

Kissing the top of her strawberry blond head, Ben reassured her the best he could. "I promise I am okay with this. I am *more* than okay with it. We need to get you back home. You've been gone long enough. Long enough to find your Prince Charming though." A twinkle lit his emerald eyes, ones that shone with a deep love and devotion for his wife.

Samantha's stomach flip-flopped under Ben's gaze. She stood on tip-toes and gave him a deep, promising, kiss.

"Ewww! Do you have to do that outside?" Lily showed her 'disgust' at her parents' show of affection causing them to kiss one more time in front of her, then reluctantly they released each other.

"Girls, let's head for Mississippi! We have a long haul in front of us."

"I'm really gonna miss Willie, Mrs. Mildred and Mr. Robert." Sadness darkened Lily's face.

"I know, Sweetie. We are too. I'm glad we got to have dinner with them and say 'good-bye' last night. Did you get your treasures Willie gave you?" Samantha referred to an old cigar box Willie had given Lily last night full of things only children would hold dear. He had drawn her a picture of the resort, added a few rocks they had collected together, one speckled and shaped like a bird's egg, including other odds and ends, completing the collection with a set of *Fitz's Soda* bottle caps, one from his root beer and one from Lily's orange crème soda.

"Yes, ma'am. I would never leave my treasure box behind." Sincerity replaced the sadness in her purple eyes.

"Remember Geoffie's waiting to see you. And Grammie and Pops. That will make the leaving easier, right?" It was Ben's turn to reassure Lily. He and Samantha had decided to wait and explain things in detail to Lily after they arrived in Mississippi. Their first stop was to Henry and Sylvia's, then to their new home two hours away. That's the part they had left out for now to protect Lily from more turmoil. They would have a couple of weeks to visit before his new job began and they could move into the house he rented for his small family.

"I know, Daddy. But it's still hard to leave."

Lifting the girl into his arms, Ben kissed her on the nose. "Ready for our adventure? I have a bag of your favorite jelly beans for our trip."

Instantly Lily's eyes lit up. "Daddy, you're the best." Lily returned a kiss on Ben's nose and hugged his neck tightly. "Okay. I think I'm ready."

## chapter 37

Ready to get out of the truck and end the two day trip of relocating to Mississippi, Samantha's stomach returned to its state of jitters every time she thought about being near her family again. The only downside was she, Ben, and Lily would be two hours away from them, but close enough to drive to see them for weekends. Excitement coursed through her as they turned into her parents' street.

Before Ben could put the truck in park, Bernice and Claudia ran out the front door of Henry and Sylvia's bottom-floor apartment. In her usual animated excitement, Bernice squealed with delight, arms waving above her head. "Sammie!! You're finally home! Get out of that truck so I can hug your neck. Oh, look at my Lily Ruth, all grown up! Hey, Ben!"

In a rush, she was out of the truck and in her sister's arms. Samantha absorbed every second of her sister's attention. "Oh, Bernie! It's so good to be home."

Peering over Bernice's shoulder, Samantha saw Claudia standing behind, waiting her turn for hugs while she dabbed at her eyes with a handkerchief. "Okay, Bernice. Let her go. It's my turn." Swallowed in Claudia's much calmer welcome, Samantha felt loved and missed all the same.

Without missing a beat, Henry and Sylvia were next in line to greet the little family with Geoffrey on their heels. "My girls! Look at the two of you!"

Henry and Sylvia gushed over them in turn while Geoffrey gave shy hugs to his returning family.

"Geoffie!" Lily ran to Geoffrey. The two cousins hugged and resumed their childhood relationship right where they left off two years ago.

"Let's get y'all inside for some supper. You must be starving. Ben, it's so good to see you again." Sylvia linked her arm through Ben's, a motion not lost on the young husband and father.

"I've been thinking about your pies all the way from Wisconsin, Sylvia. That's why we made such good timing," Ben teased his mother-in-law.

The evening passed with easy banter, each person glad to see the other. Frank and Melvin joined the rest after their work day ended just in time for supper and dessert.

After the last piece of pie was cut and served, Frank clinked his fork against his tea glass. "I have an announcement to make." Clearing his throat for dramatic flair, he winked at his wife. "It's been so hard for Bernie to keep this a secret, but somehow she managed. I'm surprised you all haven't heard by now." Bernice's playful shove interrupted him a second. "Frank and Henry and I all managed to work this surprise out without the women knowing, except for Bernice of course. My parents own some property with a large vacation home on the sweetest spot of the Mississippi River you will ever see. And they agreed to let us all stay there next weekend for two nights. The guys have already taken off work next Friday so we all can be together until Sunday evening."

The women all sucked in shocked breaths at the thought of such luxury and time with each other for three days and two nights. "Frank, you didn't! We can't afford such a trip!" Sylvia spoke for them all.

"I did and I can. Consider it an early Christmas present three months in advance. Sylvia, you can afford it because it won't cost a thing to go! The kitchen's stocked with enough groceries for a herd of families, the creek is busting with fish waiting to be caught and eaten, the house is free since it belongs to my family, and your husbands have already approved it. Any other questions? I think it will be a wonderful time for us all to be together! We've never done anything like this before, so I say it's about time. There's hiking trails, horse-back riding nearby, canoes, fishing equipment already there. I haven't been back since before Bernie and I married so I'm going if none of you do." Mock consternation crossed Frank's face while he awaited their answers.

"Of course we will go!"

"Frank, you are an angel!"

"This is a dream come true!"

All of the women chorused their agreement at once.

And with that, their family vacation was settled.

Samantha parked herself under a shade tree in a green and white striped canvas folding chair. Frank was right. The kitchen in his family's vacation home, though she thought of it more like a woodland castle, was stocked to overflowing. Thankfully she found a bottle of aspirin and fixed a pitcher of lemonade for everyone to enjoy after their fishing excursion. Retrieving the two white pills from her pocket, Samantha downed them with a huge swallow of the tart drink. Taking in a shaky breath, she watched from her perch as Ben helped Lily cast the fishing pole into the slow moving stream.

Not one hundred feet away, her father was helping Geoffrey with his pole as he dangled a small fish from the end and shouted with excitement. This weekend was beyond all of their dreams. Having three days together as a family to enjoy the great outdoors was sheer perfection.

The large wood-sided vacation home complete with front and back porches was tucked neatly in the curve of an off-shoot of the Mississippi River. Fish abounded in the stream, fire pits for cooking the day's catch, and a generous amount of picnic tables invited the visitors to relax and play. No one had to convince the children and adults alike to do just that.

Indoors was just as inviting. Huge windows were flung open to usher in the gentle breeze. Overstuffed chairs and couches sat around tables loaded with books and magazines. An impressive rock fireplace stood ready to warm the house when needed and create a cozy atmosphere even when unused. Complete with multiple bedrooms, some with bunkbeds for children and teens, the bedrooms all had thick rag rugs and plenty of chests and hooks for clothing.

Sylvia was enjoying a much needed nap in one of the upstairs bedrooms so she would be ready to help in tonight's fish fry. The rule was 'if you catch it, you clean and eat it.' The men were helping the children 'grocery shop for dinner' as they jokingly called their fishing excursion while the women stole a few hours to rest or hike the trails.

Melvin had stayed back at the house to prepare the fire pits for cooking and to make sure they had everything rounded up for the fish fry. A quick trip into town for last minute things and he was back before the fish were caught. After taking the last paper sack full of items into the house, Melvin fixed himself a glass of lemonade and joined Samantha outdoors.

"Hey, Sis!"

Samantha loved her brother-in-law dearly and appreciated how he treated her like his own sister. "Did you buy the store out?"

Easing his tall frame into a chair beside Samantha, he drawled, "Almost. There are a bunch of us to feed! I still can't believe we are all here together. This is perfect for getting to know Ben better. If I haven't told you before, Sammie, I like this guy! Good choice. Much better than that other rotten scoundrel."

A tired laugh escaped her lips. "Mel, you're not telling me something I don't already know."

"If I hadn't been gone and in the Navy, I could have saved you all of that heartache over Waylon Graves. But no, you had to run off and be stubborn." He gave her shoulder a gentle squeeze.

"I know. But think about this. If I hadn't married Waylon, I wouldn't have Lily. So all of the pain and struggle was worth it, just to have my daughter. God brought something good out of my messes."

"What do you mean, Sammie? How can good come from Waylon Graves?"

"That's not what I mean. *Good* didn't come from Waylon. Good came from *God.* I read a verse this morning in my Bible. I might not get it right but it went something like this; it's from Romans 8. 'God works everything, the good and the bad, in our lives for our good.' That's not the exact wording but I got the meaning right. See, God takes all of the things in our lives, even the mistakes, and turns them into good. Like He did with my failed marriage with Waylon. God gave me Lily Ruth. And that's beautifully good!"

"You amaze me Samantha. I like that view of yours." Melvin stroked his stubbly chin thoughtfully. "That can sure bring a man a lot of peace if he can see everything in his life in God's hands and trust that something good can come out of the bad."

"Exactly!" Samantha's face shone with the peace Melvin spoke of.

Standing to his feet, Melvin pointed to two nearby trees. "See that hammock? It's calling my name for a nap. Wake me when the fishermen return."

"Sure will, Melvin."

Laughter filled the air around Samantha as the men and children were walking closer to the house with their catch. Rising from her chair, Samantha was grateful the headache had eased up. She was now left with a slight throb in her left temple. Heading in the direction of the returning fishermen and children, she laughed at the huge amount of fish Geoffrey struggled to carry on his own. Ben clutched a string of fish in his hand as well.

Frank reached in his backpack and withdrew a Kodak 35 Rangefinder camera. "Okay, everybody stop! This catch of fish calls for a few pictures. Ben, you and Lily stand on that rock by the stream and let me snap your picture. Then I will get Geoffrey and Pops with their fish."

Ben deftly helped Lily stand on the rock and handed her the string of fish. "You hold the fish while I hold our gear."

Lily wrinkled her nose at the fish but took it from Ben. "They're a little stinky, Daddy! But it was so much fun catching them!" Her eyes were as bright as the afternoon sun, her smile as wide as the blue sky. Lily glowed and bounced with giddiness. Samantha had never seen her daughter this happy and excited before. It made her feel the same happiness and excitement Lily was feeling, only her reason wasn't over a fishing trip. She was so aware of the goodness God had shown her as it emanated from Ben and Lily.

"Okay, hold still Silly Lily! One, two, three! Got it!" Frank took Geoffrey and Henry's picture next.

Quickly they returned to show off their catch and wash up for dinner preparations after Frank snapped several more photographs. Bernice and Claudia returned from their walk and began gathering knives, cutting boards, old newspaper and bowls for the guys to clean the fish.

Samantha and her mother set to work preparing side dishes of beans and coleslaw with large slabs of cornbread. Before Sylvia had taken her nap she had quickly cooked a batch of chocolate pudding and left it to chill for dessert. They would feast tonight on each other's company and the wonderful food.

Yes, Samantha stood silently and soaked in the sheer goodness of God. The reality of the past few years of being away from her family and now returning to them was almost too much to bear. In that moment, she couldn't have found anything more beautiful in her life.

# chapter 38

*December, 1949*

Wrapping his arms tighter around Lily's foot-pajama clad body, Ben snuggled the girl up tight until his scruffy face tickled her cheek. Both were lying on the couch, stretched to their full length gazing at the lit Christmas tree. Glancing across the room at his wife, Ben watched as Samantha stared in vacant silence at the glittering tree.

Gently scrubbing his face against Lily's again, the girl emitted a round of giggles and protested against the tickling. "Daddy, stop it! You're tickly and scratchy all at the same time! That makes me laugh!"

"I love to hear my girls laugh, so no, Miss Lily, I *won't* stop!" Scooping his daughter up in his arms, Ben tossed her back onto the couch and began growling like a bear, continuing to tickle her until she begged him to quit. He loved nights like this, at home with his family.

Only, Samantha seemed a million miles away, completely oblivious to their wrestling match.

"Lily, how about you go see if there are any cookies left in the jar? You can bring a plate back for us three to share if you'd like."

"Cookies! Can I pour three milks too?"

"If you're very careful and use the plastic cups. Deal?"

"Deal, Daddy!"

Taking the moment he purposefully created to speak to Samantha alone, Ben knelt before her chair on his knees. Taking her still hands in his, Ben was surprised at how cold they felt. Samantha's eyes never left the Christmas tree.

"Sammie, are you feeling alright?" Ben rubbed her hands between his. Finally she looked his way.

A slow, deep frown creased her forehead. "What—what did you say?"

Now it was Ben's turn to frown. "Honey, I asked if you were okay. You've been very quiet tonight."

"No....yes. I'm not sure what you mean...." Tears of frustration pooled in her eyes, but she refused to let them fall.

This wasn't the first time in the past few weeks Samantha had displayed signs of confusion. "It's alright, Samantha. Does your head hurt? Can I get you anything?"

"No." Most of her answers these days were limited to a few words. Inwardly Ben vowed to take her to the doctor after Christmas. Something was wrong with his wife.

Lily walked carefully into the living room with two cups of milk. She bounced back into the kitchen and returned again slowly with one more cup and a plate piled with chocolate chip cookies. Gently Lily placed the items on the coffee table. "Mommy, I brought cookies and milk. Want one?" Lily took a cup of milk and handed it to Samantha and then gave her a cookie. "Let's dunk 'em like we always do! That's our favorite way to have cookies and milk."

Samantha stared at the cookie in one hand and the milk in the other. "What do I do with—"

Confusion settled some of Lily's excitement. "You do this, Mommy!" Lily demonstrated to Samantha how to dunk a cookie and eat it really quickly before it fell back into the milk. "It's your favorite."

Ben slowly reached up and took the milk from Samantha's hands. "I bet Mommy's too full from dinner to have dessert just yet. Here, Lily, teach me how you dunk. I don't think I do it like you. My cookie always falls back in the cup. I need you to show me the best dunking technique."

"Okay, Daddy. You do it like this." Engrossed in her dunking demonstration, Lily missed the fact that Samantha's cookie remained untouched and she had begun to stare at the Christmas tree again.

When their dessert was finished, Ben thanked Lily for the lesson on cookie dunking, had her tell Samantha 'good night,' and sent her off to brush her teeth with a promise to tuck her in soon. Worry consumed Ben's thoughts. Gathering the remains of their cookies and milk, he returned to the living room to find Samantha just as he had left her, cookie in hand, staring.

Kneeling down beside her, Ben said quietly, "Want me to take that cookie from you?"

Startled from her gazing, Samantha visibly jumped when he touched her hand. "I don't know. I think so."

Seeing his wife uncertain and confused tore at Ben's heart.

*What is going on with her, God? This is not my Samantha.*

Gently Ben led his wife to his bedroom and for the third night in a row, he helped her choose a nightgown, get undressed, and into their bed. Fear crept around the edges of his heart and mind while he helped Samantha complete such a simple task.

Then he eased her under the covers and left to check on Lily.

The next three hours, Ben sat in the living room in the same chair Samantha sat in earlier. Only he wasn't staring vacantly across the room. Instead he sat with his head in his hands pouring his heart out to God on behalf of his wife.

Thankfully Christmas Day had been completely uneventful for the family's celebrations. Ben had driven the three of them to Henry and Sylvia's to celebrate the holiday with the entire family. Samantha had been her normal self. Loving, attentive, helpful, clear-headed. None of this made sense to Ben, but he chose thankfulness for the good times they had over worrying about the bad days.

Sylvia and Henry had begged for them to let Lily stay with them for the last week of her school's winter break. Ben thought it was brilliant and would give him and Samantha time to be alone and maybe afford him the chance to talk to her and see what was troubling his wife. This was very timely though they would miss having Lily around. Delighted to stay with her grandparents, Lily embraced the idea immediately.

And thankfully the first two days of their time alone, Samantha was her old self again with only a few sporadic, mild headaches and some tiredness. This she blamed on the holiday's activities.

On their third day of being alone, Ben woke after Samantha. She was already out of bed but he didn't smell the coffee or toast that normally brought him from dreamland. Normally she was the first awake, coffee perking, Bible in her lap, and ready to serve him coffee and breakfast. Even on her bad days, as he had begun to think about them, she was up early and ready to start the day, though lately it had taken her longer than normal to prepare the coffee and morning meal. This was unusual. No scent of coffee. No Samantha and her normal noises floating around their house.

Easing himself from the bed, Ben went in search of his wife.

"Honey....where are you? Want me to start the coffee?" Walking around the end of the couch, Ben saw her lying on it, head in her hands, moaning.

Rushing to her side, Ben placed a hand to Samantha's forehead. "Sammie, are you sick?"

Another moan was the only answer he received.

Feeling her forehead, Ben could tell she didn't have a fever. Another groan escaped her lips.

"Talk to me, Samantha. Is it your head?"

"It hurts so bad, Ben." A trail of tears leaked from the corner of Samantha's tightly squinted eyes. "My head—"

Lifting her into his arms, Ben carried Samantha to the bed. "Let's get you dressed. We're going to see the doctor."

The next half hour sped by as Ben dressed his wife and drove her to the emergency room for the second time since meeting her. Inwardly he moaned and groaned with every one of Samantha's utterances of pain.

*God, this can't be happening. I knew she wasn't well. I'm so scared for my wife. Please help her, let her be okay. Heal my wife, God. Please.*

At the entrance to the emergency room doors, Ben's mind registered the startling blur of white. The white snow in drifts by the walls of the hospital, Samantha's white shirt, the white tile floors. And then her pale, white face as her body passed out limp in his arms, mercifully and momentarily relieving her from the pain.

His prayers became a chant during the waiting and the tests as Samantha's pain worsened while she drifted between conscious and unconscious. Eventually the doctor prescribed pain medications after multiple tests and x-rays which caused Samantha to remain in a state of sleep. Occasionally she would rouse and ask for Lily or himself, but Ben could hardly bear to watch her in this condition.

The doctor left them so he could visit other patients with the promise to return in a few hours. Ben spent those long moments in prayer, pacing, and worrying about his very ill wife.

Finally a light rap on the door stopped Ben in his tracks. The doctor's grim face was all Ben needed to see to know he hadn't come for a friendly chat.

Motioning to a chair next to the bed, the doctor spoke in quiet tones. "Have a seat, Mr. Wright." The doctor waited for Ben to sit before continuing. "I wish I could bring you better news. The x-rays show what appears to be a mass in your wife's head. This is causing the horrible headaches and confusion. There really is nothing we can do to treat something so large and in such a dangerous place. Her symptoms that you described and that I have witnessed lead me to believe....I'm sorry. There's not much I can do at this point."

To further punctuate the doctor's words, Samantha moaned in her sleep and tossed fitfully. "Hurts...."

Ben's heart broke at the pain etched on her face. "Can't you do something? You're a doctor! Can't you do surgery or....or give her a prescription?" Knowing he was grasping for straws, Ben continued, "You went to school to figure this kind of thing out. Can't you call a colleague? Someone who understands what's happening to my wife?"

Holding up a hand, the doctor stopped Ben. "Sir, I called in another doctor to look at your wife's x-rays and her chart. He will be happy to assess her as well, but his take on this is the same as mine. Actually he is an experienced surgeon and concluded that we would be putting your wife in further danger if we tried to operate due to the size of the mass, location, and delicacy of the operation. Please, know I wish I had better news. My job is to help people, so I am frustrated too though I know not anywhere near the level you are. Mr. Wright, at this point, you need to call any family or friends she may have and notify them of this. If any of them want to visit your wife, whether she is awake or not, they should do that very soon. Do you understand?"

Wordlessly, Ben shook his head in affirmation. Placing one hand over his eyes, the doctor left Ben alone.

"Have your wife's nurse call me if you have any questions or things change."

At the sound of the quietly closing door, Ben Wright gave way to the gut-racking sobs that he had held in for days.

Placing the black phone back in its cradle, Ben stood to face the window overlooking the street outside the hospital. A lit café sign beckoned to his stomach. Darkness was near and Ben realized he hadn't had a bite to eat or drink since the night before.

*So much can change in twenty-four hours. Last night we were enjoying a quiet meal alone and tonight my wife is laying in a hospital bed possibly....*

Turning swiftly away from the window, Ben returned to his still sleeping wife. The night nurse came in and checked Samantha's vitals. "Mr. Wright, why don't you leave this room a while and get a bite to eat. I am two doors down and promise to check on her every fifteen minutes while you go take care of yourself. She's sleeping soundly so now's a good time to get some dinner. The diner down the street makes a mean grilled cheese and tomato soup. Coffee's good too."

Without a word, Ben nodded in agreement. Exiting the front doors of the hospital, he stepped out into the growing darkness and drizzle. Unaware of the light rain, Ben set his eyes on the café and walked that way.

Near the corner of an intersection just ahead of him sat an old man dressed in a tattered jacket. At his feet lay an instrument case. Perched on the man's shoulder was an ancient fiddle that had seen better days. Gently the man pulled the bow across the strings and sang in a rich baritone the age-old words. "Amazing grace....how sweet the sound....that saved a wretch like me....I once was lost but now I'm found....'twas blind but now I see...."

Ben dropped a handful of coins in the fiddle's case and carried on the last few yards to the café's warmly lit entrance. Finding a secluded booth, he dropped wearily to the vinyl blue seat. Instantly a waitress appeared.

"What'll you have, sir?"

Not even wanting to make a decision, he answered, "Grilled cheese, tomato soup, and coffee, please."

"Coming right out." Shoving her pencil back behind an ear, the waitress left Ben to his thoughts. Instantly they turned back to the conversation he had earlier on the phone with Henry.

Bringing him a cup of coffee, the waitress quickly left to tend to more patrons.

Like the steam rising from his cup in curly wisps, snippets of his phone call to Henry drifted around his head.

*"Henry, I have some bad news....it's her head....a large mass....nothing to be done....come quick."*

*"No! Not my Sammie-girl....something left for the doctors to do....leave Lily with Claudia....on our way tonight...."*

# chapter 39

As he knew they would, Henry and Sylvia met Ben at the hospital late that evening after their two hour drive there. They stayed until the hospital staff insisted they leave to rest and then return the next morning. The nurse wrote down the phone number to Ben's house and assured them she would call if there was any change.

Giving Henry and Sylvia his bedroom, Ben opted for Lily's bed knowing he could never sleep in the bed he should be sharing with his wife. Thankfully sleep overtook him around two that morning. Sylvia's stirring in the kitchen roused Ben from a fitful sleep.

After a quick meal of coffee, eggs, and toast, the three silent adults headed straight for their loved one's bedside. Finding her in much the same condition as the night before, Ben stooped to kiss Samantha on the forehead. Henry and Sylvia followed suit and loved on their girl. Wiping constant tears, the parents were nearly beside themselves at the change in Samantha since Christmas.

Quiet conversations in the corner of the room brought Henry and Sylvia up to date on her condition during the last month. Guilt edged in on Ben as he wondered aloud if he should have insisted sooner for Samantha to see a doctor, if this was his fault for not taking immediate action when the headaches persisted.

Knowing the stubborn streak in their daughter, Henry assured Ben that he had done nothing wrong. All he had done since coming into Samantha's life was bring her good.

Quiet groans sounded from the bed. "Ben...."

Rushing to her bedside, the adults each grasped her hand or patted her leg reassuring Samantha she wasn't alone. "Honey, I'm right here. So are your parents. They came to check on you."

"What....where am...."

"You're in the hospital. Your headaches were really bad so I brought you in to see the doctor yesterday. Remember?"

Shaking her head slightly, Samantha closed her eyes again. They all stood and stared at her as her breathing became slower, signaling she slept again.

A sob sounded from Sylvia and she retreated to the farthest part of the room. Enveloping her in his arms, Henry quietly comforted his wife while he found little comfort for his own breaking heart.

Turning to the opening door, the doctor stuck his head around and motioned for them to follow him. The three entered a small room after the doctor. "I checked on Samantha early this morning after we did two x-rays during the night. She was unaware of us even doing them. Another doctor and I viewed them and both of us determined that there simply is nothing we can do to help your wife. I'm so sorry." Stopping at Henry's gasp and Sylvia's sobs, the doctor gave them a moment to gather their emotions again. Ben drew a shaking breath and raked his hands through his hair. "I will keep her comfortable and watch her closely."

Ben found his voice first. "So nothing. That's all you can tell us. Nothing. There's nothing to be done."

"I'm sorry, Mr. Wright. It won't be long now."

Rising to his feet, Ben faced the doctor head on. "So what do we do? Sit and watch her—we just can't sit here and watch her fade away...."

Standing to Ben's level, the doctor's voice full of compassion, he responded to Ben as gently as possible. "Mr. Wright, if it were my wife, I wouldn't leave her side for the next couple of days. I would hold her hand, tell her how much I love her, and—"

"I understand." Ben let the rest of the doctor's sentence dangle without finish.

Opening the door for them, the doctor ushered them back to Samantha's room. A nurse was just leaving. The doctor took the chart and looked at her vitals. "Her heart rate is slowing, Doctor." The nurse spoke in hushed tones but Ben caught every word.

The doctor nodded wordlessly and made a few notes on Samantha's chart. "I'll be in again soon to check on things."

Leaving the four of them alone, they each stood in their own personal grief staring at the woman they loved and adored. None of them wanted to see her this way, but the torture would be greater if they left her side even for a second.

"A couple of days?" Sylvia whispered the words unable to comprehend such a thought.

Wrapping an arm around her shoulders, Henry drew Sylvia to him. "I know, Sylvie. I know."

The remainder of the day was spent with the three adults taking turns going to the restroom, leaving for food and coffee, and stretching their legs to work the kinks out. No one was willing to leave Samantha alone so they rotated their time away from her bedside. Finally Ben sent Henry and Sylvia back to his house to sleep. He wanted to stay with Samantha during the night and promised to call them if anything changed.

The grieving husband slept fitfully in a chair he pulled up next to his wife's bed. Occasionally he would waken and peer at his wrist watch which only proved that regardless of one's breaking heart, time marched on. If he could have turned back time, Ben would have. To the first day Samantha complained of a headache that had proven to be more than a normal complaint. To the moment she refused his attention and waved him away with an explanation that it was nothing more than the heat. Oh, if he could only go back. Then maybe she wouldn't be lying in a hospital bed for the second time in their lives together fighting for her life.

Ben leaned his head onto their entwined hands that lay clasped on the bed. Samantha had been unconscious for most of the night, uttering an occasional sigh or moan or would call out softly for Lily. Wondering if his heart could endure any more of her plight, Ben closed his eyes and let the tears fall freely. After a moment he swiped his face against the sleeve of his shirt, unwilling to release Samantha's hand.

Placing his forehead on the crisp, white sheet that was draped over her pale body, Ben had no words to pray. He was "prayed out," as Henry called it earlier. Ben understood that reference clearly, his heart having uttered every silent cry to God he could come up with.

Samantha stirred slightly.

"Honey, I'm here. It's Ben. I'm right here with you." *Oh, if she would only wake up and talk to me.*

"It....it won't be....long." Words barely a whisper, Ben blinked back tears at the sound of Samantha's voice.

"Sammie, you're awake—can you hear me? It's Ben." Stroking her arm and hand he longed to hear her speak again to prove he hadn't imagined it. "Baby, what did you say?"

Samantha's eyes fluttered open, her purple eyes that had caught his attention the first day they met. Now she moved her head slightly towards Ben and whispered, "It won't be long now."

Confused, Ben prodded her to talk to him. "What won't be long, Samantha? This will all be over soon and you can get up out of this bed and—"

Samantha interrupted him with a surprising grip on his hand. Looking straight into the depths of Ben's soul, Samantha spoke a little clearer and louder. "I said that it won't be long. I won't be here much.....longer. And it's okay, Ben."

"We'll get you out of here just as soon as the doctor says you can go home—" Again she squeezed his hand tightly.

"No, Ben. I won't be staying. I have to go. Home."

Understanding dawned on his handsome features. Again he buried his face in the sheet. Muffled, he protested what she was saying, what his mind was urging his heart to hear. "Samantha, no."

"Listen, Ben. I love you. I need you to promise me something. Please."

"Anything, honey! What is it? Just don't leave me. And Lily. We need you." Ben let the tears fall freely.

Reaching a hand to his cheek, Samantha lightly touched Ben's face. "Promise me to love Lily and take care of her. Hold her hand tight....she likes that. Keep her safe. Help her keep finding the good in life, the lovely and beautiful. Please promise me."

The urgency in her voice was the only thing that helped Ben find the words to utter a response to his wife. "Yes, Sammie. I promise."

Slowly she closed her eyes again and her gentle breathing announced she had slipped from him again into an unseen world. He watched her chest rise and fall, willing her to keep breathing, keep living.

Henry sat bolt upright in bed. His chest hurt and his heart pounded in his ears.

"Daddy!"

Looking around the room in confusion, reality slammed him in the stomach full force. He knew he had heard Samantha call out to him. Sylvia was still sleeping beside him in the bed, his daughter and son-in-law's bed, where they should be sleeping contentedly in each other's arms. But his Sammie-girl lie in a hospital bed fighting—

He couldn't finish the thought. Again the pressure in his chest and pounding heart. An urgency pulled him from beneath the sheets with its strong fingers. They had to get back to the hospital.

"Syl! Wake up, honey. We need to go. It's Samantha Jean." Gently yet with urgency he shook her shoulder until she was awake.

"Samantha? Did Ben call?" Sitting up on the bedside, Sylvia reached for her clothes and began dressing.

"No, but I just know we need to be there. She's leaving us."

Flipping on the lamp, Sylvia looked at her watch.

4:00 a.m.

Wordlessly, within twenty minutes Henry and Sylvia were rushing in the front entrance of the hospital and to their daughter's room. Pushing through the door, they found Ben softly crying into the bedsheets.

"We're too late," Sylvia gasped.

Ben raised his head. "No. She's still with us. I was going to have the nurse call you soon."

Henry reached for Samantha's free hand while Sylvia began rubbing her face and hair. "Any change, Ben?"

Swallowing back fresh tears, Ben looked at their grief-stricken faces. He took a moment before speaking. "Nothing the doctor or nurses have noted. But she woke up and told me it wouldn't be long—" Ben's voice broke and he stopped mid-sentence.

Henry swiped at his own face in an effort to stop the tears. "I knew something was wrong."

"It was good you came now." That was all Ben could muster up to say.

Henry and Sylvia began taking turns leaning down next to their daughter's ear and kissing her face. They each whispered words of love and reassurance to her, asking her to stay with them and not to leave.

A shuddering breath coursed from Samantha's chest followed by a soft smile of peace settling over her lips. Her eyelids fluttered like two butterflies settling on a flower. "I see it....Ben, it's right there." All three adults leaned in close to hear every word from Samantha. "It's there....for everyone to see. Oh, Ben! We only have to *look!*....It's so...."

Again her eyes closed. They stood breathlessly waiting for Samantha to continue. Her eyes fluttered open again, only this time she was staring intently at something only she could see. Smiling brighter and larger than any of them had ever seen, Samantha's voice grew in strength. "There it is! I'm here now. You can go to Lily. I found it!"

Through his tears, Ben hoarsely whispered, "What did you find, Sammie? What do you see?"

Samantha's eyes closed again. "Beauty! I have found the beautiful."

With those last words, Samantha Jean Wright slipped from this world into the next, forever surrounded by the longings of her young heart.

# EPILOGUE

A slight tremble settled in her hands after Lily finished the letter from Waylon Graves. Reaching for her glass of tea, Lily took another sip and looked up into the magnolia tree's branches. The over-sized, flowers scented the air around her. Inhaling deeply, Lily noticed her heart had returned to a calming beat instead of the one that matched the rhythm of the woodpecker overhead.

She decided to re-read the short letter a second time, trying for the life of her to wrap mind and emotions around the words. *Lily, get a hold of yourself. You're a grown woman.*

The words danced before Lily's vision. Blinking a few times to clear her eyes and force them to focus, she began again.

*August 20, 1971*
*Dear Lily Ruth,*

*I know this letter will come as a surprise to you, it being twenty years or more since I last saw you or your mother Sam.*

*I don't blame anybody but myself for that. I know I ruined everything. My choices hurt you all and for that I am sorry. By now I have no doubt you know the kind of man I turned out to be. You've probably heard some things about me from your family. I won't deny any of it because I don't doubt it's all true.*

*I got word about your Mama and her passing. I'm so sorry, Lily. She was a good woman. Better than I ever deserved.*

*After my time in jail, I have tried really hard to make things better for myself and I think it would help the both of us if I say a few things. So here goes.*

*Please forgive me for being such a rotten man to your Mama and you. You were such a little thing and never deserved what I did to you and Sam. I don't expect you to ever want to see me again, but I would ask that you might could find it in your heart to forgive me if you already haven't. Not just for hurting you, but for hurting your Mama.*

*I guess that's all. My life is full of regrets where you two are concerned. I can never undo what I did. I can only ask for your forgiveness.*

*I hope your life is good and that you are happy. At the bottom of this letter, you will find my address if you ever want to write to me. I put a picture of the two of us in this letter, hoping it would remind you of our vacation and the fun we had. At least I hope it was fun. You were so tiny and sweet, Lily. I am sure you have grown into as beautiful of a woman as your Mama was.*

*I wish you well.*

*Regretfully,*
*Your father, Waylon Graves*

    Quietly, Lily slowly folded the letter from Waylon and placed it in her pocket. Waylon had been the man who fathered her, but never Lily's Daddy. That spot was reserved for another, more deserving man, Ben Wright, the love of her mother's life.

    As if it had a voice of its own, a wooden box tucked in the top of Lily's bedroom closet beckoned to her. Rising from the glider, Lily entered the back screened-in porch. Glancing at the table to her left, she noticed the wide mouthed Mason jar sitting on the table brimming with freshly cut flowers from her beds. The pink, blue, and white bachelor buttons winked up at her as she traced a hand over the jar. Memories of catching lightning bugs with her cousin and Pops flooded her mind. Touching the crocheted doily that sat beneath the jar, Lily fingered the uneven rows on its edges. Her grandmother Sylvia taught her how to crochet beginning with this very doily, its flaws only endeared the yellowing circle to her even more.

    These few items displayed on Lily's porch told part of the story of Lily's childhood after her Mama had moved on to heaven. The young girl had spent her days with her Grammy and Pops while her Daddy had worked then did his best as a grieving husband to care for his daughter the best he could. Undoubtedly, Ben Wright was one of the best things that ever entered Lily's life.

    Entering her bedroom, Lily shoved aside a flowered cardboard box that contained memorabilia from her and Stan's wedding. That wasn't the box she sought. Behind it was the wooden box she was in search of. Retrieving the box she placed it on her bedspread and slowly opened it. It had been years since Lily had gotten the box down.

    Inside its deep recesses, Lily lifted out the first thing her fingers found. It was a miniature pink and purple plaid cardboard suitcase that had been hers as a little girl. Opening the clasp, Lily's mind was flooded with the memory of her Daddy, Ben, giving Lily the gift for one of her birthdays after her Mama had died. Nestled in the suitcase was a doll complete with its own matching suitcase. The doll wore one black shoe and part of the stitching on her dress was frayed. Hugging it to her chest, Lily laid the doll aside after inhaling its familiar smell.

Next she withdrew a silver bell that still tinkled out a sound when she tugged on the ringer. Another gift from Ben. He had bought Lily a bicycle as soon as he found another place for the two of them to live. Very near to her grandparents' home, Ben got Lily the bike to ride between their house and Henry and Sylvia's. Her dark green rabbit's foot keychain came out of the box next, another memory with her Daddy attached.

A tattered, large envelope was tucked safely inside. Carefully Lily withdrew the papers that made Ben Wright her "official Daddy" as she liked to call him. Soon after her mother's death, Ben had adopted Lily as his own daughter.

Her fingers touched a canvas bag that she lifted out next. Printed on the outside in faded maroon letters were the words "*Hidden Lake Resort, Big Bend, Wis.*" Lily pulled out a cigar box and smiled at the memories. Willie Stockton had given this to her when they moved from Wisconsin to Mississippi. Opening the lid, Lily fingered a rainbow shell, two bottle caps, and other odds and ends that would only mean something to children. The cigar box also contained rocks that Lily remembered her Mama had collected over the years. Though to any other person, the trinkets were junk, to Lily these were some of her most valued treasures.

Producing two smaller envelopes, Lily found what she had been in search of since putting Waylon's letter away. The first contained the long forgotten photos that matched the one Waylon had included in the letter. Lily had remembered every detail of these pictures taken on the Mississippi coast to perfection. Her thumb in her mouth, sad eyes, scowls on her parents' faces....nothing to prove this had been a pleasant trip as Waylon hoped she would believe.

Laying that envelope aside, Lily withdrew another group of photos. A smile spread over her face for the first time since Postman Reggie had brought Waylon's letter that day. One of the photos was of Lily, her Mama, and Ben as they stood over a candle-lit birthday cake, no thumb in her mouth, only faces wreathed in smiles as they celebrated her third birthday. She fingered the edges of a second photo of Ben Wright and herself. The entire family had been on a vacation together at her uncle's family's vacation home. Lily's uncle had snapped the picture of her holding a string of fish, standing on a rock, happily nestled in the crook of Ben's arms. Lily and Ben's matching, bright smiles told of a vacation that still brought joy to Lily's heart, joy tinged with a moment of sadness as she recalled her mother having headaches during their vacation.

And that's when things had taken a drastic change in her young world.

Even in the midst of those dark changes, as clear as day, Lily could hear her Mama's voice saying "I spy something beautiful. Can you find it, Lily? It's there if you look. Good girl! You found it! That butterfly is wonderful!"

Swiping at a tear that coursed down her cheek, Lily sat down on the edge of the bed and let her mind take her back to dozens upon dozens of times her Mama had taught her, encouraged her, shown her what was beautiful in the world. Even on the darkest of days, her Mama, Samantha Jean Owens Graves Wright could find it.

Lily had learned too, but somewhere along the way, she had stopped looking. Taking the two opposing pictures, one of her and Waylon, the other with her and Ben. She stared at each photo and looked deeply in the faces of those before her. Like a rising stream after a gentle rain, thankfulness welled up in Lily's heart as she decided to begin something her mother had taught her long ago. Actually, to begin *again*.

Quietly Lily spoke into the room, "I spy something beautiful...."

Laying aside the photo with Waylon, she paused to give thanks to God for that unexpected letter. The letter had stirred deep within her soul to pick up the long-forgotten habit of looking for it. The beauty that surrounded her life. Every little and big thing.

Knowing there was one other item in the box, Lily withdrew a cloth-covered book. Her Mama's Bible. Letting the pages fall where they may, Lily gazed down and found a verse that had been underlined straight and true in red. She read the sacred words aloud from Ecclesiastes 3, verse 11. "He hath made everything beautiful in His time."

Gently replacing the treasures in the box, Lily returned it to the shelf. All except for her Mama's Bible. Tucking the Bible under her arm, Lily went out to the large magnolia tree that graced her yard. Settling now in peace, she gazed around the yard and allowed her eyes to be opened, her heart to long for and find what had been in front of her all of these years.

The good, the right, the true.

The beautiful.

# a note to my readers.....

This may be the most important part of this book. I would like to think the 91,000+ words I have written hold value, but I would be remiss to not include a piece of my heart at their ending. The past few years have taught me a few valuable lessons as they have been laced with some difficult days for myself and my family. We lost two very dear, precious souls only three months apart in our family. Lingering illnesses for many years were woven into our two loved ones last days and into the days of those left behind. Struggles and strengths, good and bad, trials and triumphs all touched each of us.

In those difficult life-seasons, it is so very easy to miss the good that surrounds us, the beauty that calls to us, and the simple treasures found in day to day living, even in the hard days.

I, like you, look for and long for what is beautiful, especially on those trying, difficult days that often turn into months and years. If you're like me, we can so easily look in the wrong places for what we need, what our soul craves. Filling our minds with distractions, social media, entertainment, and the like only leaves us feeling shallow or even empty.

Even people will leave us feeling shallow or empty if they aren't what our soul needs. Convenience and instantaneous satisfaction tend to trump patience and pure goodness in today's world. We push to be the first in line to draw from what we think will be a life-giving source in our time of great thirst only to find we have stood at the edges of a shallow mud puddle and took great gulps of emptiness, leaving us unsatisfied and even thirstier than before. We waste our time, energy, and heart plumbing the depths of what we think is a great, deep well hoping for buckets full of life-giving water only to receive mere teaspoonfuls of muddy water.

Again, some relationships, entertainment, social media, alcohol, events, shopping, possessions, accomplishments, the list can go on and on....leave us longing for what we really need.

Can I tell you the greatest source of beauty, love, peace, and joy there is on this planet? Can I lead you to the deepest of wells that can always fulfill, always quench, and never run dry?

That would be Jesus. I am a firm believer that NOTHING and NO ONE compares to Him and the life He gives! Like Samantha found, beauty can be seen in the Bible, in relationship with God, in nature, in healthy relationships with others. And sadly, at the beginning of Sammie's story she also tasted sorrow, discouragement, and great disappointment as she clung to the edges of a well run dry in the person of Waylon Graves. But that all changed for her, as you read in *Finding the Beautiful.*

And it can for you too. If you want to know the real well of life, to know Jesus, please get a Bible, find a church, surround yourself with a group of life-giving fellow believers. Or if you don't know where to start, email me at truloveswords@gmail.com.

I would love to hear from my readers and get your thoughts on *Finding the Beautiful.* Thank you for giving your time, energy, and mind to this book and its story. I pray it touched your life and brought fame to the One who gave me the words.

In Christ Alone,
Trudy Samsill

## about the author.....

Trudy Samsill is a resident of Paradise, Texas. She is wife to her best friend and soul-mate of 33 years and mother to 3 wonderful sons and 1 sweet princess, and as of 2017, a first-time grandmother to the most beautiful grandson on the planet. Trudy has been a home-school mom for 27 years. She graduated from Louisiana Baptist University with her Associates of Arts in Elementary Education in the Spring of 2013. Her first passion is writing, desiring her written words to touch her readers, to bring hope and inspiration towards greatness. She has a great love for nature, especially birds and wildflowers that flourish on their 11 acre homestead. Trudy is passionate about her relationship with God, above all else, giving Him all glory for this gift of words entrusted to her.

Connect with this author on social media or by email....

FACEBOOK: @TrudySamsill.Author
INSTAGRAM: @trudysamsill
EMAIL: trulovesword@gmail.com

**OTHER BOOKS BY THE AUTHOR:**

Please check out her first e-book venture, a short story written for teens to adults, Glass Marbles.

Don't miss RESCUED, Alaska's Aleutian Islands Series (Book 1), RETURNED, (Book 2), and REDEEMED, (Book 3). All 3 can be purchased from Amazon in e-book format or paperback from her Amazon Author Page.

THANK YOU FOR SUPPORTING ME, PURCHASING MY BOOKS, AND LEAVING REVIEWS ON AMAZON AFTER READING THEM. I ALSO GREATLY APPRECIATE IT WHEN YOU SHARE MY WORKS WITH YOUR FRIENDS AND FAMILY!

*Trudy Samsill*

Made in the USA
Monee, IL
15 May 2023

33736212R00154